The Pregnancy Pact

CARA COLTER
HELEN LACEY
KANDY SHEPHERD

MILLS & BOON

First Published in Great Britain 2018
by Mills & Boon, an imprint of HarperCollins*Publishers*
1 London Bridge Street, London, SE1 9GF

THE PREGNANCY PACT © 2018 Harlequin Books S. A.

The Pregnancy Secret © 2015 Cara Colter
The Ceo's Baby Surprise © 2015 Helen Lacey
From Paradise...To Pregnant! © 2015 Kandy Shepherd

ISBN: 978-0-263-26701-3

05-0318

MIX
Paper from
responsible sources
FSC™ C007454

This book is produced from independently certified FSC™ paper to ensure responsible forest management.

For more information visit: www.harpercollins.co.uk/green

Printed and bound in Spain
by CPI, Barcelona

THE PREGNANCY SECRET

CARA COLTER

To my friend, and mentor, Joan Fitzpatrick,
whose wisdom and compassion have guided and
inspired me for three decades.

CHAPTER ONE

A BLOCK AWAY from a destination he had no desire to reach, it pierced Kade Brennan's distracted mind that something was wrong.

Very wrong.

There were no sirens, but the strobes of the blue and red bar lights on top of half a dozen police cruisers were pulsing strenuously. It was jarringly at odds with the crystal clear morning light that filtered, a suffused lime green, through the unfurling spring leaves of the huge cottonwoods that lined the shores of the Bow River.

Now, above the sounds of a river bloated with spring runoff, above the sounds of the cheerful chirping of birds, above the sounds of the morning rush of traffic, Kade could hear the distinctive static of emergency frequency radios. A robotic female voice was calling a code he did not understand. It looked as if there was an ambulance in that cluster of emergency vehicles.

Kade broke into a run, dodging traffic as he cut across the early-morning crush of cars on Memorial Drive to the residential street on the other side.

It was one of those postcard-pretty Calgary blocks that looked as if nothing bad could ever happen on it. It was an older neighborhood of arts and crafts–style houses, many of them now turned into thriving cottage businesses. Nestled under the huge canopies of mature trees, Kade noted, were an art-supply store, an organic bakery, an antiques shop and a shoe store.

This neighborhood was made even more desirable by the fact it was connected to downtown Calgary by the Peace Bridge, a pedestrian-only walkway over the river that Kade had just crossed.

Except at this moment the postcard-pretty street that looked as if nothing bad could ever happen on it was completely choked with police cars. People walking to work had stopped and were milling about.

Kade, shouldering through them, caught bits of conversation.

"What happened?"

"No idea, but from the police presence, it must be bad."

"A murder, maybe?" The speaker could not hide the little treble of excitement at having his morning walk to work interrupted in such a thrilling fashion.

Kade shot him a dark look and shoved his way, with even more urgency, to the front of the milling crowd, scanning the addresses on the cottagey houses and businesses until he found the right one. He moved toward it.

"Sir?" A uniformed man was suddenly in front of him, blocking his path. "You can't go any farther."

Kade ignored him, and found a hand on his arm.

Kade shook off the hand impatiently. "I'm looking for my wife." Technically, that was true. For a little while longer anyway.

"Kade," Jessica had said last night over the phone, "we need to discuss the divorce." He hadn't seen her for more than a year. She'd given him the address on this

CARA COLTER   9

street, and he'd walked over from his downtown condo, annoyed at what his reluctance about meeting her was saying about him.

All this was certainly way too complicated to try to explain to the fresh-faced young policeman blocking his way.

"Her name is Jessica Brennan." Kade saw, immediately, in the young policeman's face that somehow all these police cars had something to do with her.

No, something in him screamed silently, a wolf howl of pure pain, *no*.

It was exactly the same silent scream he had stifled inside himself when he'd heard the word *divorce*. What did it mean, he'd asked himself as he hung up his phone, that she wanted the divorce finalized?

Last night, lying awake, Kade had convinced himself that it could only be good for both of them to move on.

But from his reaction to this, to the fact all these police cars had something to do with her, he knew the lie he had told himself—that he didn't care—was monstrous in proportion.

"She's okay, I think. There's been a break-in. I understand she was injured, but it's non-life-threatening."

Jessica injured in a break-in? Kade barely registered the non-life-threatening part. He felt a surge of helpless fury.

"She's okay," the young cop repeated. "Go that way."

It was upsetting to Kade that his momentary panic and rage had shown in his face, made him an open book to the cop, who had read his distress and tried to reassure.

He took a second to school himself so that he would not be as transparent to Jessica. He looked up the walk he was being directed to. Twin white lilacs in full and fragrant bloom guarded each side of a trellised gate. The house beyond the gate was the house Jessica had always wanted.

It was a cute character cottage, pale green, like the fresh colors of spring all around it. But it wasn't her home. A sign hung over the shadowed shelter of an inviting porch.

Baby Boomer, and in smaller letters, Your Place for All Things Baby.

Jessica had given him only the house number. She hadn't said a word about *that*.

And he knew exactly why. Because, for a moment, that familiar anger was there, overriding even the knife of panic that had begun to ease when the young cop had said she was okay. *Hell's bells, did she never give up?*

Or was the anger because the house, her new business and that phone call last night were evidence that she was ready to move on?

It was not as if, Kade told himself sternly, he wasn't ready to move on. In fact, he already had. He was just completely satisfied with the way things were. His company, Oilfield Supplies, had reached dizzying heights over the past year. Without the complication of a troubled relationship, he had been able to focus his attention intensely on business. The payoffs had been huge. He was a man who enjoyed success. Divorce did not fit with his picture of himself.

Divorce.

It was going to force him to face his own failure instead of ignore it. Or maybe not. Maybe these days you just signed a piece of paper and it was done. Over.

Could something like that ever be over? Not really.

He knew that from trying to bury himself in work for the past year.

If it was over, why did he still wear his ring? He had talked himself into believing it was to protect himself from the interest of the many women he encountered. Not personally. He had no personal life. But professionally he met beautiful, sophisticated, *interested* women every day. He did not need those kinds of complications.

He was aware, suddenly, he did not want Jessica to see he was still wearing that ring that bound him to her, so he took it off and slipped it in his pocket.

Taking a deep, fortifying breath, a warrior needing the opponent—when had Jessica become the opponent?—not to know he had a single doubt or fear, Kade took the wide steps, freshly painted the color of rich dairy cream, two at a time.

In startling and violent contrast to the sweet charm of the house, the glass had been smashed out of the squares of paned glass in the door. The door hung open, the catch that should have held it closed dangling uselessly.

Inside that door Kade skidded to a halt, aware of glass crackling under his feet. His eyes adjusted to the dimness as he burst out of the bright morning light. He had entered into a world more terrifying to him than an inhabited bear den.

The space was terrifying because of what was in it. It was the world he and Jessica had tried so hard to have and could not. It was a world of softness and light and dreamy hopes.

The stacks of tiny baby things made other memories crowd around Kade, of crying, and arguing, and a desperate sense of having come up against something he could not make right. Ever.

He sucked in another warrior's breath. There was a cluster of people across the room. He caught a glimpse of wheat-colored hair at the center of it and forced himself not to bolt over there.

He would not let her see what this—her injury, this building full of baby things—did to him.

Unfortunately, if he was not quite ready to see her, he had to take a moment to gather himself, and that forced him to look around.

The interior dividing walls within the house had been torn down to make one large room. What remained for walls were painted a shade of pale green one muted tone removed from that of the exterior of the house. The large space was connected by the expanse of old hardwood, rich with patina, and yet rugs and bookcases had been used to artfully divide the open area into four spaces.

Each was unique, and each so obviously represented a nursery.

One was a fantasy in pink: the crib was all done in pink flowered bedding, with pink-striped sheets and a fluffy pink elephant sprawled at the center. A polka-dot pink dress that looked like doll clothes was laid out on a change table. The letters *g-i-r-l* were suspended by invisible threads from the ceiling. A rocking chair, with pillows that matched the bedding, sat at right angles to the crib.

The next space was a composition in shades of pale blue. The crib and its bedding, again, were the main focus, but the eye was drawn to the vignette of boyish things that surrounded it. There were toy trains and tractors and trucks displayed on the shelves of a bookcase. Miniature overalls and an equally miniature ball cap hung on an antique coatrack beside it. A pair of impossibly small work boots hung from their laces off the same rack.

Next was one all done in lacy white, like a wedding dress, a basket on the floor overflowing with white stuffies: lambs and polar bears and little white dogs. The final display had two cribs, implying twins, and a shade of yellow as pale as baby duck down repeated in the bedding and lamp shades and teeny outfits.

Kade stood, sucking air into his chest, taking it all in and fighting the unmanly desire to cut and run.

How could Jessica do this? Work every day with the thing that had caused her, and him—and them—such unbelievable heartache? He felt all that anger with Jessica solidifying inside his chest. *Now* he was ready to face her.

He narrowed his eyes and looked to the cluster of people. They were at the very back of the old house, behind a counter with an old-fashioned cash register perched on it. Feeling as if his masculinity and size could damage the spaces, he passed through them quickly, holding his breath and being careful not to touch anything. Kade edged his way to the back of the room, inserting a firmness into his step that he did not feel.

It was unnecessary, because she didn't open her eyes as Kade arrived at the back of the store. Jessica was strapped to a wheeled gurney. Her eyes were tightly shut. A uniformed medic was leaning over her, splinting her right arm below her shoved-up sleeve. Two police officers, a man and a woman, stood by, notepads out.

Seeing Jessica would have been, at any time, like taking a punch to the stomach. But seeing her like this was unbearable.

It reminded him of the hardest lesson his marriage

had taught him: even though it was his deepest desire, he had been unable to protect her.

Studying her now, without her awareness, Kade could see subtle changes in her. She looked oddly grown-up in a buttoned-up white blouse and a gray pencil skirt. Her slender feet were encased in a pair of very practical and very plain flat pumps. She looked professional, and yet oddly dowdy, like that British nanny on television. Her look, if it could be called that, filled him with a certain sense of relief.

Jessica was obviously not out to capture a man.

But she looked so serious, not that he expected her to be upbeat, given the circumstances. She looked every inch the pragmatic businesswoman she had evidently become, rather than the artist she had always been. He was pretty sure the only day he'd ever seen Jessica out of jeans was the day they'd gotten married.

Her hair was the same color, untouched by dye, wheat ripening in a field, but had been bobbed off short, in a way that made her features seem elegant and chiseled and mature rather than gamine and friendly and girlish. Or maybe it was because she had lost weight that her features, especially her cheekbones, seemed to be in such sharp relief. She had on not a drop of makeup. Again, Kade felt a completely unwanted niggle of relief. She was obviously not making the least effort to play up her natural beauty.

Despite the fact she looked both the same and different, despite the fact she looked pale and bruised and despite the fact she was dressed in a way that suggested she did not like drawing attention to herself, Jessica did what she had always done, even though he tried to steel himself against reacting to her.

From the first moment he had seen her laughter-filled face on campus, he had been captivated. She had been sitting with friends at an outdoor picnic area. She had looked his way just as he was crossing a huge expanse of lawn, late for class.

His heart had done then exactly what it did now. It had stood still. And he had never made that class. Instead, he had crossed the lawn to her and to his destiny.

Jessica—then Clark—hadn't been beautiful in the traditional way. A little powder had not done anything to hide her freckles, which had already been darkening from the sun. Her glossy hair, sun streaked, had been spilling out of a clip at the back of her head. She'd been supercasual in a pink T-shirt and jean shorts with frayed cuffs. Her toenails had been painted to match her shirt.

But it was her eyes that had captivated him: as green as a leprechaun's and sparkling with just as much mischief. She had, if he recalled correctly, and he was sure he was, been wearing just a hint of makeup that day, shadow around her eyes that made them the deep, inviting green of a mountain pond. Her smile had been so compelling, warm, engaging, full of energy, infused with a force of life.

But two years of marriage had stripped her of all of that effervescent joy. And he could see, from the downturned line around her mouth, it had not returned. Kade welcomed the iciness he felt settle around his heart.

He had not been enough for her.

Still, even with that thought like an acid inside him, he could not stop himself from moving closer to her.

He was shocked that he wanted to kiss her forehead, to brush the hair back from the smoothness of her brow. Instead, he laid his palm over her slender forearm, so aware his hand could encircle it completely. He saw that she was no longer wearing her rings.

"Are you okay?" The hardness Kade inserted in his voice was deliberate. There was no sense anyone knowing the panic he had felt, just for a moment, when he had thought of a world without Jessica. Especially not Jessica herself.

Jessica's eyes flew open. They were huge and familiar pools of liquid green, surrounded by lashes so thick they looked as if they had been rolled in chocolate cake batter. She had always had the most gorgeous eyes, and even her understated look now could not hide that. Unbidden, he thought of Jessica's eyes fastened on him, as she had walked down the aisle toward him… He shook off the memory, annoyed with himself, annoyed by how quickly he had gone *there*.

Now her beautiful eyes had the shadows of sorrow mixed with their light. Still, for one unguarded moment, the look in her eyes when she saw it was him made Kade wish he was the man she had thought he was. For one unguarded moment, he wished he was a man who had an ounce of hope left in him.

CHAPTER TWO

WARINESS TOOK THE place of what had flared so briefly in Jessica's eyes when she had seen it was him, Kade. A guard equal to the one he knew to be in his own gaze went up in hers.

"What are you doing here?" Jessica asked him, her brow knit downward.

What was he doing here? She had asked him to come. "Did she hit her head?" Kade asked the ambulance attendant.

Jessica's frown deepened. "No, I did not hit my head."

"Possibly," the medic said.

"What are you doing here?" Jessica demanded again. It was a tone he remembered too well, the faintest anger hissing below the surface of her words, like a snake waiting to strike.

"You asked me to come," Kade reminded her. "To discuss—" He looked at the crowd around them, and could not bring himself to finish the sentence.

"Oh!" She looked contrite. "Now I remember. We were meeting to discuss…" Her voice drifted away, and then she sighed. "Sorry, Kade, I truly forgot you were coming." Apparently she hadn't lain awake last night contemplating the *d-i-v-o-r-c-e.*

"It's been a crazy morning," she said, as if it needed clarification.

"So I can see," he said. Jessica. Master of the understatement.

"Who are you?" the woman police officer asked.

"I'm her husband." Well, *technically*, he still was.

Kade was only inches from Jessica, but he was so aware that the small physical distance between them was nothing compared with the emotional one. It could not be crossed. That was what hissed right below the surface of her voice. There was a minefield of memory between them, and to try to negotiate it felt as if it would be risking having them both being blown to smithereens.

"I think her arm is fractured or broken," the medic said to Kade, and then returned his attention to Jessica. "We're going to transport you. They'll do X-rays at the hospital. I'm going to call ahead so they'll be ready for you in the emergency department."

"Which hospital?" Kade asked.

"You don't need to come," Jessica said, and there was *that* tone again, her apology apparently forgotten. She glared at Kade in warning when he frowned at her.

She was right. He did not *need* to go with her. And he could not have stopped himself if he tried.

"Nonetheless," he said, "I'd be more at ease making sure you were okay."

"No."

Kade knew that tone: she had made up her mind and there would be no getting her to change it.

No matter how stupidly unreasonable she was being.

"I thought he was your husband," the woman police officer said, confused.

"You don't need to come to the hospital," Jessica said.

She tried to fold her arms over her chest. The splint on her right arm made it awkward enough that after three attempts she gave up. She glared at her arm accusingly, and when that brought her no relief, she switched her glare to him.

To what he could tell was her chagrin, he accomplished what she had not been able to. He folded his arms firmly over his chest.

Battle stations.

What did this mean that he was insisting on accompanying Jessica to the hospital? That he was accepting responsibility for her?

Had he ever stopped feeling responsible for her?

"I thought he was your husband," the police officer said again.

"I am," Kade said, and heard the same firmness in his voice as that day that felt as if it was so long ago when he had said, "I do."

Jessica felt a shiver travel up and down her spine.

Her husband.

She watched Kade standing there, so close she could smell the familiar heady scent of him, his arms folded firmly over the deepness of that chest. He looked grim and formidable when he took that stance.

And even with that intimidating scowl drawing his dark brows down and pulling the edges of his mouth? Kade was the most magnificently made man Jessica had ever encountered. And she was pretty sure the female police officer wasn't immune to that fact, either.

Jessica had never tired of looking at him, not even when their relationship had become so troubled. Sometimes it had made her anger even more complicated that she still liked to look at him when he was so aggravating!

But gazing at him now, she felt resignation. This morning Kade had on a beautifully cut summer suit that she was certain was custom made. With it he had on a plain white shirt, possibly Egyptian cotton, and a subdued, expertly knotted tie, the slight luster of it screaming both silk and expense.

The ensemble made him look every inch the president and CEO of one of Calgary's most successful companies. Despite a rather mundane name, Oilfield Supplies did just that. It supplied the frantic oilfield activity of Alberta and beyond. With Kade's work ethic, ambition and smarts, the company's rise, in the past few years, had been mercurial.

And yet there was nothing soft looking about the man. There was none of the slender build or office pallor of a desk worker about him. He had learned his business from the bottom up, working on rigs to put himself through university. Despite the beautiful clothing, that rugged toughness was still in the air around him. Kade Brennan, with those long legs and those broad shoulders, and that deep chest, radiated pure power.

He had mink-dark hair. It managed, somehow, to look faintly unruly, no matter how short he cut it. And right now, that was very short.

He was clean shaven—Jessica had never known him not to be—and the close shave showed off the masculine perfection of his face: great skin, high cheekbones, straight nose, full lips, faintly jutting chin.

And his damn eyes, sexy and smoldering, were the deep sapphire of the ocean water. It was a color she had seen replicated only once, off the southernmost tip of the Big Island of Hawaii, where they had gone for their honeymoon.

But well before she'd had that reference point, from practically the moment she had met him, Jessica had spent an inordinate amount of time dreaming what their baby would look like. Would it have his eyes or hers, or some incredible combination of both?

The knife edge of that familiar pain was worse than the pain that throbbed along the length of her arm, despite the ice packs splinted in with her limb that were supposed to be giving her relief from pain.

Her husband.

She could feel her heart begin a familiar and hard tattoo at all that had once meant, and at all she knew about this man, the delicious intimacies that only a wife could know.

That he had ticklish toes, and loved the smell of lemons, and that if you kissed that little groove behind his ear, he was putty—

Jessica made herself stop, annoyed that she had gone *there* so swiftly. With everything between them, how was it she could feel this when she saw him? As if she had made the slow, chugging climb up the roller coaster and was now poised at the very summit, waiting to plunge down?

With everything between them, it felt like a betrayal of herself that she could feel such a deep and abiding hunger for the familiar feeling of his arms around her, for the scrape of his cheek across her own, for his breath in her ear, for the gentle savagery of his lips claiming her lips and his body claiming her body.

Her husband.

She felt weak. Where was her newfound sense of herself when she needed it most? Where was her fledgling self-respect? Where was her feeling that her life was working, and that she could have dreams she had set aside when Kade had walked away from her?

Jessica had discovered she could be responsible for her own dreams. It was really much easier without the complications of a man! In fact, she had decided the things she was dreaming would be so much more attainable without a man, especially one like him, who was just a little too sure that he knew the right answers for everybody.

Jessica was certain Kade would not approve of the secret she held inside herself. It was a secret that gave her pure joy, just as once an ultrasound picture tucked in a pocket close to her heart had. She had made a decision to adopt a baby.

It was at the very initial stages, little more than a thought, but she wanted things between her and Kade finalized before she even started the application process. She reminded herself that she needed to be strong for this meeting with Kade, and she despised the unexpected weakness of desire.

She'd rehearsed for a week before she'd called him, striving for just the right all-business tone of voice, planning this morning's meeting so carefully...

Of course, being caught in the middle of a breaking and entering had not been part of her plan! She could not believe, in all the chaos, she had totally forgotten he would be coming.

That was it. That explained the way she was feeling right now. She'd just had quite the shock. The pain in her arm was throbbing mercilessly, and despite denying it to the medic, it was possible she'd hit her head in the scuffle. Maybe, just maybe, a tiny bit of weakness in the department of her husband was acceptable.

Except right now she needed to be strong around him, not weak!

She stole another look at him. There was no missing how ill at ease the store made him. Something in his closed expression even suggested anger. At that realization, that he was angry, something in her hardened. She had known he might react like this when she'd invited him here.

And she had told herself firmly that it was a test she needed to pass. Divorcing Kade, not just on paper, but with her heart, would involve not caring what he liked or didn't like about her choices.

Her lawyer was absolutely right. It was time to tie up some loose ends in her life. And the lawyer was not even aware of *all* the reasons why it had become so important. Her lawyer knew only about her thriving business. Her decision to adopt was a secret, for now.

But it was a secret that required her to acknowledge that Kade Brennan, the husband she had been separated from for more than a year, was one gigantic loose end!

"What happened here?" Kade asked, but typical Kade, he wasn't asking. He was demanding, ready to take charge.

And she was never going to admit what a relief it would be to let him. "Really, Kade, it's none of your business."

The female officer, in particular, looked taken aback at her tone. "I thought he was your husband," she said again, almost plaintively.

"We're nearly divorced," Jessica explained, trying for the cavalier note of a career woman who didn't care, but

she had to physically brace herself from flinching from
the word.

Divorced.

She'd rehearsed that word, too, trying to take the bitter
edge out of it, the sense of loss and finality and failure.

"Oh." If she was not mistaken, Officer—Jessica
squinted at her name tag—Kelly took to that information like a starving hound scenting a bone.

"What happened here?" Kade asked again.

Jessica glared at him. To her relief, the medic announced they were ready to go, and she was wheeled
out past Kade before having to give in to his demand for
answers. Behind her, to her annoyance, she could hear
the police officer filling him in on what had happened.
She glanced back to see the female officer blinking help-
fully at Kade and checking her notes.

"She came in to do paperwork this morning, six
o'clock. Someone broke in around seven thirty."

"Don't come to the hospital," Jessica called over her
shoulder, feeling a childish desire to get in the last shot.
"I don't need you."

She glanced back one more time just as they crossed
through her doorway to outside, where throngs of people seemed to be gathered in front of her house. But she
didn't really even notice. What she noticed was that her
arrow had hit home.

Kade looked momentarily stricken by her words.

That she didn't need him.

And instead of feeling happy that she had drawn
blood, she felt sick about it, and some little demon inside her had to try to repair it, and let him know he was
needed after all.

"Actually, Kade, can you find a way to secure everything? Please?"

Really, after her remark that she didn't need him, he should tell her to go get stuffed. But he didn't.

"And if you could put up a closed-for-the-day sign over that broken window I'd be most appreciative."

He snorted, but didn't say no.

"I can't just leave things. The door is broken. He could come back. Anybody could come in and just start helping themselves to everything in here."

All her hopes and dreams. It was a strange twist that she was being forced to ask Kade to rescue them.

"Never mind," Jessica said, appalled that she had even asked him. "I'll call someone."

She didn't need him. She didn't! Why was she giving him this mixed message: "I need you. I don't need you." She had the stunning realization she was not as clear of her soon-to-be ex-husband as she thought she was!

"I'll look after it," he said.

She should have protested harder, but there was no denying what a relief it was to have Kade Brennan, her husband for a little while longer, say that he would look after things.

CHAPTER THREE

JESSICA WAS WHEELED out to the ambulance, and Kade prowled through her shop looking for items to repair her door. Finally, in a back drawer in a tiny kitchen area he found a hammer and regarded it thoughtfully.

"This isn't really a hammer," he muttered to himself. "It's more like a toy, a prop for one of her fake nurseries."

In a dank cellar, he found some old boards. Thankfully, they had nails in them that he could pull and reuse. Why did women never have the essentials? Nails, screwdrivers, hammers, duct tape?

He boarded up the broken front door and found a square of thick wood to write a few words on.

He had to nail it up over the broken window because of the lack of duct tape. A determined thief could still get in, but the repair, though not pretty, actually looked quite a bit more secure than her old door with its paned glass.

He surveyed his work briefly, and recognized it as temporary but passable. Then he called his personal assistant, Patty, to tell her he would be very late today, if he made it in at all. "I need you to find me a simple surveillance system. I think there's a kind that alerts to your phone. And then could you find a handyman? I need a door fixed, a window replaced and that surveillance system installed. Have him call me for the details.

"And also if you could have my car dropped at Holy Cross Hospital? Whoever brings it can just give me a call when they get there, I'll meet them for keys." He listened for a moment. "No, everything is fine. No need for concern."

Kade walked out to Memorial Drive and was able to flag a cab to take him to the hospital.

He found Jessica in a wheelchair, in a waiting room in the X-ray department.

"How are you doing?"

It was obvious she was not doing well. Her face was pale, and she looked as if she was going to cry.

He could not handle Jessica crying. There was nothing he hated more than the helplessness that made him feel. To his detriment, he had not reacted well to her tears in the past.

He felt ashamed of the fact that she felt it necessary to suck in a deep, steadying breath before she spoke to him.

"They've done an X-ray. I'm just waiting for the doctor. It is broken. I'm not sure if they can set it, or if it will need surgery." She looked perilously close to tears.

Kade fought an urge to wrap his arms around her and let her cry. But he'd never been good with tears, and it felt way too late now to try to be a sensitive guy. It would require him to be a way better and braver man than he knew how to be.

She knew his weaknesses, because she set her shoulders and tilted her chin. "You didn't have to come."

He shrugged. "Your store is secure," he told her. "I put up a sign."

The struggle—whether to be gracious or belligerent—

was evident in her eyes. Graciousness won, as he had known it would. "Thank you. What did it say?"

"Baby bummer, temporarily closed due to break-in."

A reluctant smile tickled her lips, and then she surrendered and laughed. "That's pretty good. Even though it's a major bummer, not a baby one."

Kade was pretty pleased with himself that he had made her laugh instead of cry.

"It could have been a much more major bummer than it was," he said sternly. "Tell me what happened."

Jessica couldn't help but shiver at the faintly dangerous note in Kade's voice. She could not be intimidated by it!

"Isn't it fairly obvious what happened?" she asked coolly. "I was doing some paperwork, and there was a break-in."

"But he came through the front door."

"So?"

"Is there a back door?" Kade asked. That something dangerous deepened in his tone.

"Well, yes, but we just surprised each other. Thankfully, I called 911 as soon as I heard the glass break."

"Don't you think you could have run out the back door and called 911 from safety?"

Jessica remembered what she didn't like about Kade. Besides everything. She needed a good cry right now and she was sucking it back rather than risk his disapproval. On top of that, he was a big man at work. It made him think he knew the answers to everything.

Which was why she didn't even want him to know about adoption. He was certain to have an opinion about that that she would not be eager to hear.

"Hindsight is always twenty-twenty," she informed him snootily.

"How did you end up hurt?" Kade asked.

Jessica squirmed a bit.

"Um, we scuffled," she admitted. "I fell."

"You scuffled?" Kade asked, incredulous. "You *scuffled* with a burglar? I would have thought it was hard to scuffle while running for the back door."

"I was not going to run away," she said.

"That is nothing to be proud of."

"Yes," she said, "it is. Don't you dare presume to tell me what to be proud of."

From their shared laughter over the bummers of life just moments ago to this. It was just like the final weeks of their marriage: arguments lurked everywhere.

"Why are you proud of it?" he asked, that dangerous something still deepening in his tone, that muscle jerking along the line of his jaw that meant he was *really* annoyed.

"I'm proud I took on that scrawny thief," Jessica said, her voice low, but gaining power. "I lost my mother when I was twelve. I've lost two babies to miscarriage."

And she had lost Kade, not that she was going to mention that. In some ways the loss of him had been the worst of all. The other losses had been irrevocable, but Kade was still there, just not there for her.

"Sorry?" he said, reeling back slightly from her as if she had hit him with something. "What does that have to do with this?"

"I am not losing anything else," she said, and could hear the tautness in her own voice. "Not one more thing."

He stared at her, and she took a deep breath and continued.

"You listen to me, Kade Brennan. I am not surrendering to life anymore. I am not going to be the hapless victim. I am making the rules, and I am making my own life happen."

Kade was shocked into silence, so she went on, her tone low. "So if that means scuffling with someone who was trying to take one more thing from me, then so be it."

"Oh, boy," he said, his voice low and pained. "That's not even sensible."

"I don't care what you think is sensible," she said with stubborn pride.

Though, she did plan to be more sensible soon. Naturally, there would be no more scuffling once she had adopted a baby. She would think things all the way through then. She would be the model of responsible behavior.

She hoped there were no questions about how one would handle a break-in on the adoption application.

"So you weren't running for the back door," he deduced, regaining himself. "Not even close."

"Nope." The new Jessica refused to be intimidated. She met his gaze with determination. She was not going to be cowed by Kade. She was not one of his employees. She was nearly not even his wife. In a little while, they would practically be strangers.

At the thought, a little unexpected grayness swirled inside her—she was willing to bet that was a result of her injury, a bit of shock—but she fought it off bravely.

"I was not letting him get away," Jessica said. "The police were coming."

For a moment he was stunned speechless again. He clenched that muscle in his jaw tighter. She remembered she hated that about him, too: the jaw clenching.

His voice rarely rose in anger, but that muscle, leap-

ing along the hard line of his jaw, was a dead giveaway
that he was *really* irritated about something.

"Are you telling me—" Kade's voice was low and dangerous "—that you not only scuffled with the burglar,
but you tried to detain him?"

"He was a shrimp," Jessica said defiantly.

"In case you haven't looked in the mirror recently, so
are you. And he could have had a knife! Or a gun!" So
much for his voice rarely being raised in anger.

"I wasn't going to stand by and let him steal from me!"
At the look on Kade's face, she backed down marginally.
"Okay, so maybe I didn't think it all the way through."
Something that was definitely going to have to change
once she embraced motherhood.

"Maybe?"

She was not sure why she felt driven to defend herself, even when she knew Kade was right and she was
wrong. Not just defend herself, but goad him a little bit.

"Break-ins started on this block a few nights ago. No
one can sleep at night. We all go down there and check
our businesses. That business is everything to me now.
It's my whole life."

He heard the unspoken, she was sure. That the business had replaced him as her whole life.

The jaw muscle was rippling beneath the line of his
skin. She watched it, fascinated despite herself. He was
really angry.

"You've been going down there in the middle of the
night to check your business?"

It didn't seem nearly as clever now with Kade glaring at her.

"Yes, I have," she said, refusing to back down. "And
I'll probably do it again tonight, since he got away."

Well, actually, she probably wouldn't, but there was no sense Kade thinking he could order her around, could control her with even a hint of his disapproval. Those days were over.

"You are not going down there tonight," Kade said. "For God's sake, Jessica, haven't you ever heard of security cameras?"

"Of course I've thought of security cameras. And security companies. But the options are many and the selection is huge," she said. "I've been trying to figure out what is best for me and my budget. Not that that is any of your business. And you don't have any say in how I decide to handle it. None whatsoever. You and I only have one thing left to discuss. And that is our divorce."

And unbidden, the thought blasted through her that *that* was a major bummer.

And the doctor, a lovely young woman, chose that moment to come out, X-rays in hand, and say, "Mr. and Mrs. Brennan?"

Mr. and Mrs. Brennan. That should not fill her with longing! That should not make Jessica wonder if there would ever be another Mrs. Brennan taking her place.

It was over. Their brief marriage was over. They were getting divorced. Kade's life was no longer any of her business, just as hers was no longer any of his.

She would probably change her name back to Clark. She could be Ms. Clark instead of Mrs. Brennan. The baby would be a Clark.

She wasn't thinking about a first name. She knew better than that. Or at least she should know better than that. A memory knifed through her: Kade and her poring over the baby-name books. Deciding on Lewis for a boy and Amelia for a girl.

And then the first miscarriage. And somehow, she could see now, in retrospect, what she had not seen then. From the moment Kade had asked her not to name that little lost baby, a crack had appeared between them.

No, she was determined to enjoy the success of her baby nursery design business and her new storefront as a means to an end. She could have it all.

She could fill her life with the thrill of obtaining those adorable outfits no other store would carry, those one-of-a-kind over-the-crib mobiles, those perfect lamb-soft cuddly teddy bears that everyone wanted and no one could find.

And someday, maybe sooner than later, the outfits would be for her own baby. She would design a nursery for her own baby.

"Don't," he'd whispered when she had started painting the walls of their spare room a pale shade of lavender the second time. "Please don't."

But now she didn't need his approval. She could do it all her way. She could finally, finally be happy. All the pieces were in place.

Weren't they? If they were, why did Jessica feel a sudden desire to weep? It was that crack on her head. It was the throbbing in her arm. It was her day gone so terribly wrong, nothing according to her plan.

"Mr. and Mrs. Brennan?" the doctor asked, again, baffled by the lack of response.

"Yes," Kade said.

"No," Jessica said at the very same time.

He looked stubborn, a look Jessica remembered well.

She didn't think she should admit a sudden urge to kill him in front of the doctor, so she shrugged. "We're nearly divorced," she informed the doctor. "He was just leaving."

Kade gave her a look, and then got to his feet and prowled around the small waiting area.

"Well, if you could come with me."

Jessica stood up from the wheelchair to follow the doctor. She wobbled. Kade was instantly at her side.

"Sit down," he snapped.

Really, she should not tolerate that tone of voice from him, that tendency to bossiness. But the sudden wooziness she felt left her with no choice.

Kade pushed her down the hallway with the doctor, and they entered a small examining room. The doctor put the X-rays up on a light board.

"It's not a complicated break," she said, showing them with the tip of her pen. "It's what we call a complete fracture. I'm going to set it and cast it. I think you'll be in the cast for about four weeks and then require some therapy after to get full mobility back."

Four weeks in a cast? But that barely registered. What registered was that this was her arm with the bone, showing white on the X-ray, clearly snapped in two. Her wooziness increased. She had to fight an urge to put her head between her knees.

"Is it going to hurt?" Jessica whispered, still not wanting Kade to see any sign of weakness from her.

"I wish I could tell you no, but even with the powerful painkiller I'm going to give you, yes, it's going to hurt. Do you want your husband to come with you?"

Yes, part of Jessica whimpered. But that was the part she had to fight! Aware of Kade's eyes on her, she tilted her chin. "No, I'm fine. Kade, you don't have to wait."

CHAPTER FOUR

YOU DON'T HAVE to wait was not quite as firm as *you can leave now.* Jessica forced herself not to look back at him as the doctor took her to a different room. But she had to admit she felt grateful that he did not appear to be leaving.

A half hour later, her arm in a cast and immobilized in a sling, with some prescription painkillers and some instructions in her other hand, Jessica was pushed by a nurse back to the waiting area. Her feeling of wooziness had increased tenfold.

Because she actually felt happy that Kade was still there. He sprang from a chair as soon as he saw her, and then shoved his hands into his pockets.

"You didn't have to wait," Jessica said in stubborn defiance of the relief.

"I'll make sure you get home safely," he said. "I had someone from the office drop off my car for me while I waited. I'll bring it around to that door over there."

And then, before she could protest on a number of fronts—that she didn't need him to drive her and that she was going back to work, not home—he was gone.

She didn't want to admit how good his take-charge attitude felt sometimes. By the time he'd arrived at the door, she'd realized there was no way she was going to work. She was also reluctant to concede how good it felt when he held open the door of his car for her and she slid from the wheelchair into its familiar luxury. Moments later, with the wheelchair returned, he put the car in gear and threaded through what was left of the morning rush with ease.

Why did she feel glad that he didn't have a different car? She shouldn't care at all. But he'd bought the car after they'd graduated from university, well before he'd been able to afford such a thing.

"But why?" she'd asked him when he had come and shown it to her. The high-priced car had seemed as if it should not be a priority to a recent university graduate.

"Because when I marry you, this is what we're driving away in."

And then he'd shown her the ring he couldn't afford, either. Three months later, with the roof down and her veil blowing out the back, they had driven away to a shower of confetti and their cheering friends.

One of her favorite wedding pictures was of that scene, the car departing, a just-married sign tacked crookedly to the back bumper that trailed tin cans on strings. In that picture Kade had been grinning over his shoulder, a man who had everything. And she had been laughing, holding on to her veil to keep it from blowing off, looking like a woman embracing the wildest ride of her life.

Which marriage had definitely turned out to be, just not in the way she had expected. It had been a roller-coaster ride of reaching dizzying heights and plummeting into deep and shadowy valleys.

Jessica took a deep breath. She tried to clear her head of the memories, but she felt the painkilling drugs were impeding her sense of control. Actually, she did not know which impaired her judgment more: sitting in the car, so close to Kade, or the drugs.

She had always liked the way he drove, and though it felt like a weakness, she just gave herself over to enjoying it. The car, under his expert hand, was a living thing, darting smoothly in and out of traffic.

They pulled up in front of the house they had once shared. It was farther from downtown than her business, but still in a beautiful established southwest neighborhood with rows of single-story bungalows, circa 1950.

Oh, God, if getting in his car had nearly swamped her with memories, what was she going to do if he came into the house they had once shared? There was a reason she had asked him to meet her at her business.

"Kade," she said firmly, wrestling the car door open with her left arm, "we need to get a divorce."

Kade made himself turn and look at her, even though it was unexpectedly painful having her back in the passenger seat of the car.

He forced himself to really look at her. Beneath the pallor and the thinness, he suspected *something*.

"What aren't you telling me?"

She wouldn't look at him. She got the car door open, awkward as it was reaching across herself with her left arm.

"You could have waited for me to do that," he said, annoyed, but she threw him a proud glare, found her feet and stepped out.

But her fighting stance was short-lived. She got a confused look on her face. And then she went very white. And stumbled.

He bolted from the car and caught her just as her legs crumpled underneath her. He scooped her up easily and stared down at her. And there he was, in the predicament he would have least predicated for the day—with Jessica's slight weight in his arms, her body deliciously pliant against his, her eyes wide on his face. She had a scent that was all her own, faintly lemony, like a chiffon pie.

She licked her lips, and his eyes moved to them, and he remembered her taste, and the glory of kissing Jessica.

She seemed to sense the sudden hiss of energy between them and regained herself quickly, inserted her good hand between them and shoved. "Put me down!"

As if he had snatched her up against her will instead of rescuing her from a fall. He ignored her and carried her up the walkway to the house.

Their house.

He was not going to carry her across the threshold. The memory of that moment in their history was just too poignant. He set her down on the front steps and her legs folded. She sat down on the top stair, looking fragile and forlorn.

"I don't feel well and I don't know where my keys are," she said.

He still had one, but he wasn't sure if he should use it. It felt presumptuous. It didn't feel as if he should treat it like his house anymore.

"I must have left my purse at the shop," she said, trying to get up.

"Sit still for a minute," he said.

It wasn't an order, just a suggestion, but she folded her

good arm over the one in the sling. He half expected she might stick her tongue out at him, but she didn't.

"You've lost weight," he said, watching her sit on the stoop.

"A little," she admitted, as if she was giving away a state secret. "You know me. Obsessed about my projects. Right now it's launching Baby Boomer. Sometimes I forget to eat."

He frowned at that. She was always obsessed about something. Once, it had been about him.

"What's your sudden panic to get a divorce?" he asked.

She choked and glared at him. "Over a year is not a sudden panic."

"Have you met someone?" His voice sounded oddly raw in his own ears.

Jessica searched his face but he kept his features cool.

"Not that it is any of your business, but no." She hesitated. "Have you?"

He snorted. "No, I'm cured, thanks."

"I am, too!" She hesitated again, not, he guessed, wanting to appear too interested in his life. "I suppose you're playing the field, then?"

"What? What does that mean, exactly?"

"Seeing lots of women."

He snorted and allowed himself to feel the insult of it. Jessica was painting him as a playboy? "You have to know me better than that."

"You live in that building. It has a reputation."

"The condominium has a reputation?" he asked, astounded. "The building I live in? River's Edge?"

"It does," she said firmly. "Lots of single people live there. Very wealthy single people. It has a pool and that superswanky penthouse party room. The apartments are posh."

"How do you know all that?" he asked.

She turned red. "Don't get the idea I've been sneaking around spying on you."

"That is the furthest from any idea I would ever get about you," he said drily.

"The newspaper did a feature on it."

"I must have missed that."

"It seems like a good place for a single guy to live. One who is, you know, in pursuit of fun and freedom."

That was what Jessica thought he was in pursuit of? Jeez. Well, let her think it. How could it be that she didn't know him at all?

"Rest assured—" he could hear the stiffness in his voice "—I live there because it is a stone's throw from work, which by the way is where I spend the majority of my waking hours." He hesitated, not wanting to appear too interested in her life, either. "So are *you* playing the field?"

"Don't be ridiculous," she said.

"How come it's ridiculous when I ask but not when you ask?" And there it was, the tension between them, always waiting to be fanned to life.

"I already told you I'm obsessed with my business. I don't have time for anything else."

"So you are not in a new relationship, and apparently not looking for one. You want a divorce why?"

She sighed with what he felt was unnecessary drama. "We can't just go on indefinitely like this, Kade."

He wanted to ask why not but he didn't.

"All those hours I spend working are paying off. My business is moving to the next level."

He raised an eyebrow at her.

"I did over a hundred thousand in internet sales last year."

He let out a low appreciative whistle. "That's good."

"I think it could be double that this year with the storefront opening."

So she was moving up as well as on. Well, good for her. No sense admitting, not even to himself, how happy he was that her moving on did not involve a new guy moving in.

"My lawyer has advised me to tie up any loose ends."

He managed, barely, not to wince at being referred to as a loose end. "So your lawyer is afraid of what? That you'll be wildly successful and I, as your legal partner, will come in and demand half your business?"

"I suppose stranger things have happened," she said coolly.

"I think my business is probably worth as much as your business if we were going to start making claims against each other."

"We both know your business is probably worth a hundred times what my little place is worth. It's not about that."

"What's it about, then?" He was watching her narrowly. He knew her so well. And he knew there was something she wasn't telling him.

She sighed heavily. "Kade, we don't even have a separation agreement. We own this house together. And everything in it. You haven't even taken a piece of furniture. We need to figure things out."

He rolled his shoulders and looked at *their* house, the hopeless little fixer-upper that she had fallen in love with from the first moment she had laid her eyes on it.

"It's like the cottage in *Snow White*," she had said dreamily.

It hadn't been anything like the cottage in *Snow White*. Except for the decorative shutters, with hearts cut out of them, the house had been an uninspired square box with ugly stucco. The only thing Snow Whitish about it? It needed seven dwarfs, full-time, to help with its constant need for repair.

She had not done one thing to the exterior since he had left. They hadn't been able to afford too much at the time, so they had rented one of those spray-painter things and redone the stucco white. The black shutters and door had become pale blue.

"Isn't the color a little, er, babyish?" he had asked her of the pale blue.

Her sigh of pure delight, as if the color was inviting a baby into their house, seemed now, in retrospect, as if it might have been a warning.

Their strictly cosmetic changes were already deteriorating.

Was it the same inside as it had been? Suddenly he felt driven to know just how much she had moved on. It felt as if he needed to know.

He looked on his chain and acted surprised. "I have a key."

And a moment later he was helping her into the home they had shared. He had thought she would, if sensible, rip out every reminder of him.

But she was the woman who had scuffled with a burglar, and she had not done the sensible thing.

Their house was relatively unchanged. He thought she might have tried to erase signs of him—and them—but no, there was the couch they had picked out together, and the old scarred wooden bench she had fallen in love with and used as a coffee table. She hadn't even gotten rid of the oversize fake leather burgundy recliner with the handy remote control holder built into it. He had thought it would go. When people had come over she had referred to it, apologetically, as the guy chair, her nose wrinkled up with affectionate resignation. She had even named it Behemoth.

In fact, as far as Kade could see, the only change was that the bench contained only a mason glass jar spilling purple tulips. It was not covered with baby magazines. Oh. And there was one other thing changed. Their wedding pictures, her favorite shots in different-size frames, were not hung over the mantel of the fireplace. The paint had not faded where they had hung, and so there were six empty squares where once their love for each other had been on proud display.

The fireplace didn't actually work. He remembered their excitement the first time they had tried to light it, the year's first snow falling outside. The chimney had belched so much black smoke back into the house they had run outside, choking on soot and laughter. There was still a big black mark on the front of it from that.

He led her through the familiar space of the tiny house to the back, where the kitchen was. One day, they had hoped to knock out a wall and have open concept, but it had not happened. He made her sit at the table, another piece of furniture they had bought together at the second-hand stores they had loved to haunt on Saturday mornings. Without asking her, he fetched her a glass of water, finding the glasses with easy familiarity.

He remembered trying to paint the oak cabinets white in an effort to modernize the look of the kitchen. It had been disastrous. They had fallen asleep tucked against each other, propped against a cupboard, exhausted, covered in more paint than the cabinets. The cabinets looked as awful as they always had, the old stain bleeding through the white. They'd never bothered to try painting them again. The truth was, he liked them like that, with their laughter and ineptitude caught for all time in the hardened paint dribbles. And he thought she probably did, too.

The memories all felt like a knife between his eyes.

CHAPTER FIVE

BUT OF COURSE, Kade knew, those happy memories of renovation disaster had all happened before everything went south. After Jessica had discovered she was pregnant the first time, renovation had slammed to a halt.

Chemicals. Dust. The possibility of stirring up mouse poo.

Jessica took a sip of the water, watching him over the rim. "We need to make a decision about the house."

"You can have it," he said. "I don't want it."

"I don't want you to give me a house, Kade," she said with irritating patience, as if she was explaining the multiplication tables to a third grader. "I actually don't want this house. I'd like to get my half out of it and move on."

She didn't want the house with the fireplace that didn't work and laughter captured in the paint dribbles? She'd always loved this house, despite its many flaws.

There was something more going on that she was not telling him. He always knew. She was terrible at keeping secrets.

"I'll just sign over my half to you," he repeated.

"I don't want you to give it to me." Now she sounded mad. This was what their last weeks and months together had been like. There was always a minefield to be crossed between them. No matter what you said, it was wrong; the seeds were there for a bitter battle.

"That's ridiculous. Who says no to being given a house?"

"Okay, then. I'll give it to you."

"Why are you being so difficult?"

He could not believe the words had come out of his mouth. Their favorite line from *Beauty and the Beast*. In the early days, one of them had always broken the fury of an argument by using it.

For a moment, something suspiciously like tears shone behind her eyes, but then the moment was gone, and her mouth was pressed together in that stubborn "there is no talking to her now" expression.

"Can't we even get divorced normally?" she asked a little wearily, sinking back in her chair and closing her eyes.

"What does that mean?" he asked, but was sorry the minute the words were out of his mouth.

Of course, what it meant was that they hadn't been able to make a baby *normally*.

But thankfully, Jessica did not go there. "Normal— we're supposed to fight over the assets, not be trying to give them to each other."

"Oh, forgive me," he said sarcastically. "I haven't read the rule book on divorce. This is my first one."

Then he realized she was way too pale, and that she wasn't up for this. "You're not feeling very good, are you?"

"No," she admitted.

"We need to talk about this another time."

"Why do you always get to decide what *we* need?"

That stung, but he wasn't going to get drawn into an

argument. "Look, you've had a tough morning, and you are currently under the influence of some pretty potent painkillers."

She sighed.

"You should probably avoid major decisions for forty-eight hours."

"I'm perfectly capable of making some decisions."

"There is ample evidence you aren't thinking right. You've just refused the offer of a house."

"Because I am not going to be your charity case! I have my pride, Kade. We'll sell it. You take half. I take half."

He shrugged, and glanced around. "Have you done any of the repairs that needed doing?"

Her mutinous expression said more than she wanted it to.

"Nothing is fixed," he guessed softly. "You're still jiggling the toilet handle and putting a bucket under the leak in the spare bedroom ceiling. You're still getting slivers in your feet from the floor you refuse to rip out, even though it was going to cost more to refurbish it than it would to put in a new one."

"That's precisely why I need to sell it," she said reasonably. "It's not a suitable house for a woman on her own."

Again, he heard something Jessica was not telling him.

"We'll talk about selling the house," he promised. "We'll probably get more for it if we do some fixes."

He noted his easy use of the word *we*, and backtracked rapidly. "How about if I come back later in the week? I'll have a quick look through the house and make a list of what absolutely has to be done, and then I'll hire a handyman to do it. My assistant is actually tracking one down to fix the door on your shop, so we'll see how he does there."

"I think the real estate agent can do the list of what needs to be done."

She'd already talked to a real estate agent. He shrugged as if he didn't feel smacked up the side of the head by her determination to rid herself of this reminder of all things *them*.

"Your real estate agent wants to make money off you. He is not necessarily a good choice as an adviser."

"And you are?"

He deserved that, he supposed.

"Okay. Do it your way," Jessica said. "I'll pay half for the handyman. Do you think you could come in fairly quickly and make your list? Maybe tomorrow while I'm at work?"

He didn't tell her he doubted she would be going back to work tomorrow. Her face was pale with exhaustion and she was slumped in her chair. No matter what she said, now was not the time for this discussion.

"I'm going to put you to bed," Kade said. "You're obviously done for today. We can talk about the house later." He noticed he carefully avoided the word *divorce*.

"I am exhausted," she admitted. "I do need to go to bed. However, you are not putting me to bed." She folded her one arm up over her sling, but winced at the unexpected hardness of the cast hitting her in the chest.

"I doubt if you can even get your clothes off on your own."

She contemplated that, looked down at her arm in the sling. He knew at that moment, the reality of the next four weeks was sinking in. In her mind, she was trying to think how she was going to accomplish the simple task of getting her clothes off and getting into pajamas.

"I'll go to bed in my clothes," she announced.

"Eventually," he pointed out, "you're going to have to figure out how to get out of them. You're going to be in that cast for how long?"

"A month," she said, horror in her features as her new reality dawned on her.

"I'll just help you this first time."

"You are not helping me get undressed," she said, shocked.

He felt a little shock himself at the picture in his mind of that very shirt sliding off the slenderness of her shoulders. He blinked at the old stirring of pure fire he felt for Jessica. She was disabled, for God's sake.

It took enormous strength to wrestle down the yearning the thought of touching her created in him, to force his voice to be patient and practical.

"Okay," Kade said slowly, "so you don't want me to help you get undressed, even though I've done it dozens of times before. What do you propose?"

Her face turned fiery with her blush. She glared at him, but then stared at her sleeve, bunched up above the cast, and the reality of trying to get the shirt off over the rather major obstacle of her cast-encased arm seemed to settle in.

"Am I going to have to cut it off? But I love this blouse!" She launched to her feet. He was sure it was as much to turn her back to him as anything else. She went to the kitchen drawer where they had always kept the scissors and yanked it open. "Maybe if I cut it along the seam," she muttered.

He watched her juggle the scissors for a minute before taking pity on her. He went and took the scissors away and stepped in front of her. Gently, he took her arm from the sling, and straightened the sleeve of the blouse as much as he could.

There was less resistance than he expected. Carefully, so aware of her nearness and her scent, and the silky feel of her skin beneath his fingertips, he took the sharp point of the scissors and slit the seam of the sleeve.

She stared down at her slit-open sleeve. "Thanks. I'll take it from here."

"Really? How are you going to undo your buttons?"

With a mulish expression on her face, she reached up with her left hand and tried to clumsily shove the button through a very tight buttonhole.

"Here," he said. "I'll help you."

She realized she could not refuse. "Okay," she said with ill grace. "But don't look."

Don't look? Hell's bells, Jessica, we belong to each other. Instead of getting impatient, he teased her. "Okay. Have it your way." He closed his eyes and placed his hand lightly on her open neckline. He loved the feel of her delicate skin beneath his fingertips. Loved it.

"What are you doing?" she squeaked.

"Well, if I can't look, I'll just feel my way to those buttons. I'll braille you. Pretend I'm blind." He slid his hand down. He felt her stop breathing. He waited for her to tell him to stop, but she didn't.

It seemed like a full minute passed before Jessica came to her senses and slapped his hand away.

He opened his eyes, and she was looking at him, her eyes wide and gorgeous. She licked her lips and his gaze went to them. He wanted to crush them under his own.

That old feeling sizzled in the air between them, the way it had been before her quest for a baby had begun.

"Keep your eyes open," she demanded.

"Ah, Jessica," he said, reaching for her buttons, "don't look, but keep my eyes open. Is that even possible?"

"Try your best," she whispered.

"You are a hard woman to please." But, he remembered, his mouth going dry, she had not been a hard woman to please at all. With this memory of how it was to be together, red-hot between them, his fingers on her buttons was a dangerous thing, indeed.

Kade found his fingers on the buttons of her shirt. She stopped breathing. He stopped breathing.

Oh, my God, Jessica, he thought.

He did manage to keep his eyes open and not look. Because he held her gaze the whole time that he undid her buttons for her. His world became as it had once been: her. His whole world was suddenly, beautifully, only about the way the light looked in her hair, and the scent of her, and the amazing mountain-pond green of her eyes.

His hands slowed on her buttons as he deliberately dragged out the moment. And then he flicked open the last button and stepped back from her.

"There," he said. His voice had a raspy edge to it.

She stood, still as a doe frozen in headlights. Her shirt gapped open.

"You want me to help you get it off?"

She unfroze and her eyes skittered away from his and from the intensity that had leaped up so suddenly between them.

"No. No! I can take it from here."

Thank God, he thought. But he could already see the

impracticality of it. "I'm afraid you'll fall over and break your other arm struggling out of those clothes," he told her. "The blouse is just one obstacle. Then there's, um, your tights."

"I can manage, I'm sure." Her tone was strangled. Was she imagining him kneeling in front of her, his hands on the waistband of those tights?

He took a devilish delight in her discomfort even while he had to endure his own.

"And I'm not sure what kind of a magician you would have to be to get your bra off with your left hand," he said.

She looked stricken as she went over the necessary steps in her mind.

"If you let me help you this time…" Kade suggested, but she didn't let him finish.

"No!"

"Okay." He put his hands in the air—cowboy surrender. And suddenly it didn't seem funny anymore to torment her. It just reminded him of all they'd lost. The easy familiarity between them was gone. The beautiful tension. The joy they had taken in discovering each other's bodies and the secrets of pleasing each other. In those first early days, he remembered chasing her around this little house until they were both screaming with laughter.

She blushed, and it seemed to him each of those losses was written in the contrived pride of her posture, too. Jessica headed for the hallway, the bedroom they had shared.

If he followed her there, there was probably no predicting what would happen next. And yet he had to fight down the urge to trail after her.

What was wrong with him? What could happen next? She was on drugs. Her arm was disabled. She was being deliberately dowdy.

The simple truth? None of that mattered, least of all the dowdy part. Around Jessica, had he ever been able to think straight? Ever?

"While you're in there," he called after her, trying to convince her, or maybe himself, that he was just a practical, helpful guy, and not totally besotted with this woman who was not going to be his wife much longer, "you can pick what you're going to wear for the next four weeks very carefully."

"And while you're out there, you can start making a list of the fixes. Then you won't have to come back later."

To help her. He would not have to come back later to help her. He mulled that over. "I'm not sure how you can do this on your own. Think about putting on tights one-handed. It would probably be even more challenging than getting them off."

"I can go bare legged," she called.

"I don't even want to think about how you'll get the bra on," he said gruffly. He couldn't imagine how she was going to struggle into and out of her clothes, but that was not a good thing for him to be imagining anyway.

CHAPTER SIX

JESSICA BOLTED THROUGH her bedroom and into the safety of her bathroom. She did not want Kade thinking about her bra, either!

But the reality of her situation was now hitting home.

Oh, there were practical realities. How was she going to manage all this? Not just dressing, which was going to be an inconvenience and a major challenge, but everything? How was she going to take a shower, and unpack boxes at Baby Boomer? How was she going to butter toast, for heaven's sake?

But all those practical realities were taking a backseat to the reality of how she had felt just now with Kade's hand, his touch warm and strong and beautiful, on her neck, and then on her buttons.

That was just chemistry, she warned herself. They had always had chemistry in abundance. Well, not always. The chemistry had been challenged when they—no, she—had wanted it to respond on cue.

Still, it was easier to feel as if she could control the unexpected reality of Kade being in her home—their home—while she was comfortably locked in her bathroom.

Just to prove her control, she locked the door. But as

she heard the lock click, she was very aware that she could not lock out the danger she felt. It was inside herself. How did you lock that away?

"Focus," Jessica commanded herself. But life seemed suddenly very complicated, and she felt exhausted by the complications. She wanted out of her clothes and into her bed.

She wanted her husband out of her house and she wanted the stirring of something that had slept for so long within her to go back to sleep!

Even if it did make her feel alive in a way she had not felt alive in a long, long time. Not even the excitement and success of her business had made her feel like this, tingling with a primal awareness of what it was to be alive.

Even the most exciting thing in her life—contemplating adopting a baby, and starting a family of her own—had never made her feel like this!

"That's a good thing," she told herself, out loud. "*This* feeling is a drug, a powerful, potent, addicting drug that could wreck everything."

But what a beautiful way to have it wrecked, a horrible uncontrollable little voice deep inside her whined.

"Everything okay in there?"

"Yes, fine, thanks." No, it wasn't fine. *Go away. I can't think clearly with you here.*

"I thought I heard you mumbling. Are you sure you're okay?"

"I'm fine," she called. She could hear a desperate edge in her own voice. Jessica was breathing hard, as if she had run a marathon.

Annoyed with herself, she told herself to just focus on one thing at a time. That one thing right now was removing her blouse. By herself.

Her nightie was hanging on the back of the bathroom door. She should not feel regret that the nightwear was mundane and not the least sexy. She should only be feeling thankful that it was sleeveless.

For a whole year, she had not cared what her sleepwear looked like. As long as it was comfortable she hadn't cared if it was frumpy, if it had all the sex appeal of a twenty-pound potato sack.

For a whole year, she had told herself that not caring what she slept in, that not spending monstrous amounts of money on gorgeous lingerie, was a form of freedom. She had convinced herself it was one of the perks of the single life.

"Focus on getting your blouse off!" she told herself.

"Jessica?"

"I'm okay." She hoped he would not hear the edge in her voice. Of course, he did.

"You don't sound okay. I told you it was going to be more difficult than you thought."

What? Getting dressed? Or getting divorced?

One of the things that was so annoying about Kade? He had an aggravating tendency to be right.

"Focus," Jessica commanded herself. She managed to shrug the blouse off both her shoulders, and peeled the sleeve off her left arm with her teeth. But when she tried to slide the newly slit sleeve over the cast, it bunched up around it, and refused to move.

By now, Jessica was thoroughly sick of both Kade's tendency to be right and the blouse. It wasn't one of her favorites anymore. How was she going to ever wear it again without imagining his hands on the buttons?

She tugged at it. Hard. It made a ripping sound. She liked that sound. She tugged at it harder.

"Argh!" She had managed to hurt her arm.

"Okay in there?"

"Stop asking!"

"Okay. There's no need to get pissy about it!"

She didn't want him telling her what to get pissy about! That was why she needed to divorce him.

She investigated the blouse. It was bunched up on the cast, and she had tugged at it so hard it was stuck there. She was afraid she was going to hurt her arm again trying to force it back off. Gentle prying was ineffectual. It refused to budge. The shoulder was too narrow to come down over the cast, and the fabric had ripped to the seams, but the seams held fast.

"That will teach me to buy such good quality," Jessica muttered, then waited for him to comment. Silence. One-handed, she opened every drawer in the bathroom looking for scissors. Naturally, there were none.

She would just have to forge ahead. So with the blouse hanging off her one arm increasing her handicap substantially, and by twisting herself into pretzel-like configurations, she managed to get the tights off. And then the skirt. She was sweating profusely.

Once the bra was off, she thought, it would be fairly simple to maneuver the nightgown over her head.

She reached behind her with her left hand and the bra gave way with delightful ease. She stepped out of it and let it fall in the heap with her tights and skirt.

The nightgown should be simple. If she left it hanging up as it was on the back of the bathroom door, she could just stick her head up under it, and it would practically put itself on. She grunted with satisfaction as she managed to get inside her nightie, put her left hand through the armhole and release it from its peg.

The nightie settled around her like a burka, her head covered, her face out the neck hole. That was okay. This angle should be good for getting her right arm up through the right armhole.

She tried to get her casted arm up. The nightie shifted up over her head as she found the right armhole and shoved. Of course, the blouse bunched around the cast prevented it from clearing the hole. It snagged on something.

So she was stuck with her arms in the air, and her head inside her nightgown.

She wiggled. Both arms. And her hips. Nothing happened.

With her left hand, she tried to adjust the nightie. She tugged down the neckline. Now half her head was out, one eye free. She turned to the mirror and peered at herself with her one uncovered eye. Her nightgown was hopelessly caught in her blouse, and her arm was stuck over her head.

And it hurt like the blazes.

She plunked herself down on the toilet seat and wriggled this way and that. She was sweating again.

There was a knock at the door.

She went very still.

"I made that list."

"Good," she croaked.

"Nothing on it I didn't expect. What do you think about the floors?"

She could not think about floors right now! She grunted as she tried again to free herself from her nightgown.

"Everything okay in there, Jessica?"

"I told you to stop asking!"

"I heard a thumping noise. You didn't fall, did you?"

"No."

"Are you okay?"

"Um—"

"It's a yes-or-no answer."

"Okay, then," she snapped with ill grace. "No." She unlocked the door.

He opened it. He stood there regarding her for a moment. She regarded him back, with her one eye that was uncovered, trying for dignity, her nightie stuck on her head, and her arm stuck in the air. "Don't you dare laugh," she warned him.

He snickered.

"I'm warning you."

"You are warning me what?" he challenged her.

"Not to laugh. And don't come one step closer."

Naturally, he ignored her on both fronts. Naturally, she was relieved, about him coming over anyway. Her arm was starting to ache unbearably. The smile on his lips she could have lived without.

Because there was really nothing quite as glorious as Kade smiling. He was beautiful at the best of times, but when that smile touched his lips and put the sparkle of sunshine on the sapphire surface of his eyes, he was irresistible.

Except she had to resist!

But then the smile was gone. Kade was towering over her. It occurred to her, from the draft she felt and the sudden scorching heat of his eyes, that the nightie was riding up fairly high on her legs.

Wordlessly, the smile gone, his expression all intense focus, he reached for where the blouse was stuck in the right-hand armhole of her nightgown. He began to unwind it. It gave easily to the ministrations of his fingers.

She said nothing.

"You see," he said softly, "there's nothing you can threaten me with that will work. Because the worst has already happened to me."

"What's that?" she demanded. How could he say the worst had happened to him when she was the one sitting here, humiliatingly trapped by her own clothing?

"You're divorcing me," he said softly. And then his face hardened and he looked as if he wanted to choke back the words already spoken.

CHAPTER SEVEN

THE NIGHTGOWN BROKE FREE, and her casted arm went through the right hole and the rest of the garment whispered around her. She used her left hand to tug the hem down to a decent level over her legs.

He bent his head and put his teeth on the fabric of her blouse, and the stubborn seam released. With one final, gentle tug that did not hurt Jessica's arm at all, the blouse was free from the cast.

"A good tailor can probably fix that," he said, laying the destroyed blouse in her lap.

"I'm not divorcing you," she said. "We're divorcing each other. Isn't that what you want?"

He found where her sling was discarded on the floor and looped it gently over her head.

"It seems to be what you want all of a sudden," he said. "There's something you aren't telling me, isn't there?"

She felt suddenly weak, as if she could blurt out her deepest secret to him. How would it feel to tell him? *Kade, there is going to be a baby after all.*

No, that was not the type of thing to blurt out. What would be her motivation? Did she think it would change things between them? She didn't want them to change because of a baby. She wanted them to change because he loved her.

What? She didn't want things to change between them at all. She was taking steps to close this door, not reopen it! She was happy.

"Happy, happy, happy," she muttered out loud.

"Huh?"

"Oh. Just thinking out loud."

He looked baffled, as well he should!

"Go to bed," he told her. "We'll talk later. Now is obviously not the time."

He had that right! Where were these horrible, weak thoughts coming from? She needed to get her defenses back up.

With what seemed to be exquisite tenderness, he slipped her cast back inside the sling, adjusted the knot on the back of her neck.

His touch made her feel hungry for him and miss him more than it seemed possible. He put his hand on her left elbow and helped her up, and then across the bathroom and into the bedroom.

He let go of her only long enough to turn back the bedsheets and help her slide into the bed. She suddenly felt so exhausted that even the hunger she felt for her husband's love felt like a distant pang.

He tucked the covers up around her, and stood looking down at her.

"Okay," she said. "I'm fine. You can leave."

He started to go, but then he turned back and stood in the bedroom door, one big shoulder braced against the frame. He looked at her long and hard, until the ache came back so strong she had to clamp her teeth together to keep herself from flicking open the covers, an invitation.

Just like that, the intimacies of this bedroom revisited her. His scent, and the feel of his hands on her heated skin, his lips exploring every inch of her.

"Are you okay?" he asked. "You're beet red."

Flushed with remembered passion, how embarrassing.

She would do well to remember all that passion had not been able to carry them through heartbreak and turbulence.

She had bled all the passion out of this bedroom. She had become, she knew, obsessed with having a baby after the two miscarriages. It had become so horrible. Taking temperatures and keeping charts, and their lovemaking always faintly soured with her desperation.

Seeing him standing in the doorway, she remembered she had stood in that very spot watching him pack his things after their final night together.

"Please don't," she'd whispered.

"I can't stay."

"But why?"

Those cruel words that were forever a part of her now.

"Jessica, you've taken all the fun out of it."

"Out of making love?" she had asked him, stricken.

"Out of everything."

These were the things she needed to remember when a weak part of her yearned, with an almost physical ache, to be loved by him. To be held by him. To taste his lips again, and to taste faint salt on his skin after they'd made love. To feel the glory of his well-defined muscles under her fingertips. To smell him fresh out of the shower, to laugh with him until she could barely breathe for the ecstatic joy of it.

No, she needed to remember the pain, not the glory, the loneliness and the disappointment, and all the hurtful things. She needed to remember when she had needed him—when she had felt so fragile it had seemed as if a feather falling on her could have cracked her wide-open—Kade had been unavailable in every way.

"I'm fine," she said to Kade now. "Please go."

He heard the coolness in her tone and looked offended by it, but she told herself she didn't care. She told herself she felt nothing but relief as she heard him close the door of the house behind him, and then lock the dead bolt with his key.

She told herself she didn't care that he had gone and that she was alone again. For a woman who was happy, happy, happy, she felt an overwhelming need to cry. With her good arm she grabbed her pillow and put it over her face to try to stifle her desire.

Desire. Why had that unfortunate word popped into her head? This further evidence of her weakness made her fight harder not to cry.

It was weak—it was not the woman she wanted to be. Today hardly even rated as a bad day. She'd had two miscarriages. *Those* had been bad days. She'd had the husband she loved madly leave her. *That* had been a bad day.

But despite her every effort to talk herself out of them, the tears came, and they came hard, and they came for every bad day Jessica had ever had.

Kade left the house and stood on the front step for a moment. There was a little peekaboo view of the downtown skyline. It was the only place on the property that had any kind of a view, and he and Jessica used to sit out here with a glass of wine on a summer's night, planning the deck they would build someday to capitalize on their sliver of a view.

But that had been before the pregnancy quest. Then wine, along with renovations, had been off her list.

He didn't want to go there.

He glanced at his watch and was shocked how early it was in the day. It wasn't even noon yet. It felt as if he had put in a full day, and a hard day, too. Still, there was a place he could go when he didn't want to go *there* for that walk down memory lane.

Work.

He called his assistant. The handyman had already been dispensed to Jessica's business. If he went and liked the guy's work, he could surrender the list. It might minimize encounters like the one he had just had.

He decided he liked the handyman, Jake, and he liked his work. Patty had provided him with the surveillance and security system she had found, and it was already installed when Kade arrived.

"It's really cool," Jake said. "It's motion activated, but you can program it to only send an image to your phone if a door or window is touched. Give me your phone number."

Kade had the fleeting thought it should be Jessica's number that he gave him, but on the other hand, how could he trust her not to rush right down here if her phone alerted her to an intruder?

He gave him his number, and they chortled like old friends as they experimented with setting the alarm and then touching the door, watching their images come up on Kade's phone. Along with the alarm system, a new door was nearly installed, and Jake had matched the old one very closely and even gotten one with shatterproof glass. He was reinforcing the frame so that the dead bolt would not break away.

But somehow when Kade left, the list for the fixes at the house he and Jessica shared was still in his pocket. He had not surrendered it to the obviously very capable handyman.

Why? He suspected it was not because he had not got an answer from her about the floors.

He mulled it over as he drove into the office. Somewhere between her house and there, he had decided he was doing the fixes himself.

But why?

He wasn't particularly handy. The state of the kitchen cupboards over there and the fireplace that did not work were ample evidence of that.

Then he knew. It was time to finish it. Not just the house, but all that house represented. It was time to finish his relationship with Jessica. She was absolutely 100 percent right about that.

And as much as he wanted to, he could not hand those finishes off to someone else. It would be cowardly. And he sensed it would leave him with a sense of incompletion that he could never outdistance.

He would go over there, and he would do all the fixes on the list in his pocket, and then they would get a real estate agent in to appraise the place, and then they would put a for-sale sign on it, and it would sell, and that last thing that held them together would be done.

And how should he feel about that?

"Happy, happy, happy," he said.

Though when Jessica had muttered that, obviously under the influence of whatever, she had looked about the furthest thing from happy! And he was aware that happy, happy, happy was about the furthest thing from how he was feeling, too.

But that just showed him how true it was and how urgent. They needed to be done. He called his assistant and did something he had not done for a long, long time.

He asked her to clear his weekend.

It wasn't until he hung up the phone that he was aware that, for someone who wanted to finish things, another motivation lurked just behind his need to fix the house.

Was Jessica going to be okay after being mugged? Not her arm. That would heal. But her. She had always had that artistic temperament, ultrasensitive to the world.

If he knew Jessica—and he did—she was not nearly as brave as she was trying to be.

So, on Saturday morning, feeling a little foolish in his brand-new tool belt, Kade knocked on the door of the house he had shared with Jessica. He was certain she had said she would be at work, but she opened the door.

He could see why she wasn't at work. She would scare people away from her fledgling business in the getup she had on. She was wearing a crazy sleeveless dress that was at least four sizes too large for her.

But, in truth, it was her face that worried him. Just as he suspected, her drawn features hinted she might not be doing well. There was the gaunt look of sleeplessness about her, as well as dark circles under her eyes.

"It's a maternity dress. I have three of them." Her tone was defensive. "They're easy to get on. See the buttons down the front? That is a very hard thing to find in a dress."

"I didn't say anything." Her arm was in the sling. At least she was following doctor's orders.

"But getting dressed was not that easy, even with the buttons. I'm running late."

He noticed her cast had been decorated with all kinds of signatures and drawings.

In college, she had always been surrounded by friends. But then marriage had done something to her. Her world, increasingly, had become about him and their house. When the pregnancy quest had begun, Jessica had quit the job she'd had since earning her arts degree. Admittedly, it had not been the best job. She had barely made minimum wage at that funky, fledgling art gallery in east Calgary.

At first, he'd liked it that Jessica was home, and doted on him. He'd liked it quite a lot, actually. Maybe he'd liked it enough he'd encouraged it. Who didn't want to come home to fresh-baked bread, or roast beef and Yorkshire pudding or three dozen chocolate-chip cookies still warm out of the oven?

Who didn't want to come home to the most beautiful woman in the world waiting for him, with some newly inventive way of showing she loved him? Once it had been rose petals floating in a freshly drawn tub. Another time it had been a candlelit wine tasting in the back garden, a garden that she had single-handedly wrested from a weedy demise.

But slowly, all her devotion had begun to grate on him. He was so aware that Jessica's world was becoming smaller and smaller: paint colors for rooms rather than canvases. She was always trying new recipes. She discovered shopping online and was constantly discovering useless bric-a-brac that he was supposed to share her enthusiasm for.

It had pierced even his colossal self-centeredness that she was becoming a shadow of the vibrant person she had once been. The obsession with the baby had just intensified the sense he didn't know who she was anymore.

She'd started buying things for a baby they didn't have: little shoes just too adorable to pass up, hand-crocheted samplers for the walls of a nursery they didn't have yet. The magazine racks—God forbid a magazine was left conveniently out—were stuffed with parenting magazines.

She was forever showing him articles on the best baby bottles, and strollers, and car seats. She wanted him to go over fabric samples with her because she had found a seamstress to custom make the crib bedding. But it didn't matter which one he picked. The next day she had more for him to look at. She was acquiring a collection of stuffed animals that would soon need a room of their own, not to mention require them to take out a second mortgage to pay for them all.

"Jessica," he remembered shouting at her, "nobody pays three hundred dollars for a teddy bear."

She had looked crushed, and then unrepentant.

The anger, he knew in retrospect, though he had no idea at the time, had nothing to do with the teddy bear. It had to do with the fact he felt responsible for the awful metamorphosis taking place in her. It had to do with the fact that he was aware, in her eyes, he was not enough for her.

She brought him back to the present. "You didn't have to say anything about the dress. I can see in your face how you feel about it."

He was fairly certain it was the memory of the three-hundred-dollar-teddy-bear fight that had been in his face, so he tried to banish those thoughts and stay in the mo-

ment. "I'm not sure why you would wear something so…
er…unflattering."

"Because I don't care what you think, that's why!"

Or, he thought looking at her, she was trying very,
very hard to make it appear that she didn't care what he
thought.

CHAPTER EIGHT

"I LIKE THE CAST, though," Kade told Jessica.

And he did. He liked it that she had a bigger world again. All the scribbling on the cast was evidence of friends and coworkers and a life beyond the house. Okay, it grated a bit that she had managed to make a bigger world without him, and somehow it was still about babies.

"The dress is what I could get on by myself. See? Buttons down the front."

"About the dress," he said, deadpan. "Are they all that color? What would you call that color?"

"Pink?" she suggested.

"Nausea, heartburn, indigestion…" It was the slogan of a famously pink stomach-relief medication.

"The other ones are worse—"

"No, no, they can't be."

"Spiced pumpkin and real-woods camo."

"A camo maternity dress? I guess my next question would be, how are sales?"

"They are very, very popular."

"Tell me it ain't so," he groaned.

"They are part of an extraoversize line."

"Look, you are scaring me with the visual."

"Well, your visual is a little scary, too," she said,

standing back from the door to let him by her. "A tool belt? And what is that you're driving?"

"I borrowed a truck."

"A truck worthy of a camo-wearing pregnant lady, too."

"I needed it for the vibrating floor sander I rented to refinish the floors."

"A floor sander. The scariness increases. You always thought we should just replace the floors," she reminded him.

"You always thought we should refinish them."

"But it doesn't matter now!" she said, but it felt as if it did. It felt as if it was part of all that was unfinished. In the house, and between them. But Kade did not tell her that.

"What do you know about refinishing a floor?" she asked, looking at her watch.

"Oh, ye of little faith," he said. "I went on the internet. It's easier than you think."

Jessica looked insultingly doubtful.

"I think that refinishing will be less time-consuming than ripping out the old floor and putting down a new one," he told her. He didn't add it might be more in keeping with his skill set.

"Why are you tackling it? Why didn't you just hire someone? That guy you hired to install my door was excellent. By the way, I owe you some money for that."

"Yeah, whatever."

She looked as if she was going to argue, but then remembered she already was in the middle of one argument with him and decided to stick to that one. "I mean this is not exactly your line of work, Kade. It's certainly not in keeping with your current lifestyle."

"What lifestyle is that?" he asked her.

"You know."

"I don't."

"CEO—chief everything officer—at a prestigious company, resident of River's Edge."

"I already told you I work all the time."

"That's exactly what I'm trying to say. You work all the time, and not at renovations. You have a very sophisticated lifestyle. You move in very high-powered circles. I don't understand why you want to do this."

"I started it," he said grimly. "And I'm going to finish it."

She looked at him, and he knew she got it. She got it at every level that he had meant it at.

"Well, I'd love to stay and help—"

He could tell she meant it to sound sarcastic, but instead they both heard the wistfulness there, and Jessica blushed.

"—but I have to go to work. It already took me nearly forty-five minutes longer to get ready than I thought it would, and my part-time staffer can only stay until noon today."

"You slept in," he guessed.

Jessica looked as if she was going to protest, but then didn't. She sighed. "I had trouble sleeping."

"I thought you would."

"What? Why?"

"There aren't very many people who could walk away from being assaulted without being affected by it. And you've always been more sensitive than the average person anyway."

She smiled wanly and gave in, just a little bit, to the fact that he was her husband. He *knew* her. "I'm okay till I lie down, then I feel as if I hear glass breaking. I jump at the sound of the furnace turning on, and that tree branch outside the bedroom scraping the window. Then, since I'm awake anyway, I contemplate how to protect my shop, and hate how helpless I feel."

He drew in a deep breath. The warrior in him wanted to devote his life to protecting her.

But she looked as abashed at her confessions as he was at his reaction to them. Jessica glanced again at her watch. "Yikes! Would you look at the time! Sorry, again. I can't help."

"It doesn't matter. There is a lot of legwork before I actually do anything. I have to move furniture before I get started on the floors."

She cast a look at Behemoth. She was obviously thinking moving furniture was a two-person job, but he had also rented a dolly this morning with that recliner specifically in mind.

But Jessica surprised him. The practicalities of moving furniture were not what was on her mind.

"Remember the day we brought that home?" she asked softly.

These were the conversations he didn't want to have. Because the truth was that he remembered everything.

"You protesting the whole way home how ugly it was," Kade reminded her. He thought her exact words had been that it didn't fit with her *vision* for their house. He hadn't become totally jaded with the vision yet. Or maybe he had started to, because he had brought home the chair over her strenuous protests.

"And then we couldn't get it in the door. It weighs about a thousand pounds—"

"Well, maybe fifty," he corrected her wryly.

"And I was trying to hold up one end of it and you were trying to stuff it through the door. I told you it was a sign the house did not want it, and then you shoved extra hard. The frame of the door cracked and Behemoth catapulted into the house and nearly crushed me."

"Except I saved you," he said.

She looked at his face. Her eyes were very wide. She looked as if she was going to step toward him.

Suddenly, he remembered how they had celebrated getting that chair into the house. On the chair. And she had seemed affectionately tolerant of Behemoth after that.

The memory was between them, liquid and white-hot. It didn't mean anything that she still had the chair, did it?

"Go to work," Kade said gruffly, deliberately stepping back from her. "You probably wouldn't be of any help in your delicate state anyway."

Too late, he realized that a delicate state usually referred to pregnancy, and that, of course, was the topic that was a minefield between them.

Thankfully, she seemed a little rattled, as he was himself, by the Behemoth memory. He didn't intend to share the secret of the furniture-moving dolly with her. She would come home, and the floors would be completely done, and the furniture back in place and she would be filled with complete admiration for his adeptness in all things masculine.

And she would be so sorry things had not worked between them.

That thought blasted through his brain from nowhere that he could discern.

"Where should I put the furniture?" he asked hastily.

"Oh. Good question. Try the guest room. I use it as an office. It probably has the most room in it right now."

"Okay."

She cast one last rather insultingly doubtful look around the living room, but then looked at her watch and made a squeaking noise. She disappeared and came back in a few minutes, her look improved ever so slightly by a nice handbag, ultrahigh heels and dark glasses that hid the circles under her eyes.

"All right," she called. "Good luck. See you later."

Then she turned and, with her heels clacking sexy defiance of that horrible dress, went through the kitchen and out the back door. The door seemed to snap shut behind her. Was he mistaken, or had she been eager to get away from him?

Jessica could not wait to get out of that house! Her husband was an attractive man. His executive look—the tailored suits and linen shirts and silk ties, the manicured nails and the beautifully groomed hair—was enough to make any woman give him a second glance.

And yet the man he was this morning felt like *her* Kade. Casual in jeans faded to nearly white, his plaid shirt open at the beautiful column of his throat, his sleeves rolled up over the carved muscle of his forearms, a faint shadow of whiskers on his face. It was who he had been in private—dressed down, relaxed, so, so sexy.

Add to that the tool belt riding low on his hips, his easy confidence about pitting all that masculine strength against Behemoth...

Behemoth. Back in the day. When everything was still *fun*.

Good grief, she had wanted to just throw herself

against him this morning, feel his heart beating beneath her cheek, feel his arms close around her.

The robbery had left her far more rattled than she ever could have believed. Her sleep was troubled. She started at the least sound. Her mind drifted back to that morning if she let down her guard for even a second. And she felt dreadfully alone with the stress of it.

It was making her weak. The fact that he *knew* how she would react made her lonely for him, even though the sane part of her knew wanting to lean on Kade was an insane form of weakness. She had already tried that once, and he wasn't good at comforting her. Probably what had stopped her from throwing herself at him this morning was uncertainty. Would he have gathered her to him, rested his chin on the top of her head, folded his arms around her? Or would he, after an uncomfortable moment of tolerating her embrace, have stepped away?

She did not think it would be a good idea to make herself vulnerable to Kade again.

But even with that resolve strong within her, Jessica arrived at work feeling rattled.

Her stomach was in knots.

"Good grief," said Macy, her part-time staffer, stopping in her tracks. "Where'd you get that dress?"

"You know perfectly well I got it from the rack of Poppy Puppins at the back."

"It looks horrible on you."

Jessica didn't want to look horrible. She hated it that Kade had seen her looking horrible, even though she had deliberately worn the outfit to let him know she did not care one whit what he thought of her.

Sleep deprivation, obviously, was kicking in, plus it was some kind of reaction to being the victim of a crime, just as Kade had said, because Jessica felt as if she was fighting not to burst into tears.

"It has buttons on the front!" Jessica exclaimed for the second time that day. Ignoring the pitying look from Macy, she headed to office and slammed the door behind her.

She could not focus, even before she had *the* thought. *The* thought made her stomach feel as if it had become the lead car on the world's biggest roller coaster. It plunged downward and then did a crazy double loop. She bolted out of her office and into the store.

"Jessica? What's wrong?"

Jessica stared at Macy, not really seeing her. This was the thought that was tormenting her: Had she told Kade to put the furniture in the guest room? But she used that room as an office! And if she was not mistaken, she had the names of adoption agencies and lawyers who specialized in that field strewn all over the desk.

"Are you okay?" Macy asked. She dropped a tiny stuffed football and rushed to Jessica's side. "Are you going to faint?"

Jessica looked down at the bill of lading she still had clutched in her hand. She did feel terribly wobbly. "I think I'm okay," she said doubtfully.

"I was supposed to babysit for my sister at noon, but if you want, I'll see if my mom can do it instead."

Jessica was ashamed that her distress, her weakness, was that obvious to her employee. But her soon-to-be ex-husband had always had a gift for rattling her world, in one way or another.

What did it matter if he knew she was contemplating adoption? But at some deep, deep level, she did not want him to know.

So though usually Jessica would have said a vehement no to an offer like Macy had just made, she didn't. Usually, she would have pulled herself together. She could just phone and tell Kade to put Behemoth in her bedroom instead of the office.

She looked at her watch. He'd been there, in her house, for an hour and a half. It was possible he was already in the office, poring over her personal papers, uncovering her secrets.

"Oh, Macy, could you? I'd be so grateful." She shoved the bill of lading into Macy's hand.

And it wasn't until Jessica was halfway home that she realized she had not even waited for Macy's answer, but had bolted out the door as if her house was on fire.

Which, in less than half an hour, it would be.

CHAPTER NINE

JESSICA PULLED UP to the front of her house. She usually parked in the back, but such was her sense of urgency, she had decided to cut seconds by parking out front instead.

Her sense of her life spiraling out of her control deepened at what awaited her. All the living room furniture was on the front lawn, with the exception of Behemoth, which, as she already knew, could not fit through the front door. At least she hoped the furniture on the front lawn indicated there had been no invasion of her office.

Gathering herself, Jessica went up the steps. The front door to her house was open. She peered in. Her living room was emptied of furniture.

Kade was glaring down at some instructions in his hand. There was a machine there that looked like a huge floor polisher, only it had a bag attached to it, like a lawn mower. Though it felt like further weakness, she stood there for a minute regarding him, loving the look of him.

He looked big and broad and strong. He looked like the kind of man every woman dreamed of leaning on. But that was what Jessica needed to remember.

When she had needed someone to lean on, and when that person should have been her husband? Kade had not been there. At first he had just been emotionally absent, but then he had begun working longer and longer hours, until he was physically absent, too.

By the time Kade had made it official and moved out, her abandonment by her husband had already been complete.

Remembering all that as a defense against how glorious he looked right now, Jessica cleared her throat.

"It's not for sale," he said, without looking up.

"What?"

He did look up then. "What are you doing back?" he asked with a frown.

"What's not for sale?"

"The furniture. People keep stopping and asking if there's a yard sale. The coffee table is generating quite a lot of interest."

"I always told you it was a good piece."

He was silent for a moment. She knew she had left herself wide-open for him to tease her about what a *good piece* meant to him as opposed to what it meant to her. When he didn't follow that thread—once he had found teasing her irresistible—she was not sure how she felt. But it was not relieved.

"If Behemoth was out there," Kade said, "people would be throwing their money at me. I'd be at the center of a bidding war. The newspaper would probably be here by now to find out what all the fuss on Twenty-Ninth Avenue was about."

"Which brings me to my next question," Jessica said. "Why exactly is everything out on the lawn?"

He lifted a shoulder. "Faster to toss it out there than move it all down the hall."

"Toss?" she said.

"I meant gently move."

Despite the fact it meant he had been careless with her possessions, no matter what he said—and what was to stop anyone from taking whatever they wanted?—she felt relief that he had obviously not been anywhere near the spare bedroom that served as her office. She would know by looking at him if he had seen that adoption stuff, but obviously he was preoccupied with the machine in front of him.

It didn't surprise her that he would throw her things out on the lawn if that was faster than maneuvering them down the hallway. He had always had intensity of focus. When he wanted something, he simply removed the obstacles to getting it. It had made him a tremendous success in business.

It was how he had wooed her. She had been bowled over by him. But then that same attitude had become a toxin in their relationship.

A baby wasn't going to happen? Cut your losses and move on.

"How come you're home?" he asked again.

"Things were slow," she, who never told a fib, lied with shocking ease. "I shut it down a bit early. It seemed to me I should be helping out here. After all, I started it, too."

"I don't really see how you can help. You're kind of handicapped at the moment." He regarded her with a furrowed brow. "You still look not quite right. Pale. Fragile."

"I'm fine."

He brightened as he thought of a use for her. "I know what you could do! You could order pizza. Is Stradivarius still around the corner? God, I've missed that pizza. I haven't had it since—"

His voice trailed away. *Since you left me.* Had he missed her? At all? Or had even pizza rated higher than her?

It didn't matter. Their lives were separate now. She was moving on. Which reminded her of why she had rushed home. And it was not to order him a pizza!

She sidled by Kade. She passed close enough to him to breath in the wonderful familiar scent of him, mixed with something unfamiliar. Sawdust from the floor?

It was tempting to lean just a little closer and breathe deeply of the intoxication that was his scent. But she didn't.

"I'll just go, um, freshen up." She didn't mean changing her clothes. Changing clothes had become a rather daunting undertaking with one arm out of commission. What she really meant was she would go to her office and put her life away from his prying eyes just in case he did make it in there.

Behemoth, it turned out, was in the bathroom, not her office. It would be necessary to climb over it if she was really freshening up, which she wasn't. How far did she need to take the ruse? Did she need to climb over that thing and flush the toilet?

It seemed as if it would be endangering her other arm, and unnecessarily, because when she glanced back down the hall, Kade was not paying the least bit of attention to her.

As always.

The thought was edged with so much bitterness she could practically taste it, like chewing on a lemon peel.

Jessica went into her office. The papers were all out, just as she had remembered, but they were undisturbed. She slid them into the top drawer of the desk. She considered locking it, but it fell under the category of him not paying any attention to her. She doubted Kade would find her interesting enough to pry into her closed desk.

"Interesting placement of Behemoth," she said when she came back into the living room.

"I was thinking it might start a trend. Every man would like a recliner in the bathroom. Some kind of recliner-toilet combination is probably a million-dollar idea just waiting to be developed."

"That is gross."

"It isn't. It's combining practicality with extreme luxury. You have to admit there is nothing particularly comfortable or luxurious about a toilet seat."

She remembered this about him with an ache of longing: that easy irreverence that made her want to be stuffy and disapproving, but she always gave in and laughed instead.

She could feel her lips twitching. He saw it, too.

"Think about it," Kade pressed on. "We could offer designer colors. Pickled pumpkin and redneck camo. We could throw in a free matching dress with every purchase."

She tried to be stern. She giggled. He smiled at her giggle. She succeeded in smothering her giggle. He succeeded in smothering his smile.

"I think," she said severely, Mother Superior to misbehaving novice, "we should try to get the floors done before we tackle anything else together."

"Oh, right. Okay. So come and look at this."

She went over to where he was glaring at the floor. "What do you think?"

"About what?"

"That was what I was afraid of," he groaned. "I already sanded this part. Not much is happening. I just went out and got a different grit of sandpaper. I'm going to try it again. Cover your ears."

Obediently, Jessica put her hands over her ears. The machine roared to life. It was like standing next to a jackhammer.

To her relief, Kade stopped it after a few seconds. "Better," he said, "but still…" A light came on in his face. "It's not heavy enough."

"Huh?"

"The sander. It isn't heavy enough to really dig into those floors. Get on."

"What?"

"Come on. Sit on the front of it."

"Have you lost your mind?"

"You wanted to help. You can't do much with your arm like that. Come sit on the sander."

Why hadn't she just gone and ordered a pizza? Against her better judgment, she moved a little closer. "Sit on it?" She tapped it. "Here?"

He nodded eagerly.

Oh, jeez, it had always been hard not to get caught up in his enthusiasm.

She kicked off her shoes, gathered her skirt underneath her and sat down regally on the sander. She planted her feet firmly on a part of it that looked like a front fender. "Do not do anything that will jeopardize my other arm," she warned him.

"Don't worry." Grinning happily, he started the sander. A quiver ran through her. And then a tremble.

"Oh, my God." Her voice came out shaking, as if she was trying to talk from under water. In the midst of an earthquake. With her good hand, she clutched wildly at the side of the sander. She braced her front feet.

"Ready?"

Ready? *Sheesh, Jessica, run for your life!* Instead, she clung like a bronc rider waiting for the gate to open. She nodded her head.

The machine lurched across the floor.

"That's better," Kade called. "It's working!" He swung the huge machine slowly back and forth over the floor.

"I feel like I'm on one of those machines from a seventies gym," she yelled. Her voice sounded as if she was a cartoon character. Her whole body was vibrating crazily. She could see the flesh on her arms and legs jiggling rapidly.

She started to laugh. Even her laughter was shaking. Kade also gave a shout of pure glee.

He abandoned the slow sweeping motions in the corner and swiveled the machine outward. He raced across the living room, pushing the machine in front of him. Jessica glanced over her shoulder. A wide swath of sanded wood showed behind them, like the wake behind a boat.

They rocketed toward the front door.

An older woman put her head in. Her glasses slipped down her face and her mouth fell open. She was followed by her husband. His mouth fell open, and he grabbed her arm and tried to push her back out the door, as if protecting her from a sight unsuitable for a lady.

She was having none of it, though. She stood her ground, taking in the sight, wide-eyed.

Kade jerked the machine to a halt so quickly Jessica was nearly launched. He turned off the machine. Jessica pulled her skirt down—the vibrating had made it ride dangerously up her thigh—and tried to quit laughing.

An undignified snort, caused by the suppressed laughter, came out of her mouth.

"Yes?" Kade asked their visitors, his voice dignified, as if not a thing was amiss.

"Uh, we were wondering if there's a yard sale," the man said when it was evident his wife was still shocked speechless. "We wondered about the bench."

"Not for sale," Kade said, and then Jessica heard a familiar wickedness enter his tone. "However, I'll give you a good deal on the world's best vibrator."

The woman staggered backward out the door. The man's mouth fell open so hard, his chin hit his chest.

"Sorry to disturb you," he cried as he backed out the door after his wife.

Jessica waited until they were gone. She glared up at the man who was her husband, but she could not stir any genuine annoyance with him. Instead, she remembered how funny and spontaneous he was, she remembered that irreverent edge to his humor.

A smile was tickling his lips. And then she remembered that oh-so-familiar grin. And realized she had never really forgotten that.

Kade gave a shout of pure delight and devilment. And then the laughter spilled out of Jessica, too, and they were both laughing. Hard. Until they were doubled over with it, until the walls of their little house rang with it.

Until the laughter flowed between them like a river that connected them to everything they had once been.

CHAPTER TEN

KADE LOOKED AT Jessica and realized how much he loved to make her laugh. He always had. That was what he had missed most when their relationship had begun to go sideways. Her laughter.

"Goodness," Jessica said a little breathlessly. "I have not laughed like that in a very long time."

"Me, either," he admitted.

"It reminds me of when we were younger," she said.

"Me, too."

"Before…" Her voice faded away. But he knew what she meant. Before the loss of the first baby. And then the second one. Her laughter had leached out of her like bloodred wine leaking from a wineskin with a small puncture in it.

And when she had stopped laughing, and when he had realized how powerless he was to fix that, nothing had seemed worth laughing about to him anymore, either.

Now he watched as she scrambled off the sander, brushing at that ugly skirt with her good arm. The laughter had lightened the strained look around her eyes and mouth.

But when she faced him, a different kind of strain was

there. And it wasn't, for once, the strain of remembering everything that had transpired between them.

This had been lost, too, this deep and delicious sense of awareness of each other. Or maybe not lost. Maybe it had gone underground, like a creek that ran below the surface. It didn't matter that right now, Jessica's surface was encased in that thoroughly revolting dress. Kade could see, with utter ease, to what was underneath. And not her underwear. Her spirit. He could sense that beautiful, sensual awareness of each other, a longing to touch and explore.

In their marriage, it felt as if that had gone, too. It had gone the same place the laughter had gone—into that lonely abyss. It was as if the raft of life that they had shared had snapped in two, and they had stood by helplessly, with no paddles, drifting farther and farther away, not able to stop it.

"Why babies?" he asked softly.

"What?"

She actually looked frightened by the question.

"Why Baby Boomer? Why is your business about all things baby when that caused us so much heartache?"

"Oh." She relaxed visibly. "I'm not sure it was even intentional. You know some of my friends had seen the nursery you and I—" Her voice drifted away and she squinted, as if looking at something in the distance. Then she cleared her throat. "Nicole Reynolds asked me if I could do something for her. A mural on the wall of her nursery. It was a forest scene, with rabbits and birds and a deer. It was an immersion and it kind of snatched me back from the brink. Gave me purpose and a reason to get up in the morning. I liked being part of what was happening in their family, that circle of joy and expectation. It just kind of snowballed."

He was so aware he had caused her that pain. Well, not all of it. The miscarriages had put her in a space he couldn't reach. And then she'd wanted to try again. To plunge herself into that pool of misery he could not rescue her from again. He'd thought it was his job to make her happy. To make her world perfect. At some point, to his grave detriment, he had given up trying.

"I'm sorry, Jessie. I'm sorry it wasn't me who snatched you back from the brink."

Her eyes skittered to him and then away. For a moment it looked as if she would cross that abyss between them, throw herself into his embrace, come home.

But that moment passed even before he recognized completely what was blooming inside him.

Hope.

Shouldn't he know by now that that was the worst trap of all? To hope?

She seemed to recognize it, because smiling way too brightly, she said, "How about if I go order that pizza now?"

"Oh, yeah, sure."

She retreated to the kitchen; he looked at the floors. With the extra weight on the sander, wood had disappeared quickly. The wood was bare, but wavy. If he put a level on it, it would probably rock like the little horse in one of her nursery displays. He was fairly certain that the damage caused by her wild ride on the sander was something wood filler could not fix.

But he was aware of *liking* this kind of problem over the other kind. The baffling problems of the heart.

"What kind of pizza?" she called.

"The usual," he said, before he remembered they really didn't have a usual anymore, not since their lives had become unusual.

But she didn't miss a beat, and he heard her talking into the phone, ordering a half pepperoni and mushroom and a half anchovies and pineapple and ham.

He went into the kitchen and watched her. The afternoon sunshine was painting her in gold. Even in that horrible dress, she looked beautiful. He remembered what it was to share a life with her and felt the pang of intense loss.

And suspected she was feeling it, too. Jessica had hung up the phone, but she had all the old take-out menus out of the kitchen drawer—she'd actually allowed them to have a junk drawer—and was studying them hard.

"You're too heavy," he said when she glanced up at him.

"Excuse me? Then maybe pizza isn't the right choice!"

"Oh, for heaven's sake. Not like that."

"Not like what?"

"You," he said, and could hear the gruff sincerity in his voice, "are perfect. You are too heavy for the sander! We dug some pretty good ruts in the floor."

"Oh." She blushed and looked back at the menus. She was pleased that he thought she was perfect. And he was pleased that he had pleased her, even though the road they were on seemed fraught with danger. "You should have hired it out."

"Very unmanly," he said.

"You," she said, and he could hear the sincerity in her voice, "couldn't be unmanly if you were wearing this dress."

He was pleased that she thought he was manly,

though the sense of danger was hissing in the air between them now.

She was right, and not just about the manly part. He
should have hired the floor job out. The truth, he wouldn't
have missed those moments of her laughter for the world.
Even if the floor was completely wrecked, which seemed
like a distinct possibility at the moment, that seemed a
small price to pay.

"I just need something lighter than you to put on the
sander." He deliberately walked away from the building
tension between them and went out the back door to their
toolshed. He found an old cinder block. He didn't miss
the look on her face when he came back in hefting it, as
her eyes found the bulge of his biceps and lingered there
for a heated moment.

He slowed marginally, liking her admiration of his
manliness more than he had a right to. Then he went into
the living room and found and pitted himself against a
nice comforting problem, one that he could solve. How
did you get a cinder block to sit on a sander?

Kade finally had it attached, and restarted the
machine. It wasn't nearly as much fun as waltzing around
the room with Jessica. And it wasn't nearly as dangerous, either.

Or that was what he thought until the precise moment he smelled smoke. Frowning, he looked toward the
kitchen. They were having pizza. What was she burning?

He shut off the sander, and went into the kitchen doorway, expecting crazily to find her pulling burned cookies from the oven. She had gone through a cookie phase
when she had made her world all about him. Who had
known there were so many kinds of cookies?

Once or twice, he had tried to distract her from her

full-scaled descent into domestic divahood. He had crossed the kitchen, breathed on her neck, nibbled her ear...

He remembered them laughing when he'd lured her away and they'd come back to cookies burned black. She had taken them out of the oven and thrown the whole sheet out into the yard...

But now there were no cookies. In fact, Jessica was standing right where he had left her, still studying all the take-out menus as if each one represented something very special. Which it did, not that he wanted to go there now. Kade did not want to remember Chinese food on the front steps during a thunderstorm, or a memorable evening of naked pad thai, a real dish that they had eaten, well, in the spirit of the name.

"Don't distract me," he snapped at her, and that earned him a wide-eyed look of surprise.

"What are you burning?"

"I'm not burning anything."

He turned away from her, sniffing the air. It wasn't coming from in here, the kitchen. In fact, it seemed to be coming from the living room. He turned back in and the sanding machine caught his attention. A wisp of something curled out of the bag that caught the sawdust coming off the floor.

And in the split second that he was watching it, that wisp of phantom gray turned into a belch of pure black smoke.

"The house is on fire!" he cried.

"That's not funny," she said.

He pushed by her and opened the cupboard by the stove—thank God she had not moved things around—and picked up the huge canner stored there. He dashed to the sink, then remembered the canner didn't fit well under the faucet. He tilted it precariously and turned on the water. It seemed it was filling in slow motion.

She sniffed the air. "What the—"

He glanced back at the door between the kitchen and the living room. A cloud of black smoke billowed in, up close to the top of the door frame.

"Get out of the house," he yelled at her. He picked up the pot and raced out to the living room. The first flame was just shooting out of the sawdust bag on the sander. He threw the pot of water on it. The fire crackled, and then disappeared into a cloud of thick black smoke that was so acrid smelling he choked on it.

He threw the pot on the floor, and went to Jessica, who, surprise, surprise, had not followed his instructions and had not bolted for the door and the safety of the backyard. She was still standing by the menus with her mouth open.

He scooped her up. He was not sure how he managed to think of her arm under these circumstances, but he did and he was extracareful not to put any pressure on her injured limb. He tucked her close to his chest—and felt a sense, despite the awful urgency of this situation, of being exactly where he belonged.

Protecting Jessica, looking after her, using his superior strength to keep her safe. She was stunned into silence, her green eyes wide and startled on his face.

And then he felt something sigh within her and knew she felt it, too. That somehow she belonged here, in his arms.

He juggled her to get the back door open, then hurtled down the back steps and into the yard. With reluctance, he let her slide from his arms and find her own feet.

"Is the house on fire?" she asked. "Should I call 911?"

"I want you to make note of the technique. First, you get to a safe place, then you call 911."

"But the phone's in there."

"I have one," he tapped his pocket. "But don't worry. The fire's out. I just didn't want you breathing that black guck into your lungs."

"My hero," she said drily. "Rescuing me from the fire you started."

"It wasn't exactly a fire," he said.

She lifted an eyebrow at him.

"A smolder. Prefire at best."

"Ah."

"The sander must be flawed. Sheesh. We could sue them. I'm going to call them right now and let them know the danger they have put us in." He called the rental company. He started to blast them, but then stopped and listened.

He hung up the phone and hung his head.

"What?"

Kade did not want to admit this, but he choked it out. "My fault. You need to check the finish that was on the floor before you start sanding. Some of the finishes become highly flammable if you add friction."

She was smiling at him as if it didn't matter one bit. "You've always been like that," she said. "Just charge ahead, to hell with the instructions."

"And I'm often left cleaning up messes of my own making," he said. "I'm going to go back into the house. You stay out here. Toxins."

"It's not as if I'm pregnant," she said, and he heard the faint bitterness and the utter defeat in those words.

And there it was, the ultrasensitive topic between

them. There was nothing to say. He had already said everything he knew how to say. If it was meant to be, it would be. Maybe if they relaxed. It didn't change how he felt about her. He didn't care about a baby. He cared about her.

So he had said everything he could say on that topic, most if it wrong.

And so now he said nothing at all. He just laid his hand on her cheek, and held it there for a moment, hoping she could *feel* what he had never been able to say.

CHAPTER ELEVEN

JESSICA DID SEEM to be able to feel all those things he had never been able to say, because instead of slapping his hand away, she leaned into it, and then covered it with her own, and closed her eyes. She sighed, and then opened her eyes, and it seemed to him it was with reluctance she put his hand away from her.

And so they went into the house together and paused in the doorway.

"Wow, does that stink," Jessica said. She went and grabbed a couple of dish towels off the oven handle. "We need these over our faces, not that I can tie them."

Kade took the towels from her and tied one over the bottom half of her face and one over his.

"Is mine manly?" he asked. "Or did I get the one with the flowers on it?"

He saw her eyes smile from under her mask. Now Jessica was in an ugly dress *and* had her face covered up. But the laughter still twinkled around the edges of her eyes, and it made her so beautiful it threatened to take his breath away far more than the toxic cloud of odor in the room.

Firmly, Kade made himself turn from her, and aware he looked ridiculous, like an old-time bandito, surveyed the damage to the living room.

All that was left of the sander bag was ribbons of charred fabric. They were still smoking, so he went over and picked up the sander and threw it out the front door, possibly with a little more force than was necessary. It hit the concrete walkway and pieces shot off it and scattered.

"That gave me a manly sense of satisfaction," Kade said, his voice muffled from under the dish towel. He turned back into the room.

The smile deepened around her eyes. How was this that they had narrowly averted disaster, and yet it felt good to be with her? It was as if a wall that had been erected between them was showing signs of stress, a brick or two falling out of it.

There was a large scorch mark on the floor where the sander had been, and a black ugly film shining with some oily substance coated the floor where he had thrown the water. The smoke had belched up and stained the ceiling.

"I think the worst damage is the smell," Kade said. "It's awful, like a potent chemical soup. I don't think you're going to be able to stay here until it airs out a bit."

"It's okay. I'll get a hotel."

"You're probably going to have to call your insurance company. The smell is probably through the whole house. Your clothes have probably absorbed it."

"Oh, boy," she said, "two claims in one week. What do you suppose that will do to my premiums?" And then she giggled. "It's a good thing the furniture is on the lawn. It won't have this smell in it. Do you think I'm going to have to repaint?"

"You don't have to go to a hotel," he said. "I've got lots of room."

Son, I say, son, what are you doing?

She hesitated. There was a knock at the door.

"Pizza," they said together.

Jessica contemplated what she was feeling as Kade looked after the pizza delivery. He cocked his head slightly at her, a signal to look at the delivery boy, who was oblivious, earbuds in, head bobbing. He didn't seem to even notice that he was stepping over a smoldering piece of machinery on the front walkway to get to the door. If he noticed the smell rolling out of the house, it did not affect his rhythm in any way.

As they watched the pizza boy depart, she felt like laughing again. That was impossible! She'd had two disasters in one week. She should be crying, not feeling as if an effervescent bubble of joy was rising in her.

Shock, she told herself. She was reacting to the pure shock of life delivering the unexpected. Wasn't there something just a little bit delightful about being surprised?

"Of course I can't stay with you, Kade," she said, coming to her senses, despite the shock of being surprised. "I'll get a hotel room. Or I can stay with friends."

"Why don't we go to my place and eat the pizza? You don't make your best decisions on an empty stomach. We'll figure it out from there."

Other than the fact it, once again, felt good to be *known*, that sounded so reasonable. She was hungry, and it would be better to look for a place to live for the next few days on a full tummy. What would it hurt to go to his place to have the pizza? She had to admit that she was curious about where Kade lived.

And so she found herself heading for the borrowed truck, laughing at the irony of him carefully locking the door when all her furniture was still on the lawn. Except for her precious bench, which at the last moment, she made him load into the box of the truck, they just left everything there.

She suspected leaving her furniture on the lawn was not nearly as dangerous as getting into that truck with him and heading toward a peek at his life.

His condo building sat in the middle of a parklike setting in a curve in the Bow River. Everything about the building, including its prime nearly downtown location, whispered class, wealth and arrival. There was a waterfall feature in the center of the circular flagstone driveway. The building was faced in black granite and black tinted glass, and yet was saved from the coldness of pure modern design by the seamless blending of more rustic elements such as stone and wood in the very impressive facade.

A uniformed doorman came out when Kade pulled up in front of the posh entryway to the building.

"Hey, Samuel, can you park this in the secured visitor area for me?"

Kade came and helped her out of the truck, and she was aware of the gurgle of the waterfall sliding over rocks. Something in the plantings around it smelled wonderful. Honeysuckle?

If the doorman was surprised to have a pickup truck to park among the expensive sports cars and luxury vehicles, it certainly didn't show in his smooth features.

"It's underground," Kade said to Jessica, when the truck had pulled away. "You don't have to worry about your bench."

The truth was she was so bowled over by her surroundings, the bench had slipped her mind.

Though the incredible landscape outside should have prepared her for the lobby, she felt unprepared. The entryway to the building was gorgeous, with soaring ceilings, a huge chandelier and deep distressed-leather sofas grouped around a fireplace.

No wonder he had never come home.

"Wow," Jessica said, gulping. "Our little place must seem pretty humble after this. I can see why you were just going to give it to me."

Kade looked around, as if he was puzzled. "I actually didn't pick the place," he said. "The company owns several units in here that we use for visiting executives. One was available. I needed a place to go and we had one vacant. I rent it from the company."

She cast him a glance as they took a quiet elevator up to the top floor. He really did seem oblivious to the sumptuous surroundings he found himself in. Once off the elevator, Kade put a code into the keyless entry.

"It's 1121," he said, "in case you ever need it."

She ducked her head at the trust he had in her—gosh, what if she barged in when he was entertaining a girlfriend?—and because it felt sad that she knew she would never need it. Well, unless she did stay for a couple of days until the disaster at her place was sorted.

Already, she realized with wry self-knowledge, her vehement no to his invitation was wavering.

Maybe that wasn't so surprising. Kade was charming, and he could be lethally so. She needed to remember charm was not something you could take to the bank in a relationship.

He opened the door and stood back.

"Oh, my gosh," Jessica said, stepping by him. The sense of being seduced, somehow, increased. She found herself standing in a wide entryway, floored in huge marble tiles. That area flowed seamlessly into the open-space living area, where floor-to-ceiling windows looked out over the park and pathways that surrounded the Bow River.

The views were breathtaking and exquisite, and she had a sense of being intensely curious and not knowing where to look first, because the interior of the apartment was also breathtaking. The furnishings and finishes were ultramodern and high-end. The kitchen, on the back wall of the huge open space, was a masterpiece of granite and stainless steel. A huge island had the cooktop in it, and a space-age stainless-steel fan over that.

"Let's eat," Kade said. He'd obviously gotten used to all this luxury. The fabulous interior of his apartment didn't create even a ripple in him. "Maybe on the deck? It's a nice night. I'll just get some plates."

Jessica, as if in a dream, moved out fold-back glass doors onto the covered terrace. It was so big it easily contained a sitting area with six deeply cushioned dark rattan chairs grouped together. On the other side of it sat a huge rustic plank table with dining chairs around it. It looked as if it could sit eight people with ease.

Huge planters contained everything from full-size trees to bashful groups of purple pansies. She took a seat at the table and wondered about all the parties that had been hosted here that she had not been invited to. She looked out over the river.

She felt as if she was going to cry. The apartment screamed to her that he had moved on. That he had a life she knew nothing about. After all their closeness this afternoon, she suddenly felt unbearably lonely.

Kade came out, juggling dishes and the pizza.

"What?" he said, sliding her a look as he put everything down.

"Your apartment is beautiful," she said, and could hear the stiffness in her own voice.

"Yeah, it's okay," he said. She cast him a look. Was he deliberately understating it?

"The kitchen is like something out of a magazine layout."

He shrugged, took a slice of pizza out of the box and laid it on her plate, from the pepperoni half, just as if they had ordered pizza together yesterday instead of a long, long time ago.

"I think I'll look for open concept in my next place," she said. She bit into the pizza and tried not to swoon. Not just because the pizza was so good, but because of the memories that swarmed in with the flavor.

"Don't," he said.

Swoon over pizza?

"It's not all it's cracked up to be, open concept."

"Oh," she said, relieved. "You don't like it?"

"You can't be messy. Everything's out in the open all the time. Where do you hide from your dirty dishes?"

"That would be hard on you," Jessica said. She remembered painful words between them over things that now seemed so ridiculous: toothpaste smears on the sink, the toilet paper roll put on the "wrong" way. "But I didn't see any dirty dishes."

"Oh, the condo offers a service. They send someone in to clean and make the beds and stuff. You don't think I'm keeping all those plants alive, do you?"

"Very swanky," she said. "Kind of like living at a hotel."

"Exactly. That is probably why this place," Kade said, "has never felt like home."

Jessica felt the shock of that ripple through her. This beautiful, perfect space did not feel like home to him?

"I've missed this pizza," he said.

"Me, too," she said. But she knew neither of them was talking about pizza. They sat out on his deck and watched the light change on the river as the sun went down behind them. The silence was comfortable between them.

"I should go," she finally said. "I have to make some phone calls. It's probably getting late to call a friend for tonight. I'll go to a hotel and arrange something for the rest of the week."

"You shouldn't bother. It sounds as if it's going to be a lot of hassle. There is lots of room here. There's a guest room."

Logically, Jessica knew she could not stay. But it felt so good to be here. It felt oddly like home to her, even if it didn't to Kade. Maybe it was because she was aware that, for the very first time since she had been attacked in her business, she felt safe.

And so tired. And relaxed.

Maybe for her, home was where Kade was, which was all the more reason to go, really.

"Okay," she heard herself saying, without nearly enough fight. "Maybe just for one night."

The logical part of her tried to kick in. "I should have packed a bag. I don't know why I didn't think of it."

"I told you," Kade said with an indulgent smile, "you don't think well when you're hungry. I thought of it, but then I wondered if your stuff was going to smell like that burning sander. Don't worry. Like I said, the place is set up for visiting execs. The bathrooms are all stocked up with toothbrushes and toothpaste and shampoo and stuff. And you don't need pajamas."

She could feel her eyebrows shoot up into her hairline.

He laughed. "The guest bedroom has its own en suite, not that I was suggesting you sleep naked. You can borrow one of my shirts."

Good grief, he was her husband. Why would she blush like a schoolgirl when the word *naked* fell, with such aggravating ease, from his gorgeous lips?

CHAPTER TWELVE

"AND WHAT SHOULD I do for clothes tomorrow?" Jessica asked. Her voice felt stiff with tension.

But Kade did not seem tense at all. He just shrugged, and then said, his tone teasing, "We will figure something out. It's not as though we could do worse than what you have on."

We.

She ordered herself not to give in to this. It was a weakness to let him look after her. It was an illusion to feel safe with him.

But she did. And she was suddenly aware she had not really slept or even eaten properly since the break-in. Exhaustion settled over her.

"One night," she decided. "My place will probably be aired out by tomorrow."

"Probably," he said insincerely.

"I think I have to go to bed now."

"All right. I'll show you the way, and find you a shirt to wear for pajamas."

"I'll put away the dishes."

"No, I'll do it. I've gotten better at picking up behind myself."

Was that true, or would the maid come and pick up

after them tomorrow? She found she just didn't care. She was giving herself over to the luxurious feeling of being looked after. Just for one night, though!

And then she found herself led down a wide hallway and tucked inside a bedroom that was an opulent symphony of grays. She went into the attached bathroom. Her mouth fell open. There was a beautiful bathtub shaped like an egg in here. And double sinks and granite, and a walk-in shower. And this was the guest room.

Why did she feel such comfort that he didn't feel as at home here as he had in the humble little wreck of a house they had shared?

Just tired, she told herself. As promised, there was everything she needed there, from toothbrushes to fresh towels.

When she went out of the bathroom, she saw he had left a shirt on the bed for her. Unable to stop herself, she buried her face in it, and inhaled the deep and wonderful scent of her husband. She managed to get the oversize buttons undone on the dress and get it off.

She pulled his shirt on. His buttons weren't quite so easy to do up, but she managed. When she noticed they were done up crooked, she didn't have the energy to change them. She tumbled into the deep luxury of that bed, looked out the window at the lights of the city reflecting in the dark waters of the river and felt her eyes grow heavy.

She realized, for the first time since her shop had been broken into and she had been injured in her ill-advised scuffle with the perpetrator, she was going to get to sleep easily. She suspected she would sleep deeply.

Only it wasn't really the first time in a week.

It was the first time in a year.

* * *

Kade was so aware that Jessica was right down the hall-way from him. He wished he would not have made that crack about her sleeping naked.

Because a man did not want to be having naked thoughts about the wife he still missed and mourned.

But he had developed ways of getting by all these pain-ful feelings. He looked at his watch. Despite the fact Jessica was in bed—she had always handled stress poorly, and he suspected she was exhausted—it was still early.

And he had his balm.

He had work. Plus, he had nearly wrecked her house today. He needed to look after that. He liked the sense of having a mission. This time, though, he decided to call the guy who had fixed her shop door, at least for the floors.

Jake, like all good carpenters and handymen in the supercharged economy of Calgary, was busy.

But willing to put a different project on hold when he heard Jessica's situation, and that Jessica's furniture was currently residing on the lawn.

His attitude inspired confidence, and Kade found him-self sharing the whole repair list with him. Jake prom-ised to look at it first thing in the morning, even though it was Sunday, and get back to him with a cost estimate and a time frame.

"Can she stay out of the house for a couple of days? The floor sanding and refinishing causes a real mess. It's actually kind of a hazardous environment. Even the best floor sander can't contain all the dust, and it's full of chemicals. Plus it'll be easier for me to work if she's not there."

"Oh, sure," Kade said, thinking of Jessica staying here

a few days. She probably wouldn't. She would probably
insist on getting a hotel.

But for a little while longer, anyway, he was still her
husband. And he liked having her here, under his roof.
He liked how protective he felt of her, and how he felt as
if he could fix her world.

So he gave Jake the go-ahead.

As he disconnected his phone, Kade realized he
needed to remember, when it came to larger issues, there
was a lot he could not fix. This sense of having her under
his protection was largely an illusion. They had tried it
over the fire of real life, and they had been scorched.

Tomorrow, he would get up superearly and be gone
before she even opened her eyes. He would solve all the
helpless ambivalence she made him feel in the way he
always had.

He would go to work.

He would, a little voice inside him said, abandon his
wife. The same as always.

But it didn't quite work out that way. Because in the
night, he was awakened to the sound of screaming.

Kade bolted from his bed and down the hall to her
door. He paused outside it for a minute, aware, suddenly,
he was in his underwear.

He heard a strangled sob, and the hesitation was over.
He opened her door, and raced to her side. The bedside
lamp was a touch lamp, and he brushed it with his hand.

Jessica was illuminated in the soft light. She was
thrashing around, her hair a sweaty tangle, her eyes
clenched tightly shut. When the light came on, she sat
up abruptly, and the jolt to her arm woke her up.

She looked up at him, terrified, and then the terror
melted into a look he could have lived for.

Had lived for, once upon a time, when he still believed in once upon a time.

"Are you okay?" he asked softly.

"Just a dream," she said, her voice hoarse.

He went into the adjoining bathroom and found a glass wrapped in plastic that crinkled when he stripped it off. Again, he was reminded this place was more like a hotel and not a home. He filled the glass and brought it to her.

She was sitting up now, with her back against the headboard, her eyes shut. "Sorry," she said.

"No, no, it's okay." He handed her the water. "How long have you been having the nightmares?"

"Since the break-in." She took a long drink of water. "I dream that someone is breaking into my house. My bedroom. That I wake up and—" She shuddered.

Kade felt a helpless anger at the burglar who had caused all this.

"Are you in your underwear?" she whispered.

"Yeah." He wanted to say it was nothing she had never seen before, but she looked suddenly shy, and it was adorable.

"You know I don't own a pair of pajamas," he reminded her.

He sat down on the bed beside her. Everything about her was adorable. She looked cute and very vulnerable in his too-large shirt with the buttons done up crooked. Her hair was sticking up on one side, and he had to resist the temptation to smooth it down with his hand. He noticed her eyes skittered everywhere but to his bare legs.

Sheesh. How long had they been married?

She seemed as if she might protest him getting in the bed, but instead, after a moment's thought, she scooted over, and he slid his legs up on the mattress beside her.

He felt the soft familiar curve of her shoulder touching his, let the scent of her fill up his nose.

"I'm sorry about the nightmares," he said.

"It's silly," she said. "I think I'm getting post-traumatic stress disorder. It's shameful to get it for a very minor event."

"Hey, stop that. You were the victim here. The person who should be ashamed is whoever did this. Jessica, do these people not have any kind of conscience? Decency? Can they not know how these stupid things they do for piddling sums of money reverberate outward in a circle of pain and distress for their victims?"

He felt her relax, snuggle against him. "I feel sorry for him."

He snorted. "You would."

"I don't think you or I have ever known that kind of desperation, Kade."

Except that was not true. When she had wanted to have that baby, he had been desperate to make her happy. Desperate. And her own desperation had filled him with the most horrifying sense of helplessness.

He reached over and snapped off the light. His hand found her head, and he pulled it onto his shoulder, and stroked her hair.

"Go to sleep," he said softly. "I'll just stay with you until you do. You're safe. I'll take care of you. Why don't you lie back down."

"In a minute," she said huskily. "You know what this reminds me of, Kade?

"Hmm?"

"Remember when we first met, how I was terrified of thunderstorms?"

"Yeah," he said gruffly, "I remember."

"And then that one night, a huge electrical storm was moving over the city, and you came and got me out of the bathroom where I was hiding."

"Under the sink," he recalled.

"And you led me outside, and you had the whole front step set up. You had a blanket out there, and a bottle of wine, and two glasses, and we sat on the step.

"At first I was terrified. I was quivering, I was so scared. I wanted to bolt. The clouds were so black. And the lightning was ripping open the heavens. I felt like Dorothy in the *Wizard of Oz*, as if I could be swept away.

"And then you put your hand on my shoulder, as if to hold me to the earth. You told me to count the seconds between the lightning bolt and the thunder hitting and I would know how far away the lightning strike was."

He remembered it all, especially her body trembling against his as the storm had intensified all around them.

"It kept getting closer and closer. Finally, there was no pause between the lightning strike and the thunder, there was not even time to count to one. The whole house shook. I could feel the rumble of the thunder ripple through you and through me and through the stairs and through the whole world. The tree in the front yard shook."

"Yeah, I remember."

"The whole night lit up in a flash, and I looked at you, and your face was illuminated by the lightning. You weren't even a little bit afraid. I could tell you loved it. You loved the fury and intensity of the storm. And suddenly, just like that, I wasn't afraid anymore. I loved it, too. Sitting out on the front steps with you, we sipped that wine, and cuddled under that blanket, and got soaked when the rain came."

She was silent for a long time.

"And after that," he said gently, "every time there was a storm, you were the first one out on that step."

"It's funny, isn't it? It cost nothing to go sit on those steps and storm watch. They came from nowhere. We couldn't plan it or expect it. And yet those moments?"

"I know, Jessica," he said softly. "The best. Those moments were the best."

"And today," she said, her voice slightly slurred with sleep, "today was a good day, like that."

"I nearly burned your house down."

"Our house," she corrected him. "You made me laugh. That made it worth it."

It made him realize how much pain was between them, and how much of it he had caused. He had a sense of wanting, somehow, to make it right between them. It bothered him, her casual admittance that she did not laugh much anymore. It bothered him, and he accepted responsibility for it.

So it could be a clean goodbye between him and Jessica. They could get a divorce without acrimony and without regret. So they could remember times like that, sitting in the thunderstorm, and know they had been made better for them. Not temporarily. But permanently.

He was a better man because of her.

CHAPTER THIRTEEN

PERHAPS, KADE THOUGHT, he was not the man he had wished to be or hoped to be, but still, he was better than he had been. Because of her, and because of the love they had shared.

Was there a way to honor that before they said goodbye? What if tomorrow, Sunday, he wasn't going to go to work after all?

Kade could tell something had shifted. Her head fell against his chest heavily, and he heard her breathing change.

And he knew he should get up and move, but there was something about this moment, this unexpected gift of his wife trusting him and being with him, that felt like one of those best moments ever, a moment just like sitting on the front step with her watching thunderstorms.

And so he accepted that he was reluctant to leave it. And eventually he fell asleep, sitting up, with Jessica's sweet weight nestled into him and the feel of the silk of her hair beneath his fingers.

Jessica woke to the most luxurious feeling of having slept well. The sun was spilling in her bedroom window. When she sat up and stretched, she saw that through the enormous windows of the bedroom, she had a view of the river and people jogging down the paths beside it.

Had she dreamed Kade had come into her room and they had talked about thunderstorms? It seemed as if she must have, because things had not been that easy between them for a long, long time.

And yet, when she looked, she was pretty sure the bedding beside her had been crushed from the weight of another person.

Far off in that big apartment, she heard a familiar sound.

Kade was whistling.

She realized she was surprised he was still here in the apartment. She glanced at the bedside clock. It was after nine. Sunday was just another workday for Kade. Usually he was in the office by seven. But not only was he here, he sounded happy.

Like the Kade of old.

There was a light tap on the door, and it swung open. Jessica pulled the covers up around her chin as if she was shy of him.

"I brought you a coffee."

She *was* shy of him. She realized she had not dreamed last night, because she had a sudden and rather mouth-watering picture of him in his underwear. Thankfully, he was fully dressed now, though he was still off the sexiness scale this morning.

It was obvious that Kade was fresh out of the shower, his dark hair towel roughened, a single beautiful bead of water sliding down his cheek to his jaw. Dressed in jeans, he had a thick white towel looped around his neck, and his chest and feet were deliciously bare.

She could look at that particular sight all day: the

deepness of his chest, the chiseled perfection of his muscles, the ridged abs narrowing and disappearing into the waistband of jeans that hung low on slender hips. Her mouth actually went dry looking at him standing there.

He came in and handed her the coffee. It smelled wonderful—though not as wonderful as his fresh-from-the-shower scent—and she reached out for it. Their fingers touched, and the intensity sizzled in the air between them.

She knew that no part of last night had been a dream. He had slipped onto the bed beside her, and they had talked of thunderstorms, and she had fallen asleep with his big shoulder under her head.

She took a steadying sip of the coffee. It was one of those unexpectedly perfect moments. Kade had always made the best coffee. He delighted in good coffee and was always experimenting with different beans, which he ground himself. It had just the right amount of cream and no sugar.

He remembered. Silly to feel so wonderful that he remembered how she liked her coffee. The luxury of the bed, the sun spilling in the window, the coffee, him delivering it bare chested—yes, an unexpectedly perfect moment.

"I just talked to Jake," he said, taking a sip of his own coffee, and eyeing her over the rim of it.

"Who?"

"Jake. The contractor who fixed the door at your shop. He's over at your house."

"He's at my house at, what is it, seven o'clock on Sunday morning? How do you get a contractor, especially a good one, to do that?"

"I used my substantial charm."

"And your substantial checkbook?" she asked sweetly.

He pretended to be offended. "He's going to do the list of all the things that need fixing—the leak in the roof and the toilet handle and the floors, which really need refinishing now. And he'll fix the new smoke damage on the ceiling, too. That's the good news."

"Uh-oh, there's bad news."

"Yeah. There always is, isn't there? It's going to take him the better part of a week to get everything done. And he says it will go a lot smoother if you aren't there."

She concentrated hard on her coffee. "Oh," she finally squeaked out. A week of this? Coffee delivered by a gorgeous man whom she happened to know intimately? Who had joined her last night in bed in his underwear? She'd be a basket case. "Look, obviously I can't stay here. I'll call a friend. Or get a hotel."

"Why is it obvious you can't stay here?" he asked.

"Kade, we're getting a divorce. We're supposed to be fighting, not setting up as roommates." Certainly she should not be feeling this way about the near nudity of a man she was about to divorce!

"'From where the sun now stands, I will fight no more forever,'" he said softly.

"I hate it when you quote Chief Joseph." No, she didn't. She loved it. She loved it as much as she loved that he had made her coffee exactly as she liked it, without even having to ask.

She loved that he remembered she had once bought a piece of art—that they couldn't afford—with a part of that quote as its name. She remembered that he hadn't been mad. He'd turned the piece over in his hands—a shard of gourd, burned with an Appaloosa galloping across it toward the sun—and he'd smiled and said, "Worth starving for a few weeks."

And, of course, they hadn't starved.

But of course, that had been at the beginning, when her staying home and having a house of her own and a husband to look after had been so novel. Later, it seemed as if Kade was nothing but annoyed when she bought things for the house. She thought of reminding him of that.

But it seemed too petty. She slid him a look now. Was he quoting that because they were turning over a new leaf? Because they were not going to squabble anymore?

Everybody squabbled when they got divorced.

"You want to do something fun today?" he asked. "Since fixing the house has been removed from our list?"

No, she did not want to do something fun! She wanted to get a divorce. She wanted to sell the house they had shared. She wanted to cut ties with him. She wanted to adopt a baby and get on with her life, without him. Fun? Who had fun in the middle of a divorce?

"I thought I took the fun out of everything," she said. She put the coffee down and folded her arms over the largeness of his shirt, which she suddenly wished was at least a little sexy. She recognized the treachery of her thoughts.

He looked bewildered. "You took the fun out of everything?"

"That's what you said. The day you left."

Kade looked genuinely shocked. "I didn't say that."

"Yes, you did." The words, in fact, felt burned into her, as if they had become part of who she was.

"Are you sure?"

"Oh, yeah."

He looked genuinely distressed, but she found she couldn't let it go.

"So," she said, trying for a bright, light note, "what do you do for fun? You're probably an expert at it, now that the dead weight isn't around your neck anymore."

"Jessica, I don't remember saying that. It must have been one of those mean, in-the-heat-of-the-moment things. I'm sorry."

She shrugged, as if it didn't matter one little bit, as if she had not mulled over those words every single day for a year.

"So if we *were* going to do something fun today— and I'm not saying that we are—what would you suggest?" Did it sound as if she was forgiving him? *Was* she forgiving him? "Remember, I have one arm out of commission. Skydiving is out. Ditto for rock climbing. And bull riding."

"I said that? That you took the fun out of everything?"

"Yes! And then you packed your bag, and you left, and you never looked back."

"I thought you'd call, Jessica."

"Why would I call? You were the one who left." She hesitated. She tried to strip any hurt from her voice. "I thought you'd call."

"I didn't know what to say."

"Neither did I. I wasn't going to beg you to come back."

"Why would you beg me to come back?" he asked wearily. "And I guess that's why I didn't call, either. We had reached a complete impasse. We were utterly and exhaustingly miserable. We just seemed to go in endless circles. You wanted a baby. I'd had enough."

She could see the very real pain in his face. For the first time? Had she really been so wrapped up in herself and what she wanted that she could not see what it was doing to him? She'd accused him of being insensitive to her, but she saw now it had been a two-way street. She felt an odd little shiver of awareness go up her spine.

"So," Jessica said carefully, trying to navigate the minefield between them without getting blown up, "answer the question. What do you do with a one-armed woman for fun?"

His eyes fastened on her lips.

"Stop it," she said.

"Stop what?" he asked innocently.

"Looking at me like that. I think *that* would be quite a challenge one armed."

"What?" he asked innocently.

"You know."

He smiled wickedly. "I think *that* could be quite a lot of fun.

"I think it would be darn near impossible."

"I don't. I like a challenge. I like figuring things out."

Good grief, she could not stay here for days with this kind of delicious sensual tension in the air between them.

"I could start by offering to help you shower," he said, his voice a low growl.

She threw the pillow at him. It was a clean miss, but he dodged anyway, managing to save his coffee. He laughed and made a face at her. "So are we agreed? We'll do something fun today?"

"I suppose, if you promise to be good," she said warningly, reaching for the other pillow.

"Do I have to? Okay, okay." And then he backed away from her, closed the door and was gone.

She freshened up in the bathroom and put on the maternity dress. When she saw her reflection in the full-length mirror of his opulent guest bathroom, she felt she had succeeded just a little too well in her goals.

She had wanted to look as if she didn't care! She was not sure she had wanted to look quite this bad! She looked like a waif abandoned outside an orphanage. Still, defiantly, refusing to give in to the temptation to win his approval in any way, least of all by trying to make herself attractive to him, she stepped out of the bathroom.

The truth was she hadn't brought anything else anyway. She had thought her stay here was going to be brief. Given the shakiness of her resolve, looking pathetic seemed as if it could only be a good thing.

He was behind the kitchen counter putting croissants—obviously freshly delivered—on a plate.

"Wow. Excuse me while I pluck out my eyes. I'd forgotten the full ugliness of that dress. Or maybe I blocked it. Trauma."

"It is not that bad." He still had not put on a shirt. In the "life was unfair" department, this seemed to rate quite high: that he wanted to pluck out his eyes and she wanted to gaze at him endlessly.

"It is. That bad. Believe me. At least its awfulness helps me figure out the agenda for the day. We need to go shopping first."

"I am not going shopping. I love this dress." She didn't actually. She thought it was quite hideous. "I'm sorry you'll be embarrassed by me, but that's the way it is."

"I'm not embarrassed by you. But in the 'find something to be grateful for' department—"

She squinted at him suspiciously. He was not a "find something to be grateful for" kind of guy.

"I'm just glad you didn't bring the camo one. If we end up in the woods today, I don't want to misplace you."

"What are the chances we'll end up in the woods?"

"Anything can happen when you just let the day unfold."

She should not feel nearly as thrilled by that as she did! But spontaneity had not been part of her world for a long time, and Jessica suddenly felt eager for it.

CHAPTER FOURTEEN

ONE THING THAT Jessica remembered about Kade with complete fondness was that he always seemed open to what the world could bring him.

They had a simple breakfast at his apartment. He had had the still-steaming croissants and preserves delivered, and they sat out on the terrace and ate in the new warmth of the spring light. What was it about spring that brought hope to even the most wounded heart?

He seemed to forget she looked ugly. She seemed to forget he looked gorgeous. The old comfort rose up between them.

They talked as if nothing had ever gone wrong between them. It was like the old days, when spending time with him felt as if she was spending time with her best friend. The conversation flowed easily and naturally, words spilling out of them, as if they were anxious to catch up. They talked about mutual friends, his aunt Helen and her cousin Dave. They talked a bit about their businesses.

And then they left his place and walked downtown. Jessica became self-consciously aware of the ugliness of her dress again as she walked beside him. Kade was dressed casually in a sports shirt and summer khaki pants, and yet she could not help but notice how he got *that* look from women. Interested. Admiring. Hungry for a taste of that particular delight. They would glance at her, too, and then dismiss her.

When he came around to her good arm and his hand found hers, her own sense of hunger deepened. She was so aware of how much she had missed this, the small intimacies that made a relationship, the feel of his hand, strong, closing possessively around her own, sending that message to all who passed: *taken*.

She was determined to make a go of it on her own, but that simple thing, him taking her hand, filled her with a longing that felt physical in its intensity, like a shiver going up and down her spine that would not go away.

If she was smart, she would drop his hand and turn and run.

But smart seemed to have abandoned her. She wanted these moments. It felt as if she was stealing them to store away, as a part of her, for when she did not have him anymore. She actually felt thankful that *these* memories might overlay the old ones. Their history, leading up to the separation, was so filled with bitterness and anger and frustration that it had become as if the dark colors of a new painting had completely obliterated the light of the old painting that existed right underneath it.

They entered the downtown. It was a beautiful day so they avoided the Plus 15 Skywalk and instead strolled the pedestrian mall on Stephen Avenue. Downtown did not have its weekday bustle, the throngs of men and women in business attire, but there was still a colorful conglomeration of shoppers and activities on the streets.

A cowboy-hatted busker had set up close to Stephen Avenue Walk and was singing lustily. They stopped and watched for a few minutes. Kade dropped a five into his guitar case and they moved on.

They enjoyed the historic sandstone buildings of one of Canada's few designated National Historic Sites. Calgarians had been conducting their commerce here on Eighth Avenue for over a hundred years. They passed the building where Kade worked, in the heart of Calgary's financial district, and then walked along the column-fronted arcade of the very impressive Hudson's Bay Company building. The building had always anchored Calgary's downtown core.

"How about there?"

She looked at the store Kade had paused to point out. It was a tiny but very upscale boutique called Chrysalis, which Jessica knew of but had never set foot in. "I can't go in there."

"Why?"

Mostly because of how she was dressed right now! "I can't afford anything in there."

"I can."

"No."

"Come on. It will be fun. Remember that scene we liked in that movie?"

"Pretty Woman?" she guessed.

He nodded happily. "Let's reenact that."

"I'm no Julia Roberts," she said, but she could feel herself being drawn into his playfulness. Where had all the playfulness gone between them?

"You are way better than her," he said, and he looked at her with such genuine male appreciation that she nearly melted.

They went into the shop. It was understated and tasteful. But the salesclerk was a very chic young woman with an outrageous purple streak in her blond hair. She rushed at them, probably, Jessica thought, to get rid of her, the same as in the movie.

"My first customers of the day," she said gleefully. Then she eyed Jessica with the look of a seasoned fashion aficionado. Rather than judgment or snobbery, Jessica sensed friendliness and very genuine concern. "What is that you are wearing?"

In a tone that should be reserved for "I'm so sorry to hear about the death in your family."

"I'm having a little trouble with my arm," Jessica said defensively.

"Even so, you're lovely! And just a little bit of a thing. You have to show off your assets!" She cast Kade a look that clearly said, "Especially if you are with a guy who looks like that," and that she clearly considered him an asset worth keeping.

"Thank you. We'll just have a quick look around," Jessica said.

"No, no, *no*. I am going to guide you through your Chrysalis experience."

"Oh, dear," Jessica mumbled, and sent Kade a pleading look. *Get me out of here.* But Kade folded his arms over his chest and shrugged slightly. *Let's just go with it.*

"I will have you fixed up in no time. In fact, I will love working with you. Caterpillar to butterfly, as our name suggests. I'm Holly, by the way."

The girl's enthusiasm was so genuine that Jessica could not even stir herself to annoyance at being called, basically, an insect pupa.

"Usually, I would ask about your lifestyle, but today I think you're looking for some things that are easier to get in and out of, aren't you?"

Kade frowned at Holly. "We were hoping for some-one more like the salesclerk in *Pretty Woman*. You know? If you could just be snotty, and then I flash my gold card at you and you fall all over yourself trying to help us out."

Holly laughed. "Well, I like the gold card part. And I always fall all over myself trying to help people out." She looked at Jessica. "How would you feel if I just put you in a change room and found some things that I think would work for you?"

Jessica should be insulted. She was obviously being told she could not be trusted to pick out her own things, but given the dress she had on, could she blame the girl?

"I like to encourage everyone to let me pick some things for them," Holly said. "You know, people get in shopping ruts."

Out of the corner of her vision, Jessica saw Kade roll his eyes at the near religious fervor Holly apparently had for the shopping experience.

Undaunted, Holly went on. "They pick variations of the same thing for themselves over and over. Sometimes a fresh eye can be amazing. And then, you can model what I pick out for you for your extremely handsome boyfriend."

"Husband," Kade said. "Though I like the handsome part."

"Oh, sorry. No rings," Holly said. She squinted at him. "Though you look as though you've had one on recently."

Jessica's gaze flew to Kade's ring finger. Sure enough, a white band of skin marked where his wedding ring had been. The band had been there recently, obviously, since such marks faded rather quickly. What did it mean that he had worn his ring so recently?

Stay in the moment, she ordered herself sternly. She had one mission today. To have fun. To let go. To be free. And if she ended up, with Holly's help, looking a little bit better than she looked right now, she'd go with that, too.

For once, Jessica felt no desire at all to hide behind their upcoming divorce.

She followed Holly obediently to the back of the store. There was a classy sitting area there for Kade, complete with a comfy deep upholstered chair and a huge flat-screen TV. Holly handed him the remote, and then shooed Jessica into an opulent change room.

Minutes later, she was back. "I don't mean to be presumptuous, but I brought you this." She held up a bra. "Front closing."

And sexy as all get out. Jessica took the bra with her good hand and suddenly ached to put it on. To give herself permission to be feminine and beautiful.

She had not felt like a beautiful woman since her husband had left her. Despite career success, somehow she carried loneliness and defeat within her.

A thought, unwelcome, came out of nowhere.

Had she been planning on using a child to combat her pervasive feeling of inadequacy? She shook off the shadow that passed over her. Today was just about fun. She had given herself over to introspection quite enough in the past year.

"You are a lifesaver," Jessica told Holly, and then surrendered to the process. She allowed herself to be spoiled completely. Holly did have an exceptional eye for fashion, and along with the bra, she had soon provided Jessica with a stack of clothing topped by a filmy jade silk top.

None of it was anything Jessica would have chosen

for herself. She had become the master of understated. Almost all her clothes were in neutrals, grays and taupes, as if, she realized with a start, she was trying to make herself invisible.

Jessica fingered the silk and felt a pure and simple longing. To be pretty.

It occurred to her she had not cared about being pretty since long before Kade had left her. Since she had lost the second baby.

"This will be amazing with your eyes. And look—Velcro fasteners!"

"You found a top with a Velcro closure? Is this really silk? Where's the price tag?"

"Your Prince Charming out there told me to take the price tags off."

"Humph," she said, but she didn't feel nearly as annoyed as she should have. She didn't have to buy it, she reminded herself. She just had to have fun with it.

Soon, the ensemble was completed with an easy-to-pull-on skirt with a flirty hemline and a delicate pair of sandals that Jessica could just slip her feet into.

"You look awesome," Holly said. "Go show him."

Jessica stared at herself in the mirror. "Um, I think I look a bit too young." Plus, the blouse was extremely sheer, which explained Holly bringing a sexy bra with it.

"Nonsense."

"This looks like something a teenager would wear. Don't you think the skirt is a little, um, short? Not to mention the blouse is a little, er, see-through."

"When you have legs like that? Show them off, girlfriend. Same with your other assets. Now go show him! He'll let you know how right that look is for you."

Feeling strangely shy about sharing this oddly intimate moment with Kade, the same as she had felt this morning sharing space with him, Jessica exited the change room. Kade had found a football game on TV and didn't even look impatient. He looked content.

And then he noticed her. He flipped off the sound. His eyes darkened. She suddenly didn't care how short the skirt was or if the blouse was see-through. She did a saucy little spin.

"Wow," he said, his voice hoarse. "You look incredible. Two thumbs-up to that one."

Jessica didn't just feel beautiful for the first time in a long time. She felt sexy. It felt unbelievably good to feel sexy with no agenda, no calendar lurking in the back of her mind, no temperature to take. It felt, well, fun. And after that, she just gave herself over to the experience completely.

It was fun, having Holly help her in and out of outfits, and then modeling them for Kade, who was a great audience. He raised his eyebrows, and did low wolf whistles and louder ones. He made her feel as if she was not only sexy and beautiful, but as if she was the only woman in the world he felt that way about.

But even so, Jessica had to draw the line somewhere, and she drew it at an evening dress Holly hauled in.

"I have absolutely nowhere to wear such a thing," she said. Still, she touched it wistfully. Like everything in Chrysalis, the cut and the fabric were mouthwatering. "I won't be able to get it on over my arm."

"Sure you will," Holly said. "It's back fastening, so I'll just drop it over your head, like this, and poof. Ooh, butterfly."

It took a bit more work for them to get her arm out

the sleeve, but then she was standing there looking at herself, stunned.

Her hair was flyaway from all the in-and-out of trying on clothes, but somehow that added to the sense of electricity in the air. The dress, the color of licking flame, fit her like a glove, then flared out at the bottom in a mermaid hemline.

"Here." Holly crouched at her feet. "Let me slip these on you."

As if in a dream, Jessica lifted one foot and then the other. She stared at herself in the mirror. The heels had added three inches to her height. The cast and sling on her arm might as well have disappeared, the outfit was so attention grabbing, especially with a very deep, plunging neckline.

Holly stood back and looked at her with satisfaction. "*This* is exactly what I envisioned from the moment you walked through the door. Go show him."

Should she? What was the point? It didn't feel fun anymore. It felt strangely intense, almost like the moment she had walked toward him down that long aisle in her wedding dress.

She was going to protest, but when Holly held open the door for her, Jessica sucked in her breath and walked out. Holly slid away.

Kade didn't look right away. "Don't drop it!" he yelled at the TV. And then he turned and saw her. Without taking his eyes off her, he turned off the remote. The television screen went blank. He stood up. His mouth fell open and then he shut it, and rocked back on his heels, looking at her with eyes narrowed with passion.

This was what she had missed when that moment she had glided down the aisle toward him had been replaced by the pressures of everyday living, by disappointments, by hurts, by misunderstandings.

"Jessie," he whispered.

This was what she had missed. She leaned toward him.

CHAPTER FIFTEEN

JESSIE LEANED TOWARD HIM, looking at him with heavy-lidded eyes.

*Pretty woman...walking down the street...*The music seemed to explode into the small dressing room and waiting area. Jessica gasped and put her hand to her throat, wobbled on the high heels.

Kade was in front of her instantly, looking down at her with concern.

"Sorry," she said. "I keep startling from loud noises."

He cocked his head at her. The room flooded with Roy Orbison's distinctive vocals. Kade took one step closer to her. He held out his hand, and she didn't hesitate, not for one second. She took his hand. Kade drew her to him and rocked her against him.

And then, as if they had planned it, as if they had never stopped dancing with each other, they were moving together. Even though the tempo of the song was fast, they did not dance that way.

They slow danced around the waiting area, their bodies clinging to each other, their gazes locked. The music faded, but they didn't let go, but stood very still, drinking each other in, as if they could make up for a whole year lost.

Holly burst in. "How cool was that, that I found—" She stopped. "Whoa. You two are *hot*."

Kade's arms slid away from Jessica. He stepped back. He swept a hand through his hair. "We'll take it," he said.

"That dress?" Holly said.

"No. Everything. Every single thing she tried on."

Jessica's mouth opened, but the protest was stuck somewhere in her throat, and not a single sound came out. She turned and went back into the change cubicle.

"Wear this one," Holly suggested, following her in. She dug through the pile of clothing to the very first outfit Jessica had tired on, the jade top and skirt.

But she didn't want to wear that one. Her world felt totally rattled by what had just happened, by how spontaneously she and Kade had gone into each other's arms. She wanted to feel safe again.

"Where's the dress I came in here with?"

Holly giggled. "He told me to throw it away."

"What?"

"Yeah, he said to grab it at my first opportunity and dispose of it."

"And you just listened to him? That's outrageous."

"He's very masterful," Holly said with an unapologetic sigh. "Besides—" she winked "—he's the one with the credit card."

Jessica thought of the frank male appreciation in his eyes as she had modeled her new outfits, and she contemplated how she was feeling right now.

Alive. One hundred percent in the land of the living, the life force tingling along the surface of her skin. Did she want to go back to safety? To reclaim that familiar wooden feeling she had lived with for so long?

Why not, just for today, embrace this? That she was

alive? And that her life was alight with the unexpected element of fun? And with the unexpected sizzle of attraction between her and the man she had married.

They left the store with Kade's arms loaded with parcels, and with her feeling fresh and flirty and like a breath of spring in the first outfit she had tried on. He had paid for everything.

"I'll pay you back," she said. He had insisted on buying every single thing she had donned, even the evening gown.

Since the theme of the day was fun, she'd given in. But buying the gown? That was just silly. She had nowhere to wear an evening gown. Her future plans did not involve anything that would require formal wear. In fact, she needed to be stocking up on comfy pants and sweatshirts that could hold up to baby puke and other fluids associated with the delights of motherhood.

But she had been so caught up in the moment, and the dress had made her feel so uncharacteristically glamorous—sexy, even—that she had actually wanted to be silly. She had wanted to purchase that piece of silk and gossamer that had made her feel better than a movie star.

She should have protested more—she knew that when the bill was totaled—but the look in his eyes when he had seen her had sold every single outfit to her. She'd had a ridiculous sense of *needing* those clothes, though in her heart, she knew what she wanted was the look in his eyes. "Once we sell the house, I'll pay you back," she said firmly.

"Whatever. Hey, this stuff is already heavy. Look. There's one of those rickshaw things being pulled by a bike. Have you ever been in one of those?"

"No."

He juggled the packages to his left arm, put his two fingers to his lips and let out a piercing whistle. The driver, a fit-looking twentysomething guy, pulled over.

"Where to?"

"Ah, we aren't sure yet. I think we need you for the day. Have you got a day rate?"

"I do now!"

Jessica knew she should have protested when the driver named his rate, but somehow she just couldn't. She and Kade piled into the narrow seat of the rickshaw, squished together, all their packages bunched in with them.

"Where to?"

"We need a picnic lunch," Kade decided. "And a bottle of wine. And a forest. Maybe Yan's for the lunch. Do you feel like Szechuan?"

She thought of all those menus she had sorted through yesterday, each one representing a memory. She loved Szechuan-style Chinese food. "Two orders of ginger beef," she reminded him.

Their driver took off across the downtown, darting in and out of traffic, getting them honked at, shaking his fist and yelling obscenities at drivers of vehicles.

It was hysterically funny, and she could not stop laughing. That wondrous feeling of being alive continued to tingle along the surface of her skin.

"You're going to get us killed," she said with a laugh as a cab they had cut off laid on the horn. She clung to Kade's arm as the rickshaw swayed violently, and then their driver bumped up on a curb. "Or get my other arm broken."

He twirled an imaginary moustache. "Ah, getting

you right where I want you. Helpless. And then I can ply my lethal charms against you."

Kade flopped down on the blanket that he had purchased. The driver had found them a quiet spot on Prince's Island, and had managed to make himself scarce while Kade and Jessica enjoyed their picnic under a leafy tree, with the sound of the river in the background. Now, after too much food, and most of a bottle of wine, Kade felt sleepy and relaxed.

"Two orders of ginger beef," he moaned. "It's masochistic."

"Nobody was forcing you to eat it."

"You know why we always have to buy two, though." *Always*, as if there was not a yearlong blank spot in their relationship, as if they could just pick up where they had left off. He considered where they had left off, and thought, despite his current level of comfort with Jessica, why would they want to?

"Yes, we always have to buy two because you eat the first one by yourself, and most of the second one."

"Guilty," he moaned. "My tummy hurts, Jessie."

"And three spring rolls," she reminded him. "And most of the sizzling rice." Despite the sternness in her tone, when he opened one eye, she was smiling. She looked as utterly content as he could remember her looking in a long, long time.

He lifted up his shirt and showed her his tummy. She sighed, and scooted over beside him, that teeny-tiny skirt hitching way up her legs, and rubbed his stomach with gentle hands.

"Ah," he said, and closed his eyes. Maybe it was because he had not slept well last night, or maybe it was because he had eaten too much, or maybe it was because his world felt right for the first time in over a year, but with a sigh of contentment, he went to sleep.

When he woke up, she was sleeping curled up beside him. He slid his arm around her shoulders and pulled her into his side, being careful of her arm.

"Did we fall asleep?" she asked.

"Yeah."

"Is our driver still here? Or did he take off with all my new stuff?"

Kade got up on one elbow. He could see the rickshaw over by the riverbank. When he craned his head, he could see the driver tapping earnestly at his phone with his thumbs.

"I haven't paid him yet. He's not going anywhere." He slid his own phone out of his pocket and checked the time. "Holy, it's four o'clock already."

"It's been a perfect day," she said.

"Agreed. What was the best part for you? The shopping? I love the long dress."

"I don't have a single place to wear a dress like that," she said. "I shouldn't have bought it."

"Yes, you should have. I want you to accept it as a gift from me. You can pay me back for the rest of that stuff if you insist—"

"Which I do!"

"But I want to buy that dress."

"Why do you want to buy me a dress that I probably will never wear?"

"Wear it around the house. Put a movie on, and wear it to watch it. Eat popcorn in it."

She laughed. "That seems eccentric and foolhardy. What if I got butter on it?"

"That's what I liked about it. You know what it reminded me of, Jess?"

"No. What?" She held her breath.

"It reminded me of those paintings you used to do, the ones that were all swirling colors and amazing motion."

"I haven't thought about those for years," she said.

"Save the dress and wear it to the unveiling of your first art show."

She laughed a little nervously. "I'm not having a first art show."

"But that's what I've always wondered. Where did that part of you go?"

"I paint murals," she said. "That's my creative outlet."

"I don't think bunnies on walls do justice to your gifts," he said.

"I don't care what you think!" she snapped. "Sorry. Let's not ruin the moment with you telling me how to live my life."

She was right. This was not any of his business, not anymore. Maybe it never had been.

"Is there any ginger beef left?" he asked wistfully.

"No."

"How about sizzling rice?"

And then the moment of tension was gone, and she laughed and passed him the container. It seemed like the most natural thing in the world to go home to his place together. And then to say good-night with unnatural formality and to go to their separate bedrooms.

The next morning, they both got up. He ordered croissants again. She came out to eat one in the too-large shirt.

"I guess I should have been shopping for pajamas instead of evening dresses," she said.

What kind of kettle of worms would it open up, he

wondered, if he said he liked what she had on—his shirt—way better than pajamas?

"Are you coming back here after you've finished work?" he asked her. He was holding his breath waiting for her reply.

"I guess," she said, and he heard in her voice the very same things he was feeling. What were they reopening, exactly, by living under the same roof? What were they moving toward? Were they putting a framework in place for their future relationship? Was it possible they could be one of those rare amicably divorced couples who were friends?

He hoped things would become clear in the next few days, because he did not like uncertainty. And at the moment, his future seemed murky, like looking into a most uncooperative crystal ball.

CHAPTER SIXTEEN

MONDAY, AFTER WORK, Jessica returned to Kade's apartment. She was somewhat ashamed that she had not done a single thing to make new living arrangements for herself. And now here she was, aware she was waiting for the door of the apartment to open.

Why? Kade never came home at regular hours. What was she waiting for? Hadn't this been part of their whole problem? That she waited, as if her whole life depended on him, and he had a whole life that had nothing to do with her?

Surely she'd come further than this, still waiting for him to come home! It was pathetic, and she was not being pathetic anymore. And so, instead of sitting in the apartment, she went and explored his building.

There was a good-size pool that they were conducting a kayaking class in, and beside that was a climbing wall. She went and sat on a bench and watched people climb the wall.

A good-looking man came over and introduced himself as Dave and asked her if she was going to try it.

She held up her arm. "Already did," she said, deadpan. He laughed and flirted with her a bit, and she realized whatever had happened when she had put on all those clothes had been good. She was wearing one of her new outfits, and it seemed to fill her with confidence she hadn't had for some time. Dave went up the wall, obviously showing off, and she was content to let him.

She watched for a while, and decided as soon as her arm got better, she would try climbing. The wall looked really fun.

After doing a thorough tour of the building and the gorgeous gardens outside, which included that impressive waterfall at the front, she wandered back to the apartments.

Kade was there. Did he look pleased when she let herself in using the code he had given her?

"Hey," he said. "How was your day?"

"Oh, I struggled through."

"Work late?"

"Oh, no, I've been back for a while. I thought I'd check out your building. It's great. I love the climbing wall."

"Really? I've never been on it. Is that one of the outfits we bought yesterday?"

"Yeah, I've had lots of comments on it. A guy named Dave, down at the climbing wall, stopped to talk to me. I don't think he normally would have mistaken me for his type."

She felt just the littlest thrill of pleasure that Kade could not hide his annoyance at Dave's attention.

"Want to order something for dinner? I don't have much here to cook." He snapped his fingers. "Unless you want an omelet."

He'd always made the best omelets.

"Perfect," she said.

And it was perfect. After dinner they watched the

news together, and it felt so utterly easy, as if they were an old married couple.

Which they were, sort of.

Of course, when they'd been a newly married couple, they hadn't sat around watching television. They couldn't keep their hands off each other. Later, when that stage had passed—or when she'd killed it, by bringing out the dreaded chart—they had played cards sometimes in the evening.

She suddenly longed for that.

"You have a deck of cards, Kade?"

"Why? You want to play strip poker?" he asked with such earnest hopefulness she burst out laughing.

"No!"

"How about a strip Scrabble game, then?"

"How about just an ordinary Scrabble game?" she said, trying not to encourage him by laughing.

"Can we use bad words?"

"I suppose that would be okay. Just this once."

"How about if we use only bad words?"

She gave him a slug on his arm. "That falls into the 'give him an inch and he'll take a mile' category."

Suddenly, she wanted to play a bad-words Scrabble game with him. She wanted to not be the uptight one, the stick-in-the-mud. "A bad-words Scrabble game it is," she said.

"I don't actually have a Scrabble board."

"That figures."

"But I bet we can find it on the computer."

And so that was what they did, sat side by side on his sofa, playing a bad-words Scrabble game on the computer until she was laughing so hard it felt as if she could die from it.

"So," he said casually, after he had just played *phaut*, "tell me why you want a divorce all of a sudden."

"I told you, it's not all of a sudden."

"But there's something going on."

And, maybe he'd done this on purpose, reminded her of what it was like to have a best friend, because she wanted to tell him. Crazily, she wanted to know what he thought.

"I'm thinking of adopting a baby," she said quietly.

He was staring at her. "Aw, Jess," he said, not as if he was happy for her, but as if he pitied her.

"What does that mean?" she asked.

"It's the Old English spelling of *fart*," he said. "*P-h-a-u-t*. You can challenge it if you want. But you miss a turn if you're wrong."

She had just told him something very important! How could he act as if the stupid word he'd made up was more engrossing?

"Not *that*. What does 'aw, Jess' mean?"

"Never mind. I'm sorry I said it."

She saw, suddenly, that he was using his stupid made-up word as a way not to get into it with her. "No, I want you to tell me."

"But then when I do, you'll be mad," he said, confirming his avoidance strategy.

"Will I?" When had she become that person? The one who invited opinions, but then was angry if they were not what she wanted to hear? She wanted it not to be a truth about her, but in her gut, she knew it was.

"You don't want to hear what I have to say, but maybe I'm going to say it anyway, for the sake of the baby."

She felt as if she was bracing herself.

"A baby isn't supposed to fill a need in you, Jessica," he said quietly. "You're supposed to fulfill its needs."

Jessica felt the shock of it. She felt as if she should be very, very angry with him. But she was not. Instead, she remembered the revelation she'd had in the change room of Chrysalis, the one she had tried to shake off.

That she was using a child to try to fight off her own pervasive feeling of inadequacy. Instead of being angry with Kade, Jessica was, instead, sharply aware she had carried a certain neediness in her since the death of her mother. The miscarriages had made it worse.

So Kade had called a spade a spade. She saw, from the look on his face, it was not a put-down at all. She had a deep sense of his courage, that he had handed her a simple truth, knowing it might make her angry, but also believing she needed to hear it. And maybe also believing she would know what to do with it.

Jessica remembered how before she had hated everything about Kade, she had loved everything about him. And this was one of the things she had loved, that he had a way of seeing right to the heart of things. He would have shrugged it off, uncomfortable, if she called it intuition, but that was exactly what it was.

It was part of what made him so good at business. He was brilliantly insightful. Before things had gone sideways between them, Jessica had loved his input, so different from her own.

"I've been too blunt," he said. "I'm sorry."

"No, Kade," she said, "it's what I needed to hear, even if it's not what I wanted to hear."

She suspected this was why she had not wanted to tell him about the adoption, because he could shed a light on her plans that could change everything.

"You and I," she said, "we've always been so different. It's as if we each have the pieces of half of a puzzle.

It's when we're together that we can piece together the whole thing."

She thought of those adoption papers at home, and it occurred to her this was what he had shown her: she was still wanting a baby to fill gaps in her life.

She had probably never been less ready for a baby than she was right now.

"I'm very tired now," she whispered, feeling as if she was holding the remnants of another shattered dream within herself. "I'm going to bed."

"Jess, I'm sorry. I didn't want to hurt you."

She smiled wanly. "Oh, Kade, I don't think we ever wanted to hurt each other. And yet, somehow we always do."

And yet, over the next few days it was as if something had broken free between them; a wall of ice had crumbled, and what was held behind it flowed out. As they shared his beautiful space, there were moments of spontaneous laughter. And quiet companionship. As they shared meals and memories and old connections, they rediscovered their comfort with one another. And caught glimpses of the joy they had once shared. And relaxed into that rare sensation of having found someone in the world with whom it was possible to be genuine.

And so when Jake called Kade on Thursday afternoon and told him that the house was done, Kade felt not happy that the work had been finished so quickly, but a sense of loss. He wanted to give Jake a list of ten more things to do. No, a hundred. No, a thousand.

He brought her the news after work. Jessica had arrived at the apartment before him. She was wearing one of the outfits they had bought together—a lively floral-print dress with a belt and a wide skirt that reminded him of something someone might wear to dance the jive.

She had her arm out of the sling and was wiping down his counters. Once it had bugged him so much that she felt driven to wipe up every crumb.

But now, watching her, he could see it gave her a kind of contentment to be bringing order to her space, and he found he liked watching her.

She looked up and saw him standing there, and she smiled a greeting.

"Hey! You are not supposed to be out of that sling yet."

"You know me."

It was the most casual of statements, but it filled him with some sense of satisfaction that, yes, he did know her.

"I could not handle the mess on the counter. I needed both hands free to wring out the dishcloth."

"You've always been such a stickler for tidy."

"I know. You used to protest daily, *too many rules*."

"Did I? I don't remember that."

Jessica cast Kade a look. Could he really not remember the mean things he had said to her?

"You called me the sock Nazi," she remembered ruefully. Was she hoping he would apologize? He didn't. He cocked his head at her, and looked at her in that way that made her stomach do the roller-coaster thing.

"I couldn't understand the changes in you," he said. "We said 'I do' and overnight you went from being this kind of Bohemian free-spirited artist to Martha Stewart's understudy."

"And you," she reminded him, "resisted me at every turn. It drove me crazy. If I put out a laundry hamper,

you would throw your dirty clothes on the floor beside it."

It had driven her crazy that she had been creating this
perfect little nest for them—a perfect world, really—and
he'd resisted her at every turn. He'd left his socks in the
living room. He'd hung his towels crooked in the bathroom. He'd left dishes in the sink, and if he'd been working outside and forgot something in the house, he'd just
traipsed in, leaving a pathway of leaves and grass and
mud in his wake.

"I know I could be inconsiderate," he said, but he
didn't sound very remorseful. "I felt as if you were trying to control me all the time, I felt as if you thought the
way you wanted to live was the only correct way, and
what I wanted, to be a little relaxed in my own space,
didn't count at all."

Jessica felt shocked by that. It was certainly true. She
had always wanted things her way.

"And then I'd come home from working all day, and
you'd have some elaborate meal all prepared and candles
on the table and the best dishes out. I would have been
just as happy with a hamburger and my feet up on the
coffee table in front of the TV. Not that I was allowed
to put my feet up on the coffee table, even though it was
really a bench that was sturdy enough to have survived
one war, a fire and two floods."

She was aghast at the picture he was painting. He
looked as if he was going to stop, but now that the flood-
gates were open, he was completely unable to.

"I wanted to talk to you the way we had always
talked—about ideas and dreams and your art. I wanted
to laugh with you and be lighthearted.

"But suddenly all you wanted to talk about was paint

colors for the nursery and could we please get a new sofa, and did I think there was too much tarragon in the recipe. *Tarragon*, Jess."

And so this was how their relationship had started to show cracks, she thought. She had known it was all going dreadfully wrong.

"I wanted to shake you, and say, 'Who are you and what the hell have you done with Jessica?'"

It wasn't until after he'd gone from her life that she realized how stupid it had been to make an issue out of the very things she then had missed.

"But you—" Jessica's defensive response died on her lips. She considered the possibility he was right. Instead of feeling defensive, she let what he had just said sink in. Suddenly, for the first time, it occurred to her maybe she should be the one who was sorry. If she was going to move on, if she was going to be a good parent—no, a great parent—to a child someday, she had to start working on herself now. And part of that meant facing her role in the relationship going wrong.

Up until this point, had she really told herself she had no part in it? That it was all his fault?

"What happened to you?" he asked. "And worse, what did I have to do with it?"

"Nothing," she said softly, and with dawning realization. "You had nothing to do with it. I think, Kade, ever since my mom died, I longed to have *that* world again.

"I was only twelve when she was diagnosed with a rare form of cancer. She went from diagnosis to dead in three weeks."

"I know that," he said, reminding her he knew so much about her.

"But what you didn't know—maybe what I didn't

even know until this minute—was that I wanted my world back. After she died, it was just my dad and my brother and me. Everything went south. The house was a catastrophe. We ate takeout and macaroni and cheese. I couldn't even invite a friend over, our house was such a disaster. I wanted my lovely, stable family back."

"Oh, Jessie," he said. "I probably should have figured that out."

"And then we got married," she said slowly, "and I already had this idea in my head what a perfect life looked like, and I set out to make our life together look like that. And when I could sense you were dissatisfied, I thought it was because we needed to take the next step—to solidify ourselves as a family."

"You decided you wanted to have a baby."

"Didn't you want to have a baby?" she asked.

"Of course I did," he reassured her. "But maybe not for me. I wanted you to be happy. It didn't seem as though paint chips and the creative use of tarragon were making you happy. It certainly didn't seem as though I was making you happy."

CHAPTER SEVENTEEN

So HERE WAS a painful truth looking Jessica in the face. She'd had a wonderful husband who loved her, and somehow she had managed to manufacture misery.

Not that their challenges had not been real, but why hadn't she been able to focus on everything that was right and good, instead of working away at the tiny cracks until they had become fractures between Kade and her?

As painful as this conversation was, Jessica was relieved by it. This was the conversation they had needed to have a year ago, when everything had fallen apart so completely between them. Maybe if they had had it even before that, they could have stopped things from progressing to a complete fallout.

"When the first miscarriage happened," Jessica admitted softly, "I think it was a cruel reminder of what I'd already learned from my mother's illness—I was not in control of anything. And yet instead of surrendering to that, I fought it hard. The more out of control I felt, the more I started trying to control everything. Maybe especially you."

"Jessica," Kade said, and his voice was choked, "I always saw the failure as mine, not yours."

Her eyes filled with tears. It was not what she needed to hear, not right now, just as she was acknowledging her part in their marriage catastrophe.

"When I married you," Kade said, his voice low and pain-filled, "it felt as if that was a sacred vow and that I had found my lifelong duty. It was to protect you. To keep you safe. To stop bad things from happening. I felt as if my love should be enough to protect us—and you—from every storm.

"When it wasn't? When the growing chasm between us was made impassable by the two miscarriages, I could not enter your world anymore. I felt as if I was losing my mind. Those miscarriages, those lost babies, made me admit to myself how powerless I was. I couldn't do the most important thing I'd ever wanted to do. I could not save my own babies.

"And that compounded the fact I was already dealing with a terrible sense of failure at lesser levels."

"What levels?" she asked.

"I had failed to even make you happy. I wanted you to stop trying to get pregnant. But you wouldn't. It made me feel as if I was not enough to meet your needs. It felt as if the bottom fell out of our whole world. When you wanted to keep trying—keep subjecting yourself and us to that roller-coaster ride of hope and joy and grief and despair—I just couldn't do it. And so I retreated to a world where I could be in control."

"And abandoned me," she whispered.

"Yes," he said quietly. "Yes. Yes, I did abandon you. But I think not nearly so thoroughly as you abandoned yourself. It was as if a baby was going to become your whole reason and your whole life."

She realized that she had not been ready then, and she

was not really ready now, either. She began to cry. She had vowed no more losses, and now she faced the biggest one of all. Somehow in marriage, she had lost herself. She had become the role she played instead of the person she was.

Kade had always hated tears.

Always. If they argued and she started crying, he left.

Except when they had lost the first baby. They had crawled into bed together and clung to each other and wept until there were no tears left.

But after that, it was as if he steeled himself against that kind of pain, against feeling so intensely ever again. Even after the devastation of the loss of the second baby, he had been capable of only a few clumsy claps on the shoulder, a few of the kinds of platitudes she had come to hate the most.

It had seemed as if her grief had alienated him even more, had driven him away even more completely.

The tears trickled down her cheeks. She could not stop them now that they had been let loose.

She expected him to do what he had always done: escape at the first sign of a loss of control on her part. But he didn't.

"Jessie," Kade said softly. "In retrospect, we weren't ready for those babies. Neither of us was. We thought our relationship was on firm ground, but at the first stress, it fractured, so it wasn't. Babies need to come into a stronger place than that."

He came and he put his arms around her. He drew her deep against him, doing what she had needed so desperately from him all along. He let her tears soak into his shirt.

"I'm okay now," she finally sighed against him. "Thank you."

"For what?" he growled.

"For holding me. It's all I ever needed. Not for you to fix things, but for you to be there, as solid as a rock, when things went sideways."

He looked at her. He nodded. She could see the regret in his face. She could see that he got it. Completely.

And then something changed in his eyes, and he reached down and lifted a tear off her cheek with his finger, and scraped his thumb across her lip.

Jessica could feel the move into the danger zone. And she should have stepped back from it. But she could not.

A part of her that would not be controlled missed him—and missed this part of their life together—with a desperation that made her think she knew how heroin addicts felt. The *need* overshadowed everything. It overpowered common sense and reason. It certainly overpowered the need to be in control and the need to be right.

They were all gone—common sense and reason, control and the need to be right. They were gone, and in their place his thumb scraping across her lip became her whole world. Her lips parted, and she drew his thumb into her mouth. His skin tasted of heaven.

He went very still. She gazed up at him. And then she stood on her tiptoes, and she pulled his head down to her. She kissed that beautiful, familiar little groove behind his ear. He groaned his surrender and placed his hands on each side of her face and looked down at her, and then lowered his mouth to hers.

Welcome.

Welcome home.

His hunger was as apparent as hers. He crushed her lips under his own. His tongue found the hollow of her mouth, and she melted against him as he devoured her. His lips moved away from hers and he anointed the hollow of her throat and the tip of her nose and her eyelids.

"Jessica," he said hoarsely. "Oh, Jessica."

He scooped her up in his arms and went to the hallway to his bedroom. He tapped open the partially closed door with his foot, strode across the room and laid her on his king-size bed. It gave luxuriously under her weight. She stared up at him.

And wanted her husband, Kade, as she had never wanted anything else in her entire life. The wanting sizzled in her belly, and curled around her heart, and came out her lips as a moan of desire and invitation. She held out her good arm to him.

And he came willingly down to her, laying his body over hers, careful to hold his weight off her broken wing. He found the lobe of her ear and nipped it with delicate precision. He rained tiny kisses down on her brow and her nose and her cheeks and her chin.

Finally, when she was gasping with wanting and longing, he captured her lips and nuzzled teasingly. And then he took her lips more deeply, laying his claim, stoking the fire that was already there to white-hot.

"I am going to melt," she said hoarsely.

"Melt, then," he whispered. "Melt, and I will come with you."

His mouth on hers became a fury of possession and hunger. His tongue plunged the cool cavern of her mouth, exploring, darting, resting, tasting. He left her mouth and trailed kisses down the open collar of her shirt. He laid his trail of fire down her neck and onto her breastbone. His fingers found the buttons of her blouse and released them one by one. His lips found the nakedness of her flesh where it mounded above her bra, then blazed down the rise of her ribs to the fall of her belly. His lips went to all the places on her that only his lips had ever been before.

She did not melt. Rather, the heat built to a near explosion. The first of July, Canada Day, was weeks away, but the fireworks had begun already. They started, always, with the smaller ones, delightful little displays of color and noise, smoke and beauty. But they built and built and built to a fiery crescendo that lit the entire sky and shook the entire world.

It was obvious from the need that ached within her, from the way her body arched against him in welcome and anticipation, that this particular set of fireworks was heading toward only one possible climax.

"My arm— I don't know..." she whispered. It was her only uneasiness. She felt no guilt and no regret. He was her husband, and they belonged to each other in this way. They always had.

Kade took his weight off her and drank her in deeply.

"Do you want to do this?" he asked, and his voice was a rasp of raw need.

She knew her answer, her certainty, was in her face, and vibrating along the whole length of her body.

"I do. It's just with my arm like this, I don't know how we're going to manage," she said.

"I do," Kade whispered, his voice a growl of pure and sensual need. He had, intentionally or not, echoed their vows. *I do.* "Do you trust me, Jessie?"

"Yes."

"I know exactly how we are going to do this," he told her.

And he did. And so did she.

When they were done, in the sacred stillness that followed, the truth hit her and hit her hard.

It was not that she loved her husband again. It was that she had never stopped. Cradling the warmth of that truth to her, in the arms of her beloved, *home* for the first time in more than a year, Jessica slept.

Kade woke deep in the night. Jessica was asleep beside him, curled tightly against him, like a puppy seeking warmth. He felt tenderness toward her unfurl in him with such strength it felt as if his throat was closing. He'd known, in some deep place inside himself, ever since he'd seen the police cars in front of her store that morning, that he still loved her.

That he could not imagine a world without her. Not just *a* world. *His world.*

Something buzzed by his ear, and Kade realized it was that sound that had woken him up, and he was momentarily confused. His phone was automatically set to Do Not Disturb during the evening hours. He picked it up off the nightstand and squinted at it. It was four-thirty in the morning.

The phone buzzed again, vibrating in his hand. It was not his normal ring. Suddenly it occurred to him they had programmed the alarm at Baby Boomer to this phone to override his do-not-disturb settings. He unlocked the screen. Sure enough, there was a live-feed image of someone at the door of Baby Boomer.

Glancing at Jessica and seeing how peaceful she looked, Kade slipped from the bed, grabbed his clothes off the floor and went out into the hall. He called 911, with his phone tucked in against his ear, pulling on his pants at the same time. He explained what was happening, but the operator sounded particularly bored with his news of an alarm going off and a possible break-in in progress.

He thought of Jessica with her arm immobilized and he thought of her ongoing sleep disturbances and about the way she startled every time there was a loud sound. Even in the cubicle of the dress shop, when the music had started unexpectedly, she had nearly jumped out of her skin. Thinking of that, Kade felt really, really angry. Dangerously angry.

Jessica needed to know that he would look after her. That he would protect her. If her world was threatened, he would be there. He would put his body between her and a bullet if he had to.

And so, like a soldier getting ready to do battle for all he believed in, Kade went out the apartment door, got in his car and headed at full speed to her store.

At first it appeared no one was there. But then he noticed the newly repaired door hanging open and a sliver of light moving inside the store.

Without a single thought, he leaped from the car and took the stairs two at a time. He burst in the door and raced across the room and tackled the shadowy figure by the cash register.

Jessica was right. The thief was scrawny! Holding him in place was ridiculously easy. The anger at all the grief this guy had caused Jessica seemed to seep out of him. The thief was screaming, "Please don't hurt me."

He seemed skinny and pathetic, and just as Jessica had guessed, desperate with a kind of desperation Kade did not know.

Kade heard sirens and saw flashing lights, and moments later the police were in the doorway, telling *him* to put his hands in the air. It seemed to take forever to sort it all out, but finally, he finished filling out reports and doing interviews.

It was now nearly seven. Jessica was probably awake and probably wondering where he was.

He called her, and could hear the anxiety in her voice as soon as she answered the phone.

"Where are you?"

"The alarm at your business alerted to my phone a couple of hours ago. I headed over here."

"*You* answered the alarm?"

"Well, I called the police, but I just wanted to make sure they caught him." He laughed, adrenaline still coursing through his veins. "You were right, Jessie. He was scrawny."

She cut him off, her voice shrill. "You caught the thief?"

"Yeah," he said proudly.

"But you are the one who lectured me about being foolhardy!"

He frowned. He wanted to be her hero. He wanted her to know her world was safe with him. Why didn't she sound pleased? Why wasn't she getting the message?

"You could have been killed," she said. "He could have had a gun or a knife. You're the one who pointed that out to me."

"Jessica, it all worked out, didn't it?"

"Did it?" she said, and he did not like what he heard in her voice. "Did it, Kade?"

"Yes!"

"Kade, being in a relationship means thinking about the other person."

"I *was* thinking about you."

"No, you weren't."

"How about if you don't tell me what I was think-ing about? We had a great night last night. It doesn't mean you own me. It doesn't mean you get to control me. You know what this conversation feels like? *Here we go again*."

"Does it?" she said, and her voice was very shrill. "Well, try this out—here we *don't* go again!"

And she slammed down the phone. He stared at his phone for a long time, and finally put it back in his pocket. He already knew, when he got back to his apart-ment, she would be gone.

CHAPTER EIGHTEEN

JESSICA HUNG UP the phone. She was shaking violently. She hugged herself against the feeling of being cold.

And she faced an awful truth about herself. Her courage was all used up. She did not have one drop left. This love made her feel so vulnerable, and she did not want to feel that way anymore.

She thought of how it had been last night, of Kade's heated lips anointing every inch of her fevered flesh.

In the cold light of dawn, her heart swelled with loving him.

But it didn't feel good at all. It felt as if that love could not make her whole and could even destroy what was left of her.

It was her curse: her mother, whom she had loved so deeply, taken from her. And then each of those babies, whom she had loved madly and beyond reason, without even having met them, gone from this earth.

Loving Kade felt as if it was leaving herself open to one more loss. And he could be reckless. Impulsive. Look what he had just done! That could have been a far different phone call. It could have been the police calling to tell her Kade was dead.

Was he right? Was she trying to control him? Whatever—she had a deep sense that she could not sustain one more loss.

Quietly, Jessica walked through his beautiful apartment. With each step a memory: pizza and warm croissants and sitting on the sofa and playing a Scrabble game. She went back to the guest room, put on the nearest thing she could find, but left all the rest of the clothing they had bought together, because it, too, held too many memories.

Of dancing with him in Chrysalis. She should have recognized the danger right that second, before rickshaw rides, and Chinese food in the park, and falling asleep on a blanket with the trees whispering their names. Before it had all built to that moment last night of unbridled passion, of *hoping* for the most uncertain thing of all.

The future.

Feeling like a thief who had stolen the most precious thing of all, a moment of the pure pleasure of love, Jessica slipped out the door of Kade's empty apartment and locked it behind her. She went down to the lobby and had the concierge call her a cab.

In minutes, she was being whisked through the dawn-drenched city. As soon as they pulled up in front of her house, she wished that she had thought to go to a hotel.

Because this was more of them, of her and of Kade. It was the house they had chosen together and lived in together and loved in together.

And fought in together, she reminded herself, and watched love make that torturous metamorphosis to hate.

She could not survive that again. She could not survive losing him again.

When she let herself in the house, she felt relief. It wasn't really *their* house anymore. Though all her familiar furniture was back, except her bench, which was still in the back of a truck somewhere, everything else felt new.

Except Behemoth, which seemed to be squatting on the new floor glaring accusingly at her.

It even smelled new, of floor varnish and paint. The floors glowed with soft beauty; the walls had been painted a dove gray. The soot was gone from where they had tried to use the fireplace that one time, and it was gone off the ceiling.

Jessica went through to the kitchen, and it was as she had dreaded. She reached up and touched the cabinets. The oak stain was no longer bleeding through the white, and that, more than anything else, made her feel like crying.

She kicked off her shoes and passed her bedroom. There would be no going back to bed. She was sure of that. She went to her office and slid open the desk drawer.

Jessica took out all the documents she needed to start filling out to begin the adoption procedure, to get on with her dreams of a life in a way that did not involve him.

But as she stared at the papers, she realized she was terrified of everything that love meant, and especially of the built-in potential for loss and heartbreak.

She was not whole. She had never been whole. She had brought a neediness to her and Kade's relationship that had sucked the life out of it. And if she did not get herself sorted out, she would do the same to a child.

She thought of putting the documents back in the desk drawer, but it seemed to her they would be just one more thing to move, to sort through when the time came to leave here. It seemed to her she was not at all sure what she wanted anymore.

She dumped the papers in the garbage, and then she went and sat on the couch and hugged her knees to herself, and cried for who she was not, and what she was never going to have.

Finally, done with crying, done with Kade, done with dreams, she called the real estate office. An agent was there promptly, and Jessica calmly walked through the house with him as he did his appraisal. She felt numb and disconnected, as if the agent was on one side of a thick glass wall, and she was on the other. She didn't really care what price he put on the house. In fact, she barely registered the number he had given her. She gave him the listing, signed the papers, and he pounded the for-sale sign into her lawn.

She kept hoping her phone would ring, but it didn't. She and Kade had arrived at the same place, all over, an impasse that neither of them would be willing to cross. If it was a good thing, why did she feel so bereft?

After she had watched the agent pound the sign in in front of her house, she went outside and invited him to come by Baby Boomer and do the very same thing.

In the brutal light of this heartbreak, Jessica could see herself all too clearly. The business had risen from her neediness, from her need for something outside herself to fill her. It had been part of that whole obsession that she had not been able to let go of, not even after it had cost her her marriage to the man she loved.

Jessica expected to feel sad when the for-sale sign went up in front of Baby Boomer.

Instead, she felt relief. She felt oddly free.

It was going to be different now. She thought about what she really wanted, and she remembered when she had first met Kade, before she had lost herself, who she had been. An artist, not drawing pictures of bunnies on nursery walls, but drawing from a place deep within her.

That night, after she had closed the shop for the day, she went into the art-supply store next door. As soon as she walked in the door, the smells welcomed her—the smell of canvases and paints and brushes.

It smelled of home, she told herself firmly, her true home, the self she had walked away from again and again and again.

But home conjured other images: Kade laughing, and Kade with his feet up on the coffee table, and Kade's socks on the floor, and Kade opening a box of pizza, and her sitting on a sander laughing so hard she cried. She shook that off impatiently.

She had made her vow, her new vow. And it was not to have and to hold. The vow she intended to obey was that she would not lose anything else. Not one more thing. And that meant not doing anything that would open her to loss.

Possibly more than any other single thing, loving Kade fell into that category.

Over the next weeks Jessica had to relearn a terribly hard lesson: you didn't just stop loving someone because you wanted to, because it had the potential to hurt you.

Love was always there in the background, beckoning, saying you can have a larger life if you risk this. But she thought maybe it was from living in the house they had shared together that she could not shake her sense of grief and torment.

Not even painting could fill her.

So she did other things she had always wanted to do and held back from. She signed up for a rock-climbing course, and a kayaking program, and a gourmet-cooking class. She had a sense of needing to fill every second so that she would not have time to think, to be drawn into the endless pool of grief that was waiting to drown her. Jessica was aware she was searching frantically to find things she could be passionate about that did not involve that sneaky, capricious, uncontrollable force called love.

But the more she tried to do, the more exhausted she became. If these efforts to fill her life were right, wouldn't she feel energized by them, instead of completely drained? At rock climbing, her limbs were so weak she could not hold herself on the wall. At kayaking—which was only in a local swimming pool for now—she fell out of the kayak and had a panic attack. At cooking class, she took one taste of her hollandaise sauce and had to run to the bathroom and be sick.

The feeling of weakness progressed. Jessica felt tired all the time. She had fallen asleep at work. She cried at the drop of a hat. Her stomach constantly felt as if it was knotted with anxiety.

Obviously, she had been absolutely correct when she had told him, "Here we *don't* go again." She took this as evidence that she was doing the right thing. If she was having this kind of reaction to a weeklong reunion with her husband, what would happen to her if they tried it for another year? Or two? And *then* it didn't work? Obviously, she could not survive.

"You need to go see a doctor," Macy said to her after finding her fast asleep, her head on her arms on her desk. "Something is wrong with you."

And so she went to see the doctor. She knew nothing was wrong with her. Love was not an ailment a doctor could cure. You could not take a pill to mend a broken heart. The doctor ordered a raft of tests, and Jessica had them all done, knowing nothing would come of it.

But then the doctor's office phoned and asked her to come back in. There were test results they needed to discuss with her in person.

And that was when she knew the truth. Jessica knew that, like her mother, she was sick and dying. Thank God she had not proceeded with her adoption idea. Thank God she had not proceeded with loving Kade.

It was just another confirmation that she could not allow herself to love. People could leave her, but she could leave people, too. It was all just too risky.

The doctor swung into the room, all good cheer. Jessica guessed he'd had a fantastic golf game that completely overrode the news he was about to give her.

She waited for him to remember the gravity of breaking it to someone that they were dying.

But that foolish grin never left his face!

"I have wonderful news for you," he said. "You're pregnant."

She stared at him. Life was too cruel. All those years of charts and temperatures and schedules, and now she was pregnant. Plus, she knew a terrible truth. Being pregnant did not necessarily mean walking away with a baby at the end.

Hadn't she decided she was unsuited for motherhood? She called Macy and told her she wouldn't be in for the rest of the day. She went home.

Her real estate agent was on the steps. "I've been trying to call you all morning. We have an offer on your house! A great offer."

Numbly she signed the paper he shoved at her. She went into the house and closed the door. Despite all her efforts to control everything, to keep change at bay, everything was changing anyway.

What was she going to tell Kade?

Nothing. He would feel trapped. He would feel as if he had to do the honorable thing, be sentenced to a life of bickering with her.

No. There had been no pretense in their last night together. He did love her. She knew that.

And now they were in the same place all over again. Where that love would be tested by life. What would make it different this time? If they lost another baby, how would it be any better this time?

"It won't," Jessica told herself. "It won't be better. It will be worse."

She lay down on the couch and cried and cried and cried. She hoped she had cried until there were no tears left, but from experience, she knew. There were always tears left. There was always an event waiting to blindside you, waiting to make you find that place where you had hidden a few extra tears.

CHAPTER NINETEEN

KADE DISCONNECTED FROM the phone call. He was part owner in his and Jessica's house, so he had been notified. It had just sold. Jessica, apparently, could not even tell him that herself. That had been a secretary at the real estate company asking him to come in and sign some documents.

He had not seen or heard from Jessica since that night when they had made love, and then he had made the fateful decision to go and tackle the breaking and entering at her business himself.

For a guy who thought he had the emotional range of a rock, he was stunned by how he felt.

Angry. And then sad. Frustrated. Powerless. And then sad some more.

He loved his wife. He loved her beyond reason. They were two intelligent people. Why could they not build a bridge across this chasm that divided them?

He mulled over the news about the house. What was he going to do now? Should he be the one to try to cross the minefield between them? A man had to have his pride.

But it seemed to Kade pride might have had quite a bit to do with why they could not work things out in the first place.

Maybe a man didn't have to have his pride.

Maybe a man having his pride really had nothing to do with being strong, with doing what needed to be done, with doing the right thing. Maybe a man had to swallow his pride.

Jessica, Kade knew, would never take the first step toward reconciliation, and for a second he felt angry again.

But then he relived her voice on the phone that morning of the break-in. It occurred to him that Jessica had not been trying to control him. She had been genuinely terrified.

Suddenly, he felt ashamed of himself. Wasn't this part of what was destroying them? Pride? Okay, it was a guy thing. It was always all about him. Even when he told himself it was about her. For example, he would go and save her store. But it had really been about him. He'd wanted to be the hero. He'd wanted to see her eyes glowing with admiration for him.

Maybe it was time for him to grow up.

To see things through her eyes, instead of through the warp of his own colossal self-centeredness.

She had been terrified.

And right from the beginning, from the day he had first seen her again, after she had tried to take out the thief herself at her store, she had given him clues where all that terror came from.

I lost my mother when I was twelve. I've lost two babies to miscarriage. I am not losing anything else. Not one more thing.

Kade had seen what losing those babies had done to her. He had seen the intensity of her own love tear her apart.

He had seen photos of her when she was a girl. In her

fifth-grade class photo, she had been grinning merrily at the camera, all leprechaun charm and joyous mischief. But by the following year, when her mother had died, she had looked solemn and sad, the weight of the whole world on her shoulders.

He tried to imagine her at twelve, her sense of loss, her sense of the world being a safe place being gone.

The loss of each of those babies would have triggered that old torment, that sense of the world not being safe.

As would the man she loved putting himself at risk.

And suddenly, he despised himself. So what if she tried to control him?

"Kade," he said and swore to himself. "Don't you get it? It's not all about you."

He loved her. He loved Jessica Clark Brennan, his wife, beyond reason. He had cut her loose to navigate her heartbreaks on her own. When she had disappeared into that dark world of her own heartache, instead of having the courage to go in with her, to help her find her way back out, he had abandoned her.

That was not love.

But how was he going to make her see that he understood that now? He suspected she had spent the past weeks building up her defenses against him—against love. How was he going to knock them back down?

They had just sold a house together. The most natural thing in the world would be to bring a bottle of champagne over there and celebrate with her.

And it was time for honesty. Not pride. Pride didn't want her to know how he felt, pride did not want to be vulnerable to her.

But love did. Love wanted her to know how he felt and love wanted to be vulnerable to her.

Pride had won throughout their separation.

Now it was time to give love, their love, a chance. A second chance.

With his mind made up, a half hour later, Kade knocked on the door of the house they had shared. He saw Jessica come to the window, and then there was silence. For a moment, he thought she was not going to open the door.

But then she did.

What he saw made him feel shattered. She was in one of those horrible dresses again. He thought she had been kidding about one being available in camo, but no, she hadn't been. Aside from the horror of the dress, Jessica looked awful—tired and pale and thin.

"Hello, Jessica," he said quietly. His voice sounded unnatural to him.

"Did you come to get your check?"

"My check?" he asked, genuinely confused. Obviously there would be no money yet from a house that had barely sold.

"I told you I'd pay you for those clothes from Chrysalis once the house sold."

"You didn't even take the clothes with you."

"What? Are you wearing them?"

"Are you crazy?"

"Because if you're not, I'm paying for them."

"Okay," he said. "I am, then. Wearing them."

Just a glimmer of a smile, before she doused it like a spark of a fire in a tinder-dry forest. Still, despite her look of studied grimness, was there a shadow of something in her eyes? Something that she did not want him to see? Despite all her losses, and despite the fact she wanted not to, he could tell she *hoped*.

And her hope, to him, was the bravest thing of all.

"Well, then, did you bring back my bench?"

"No."

"What are you doing here, then?"

"Isn't it obvious? I brought a bottle of champagne. I thought we should celebrate the sale of our house."

"Oh."

"This is the part where you invite me in," he told her gently.

"What if I don't want you to come in?" she said.

But he could still see that faint spark of hope in her eyes.

"We still have some business to complete, Jessie." Ah, she'd never been able to resist him when he called her Jessie.

She stood back from the door, her chin tilted up in defiance of the hope he had seen in her eyes. He went in.

He tried to hide his shock at what he found inside the house. The house was not a reflection of Jessica. And it wasn't just that the floors had been refinished, either. There were things out of place. There was a comforter and a pillow on the sofa. Empty glasses littered the coffee table. There were socks on the floor.

Really? It was all very frightening. "Are you okay?" he asked her.

She went and sat down on the sofa, crossed her arms over her chest in defense. Against him. "I'm fine. What do you want to discuss?"

"Ah." He went through to the kitchen with his bottle of wine. "How's your arm?" he called. Maybe that was the explanation for the mess. She was not completely able-bodied.

"It's okay. The cast has been off for a bit. I have some exercises I do to strengthen my muscles."

The corkscrew was in a familiar place. How was it this kitchen felt so much more like home than his own masterpiece of granite and stainless steel? He opened the bottle, got glasses down and poured. He hated it that the cabinets had been fixed.

He went back and handed her a wineglass, and sat down beside her. He noticed the black soot stain up the front of the fireplace had been fixed, too.

It was as if their memories were being erased, one by one. "Here's to the sale of the house," he said.

"To moving on," she agreed hollowly. But she set her glass down without taking a sip.

He took a sip of his own wine, watching her carefully over the rim of his glass. A bead of perspiration broke out over her lip, and her face turned a ghastly shade of white.

He set his glass down and reached for her, afraid she was going to tumble off the sofa. "Jessica?"

She slid away from his touch and found her feet. She bolted for the bathroom, and didn't even have time to shut the door. The sound of her getting violently sick filled the whole house.

No wonder the place was a wreck. She wasn't feeling well.

She came back into the room, looking weak and wasted. She sat on the couch, tilted her head against the back and closed her eyes.

"Why did you say you were fine? Why didn't you just tell me you had the flu?"

"Sorry," she mumbled. "I should have told you. I don't want you to catch anything."

Her eyes were skittering all over the place. She was

a terrible liar. She had the same look on her face right now that she'd had the year she'd denied buying him the golf clubs he'd wanted for a long time, when she really had.

But why would she lie about having the flu? Or maybe the lie would be that she didn't want him to catch anything.

He looked at her hard. After a long time, she looked back at him, proud and...right beneath that, what? *Scared?* Of what? Him?

Kade felt a strange stillness descend on him, the kind of stillness you might feel in a church with sun pouring through a stained glass window.

He *knew*. He knew right to the bottom of his soul. Jessica was pregnant. He was being given a second chance.

She looked away. "Yeah," she finally said, the word obviously an effort from the lie inherent to it. "The flu."

"Uh-huh."

Her eyes flew to his face, then moved away again.

"You're pregnant, aren't you, Jessica?"

She was silent for a bit and then she sighed with a kind of relief. "Imagine that," she said quietly. "All those charts and temperatures and schedules, all that taking all the fun out of it, and then one night. One single night..."

"Are you happy at all?" he asked her quietly.

"It's pretty hard to be happy when you're terrified," she said. "You know what the cruelest irony is, Kade? I'd just realized, with your help, that I am not ready for a baby!"

It came out very close to a wail of pure panic.

"Aw, Jess," he said quietly, "maybe that *is* when you are ready. When you can see your own imperfections and embrace them. Maybe it's when you can see it's an imperfect world, and instead of trying to impose perfection on it, you just embrace that, too. Maybe that's the only real lesson we can give a baby. It's the one I learned from the failure of us. The world is not going to be perfect. Life is not going to be easy. I can't control everything. But together, with love for each other, we can handle whatever it throws at us."

"We?" she whispered.

"Jessie, I am not leaving you alone with this. And maybe that's what I really wanted to say that night when you told me you were planning to adopt a baby. Not that you weren't ready, or that you had issues to work on, because who could ever be ready for a baby? And who does not have issues to work on? I guess what I was trying to say that night was that it's a lot to take on alone. I didn't want to think about you taking it on without me. It's going to take two people, stumbling through, to bring this baby into the world.

"I'm going to be there for you this time."

Her eyes went to his face, and this time they stayed there, wide and hopeful. She wanted to believe—the capacity for hope was there—but she was frightened, too. And who could blame her?

"I know my track record stinks," he said.

She didn't disagree with that.

"And I know I can't protect you from life. Or from loss. I know we're months away from holding a baby in our arms, and I know you're scared this is going to end like all the other times. All I can really protect you from is walking through difficult times alone."

She was crying now.

"Jessica, I've been given a second chance to be a better man. And I'm taking it. I'm proving to you—and to myself—that I can live up to those vows we took. I remember those vows. I remember each word of them. So listen to me. Because I'm doing this again. And I'm doing it right this time."

His voice was hoarse with emotion, almost a whisper at first, and then with it growing stronger and stronger, he spoke.

"I, Kade Brennan, take you, Jessica, to be my wife, my heart and my soul, my companion through life and my one and only love. I will cherish you and I will nurture a friendship based in trust and honor. I will laugh with you and, especially, I will cry with you. I will love you faithfully, today, tomorrow and forever. Through the best and the worst, through the difficult and the easy, whatever may come, I will always be there for you. I have given you my hand." Kade held out his hand to her, cleared his throat and said, "I have given you my hand to hold, and so I give also my life into your keeping."

To him, it seemed like forever that she looked at him, her eyes sparkling with unshed tears. And then her hand slipped into his, as if it had never left it, as if this was where her hand was meant to be.

Jessica spoke. Her voice was husky and tears were set free and flowed down her face, just as they had that day all those years ago, when he had cherished her tears instead of seeing them as a sign of his own powerlessness.

She said, "I, Jessica Clark-Brennan, take you, Kade, to be my husband, my heart and my soul, my companion in life and my one and only true love. I will cherish you and I will nurture our friendship, based in trust and honor. I will laugh with you, and, yes, I will cry with you. I will love you faithfully, today, tomorrow and forever.

Through the best and the worst, through the difficult and the easy, whatever may come, I will always be there. I have given you my hand to hold, and so I give also my life into your keeping."

She had her knuckles in her eyes, scrubbing like a child who just wanted the tears to go away.

But that was their past. Her tears had upset him and made him feel helpless and hopeless, and so he had turned away. And so she had begun to try to hide how she felt from him, the very one she should have been able to lean on, the one she should have been able to be completely transparent and completely herself with.

Not this time. This time he was walking right into the fire. He slid over on the sofa and crossed the small space that remained between them. Gently, he scooped her up and put her on his lap. She did not resist. She sighed against him as if she had waited her whole life for this moment.

To feel safe, to feel looked after, to feel as if there was a slight possibility everything would be okay. He tucked her head into his shoulder, and felt her tears soak through his shirt.

It wasn't until a long time later that he realized that it was not only her tears soaking his shirt. His own, locked inside him for way too long, had joined hers.

He could not know how this pregnancy would end. But he did know, however it concluded, they were in this together this time. For all time.

"I love you," he said. "Jessie, I love you."

And then he held his breath.

Until he heard the words he needed to hear.

"Kade, I love you."

At that precise moment, the sound of her voice and

her words washed over him, and he felt like a desert that had not seen rain for the longest time. He felt as if the moisture had come, fallen on the parched place that was his soul. He could feel the color and the life seeping back into his world.

CHAPTER TWENTY

"HEY, I LIKE IT."

"The dress?" Jessica said, turning to Kade. She was teasing. She knew he hated this dress, and every dress from her Poppy Puppins collection. But it did great as a paint smock, and it covered her growing girth beautifully. Jessica watched him shrug out of his jacket at the door.

"Of course not that dress." He wrinkled his nose. "I have to find your secret cache of those dresses. Every time I throw one out, three more appear."

She laughed. It was the small things that she had come to love the most: him coming through the door at night, playing a Scrabble game together, watching TV and eating popcorn together, him licking her fingers, slick with butter.

Sometimes she wondered, if they had never had a bad spell, if she had never known what it was like to live without him as part of her daily life, would she love these little things as much as she did? Would she have known to appreciate them?

She had moved into his place at River's Edge after her house had been turned over to the new owners. Eventually, after the baby was born, they would buy a house for the three of them.

But at the moment, they were both cautious about making decisions based on a baby. This caution remained, even though her due date was looming large. They didn't even have a nursery, and the guest room was untouched. No lavender paint or murals this time. No crib, no mobiles, no teddy bears.

They had a beautiful handmade crate they could line with blankets and put beside their bed. When the time came. She loved the idea of the baby sleeping next to them, so close they could breathe in each other's breath, exchange air, become even more a part of one another.

Kade came over and put his hand on the gentle swell of her belly under the paint smock.

He put his head down and spoke directly to her stomach. "Hello, baby. Do you hear me in there? Moving," he said with satisfaction. "A football player."

"Or a ballerina."

"Nah, it's a boy."

It was only in the past few weeks that they had dared to play this game, so afraid were they of jinxing this incredibly magical and miraculous experience. But this time, the fear was different. They would lie awake with it, deep into the night, holding hands, leaning on each other.

They had chosen not to know the sex of their child. This baby was a miracle, boy or girl. Besides, it was endlessly fun debating it, even as they carefully avoided the baby sections of the stores. It was like a superstition, but she did not care. She was not buying one thing for that baby until she had held it in her arms.

She had barely set foot in Baby Boomer since selling it to Macy. But she knew Macy had her covered. She knew there was a shelf there filled with things Macy was quietly selecting for her: bottles and blankets and tiny disposable diapers and little outfits. *If* the time came this time—that hope fluttered in Jessica's chest, they were so close now, and the doctor smiled and shook his head at Jessica's fears—they had a whole nursery that could be put in a box and delivered to them.

There was an unexpected new dimension to Jessica's relationship with Macy and with her old place of business.

Macy was selling paintings almost as fast as Jessica could produce them. Jessica was working largely in abstract, the colors and motion flowing out of her like rivers of light. It was as if this part of her, dammed up for too long, was bursting forth now that it had been set free.

And for some reason, that kind of art appealed to people shopping for baby stuff, not for nurseries, necessarily, though there was a whole move away from the cute traditional look of babies' rooms.

No, people having babies these days, and especially the ones who shopped at an upscale store like Baby Boomer, were largely established professional couples. They had whole gorgeous big houses to decorate, not just nurseries.

And the name Jessica Brennan was causing a surprising stir in the Calgary art scene.

"I like it," Kade said. Having greeted the baby, he turned his attention to the canvas. "What's it called?"

She didn't have a studio. The light pouring through the windows of his apartment had proved perfect. When it was too strong, she closed the curtains and had lights set up to point to the canvas. Between the canvases, paints, lights and paint tarps on the floor, the place looked very messy. Add to that a sock of Kade's, menus out on the counter and magazines on the coffee table, and the effect was one of moderate disarray. And she loved it.

Kade had, with gentle strength, helped her probe the origins of that terrible need to feel in control.

Perhaps, she thought, eyeing their space, she had gone a little too far the other way.

She lifted her shoulder. *Oh, well.*

She turned her attention to the canvas. She was not sure where this came from, this endless current of inspiration, but she was pretty sure it came from love.

"Today it's called *Joy Rising*." She shrugged. "Who knows if it will still be called that tomorrow."

"Joy Rising," Kade said, and stood back from it.

The backdrop of the canvas was a light gray neutral. The rest of it was filled with hundreds of bubbles—like soap bubbles—rising, starting small at the bottom left of the canvas, growing larger at they reached the right-hand corner.

"It's good," he said. "Now, what's for dinner?"

It was a standing joke between them, a light tease about what she liked to call her Martha Stewart phase. "The pizza menu is on the counter."

He laughed.

And his laughter shivered along her spine. They had almost lost this. They had almost walked away from it. And that was what made it even more precious today.

And maybe that was what all loss did, if you were brave, if you were open to its lessons. Maybe all loss sharpened your sense of the now, of the gifts of this very moment.

He had moved over and was studying the menu.

"Kade?"

"Huh?"

Jessica put her hand to her swollen belly. "Ah."

He was at her side in an instant, scanning her face.

"It's time," she said. "Oh, my God, it's time."

And even this moment, with intense ripples of pain possessing her body, was awash with light, with joy rising. Jessica looked into the face of the man who was her husband, and she read the strength there and knew, together, whatever happened next, it would be just fine.

Kade woke up. His neck was sore. He had fallen asleep in the chair. For a moment, he was disoriented, but then he heard a little sound, like a kitten mewing, and it all came back to him.

His eyes adjusted to the dark, and there they were. His wife and his daughter, the baby on Jessica's chest.

He had thought over the past few months with Jessica as they came together as a couple again, as they celebrated their second chance, that he had come to know the depth and breadth of love completely.

Now, looking at his child, he knew he had only kidded himself. He had only scratched the surface of what love could be.

The baby made that mewing sound again.

Jessica stirred but did not wake.

Jessica. How could someone that tiny, someone who appeared that fragile, be so damned brave? Men thought they were courageous, but that was only until they'd seen a baby born. And then they had to admit how puny their strength was, how laughable this thing they had passed off as courage was.

Courage certainly was not tackling a thief!

Kade got up from his chair. Jessica needed to rest. She

had done her bit. Thirteen hours of the most unbelievable pain Kade could imagine.

How he had wanted to take that pain from her, to take her place.

But that was one of the lessons of this remarkable second chance. He could not take her pain away. He could not fix everything, or really, even most things.

He had to be there. He had to stand there in his own helplessness, and not run from it. He had to walk with her through her pain, not try to take it away from her. Admitting his own powerlessness sometimes took more courage than anything he had ever done before.

The baby mewed again, and stirred again.

He touched the tiny back of his baby girl. It was warm beneath his fingers. He could feel the amazing miracle of the life force in that tiny little bundle.

He had been the first to hold her, the nurse showing him how. He had looked into that tiny wrinkled face, the nose crunched and the eyes screwed tightly shut in outrage, and he had recognized her.

Love.

Love manifest.

And so, summoning his courage, he lifted the baby off the gentle rise and fall of his wife's sleeping chest.

He could hold her in the palm of one hand, his other hand supporting her neck, as the nurse had shown him.

Destiny.

They had decided to call her Destiny.

Her eyes popped open, a slate gray that the nurse had told him would change. They didn't know yet if she would have green eyes like Jessica's or blue like his, or some amazing combination of both.

The nurse had said, too, that this little baby probably could not see much.

And yet, as Kade held her, her eyes seemed to widen with delighted recognition.

"That's right, sweetie, it's me. Daddy."

Daddy. The word felt incredibly sweet on his tongue, and the baby squirmed in his hand. He drew her close to his chest and went and sat back down on the chair, awkwardly stroking her back.

He was so aware of how tiny she was, and helpless. How she was relying on him.

He felt a moment's fear. The world always seemed to be in such a fragile state. The weather changed and wars broke out, and floods came and fires.

People could be fragile, too, held in the trance of long-ago hurts, hiding the broken places within them.

There was so much that he was powerless over, and yet this little girl would see him as all-powerful. Her daddy.

This was what he needed to teach her: that yes, the world could be fragile and easily broken. And people could be fragile and easily broken, too.

But there was one thing that was not fragile, and that was not easily broken.

And that thing was love.

It was the thread that ran, strong, through all the rest. It was what gave strength when strength failed, what gave hope when it was hopeless, what gave faith when there was plenty of evidence that it made no sense at all to have faith. It was what healed the breaks, and made people come out of the trance and embrace all that it was to be alive.

"Welcome to this crazy, unpredictable, beautiful, amazing life," Kade whispered to his little girl. "Welcome."

He closed his eyes, and when he opened them, Jessica's hand was on his shoulder, and she was awake, looking at them both.

"I need to confess something to you," Kade growled.

"What?"

"I've broken one of my vows to you."

"Impossible," she whispered.

"No. You are not my one and only true love anymore. I have two of you now."

And the smile on Jessica's face—radiant, a smile that shamed the very sun—said it was worth it. Every piece of pain they had navigated was worth it.

Because it had brought them here.

To this place. To this moment.

Where they knew that all else might pass away, but that love prevailed.

* * * * *

THE CEO'S
BABY SURPRISE

HELEN LACEY

For my mother, Evelyn
Who believes in me no matter what.

Prologue

Mary-Jayne Preston yawned, opened her eyes and blinked a few times. The ceiling spun fractionally, and she drew in a soft breath.

I'm not hungover.

She closed her eyes again. The two glasses of champagne she'd drunk the night before weren't responsible for the way she felt. This was something else. An unusual lethargy crept into her limbs and spread across her skin. Her lids fluttered, and she glimpsed a sliver of light from between heavy drapes.

An unfamiliar room.

Her memory kicked in. The Sandwhisper Resort. Port Douglas.

But this isn't my bedroom.

This was a villa suite. And a top-end one, judging by the plush feel of the giant king-size bed and lavish damask drapes. Extravagance personified. Her eyelids drooped before opening again as she stretched her spine—and then nearly jumped out of her skin when she realized she wasn't alone in the big bed.

A man lay beside her. She twisted her head and saw a long, perfectly proportioned back. Smooth skin, like the sheerest satin stretched over pressed steel, broad shoulders, strong arms and dark hair. He lay on his stomach, one arm flung above his head, the other curved by his side. And he was asleep. The soft rhythm of his breathing was oddly hypnotic, and she stared at him, suddenly mesmerized by his bronzed skin and lean, muscular frame.

And then, in stunning Technicolor, it came rushing back.

The party.
The kiss.
The one-night stand.
Her first. Her *last*.

She needed to get up. To *think*. She shimmied sideways but quickly stopped moving when he stirred. She wasn't quite ready for any kind of face-to-face, morning-after awkwardness. Not with *him*. She took a deep breath and tried again, inching her hips across the cool sheet so slowly it was agonizing. Finally one leg found the edge of the mattress and she pushed the cover back. He moved again and she stilled instantly. He made a sound, half groan, half moan, and flipped around, the sheet draping haphazardly over his hips as he came to face her.

But still asleep.

Mary-Jayne's breath shuddered out as she caught sight of his profile. He was ridiculously handsome. No wonder she'd lost her head. The straight nose, chiseled cheeks and square jaw was a riveting combination. And she quickly recalled those silver-gray eyes of his…just too sexy for words. As her gaze traveled lower her fingertips tingled.

His body was incredibly well cut, and she fought the urge to touch him just one more time. She spotted a faint mark on his shoulder. Like a love bite.

Did I do that?

Heat surged through her blood when she remembered what they'd done the night before, and again in the small hours of the morning. No sweet wonder her muscles ached and her skin seemed ultrasensitive. She'd never had a night like it before, never felt such intense desire or experienced such acute and mindboggling pleasure.

It was like a dream. A fantasy.

And she needed to wake up from this particular dream. Quickly.

She managed to ease off the bed and quickly looked around for her clothes. Her underwear was by the bed, and she snatched it up with guilty fingers and then quickly dressed into the thong and bra. The shoes were easily spotted—one was by the window, the other under a chair in the corner of the room. But the black dress was nowhere to be seen. The smooth fabric had clung to her curves, and the man in the bed had told her how beautiful and desirable she'd looked. No one had ever said those words quite that way to her before. She found her purse on the chair and continued looking for the dress, keeping a mindful eye on him.

Please don't wake up...

He didn't, thankfully, and a few moments later she found the dress, scrunched in a ball and hidden beneath the quilt that had fallen to the foot of the bed. She stepped into it and slipped it up and over her hips, settling her arms through the bodice before she twisted herself into a pretzel to do up the zipper. Breathless, she cast another look toward the sleeping man.

I'm such a fool...

For weeks she'd stayed resolute, determined to avoid crashing into bed with him. But the moment he'd touched her, the moment he'd made his move she'd melted like an ice cube in hell.

Mary-Jayne pushed her feet into her patent pumps, grabbed her purse and ran.

Chapter One

Pregnant.

Not a bout of food poisoning as she'd wanted to believe.

Mary-Jayne walked from the doctor's office and headed for her car. Her head hurt. Her feet hurt. Everything hurt. The snap on her jeans felt tight around her waist. Now she knew why.

She was three months and three weeks pregnant.

She opened the door of the borrowed Honda Civic and got inside. Then she placed a hand over her belly and let out a long, heavy breath.

Twenty-seven. Single. Pregnant.

Right.

Not exactly the end of the world…but not what she'd been expecting, either.

One day she'd imagined she'd have a baby. When she was married and settled, not while she was trying to carve out a career as a jewelry designer and wasn't exactly financially stable.

She thought about calling her older sisters, Evie and Grace, but quickly shrugged off the idea. She needed time to think. Plan. Sort out what she was going to do, before she told anyone. Especially her sisters, who'd want to know *everything*.

She'd have to tell them about that night.

She gripped the steering wheel and let out a long, weary sigh. She'd tried to put the memory from her mind countless times. And failed. Every time she walked around the grounds of the Sandwhisper Resort she was reminded. And every time she fielded a telephone call from *him* she was thrust back to that crazy night.

Mary-Jayne drove through the gates of the resort and took a left down the road that led to the employees' residences. Her villa was small but well appointed and opened onto the deck and to the huge heated pool and spa area. The Sandwhisper Resort was one of the largest in Port Douglas, and certainly one of the most luxurious. The town of Port Douglas was about forty miles north of Cairns, and its population of over three thousand often doubled during peak vacation times. Living and working at the luxurious resort for the past four and half months hadn't exactly been a hardship. Running her friend Audrey's boutique was mostly enjoyable and gave her the opportunity to create and showcase her own jewelry. Life was a breeze.

Correction.

Life *had* been a breeze.

Until she'd had an uncharacteristic one-night stand with Daniel Anderson.

CEO of Anderson Holdings and heir apparent to the huge fortune that had been made by his grandfather from ore and copper mining years earlier, he owned the Sandwhisper Resort with his two brothers. There were four other resorts around the globe—one in Phuket, another along the Amalfi coast in Italy, another in the Maldives and the flagship resort in the San Francisco Bay Area.

He was rich, successful, uptight and absurdly arrogant. Everything she'd always abhorred in a man.

He was also reported to be kind, generous and honest. Well…according to his grandmother.

Eighty-year-old Solana Anderson adored her grandsons and spent her retirement flying between the east and west coasts of Australia and America, living at the resorts during the spring and summer months in alternating time zones. Mary-Jayne liked the older woman very much. They'd met the first day she'd arrived at the resort after the desperate emergency call from her old school friend Audrey had sent her flying up to Port Douglas with barely a packed suitcase. Audrey had moved into Mary-Jayne's small house in Crystal Point so she could be close to her ill mother while Mary-Jayne moved into Audrey's condo at the resort. Once she was in residence, she read the scribbled note with instructions her friend had left and opened the boutique at an unrespectable eleven o'clock. It was meant to be a temporary gig—but Audrey insisted her mother needed her. So her planned three weeks ended up being for six months.

And Solana, straight backed and still vibrant at nearly eighty years of age, had come into the store looking for an outfit to wear to her upcoming birthday party, and within the hour they were chatting and laughing over herbal tea and several outfit changes. It was then she learned that Solana's American-born husband had died a decade earlier and how she'd borne him a son and daughter. Mary-Jayne had listened while Solana talked about her much-loved grandsons, Daniel, Blake and Caleb and granddaughter Renee. One hour ticked over into two, and by three o'clock the older woman had finally decided upon an outfit and persuaded Mary-Jayne to let her see some of her hand-crafted jewelry pieces. Solana had since bought three items and had recommended Mary-Jayne's work to several of her friends.

Yes, she liked Solana. But wasn't about to tell the other woman she was carrying her great-grandchild. Not until she figured out what she was going to do. She was nearly four months along, and her pregnancy would be showing itself very soon. She couldn't hide her growing stomach behind baggy clothes forever.

He has a right to know...

The notion niggled at her over and over.

She could have the baby alone. Women did it all the time. And it was not as if she and Daniel had any kind of relationship. If she wanted, she could leave the resort and go home and never see him again. He lived mostly in San Francisco. She lived in Crystal Point, a small seaside town that sat at the southernmost point of the Great Barrier Reef. They had different lives. Different worlds.

And she didn't even like him.

She'd met him three times before the night of Solana's birthday. The first time she'd been in the store window, bent over and struggling to remove a garment from the mannequin. When she was done she'd straightened, turned to avoid knocking the mannequin over and came face-to-face with him on the other side of the glass. He'd been watching her, arms crossed.

Of course she'd known immediately who he was. There were several pictures of him and his brothers in Solana's villa, and she'd visited the older woman many times. Plus, he looked enough like his younger brother Caleb for her to recognize the family resemblance. Caleb ran the resorts in Port Douglas and Phuket while his twin Blake looked after Amalfi, Maldives and San Francisco. And according to staff gossip Daniel lorded over the resorts, his brothers and the staff from his private jet.

Still, it was hard not to be impressed by his ridiculous good looks, and despite the fact he was not her type, Mary-Jayne was as susceptible as the next woman. The impeccably cut suit, creaseless white shirt and dark tie were a riveting combination on his broad, tall frame, and for a second she'd been rooted to the spot, unable to move, unable to do anything other than stare back, held captive by the look in his gray eyes. For a moment, at least. Until he'd raised one brow and a tiny smile whispered along the edges of his mouth. He'd then looked her over with a kind of leisurely conceit that had quickly sent alarm bells clanging in her head.

There'd been interest in his expression and if he'd been anyone else she might have made some kind of encouraging gesture. Like a smile. Or nod. But Daniel Anderson was out of her league. A rich and successful corporate shark with a reputation for having no tolerance for fools in business, and no proclivity for commitment in his private life. He was the kind of man she'd always planned to avoid like the plague. The kind of man that had never interested her before.

But something had passed between them in that first moment. A look… Recognition.

Awareness…

Heat…

Attraction…

When her good sense had returned she'd darted from the window and got back to the customer waiting in the changing room. By the time she'd moved back to the front of the store and began ringing up the sale he was gone.

Mary-Jayne saw him a day later, striding across the resort foyer with his brother at his side. She'd been coming from the day spa, arms loaded with jewelry trays, when Caleb had said her name. She'd met the younger Anderson many times over the previous weeks. He was rich, charming and handsome and didn't do a solitary thing to her libido. Not so his older brother. She'd fumbled with the trays and stayed rooted to the spot as they approached and then managed to nod her way through an introduction. He was unsmiling, but his eyes regarded her with blistering intensity. Caleb's attention had quickly been diverted by the day-shift concierge and she'd been left alone with him, silent and nervous beneath his unfaltering gaze.

Then he'd spoken, and his deep voice, a smooth mix of his American upbringing and Australian roots, wound up her spine like liquid silk. "My grandmother tells me you're here for six months rather than the few weeks you'd originally planned on?"

He'd talked about her with Solana? "Ah, that's right," she'd croaked.

"And are you enjoying your time here?"

She'd nodded, feeling stupid and awkward and not in the least bit like her usual self. Normally she was confident and opinionated and more than comfortable in her own skin. But two seconds around Daniel Anderson and she was a speechless fool. Übergood looks had never interested her before. But he stirred her senses big time.

"Yes, very much."

"And I trust your friend's parent's health is improving?"

He knew about Audrey's mother? Solana *had* been busy sharing information.

"A little...yes."

A small smile had crinkled the corner of his mouth and Mary-Jayne's gaze had instantly been drawn to his lips. He had seen her reaction and his smile had increased fraction- ally. There was something extraordinarily hypnotic about him, something she couldn't quite fathom. Something she'd known she had to extricate herself from…and fast.

She'd hastily excused herself and taken off as fast as she could.

And hadn't seen him again for two days.

She'd left the resort for a run along the beach and had come upon him jogging in the other direction. He'd slowed when he was about twenty feet from her and come to a halt right next to her. And the look between them had been electric. Out of this world and all-consuming. She'd never experienced such blatant and blistering physical attraction for anyone before. And it shocked her to the core. He wasn't her usual type. In fact, Daniel Anderson was the epitome of everything she *didn't* want in a man. Money, power, arrogance… They were attributes her small-town, middle-class self had decided long ago were not for her. She dated musicians and out-of-work artists. Not corporate sharks.

His expression had been unwavering and contained hot sexual appreciation. He wanted her. No doubt about it. And the look in his eyes had made it clear he thought he'd get her.

"You know," he'd said with a kind of arrogant confidence that made her tremble. "My villa is only minutes away."

She knew that. The family's quarters were secluded and luxurious and away from the main part of the resort and had a spectacular view of the beach.

"And?" she'd managed to say, despite the way her heart had thundered behind her ribs and her knees wobbled.

He'd half smiled. "And we both know that's where we're going to end up at some point."

Mortified, she'd quickly taken off like a bullet. But her body was thrumming with a kind of intoxicating aware-

ness that stayed with her for hours. For days. Until she'd
seen him again two days later at Solana's birthday party.
The older woman had insisted she attend the celebration
and Mary-Jayne respected Solana too much to refuse the
invitation. She'd ditched her usual multicolored skirts and
long tops and rummaged through Audrey's wardrobe for
a party dress. And she'd found one—a slip of silky black
jersey that clung to her like a second skin. The huge ball-
room was easy to get lost in...or so she'd thought. But it
had only taken ten minutes until she'd felt him watching
her from across the room. He'd approached and asked if
she wanted a drink. Within half an hour they had been out
on the balcony, talking intimately. Seconds later they'd
been kissing madly. Minutes later they'd been in his villa
tearing each other's clothes off.

But Mary-Jayne wasn't under any illusions.

She knew enough about Daniel Anderson to realize she
was simply another notch on his bedpost. He was handsome, successful and wealthy and played the field mercilessly. Something he had done without compunction since
the death of his wife and unborn child four years earlier.
He certainly wouldn't be interested in her for anything
other than a one-night stand. She wasn't his type. Oh, he'd
knocked on the door of her villa the day after Solana's
party and asked her out. But she'd shut him down. She'd
piqued his interest for a moment and that was all. Thankfully, he'd left the resort the following day and returned
to San Francisco, exactly as she'd hoped. But she hadn't
expected that he'd call the store two weeks later and an-
nounce that he wanted to see her again when he returned
from California.

See her?

Yeah...right. The only thing he wanted to see was her
naked body between the sheets. And she knew that for a

man like Daniel Anderson, the chase was all that mattered. She'd refused him, and that was like pouring oil onto a fire.

When he'd called her again two weeks later she'd been in South Dakota for a friend's wedding. Annoyed that he wouldn't take the hint and all out of patience, she'd lost her temper and told him to go to hell. Then she'd returned to the Sandwhisper Resort and waited. Waited for another call. Waited for him to arrive at the resort and confuse and seduce her with his steely-eyed gaze and uncompromising intensity. But he hadn't called. And hadn't returned. As one week slipped into another, Mary-Jayne had slowly relaxed and convinced herself he'd lost interest.

Which was exactly what she wanted.

Only now, the tables had turned. She was having his baby. Which meant one thing—she'd have to see him and tell him she was having his baby. And soon.

Daniel had struggled with the remnants of a headache for two days. The three other suits in the conference room were grating on his nerves. Some days he wanted nothing more than to throw off the shackles of his name, his legacy and everything else and live a simple, quiet life.

Like today.

Because it was his birthday. He was turning thirty-four years old. He had money and power and a successful business at his command. He had apartments in San Francisco, another in London and then there was the family-owned hilltop chateau in France that he hadn't been near for over four years. He also had any number of women willing to warm his bed with minimal notice and who understood he didn't want commitment or anything resembling a serious relationship. He traveled the world but rarely saw anything other than the walls of boardrooms and offices at the resorts he'd helped build into some of the most successful around the globe. Nothing and no one touched him.

Well…except for Mary-Jayne Preston.

She was a thorn in his side. A stone in his shoe. A pain in his neck.

Months after that one crazy night in Port Douglas and he was still thinking about her. She was incredibly beautiful. Her green eyes were luminous; her lips were full and endlessly kissable. But it was her hair that had first captured his attention that day in the store window. She had masses of dark curls that hung down past her shoulders. And of course there were her lovely curves, which she possessed in all the right places.

He'd checked out her history and discovered she came from a middle-class family in Crystal Point, had studied at a local technical college and had an online business selling her handcrafted jewelry. She rented her home, owned a dog, volunteered at a number of animal shelters, had strong opinions about the environment and politics and liked to dress in colorful skirts or jeans with holes in the knees. She had piercings in her ears and navel and a butterfly tattoo on one shoulder.

She wasn't his type. Not by a long shot.

Which didn't make one ounce of difference to the relentless effect she had on him whenever she was within a twenty-foot radius. And the night of his grandmother's birthday party he'd almost tripped over his own feet when he'd caught a glimpse of her across the room. She'd looked incredible in a dress that highlighted every dip and curve of her body. And with her dark hair cascading down her back in a wave he just about had to cleave his tongue from the roof of his mouth. She looked hot. Gorgeous. Desirable.

And he knew then he wanted to get her in his bed.

It took half an hour to get her alone. Then he'd kissed her. And she'd kissed him back.

And before either of them had a chance to come up for air they were in his villa suite, tearing off clothes with little finesse and more eagerness than he'd felt in years. It had been a hot, wild night, compounded by months of abstinence and the fact he'd had Mary-Jayne Preston very much on his mind since the first time he'd seen her.

"Are you listening?"

Daniel shook off his thoughts and glanced to his left. Blake was staring at him, one brow cocked. "Always."

Blake didn't look convinced and quickly turned his attention to the other suits in the room. After a few more minutes, he dismissed the two other men, and once they were alone his brother moved to the bar and grabbed two imported beers from the fridge.

Daniel frowned. "A little early, don't you think?"

Blake flicked the tops off the bottles and shrugged. "It's after three. And you look as if you need it."

He didn't disagree, and stretched back in his leather chair. "Maybe I do."

Blake passed him a beer and grabbed a seat. "Happy birthday," his brother said, and clinked the bottle necks.

"Thanks," he said but didn't take a drink. The last thing he wanted to do was add alcohol to the remainders of a blinding headache.

His brother, who was probably the most intuitive person he'd ever known, looked at him as if he knew exactly what he was thinking. "You know, you should go home."

"I live *here*, remember?"

Blake shook his head. "I meant *home*...not here. Port Douglas."

Except Port Douglas didn't feel any more like home than San Francisco, Phuket or Amalfi.

Nowhere did. Not since Simone had died. The bay-side condo they'd bought still sat empty, and he lived in a villa at the San Francisco resort when he wasn't at any of the other four locations. He'd been born in Australia and moved to California when he was two years old. The San Francisco resort was the first, which made it home, even though he'd spent most of his adult life shifting between the two countries.

He scowled. "I can't do that right now."

"Why not?" Blake shot back. "Caleb's got the Phuket renovation under control. Things are sweet here in San Francisco." His brother grinned. "You're not really needed. CEOs are kind of superfluous to the running of a company anyhow. We all knew that when Gramps was at the helm."

"Superfluous?"

Blake's grin widened. "Yeah...like the foam on the top of an espresso to go... You know, there but not really necessary."

"You're an ass."

His brother's grin turned into a chuckle. "All I'm saying is that you haven't taken a real break from this gig for years. Not even when..."

Not even when Simone died.

Four years, four months and three weeks ago. Give or take a day. She'd been driving back from a doctor's appointment and had stopped at the mall for some shopping. The brakes on a car traveling in the opposite direction had failed. Simone had suffered terrible injuries and died an hour later in hospital. So had the baby she carried. He'd lost his wife and unborn daughter because of a broken brake line. "I'm fine," he said, and tasted the lie on his tongue.

"I'm pretty sure you're not," Blake said, more serious. "And something's been bugging you the past few months."

Something. Someone. *Green eyes... Black curling hair... Red lips...*

Daniel drank some beer. "You're imagining things. And stop fretting. You're turning into your mother."

His brother laughed loudly. They both knew that Blake was more like their father, Miles, than any of them. Daniel's mother had died of a massive brain hemorrhage barely hours after his birth, and their father had married Bernadette two years later. Within six months the twins, Blake and Caleb, were born. Bernie was a nice woman and had always treated him like her own, and wasn't as vague and hopeless as their father. Business acumen and ambition had skipped a generation, and now Miles spent his time painting and sculpting and living on their small hobby farm an hour west of Port Douglas.

Daniel finished the beer and placed the bottle on the table. "I don't need a vacation."

"Sure you do," Blake replied. "If you don't want to go to Australia, take a break somewhere else. Maybe Fiji? Or what about using that damned mausoleum that sits on that hill just outside Paris? Take some time off, relax, get laid," his brother said, and grinned again. "Recharge like us regular folk have to do every now and then."

"You're as tied to this business as I am."

"Yeah," his brother agreed. "But I know when to quit. I've got my cabin in the woods, remember?"

Blake's *cabin* was a sprawling Western red cedar house nestled on forty hectares he'd bought in small town Colorado a few years back. Daniel had visited once, hated the cold and being snowbound for days on end and decided that a warm climate was more his thing.

"I don't need a—"

"Then, how about you think about what the rest of us need?" Blake said firmly. "Or what Caleb and I need, which isn't you breathing down our necks looking for things we're doing wrong because you're so damned bored and frustrated that you can't get out your own way. Basically, *I* need a break. So go home and get whatever's bugging you out of your system and spend some time with Solana. You know you've always been her favorite."

Daniel looked at his brother. Had he done that? Had he become an overzealous, critical jerk looking for fault in everything and everyone? And bored? Was that what he was? He did miss Solana. He hadn't seen his grandmother since her birthday weekend. And it was excuse enough to see Mary-Jayne again—and get her out of his system once and for all.

He half smiled. "Okay."

Chapter Two

"Everything all right?"

Mary-Jayne nodded and looked up from the plate of food she'd been pretending to give way too much attention. "Fine."

"Are you still feeling unwell?" Solana asked. "You never did tell me what the doctor said."

"Just a twenty-four-hour bug," she replied vaguely. "And I feel fine now."

Solana didn't look convinced. "You're still pale. Is that ex-boyfriend of yours giving you grief?"

The *ex-boyfriend*. The one she'd made up to avoid any nosy questions about what was becoming her rapidly expanding middle. The ex-boyfriend she'd say was the father of her baby until she summoned the nerve to tell Solana she was carrying her grandson's child. Raised to have a solid moral compass, she was torn between believing the father of her baby had a right to know, and the fear that telling him would change everything. She was carrying Solana's great-grandchild. An Anderson heir. Nothing would be the same.

Of course, she had no illusions. Daniel Anderson was not a man looking for commitment or a family. Solana had told her enough about him, from his closed-off heart to his rumored no-strings relationships. He'd lost the love of his life and unborn child and had no interest in replacing, either.

Not that she was interested in him in *that* way. She didn't like him at all. He was arrogant and opinionated and as cold as a Popsicle. Oh, she'd certainly been swept away that one night. But one night of hot and heavy sex didn't make them *anything*.

Still…they'd made a baby together, and as prepared as she was to raise her child alone, common courtesy made it very clear to her that she had to tell him. And soon. Before Solana or anyone else worked out that she was pregnant.

She had another two weeks at the store before Audrey returned, and once that was done, Mary-Jayne intended returning to Crystal Point to regroup and figure out how to tell Daniel he was about to become a father.

"I'm going to miss you when you leave," Solana said and smiled. "I've grown very fond of our talks."

So had Mary-Jayne. She'd become increasingly attached to the other woman over the past few months, and they lunched together at least twice a week. And Solana had been incredibly supportive of her jewelry designing and had even offered to finance her work and help expand the range into several well-known stores around the country. Of course Mary-Jayne had declined the offer. Solana was a generous woman, but she'd never take advantage of their friendship in such a way…good business or not.

"We'll keep in touch," Mary-Jayne assured her and ignored the nausea scratching at her throat. Her appetite had been out of whack for weeks and the sick feeling still hadn't abated even though she was into her second trimester. Her doctor told her not to worry about it and assured her that her appetite would return, and had put her on a series of vitamins. But most days the idea of food before three in the afternoon was unimaginable.

"Yes, we must," Solana said warmly. "Knowing you has made me not miss Renee quite so much," she said of her granddaughter, who resided in London. "Of course, I get to see Caleb while I'm here and Blake when I'm in San Francisco. And Daniel when he's done looking after things and flying in between resorts. But sometimes I wish for those days when they were kids and not spread all over the world." The older woman put down her cutlery and sighed. "Listen to me, babbling on, when you must miss your own family very much."

"I do," she admitted. "I'm really close to my sisters and brother and I miss my parents a lot."

"Naturally." Solana's eyed sparkled. "Family is everything."

Mary-Jayne swallowed the lump of emotion in her throat, like she'd done countless times over the past few months. Her hormones were running riot, and with her body behaving erratically, it was getting harder to keep her feelings under wraps. One thing she did know—she wanted her baby. As unplanned as it was, as challenging as it might be being a single mother, she had developed a strong and soul-reaching love for the child in her womb.

Family is everything...

It was. She knew that. She'd been raised by wonderful parents and loved her siblings dearly. Her baby would be enveloped in that love. She *could* go home, and Daniel need never know about her pregnancy. She'd considered it. Dreamed of it.

Except...

It would be wrong. Dishonest. And wholly unfair.

"I should very much like to visit your little town one day," Solana said cheerfully.

Crystal Point. It was a tiny seaside community of eight hundred people. From the pristine beaches to the rich soil of the surrounding farmlands, it would always be home, no matter where life took her.

"I'd like that, too," she said, and pushed her plate aside.

"Not hungry?" Solana asked, her keen light gray eyes watching everything she did.

Mary-Jayne shrugged. "Not really. But it is delicious," she said of the warm mango salad on her plate. "I'm not much use in the kitchen, so our lunches are always a nice change from the grilled-cheese sandwich I'd usually have."

Solana grinned. "Didn't your mother teach you to cook?"

"She tried, but I was something of a tomboy when I was young and more interested in helping my dad in his workshop," she explained.

"Well, those skills can come in handy, too."

Mary-Jayne nodded. "For sure. I can fix a leaking tap and build a bookcase...but a cheese toastie is about my limit in the kitchen."

"Well, you'll just have to find yourself a husband who can cook," Solana suggested, smiling broadly.

"I'm not really in the market for a husband." *Not since I got knocked up by your grandson...*

Solana smiled. "Nonsense. Everyone is looking for a soul mate...even a girl as independent and free-spirited as you."

Mary-Jayne nodded vaguely. Independent and free-spirited? It was exactly how she appeared to the world. And exactly how she liked it. But for the most part, it was a charade. A facade to fool everyone into thinking she had it all together—that she was strong and self-sufficient and happy-go-lucky. She'd left home at seventeen determined to prove she could make it on her own, and had spent ten years treading water in the hope no one noticed she was just getting by—both financially and emotionally. Her family loved her, no doubt about it. As the youngest child she was indulged and allowed to do whatever she liked, mostly without consequence. Her role as the lovable but unreliable flake in the Preston family had been set from a young age. While her older brother, Noah, took over the family business, perennial earth-mother Evie married young and pursued her art, and übersmart Grace headed for a career in New York before she returned to Australia to marry the man she loved.

But for Mary-Jayne there were no such expectations, and no traditional career. She'd gotten her first piercing at fourteen and had a tattoo by the time she was fifteen. When school was over she'd found a job as a cashier in a supermarket and a month later moved out of her parents' home and into a partly furnished cottage three streets away. She'd packed whatever she could fit into her battered Volkswagen and began her adult life away from the low expectations of her family. She never doubted their love... but sometimes she wished they expected more of her. Then perhaps she would have had more ambition, more focus.

Mary-Jayne pushed back her chair and stood up. "I'll take the dishes to the kitchen."

"Thank you. You're a sweet girl, Mary-Jayne," Solana said, and collected up the cutlery. "You know, I was just telling Caleb that very thing yesterday."

It was another not-so-subtle attempt to play match-maker.

Solana had somehow got it in her head that her younger grandson would be a good match for her. And the irony wasn't lost on Mary-Jayne. She liked Caleb. He was friendly and charming and came into the store every couple of days and asked how things were going, and always po-litely inquired after Audrey. The resort staff all respected him, and he clearly ran a tight ship.

But he didn't so much as cause a blip on her radar.

Unlike Daniel. He was the blip of the century.

Mary-Jayne ignored Solana's words, collected the dishes and headed for the kitchen. Once there she took a deep breath and settled her hips against the countertop. Her stomach was still queasy, and she took a few deep breaths before she turned toward the sink and decided to make a start on the dishes. She filled the sink and was about to plunge her hands into the water when she heard a decisive knock on the front door, and then seconds later the low sound of voices. Solana had a visitor. Mary-Jayne finished the washing up, dried her hands and headed for the door.

And then stopped in her tracks.

Even though his back was to her she recognized Daniel Anderson immediately. The dark chinos and white shirt fitted him as though they'd been specifically tailored for his broad, well-cut frame. She knew those shoulders and every other part of him because the memory of the night they'd spent together was etched into her brain, and the result was the child growing inside her.

Perhaps he'd tracked her down to confront her? Maybe he knew?

Impossible.

No one knew she was pregnant. It was a coincidence. He'd forgotten all about her. He hadn't called since she'd told him to go to hell. He'd returned to see his grand-mother. Mary-Jayne's hand moved to her belly, and she puffed out the smock-style shirt she wore. If she kept her arms to her sides and kept her clothing as loose as possible it was unlikely he'd notice her little baby bump. She lingered by the doorway, her mind racing at a trillion miles an hour.

Solana was clearly delighted to see him and hugged him twice in succession. "What a wonderful surprise," his grandmother said. "Why didn't you tell me you were coming?"

"Then it's not a surprise," he replied. "Is it?"

As they chatted Mary-Jayne moved back behind the architrave and considered her options. Come clean? Act nonchalant? Make a run for it? Running for it appealed most. This wasn't the time or place to make any kind of announcement about being pregnant, not with Solana in the room. She needed time to think. Prepare.

I have to get out of here.

The back door was through the kitchen and off the dining room. But if she sneaked out through the back Solana would want to know why. There would be questions. From Solana. And then from Daniel.

"Show some backbone," she muttered to herself.

She'd always had gumption. Now wasn't the time to ditch her usual resolve and act like a frightened little girl. Mary-Jayne was about to push back her shoulders and face the music when an unwelcome and unexpected wave of nausea rose up and made her suddenly forget everything else. She put a hand to her chest, heaved and swallowed hard, fighting the awful feeling with every ounce of will-power she possessed.

And failed.

She rushed forward to the closest exit, racing past Solana and *him* and headed across the room and out to the patio, just making it to the garden in time.

Where she threw up in spectacular and humiliating fashion.

Daniel remained where he was and watched as his grandmother hurried through the doorway and quickly attended to the still-vomiting woman who was bent over in the garden. If he thought he was needed Daniel would have helped, but he was pretty sure she would much prefer his grandmother coming to her aid.

After several minutes both women came back through the door. Mary-Jayne didn't look at him. Didn't even acknowledge he was there as she walked to the front door and let herself out, head bowed, arms rigid at her sides. But he was rattled seeing her. And silently cursed himself for having so little control over the effect she had on him.

"The poor thing," his grandmother said, hovering in the doorway before she finally closed the door. "She's been unwell for weeks. Ex-boyfriend trouble, too, I think. Not that she's said much to me about it…but I think there's been someone in the picture."

Boyfriend?

His gut twinged. "Does she need a doctor?" he asked, matter-of-fact.

"I don't think so," his grandmother replied. "Probably just a twenty-four-hour bug."

Daniel ignored the twitch of concern. Mary-Jayne had a way of making him feel a whole lot of things he didn't want or need. Attraction aside, she invaded his thoughts when he least expected it. She needled his subconscious. Like she had when he'd been on a date a couple of weeks back. He'd gone out with the tall leggy blonde he'd met at a business dinner, thinking she'd be a distraction. And spent the evening wishing he'd been with someone who would at least occasionally disagree and not be totally compliant to his whims. Someone like Mary-Jayne Preston. He'd ended up saying good-night to his date by nine o'clock, barely kissing her hand when he dropped her home. Sure, he didn't want a serious relationship, but he didn't want boring conversation and shallow sex, either.

And since there had been nothing boring or shallow about the night he'd spent with the bewitching brunette, Daniel still wanted her in his bed. Despite his good sense telling him otherwise.

"So," Solana said, and raised her hands. "Why have you come home?"

"To see you. Why else?"

She tutted. "Always a question with a question. Even as a toddler you were inquisitive. Always questioning everything, always asking *why* to your grandfather. Your brothers were never as curious about things as you were. Do you remember when you were eight and persuaded your grandfather to let you ride that mad, one-eyed pony your dad saved from the animal rescue center?" She shook her head and grinned. "Everyone wanted to know why you'd want to get on such a crazy animal. And all you said was, *why not?*"

Daniel shrugged. "As I recall I dislocated my collarbone."

"And scared Bernie and me half to death," Solana said and chuckled. "You were a handful, you know. Always getting into scraps. Always pushing the envelope. Amazing you turned out so sensible."

"Who say's I'm sensible?" he inquired lightly.

Solana's smile widened. "Me. Your brothers. Your grandfather if he was still alive."

"And Miles?"

His grandmother raised a silvery brow. "I think your dad would like you to be a little *less* sensible."

"I think my father would like me to eat tofu and drive a car that runs on doughnut grease."

"My son is who he is," Solana said affectionately. "Your grandfather never understood Miles and his alternative ways. But your dad knows who he is and what he wants from life. *And* he knows how to relax and enjoy the simple things."

Daniel didn't miss the dig. It wasn't the first time he'd been accused of being an uptight killjoy by his family. "I can relax."

His grandmother looked skeptical. "Well, perhaps you can learn to while you're here."

Daniel crossed his arms. Something about her tone made him suspicious. "You knew I was coming?"

Solana nodded, clearly unapologetic. "Blake called me. And of course it was my idea." She sat down at the table. "Did you know your grandfather had his first heart attack at thirty-nine?"

Daniel sighed. He'd heard it before. Mike Anderson died at sixty-nine from a massive coronary. His fourth. After two previous bypass surgeries the final heart attack had been swift and fatal, killing him before he'd had a chance to get up from his desk. "Gran, I—"

"Don't fob me off with some vague assurance that it won't happen to you," she said, cutting him off. "You work too hard. You don't take time off. You've become as defined by Anderson Holdings as your grandfather was… and all it got him was an early grave. There's more to life than business."

He would have dismissed the criticism from anyone else…but not Solana. He loved and respected his grandmother, and her opinion was one of the few that mattered to him.

"I know that. But I'm not ready to—"

"It's been over four years," Solana reminded him gently. "And time you got back to the land of the living. Simone wouldn't want you to—"

"Gran," Daniel said, hanging on to his patience. "I know you're trying to help. And I promise I'll relax and unwind while I'm here. I'm back for a week so I'll—"

"You'll need more than a week to unwind," she said, cutting him off again. "But if that's all you can manage then so be it. And your parents are expecting you to visit, in case you were thinking you'd fly under the radar while you're here."

Guilt spiked between his shoulder blades. Solana had a way of doing that. And he hadn't considered *not* seeing his father and stepmother. Not really. True, he had little in common with Miles and Bernadette…but they *were* his parents, and he knew they'd be genuinely pleased that he'd come home for a visit.

From a young age he'd known where his path lay. He was who his grandfather looked to as his protégé. At eighteen he'd been drafted into Anderson's, studying economics at night school so he could learn the business firsthand from his grandfather. At twenty-three, following Mike Anderson's death, he'd taken over the reins and since then he'd lived and breathed Anderson's. Blake and Caleb had followed him a few years later, while Daniel remained at the helm.

He worked and had little time for anything resembling a personal life. Simone had understood that. She was a corporate lawyer and worked seventy-hour weeks. Marrying her had made sense. They were a good match…alike in many ways, and they'd been happy together. And would still be together if fate and a faulty brake line hadn't intervened. She'd still be a lawyer and he would still spend his waking hours living and breathing Anderson Holdings. And they would be parents to their daughter. Just as they'd planned.

Daniel stretched his shoulders and stifled a yawn. He was tired. Jet-lagged. But if he crashed in the afternoon he'd feel worse. The trick to staying on top of the jet lag was keeping normal sleep patterns. Besides, there were two things he wanted to do—take a shower, and see Mary-Jayne Preston.

Mary-Jayne knew that the knock on her door would be Daniel. She'd been waiting for the sound for the past hour. But the sharp rap still startled her and she jumped up from the sofa, where she'd been sitting, hands twisted and stomach churning.

She walked across the living room and down the short hallway, grappling with the emotions running riot throughout her. She ruffled out her baggy shirt and hoped it disguised her belly enough to give her some time to work out how she was going to tell the man at her door he was going to become a father. She took a deep breath, steadied her knees, grabbed the handle and opened the door.

His gray eyes immediately looked her over with unconcealed interest. "How are you feeling?"

His lovely accent wound up her spine. "Fine."

"My grandmother is worried about you."

"I'm fine, like I said."

He tilted his head slightly. "You sure about that?"

Her chin came up. "Positive. Not that I have to explain myself to you."

"No," he mused. "I guess you don't."

"Is there something else you wanted?"

A tiny smile creased one corner of his mouth. "Can I come in?"

"I'd rather you didn't," she said, and stepped back, shielding herself behind the door. "But since you own this resort I guess you can do whatever the hell you want."

There was laughter in his eyes, and she realized the more hostile she got, the more amused he appeared. Mary-Jayne took a deep breath and turned on her heels, quickly finding solace behind the single recliner chair just a few feet away. She watched as he closed the door and took a few easy strides into the room.

"I hear you've been taking my grandmother to see fortune-tellers?"

Solana had told him about that? The older woman had sworn her to secrecy, saying her grandsons would think her crazy for visiting a clairvoyant. "It was *one* fortune-teller," she informed him. "And a reputable one, I might add."

His brows came up. "Really? You believe in all that nonsense?"

She glared at him. "Well, she did say I'd meet a man who was a real jerk...so I'd say she was pretty accurate, wouldn't you agree?"

"Is that a question?" he shot back. "Because I'm probably not the best judge of my own character. Other people's characters, on the other hand, I can usually peg."

"Don't start with—"

"Why did you hang up on me when I called you?"

She was genuinely surprised by his question. And didn't respond.

"You were in South Dakota at your friend's wedding," he reminded her. "I was in San Francisco. I would have flown you to the city."

Into the city. And into his bed. Mary-Jayne knew the score. She might have been a fool the night of Solana's birthday party, but she certainly wasn't about to repeat that monumental mistake.

"I wasn't in the market for another meaningless one-night stand."

His mouth twitched. "Really? More to the point, I guess your boyfriend wouldn't have approved?"

She frowned. "My what?"

"My grandmother can be indiscreet," he said and looked her over. "Unintentionally of course, since she has no idea we had that *meaningless one-night stand.*"

Color rose and spotted her cheeks. And for several long seconds she felt a kind of riveting connection to him. It was illogical. It was relentless. It made it impossible to ignore him. Or forget the night they'd spent together. Or the way they'd made love. The silence stretched between them, and Mary-Jayne was drawn deep into his smoky gray eyes.

"I don't have a boyfriend or lover," she said quietly. "I made that up to stop Solana from asking questions about…" Her words trailed off and she moved back, putting distance between them.

"About what?"

She shook her head. "Nothing. I really can't… I can't do this."

"Do what?" he asked.

"I can't do this with you."

"We're not doing anything," he said. "Just talking."

"That's just it," she said, her voice coming out a little strangled. "I'm not ready for this. Not here. Not today. I feel unwell and I—"

"I thought you said you were feeling better?" he asked, cutting her off.

"Well, I'm not, okay? I'm not better. And seeing you here only makes me feel worse."

"Such brutal honesty. I don't know whether to be flattered or offended."

She let out an agonized moan. "That's just it. I am honest. *Always*. And seeing you now makes it impossible for me to be anything else. And I'm not ready for it... I can't do this today. I simply can't—"

"What are you talking about?" he asked impatiently and cut her off again.

"I'm talking about... I mean... I can't..."

"Mary-Jayne," he said, saying her name like he had that night, when he'd said it over and over, against her skin, against her breath. "I'm not sure what's going on with you, but you're not making much sense."

The truth screamed to be told. There was no other way. She couldn't stop being who she was. She was an honest, forthright person who wore her heart on her sleeve. Mary-Jayne stepped out from behind the chair and spread her hands across her stomach, tightening the baggy shirt over her middle. Highlighting the small bump that hadn't been there four months ago.

"I'm talking about *this*."

Daniel quickly refocused his gaze onto her middle and frowned. "You're pregnant?"

She nodded and swallowed hard. "Yes."

"And?"

She shrugged and her hair flipped around her shoulders. Now or never.

"And isn't it obvious? You're the father."

Chapter Three

He hadn't moved. Mary-Jayne looked at him and took a long breath. "This isn't how I wanted you to find out. I was going to call and tell you and—"

"You're not serious?" he asked, cutting through her words with icy precision.

She nodded. "I'm perfectly serious. I'm pregnant."

He raised a dark brow. "We used protection," he said quietly and held up a few fingers. "Three times, three lots of birth control. So your math doesn't quite work out."

"My math?" She stared at him. "What exactly are you accusing me of?"

"Nothing," he replied evenly. "Simply stating an irrefutable fact."

A fact?

Right. There was no possible way of misunderstanding his meaning. "I'm not lying to you. This baby is—"

"Yours," he corrected coldly. "And probably the ex-boyfriend who my grandmother said is giving you grief at the moment."

She fought the urge to rush across the room and slug him. "I don't have a *boyfriend*. Ex or otherwise."

"You do according to my grandmother," he stated. "Who I trust more than anyone else."

No punches pulled. He didn't believe her. *Okay.* She could handle it. She didn't care what he thought. "I only told Solana that to stop her from asking questions about why I've been unwell."

He crossed his arms, accentuating his broad shoulders, and stood as still as a statue. He really was absurdly good-looking, she thought, disliking him with every fiber in her body. His gray eyes had darkened to a deep slate color and his almost black hair was short and shiny, and she remembered how soft it had been between her fingertips. His face was perfectly proportioned and he had a small cleft in his chin that was ridiculously sexy. Yes, Daniel Anderson was as handsome as sin. He was also an arrogant, overbearing, condescending so-and-so, and if it weren't for the fact he was the biological father of her child, she'd happily *never* see him again.

"Do I really appear so gullible, Miss Preston?"

Miss Preston?

"Gullible? I don't know what you—"

"If you think naming me in a paternity claim will fatten your bank balance, think again. My lawyers will be all over you in a microsecond."

His pompous arrogance was unbelievable. "I'm not after your money."

"Then, what?" he asked. "A wedding ring?"

Fury surged through her. "I wouldn't marry you if you were the last man left on the planet."

Her words seemed to amuse him and he looked at her

in such a haughty, condescending way that her palms actually itched with the urge to slap his face. In every way she'd played the scene out in her head, and not once had she imagined he wouldn't believe that her baby was his. Naive perhaps, but Mary-Jayne had been raised to take someone at their word.

"That's quite a relief, since I won't be proposing anytime soon."

"Go to hell," she said quietly as emotion tightened her chest, and she drew in a shuddering breath. He pushed her buttons effortlessly. He really was a hateful jerk.

"Not until we've sorted out this little mix-up."

"Mix-up?" She glared at him. "I'm pregnant and you're the father. This is not a mix-up. This is just how it is."

"Then, I demand a paternity test."

Daniel hadn't meant to sound like such a cold, unfeeling bastard. But he wasn't about to be taken for a ride. He knew the score. A few months back his brother Caleb had been put through the ringer in a paternity suit that had eventually proved the kid he'd believed was his wasn't. And Daniel wasn't about to get pulled into that same kind of circus.

Mary-Jayne Preston's baby couldn't possibly be his... could it? He'd never played roulette with birth control. Besides, now that he could well and truly see her baby bump she looked further along than four months. Simone hadn't started showing so obviously until she was five months' pregnant.

"I'd like you to leave."

Daniel didn't move. "Won't that defeat the purpose of your revelation?"

She scowled, and he couldn't help thinking how she still looked beautiful even with an infuriated expression.

"You know about the baby, so whatever you decide to do with the information is up to you."

"Until I get served with child-support demands, you mean?"

She placed her hands on her hips and Daniel's gaze was immediately drawn to her belly. She was rounder than he remembered, kind of voluptuous, and a swift niggle of attraction wound its way through his blood and across his skin. Her curves had appealed to him from the moment they'd first met, and watching her now only amplified that desire.

Which was damned inconvenient, since she was obviously trying to scam him.

"I don't want your money," she said stiffly. "And I certainly don't want a wedding ring. When I get married it will be to someone I actually like. I intend to raise this baby alone. Believe me, or don't believe me. Frankly, I don't care either way."

There was such blatant contempt in her voice that he was tempted to smile. One thing about the woman in front of him—she wasn't afraid to speak her mind. And even though he knew it was crazy thinking, it was an interesting change from the usual lengths some women went to in order to get his attention. How sincere she was, he couldn't tell.

"We spent the night together a little over four months ago," he reminded her. "You look more than four months pregnant."

Her glare intensified. "So it's clearly a big baby. All I know is that the only possible way I got pregnant was from that night I spent with you. I hadn't been with anyone for a long time before that night. Despite what you think of me, I'm not easy. And I don't lie. I have no reason to want this child to be yours. I don't like you. I'm not interested in you or your money or anything else. But I am telling you the truth."

He still wasn't convinced. "So the ex-boyfriend?"

"A figment of my imagination," she replied. "Like I said, Solana was asking questions and I needed a little camouflage for a while."

He kept his head. "Even if there is no boyfriend and you are indeed carrying a supersize baby...we used contraception. So it doesn't add up."

"And since condoms are only ninety-eight percent effective, we obviously managed to slip into the two percent bracket."

Ninety-eight percent effective?

Since when?

Daniel struggled with the unease clawing up his spine. "You cannot expect me to simply accept this news at face value."

She shrugged, as if she couldn't care either way. "Do, or don't. If you want a paternity test to confirm it, then fine, that's what we'll do."

He relaxed a little. Finally, some good sense. "Thank you."

"But it won't be done until the baby is born," she said evenly and took a long breath. "There are risks associated with tests after the fifteen-week mark, and I won't put my baby in jeopardy. Not for you. Not for anyone."

There was such unequivocal resolve in her voice, and it surprised him. She was a flake. Unreliable. Unpredictable. Nothing like Simone. "Of course," he said, and did his best to ignore the stabbing pain in his temple. His shoulders ached, and he could feel the effects of no sleep and hours flying across the globe begin to creep into his limbs. "I wouldn't expect you to put your child at risk."

Her child.

Her baby.

This wasn't what he'd expected to face when he'd decided to come home. But if she was telling the truth? What then? To share a child with a woman he barely knew. It was a train wreck waiting to happen.

And he hated waiting. In business. In his personal life.

He'd waited at the hospital when Simone was brought in with critical injuries. He waited while the doctors had tried to save her and their unborn daughter. He'd waited, and then received the worst possible news. And afterward he'd experienced a heartbreaking despair. After that night he became hollow inside. He'd loved his wife and daughter. Losing them had been unbearable. And he'd never wanted to feel that kind of soul-destroying anguish again.

But if Mary-Jayne *was* carrying his child, how could he turn his back?

He couldn't. He'd be trapped.

Held ransom by the very feelings he'd sworn he never wanted to feel again.

"So what do you want from me until then?"

"Want? Nothing," she replied quietly. "I'll call you when the baby is born and the paternity test is done. Goodbye."

He sighed. "Is this how you usually handle problems? By ignoring them?"

Her cheeks quickly heated. "I don't consider this baby a problem," she shot back. "And the only thing I plan to ignore is you."

He stared at her for a moment, and then when he laughed Mary-Jayne realized she liked the sound way too much. She didn't want to like *anything* about him. Not ever. He had become enemy number one. For the next five months all she wanted to do was concentrate on growing a healthy baby. Wasting time thinking about Daniel and his sexy laugh and gray eyes was off her agenda.

"You don't really think that's going to happen, do you?" he asked, watching her with such hot intensity she couldn't look away. "You've dropped this bombshell, and you know enough about me to realize I won't simply fade away for the next five months."

"I can live in hope."

"I think you live in a fantasyland, Mary-Jayne."

The way he said her name caused her skin to prickle. No one called her that except her parents and her older brother, Noah. Even her sisters and closest friends mostly called her M.J. To the rest of the world she was M. J. Preston—the youngest and much loved sibling in a close-knit middle-class family. But Daniel had always used her full name.

Mary-Jayne took a deep breath. "A fantasyland?" She repeated his words as a question.

"What else would you call it?" he shot back as he looked her over. "You're what, twenty-seven? Never married or engaged. No real career to speak of. And a barely solvent online business. You've rented the same house for nearly ten years. You drive a car that's good for little else but scrap metal. You have less than a thousand dollars in the bank at any given time and a not-so-stellar credit rating thanks to a certain dubious ex-boyfriend who ran up a debt on your behalf over five years ago. It looks very much like you do—"

"How do you know that?" she demanded hotly, hands on hips. "How do you know all that about me? I've not told Solana any of…" She trailed off as realization hit. And then she seethed. "You had me investigated?"

"Of course," he replied, unmoving and clearly unapologetic.

"You had no right to do that," she spat. "No right at all. You invaded my privacy."

He shrugged his magnificent shoulders. "You are working at this resort and have befriended my grandmother—it was prudent to make sure you weren't a fortune hunter."

"Fortune hunter?" Mary-Jayne's eyes bulged wide and she said a rude word.

He tilted his head a fraction. "Well, the jury's still out on that one."

"Jury?" She echoed the word in disbelief. "And what does that make you? The judge? Can you actually hear yourself? Of all the pompous, arrogant and self-important things I've ever heard in my life, you take the cake. And you really do take yourself and the significance of your opinions way too seriously."

He didn't like that. Not one bit. She watched, fascinated as his eyes darkened and a tiny pulse in his cheek beat rapidly. His hands were clenched and suddenly his body looked as if it had been carved from granite. And as much as she tried to fight it, attraction reared up, and heat swirled around the small room as their gazes clashed.

Memories of that night four months ago banged around in her head. Kissing, touching, stroking. Possession and desire unlike any she had known before. There had been a quiet intensity in him that night, and she'd been swept away into another world, another universe where only pleasure and a deeply intimate connection existed. That night, he hadn't been the rigid, unyielding and disagreeable man who was now in her living room. He'd been tender and passionate. He'd whispered her name against her skin. He'd kissed her and made love to her with such profound eagerness Mary-Jayne's entire mind and body had awakened and responded in kind. She'd never been driven to please and be pleasured like that before.

But right now she had to get back to hating him. "I'm going to get changed and go for a walk to clear my head. You know the way out."

He didn't move. And he looked a little pale, she thought. Perhaps the shock that he was going to be a father was finally hitting home. But then she remembered that he didn't believe he actually was her baby's father, so that probably wasn't it.

"We still have things to discuss."

"Not for another…" Her words trailed off and she tapped off five of her fingers in her palm. "Five months. Until then, how about you treat me with the disdain that you've clearly mastered, and I'll simply pretend that you don't exist. That will work out nicely for us both, don't you think?"

Of course, she knew saying something so provocative was like waving a red cape at a bull. But she couldn't help herself. He deserved it in spades. And it was only the truth. She didn't want to see him or spend any more time in his company.

"I don't treat you with disdain."

And there it was again—his resolute belief in the sound of his own voice.

"No?" She bit down on her lip for a moment. "You've admitted you had me investigated and just accused me of being a fortune hunter. Oh, and what about what you said to me on the phone when I was in South Dakota?" She took a strengthening breath. "That I was a flake who dressed like a hippie."

His eyes flashed. "And before you told me to go to hell you called me an uptight, overachieving, supercilious snob, if I remember correctly." He uncrossed his arms and took a step toward her.

"Well, it's the truth. You are an uptight snob."

"And you dress like a hippie."

"I like to be comfortable," she said, and touched her head self-consciously. "And I can't help the way my hair gets all curly in the humidity."

His gaze flicked to her hair and she saw his mouth twitch fractionally. "I didn't say a word about your hair. In fact it's quite…it's…it's…"

"It's what?" she asked.

"Nothing," he said, and shrugged. "I would like to know your plans."

Mary-Jayne stared at him. "I don't have any plans other than to have a healthy baby in five months' time."

He looked around the room. "When are you leaving here?"

"Audrey's back in two weeks. I'll go home then."

"Have you told your family?"

She shook her head. "Not yet."

"Have you told anyone?"

She met his gaze. "You."

His expression narrowed. "And since she didn't mention it while you were throwing up in her garden, I'm guessing you haven't told my grandmother, either?"

"Just you," she replied, fighting the resentment fueling her blood. "Like I said. Incidentally, Daniel, if you're going to disbelieve everything that comes out of my mouth, it's going to be a long five months."

He grinned unexpectedly. "So you do know my name? I don't think you've ever used it before. Well, except for that night we spent together."

Her skin heated. She remembered exactly how she'd said his name that night. Over and over, whispered and moaned, as though it was the only word she'd known.

"Like I said, you know the way out."

He didn't budge. "We still need to talk."

"We've talked enough," she said tensely. "You don't believe me and you need a paternity test. *And* you think I'm after your money. Believe me, I've got your message loud and clear."

"You're angry because I want proof of paternity?"

He actually sounded surprised. Mary-Jayne almost laughed at his absurd sense of entitlement. "I'm angry because you think I'm lying to you. I don't know what kind of world you live in where you have this compulsion to question someone's integrity without cause, but I don't live in that world, Daniel. And I would never want to."

She spun on her heel and left the room, barely taking a breath until she reached the sanctuary of the main bedroom. She leaned against the closed door and shuddered.

It's done now. He knows. I can get on with things.

She pulled herself together, changed into sweats and sneakers and loitered in the room for more than ten minutes to ensure he'd be gone.

She strode into the living room and then stopped in her tracks. The room was empty. He'd left. As if he'd never been there.

A strange hollowness fluttered behind her ribs. She was glad he was gone—arrogant and disbelieving jerk that he was. She was well rid of him. With any luck she'd never have to see him again. Or speak to him. Or have to stare into those smoky gray eyes of his.

She could go home and have her baby.

Simple.

But in her heart she knew she was dreaming to believe he'd just disappear from her life. She was having his baby—and that made it about as complicated as it got.

When Daniel woke up he had a crick in his neck and his left leg was numb. It was dark out. He checked his watch: six-forty. He sat up and stretched. When he'd left her condo, he'd walked around the grounds for a few minutes before heading back to his own villa. Once he'd sat down, the jet lag had hit him with a thud. Now he needed coffee and a clear head.

He got to his feet and rounded out his shoulders. The condo was quiet, and he walked from the living room and headed for the kitchen. He had to refocus and figure what the hell he was supposed to do for the next five months until the baby came into the world.

The baby.

His baby...

I'm going to be a father.

Maybe?

Daniel still wasn't entirely convinced. Mary-Jayne potentially had a lot to gain by saying he'd fathered her child. He wasn't naive and knew some people were mercenary enough to try to take advantage of others. He remembered how devastated Caleb had been when he'd discovered the boy he'd thought was his son turned out to belong to his *then* girlfriend's ex-husband. And Daniel didn't want to form a bond with a child only to have it snatched away. Not again. Losing Simone and their unborn daughter had been soul destroying. He wasn't going to put himself in a position to get another serving of that kind of loss.

He made coffee and drank it. Damn...he felt as if his head was going to explode. He'd had it all planned out... come back to Port Douglas, reconnect with Mary-Jayne for a week and get her out of his system once and for all.

Not going to happen.

Daniel rounded out his shoulders and sucked in a long breath. He needed a plan. And fast. He swilled the cup in the sink, grabbed his keys and left the villa.

By the time he reached her condo his hands were sweating. No one had ever had such an intense physical effect on him. And he wasn't sure how to feel about it. The crazy thing was, he couldn't ignore it. And now that had amplified a hundredfold.

They needed to talk. There was no way around it. Daniel took another breath and knocked on the door.

When she answered the door she looked almost as though she'd been expecting him to return. He didn't like the idea that he was so transparent to her.

"I'm working," she said, and left him standing in the doorway. "So you'll need to amuse yourself for ten minutes before we get into round two."

The way she dismissed him so effortlessly *should* have made him madder than hell. But it didn't. He liked her spirit, and it was one of the things he found so attractive about her.

He followed her down the hall, and when he reached the dining room she was already standing by a small workbench tucked against the wall in one corner. She was bent over the narrow table, one elbow resting, using a small soldering iron. There was enough light from the lamp positioned to one side for him to see her profile, and despite the protective glasses perched on her nose he couldn't miss the intense concentration she gave her craft. There were several boards fashioned on easels that displayed her jewelry pieces, and although he was no expert, there was certainly style and creativity in her work.

She must have sensed him watching her because she turned and switched off the soldering iron. "So you're back?"

He nodded. "I'm back."

"Did you call your lawyer?"

"What?"

She shrugged a little. "Seems like something you'd do."

Daniel ignored the irritation clawing at his spine. "No, Mary-Jayne, I didn't call my lawyer. Actually, I fell asleep."

She looked surprised and then frowned a little. "Jet lag?"

He nodded again. "Once I sat down it hit me."

"I had the same reaction when I returned from Thailand last year. It took me three days to recover. The trick is to stay awake until bedtime."

There was something husky and incredibly sexy about Mary-Jayne's voice that reached him deep down. After they'd slept together, he'd pursued her and she'd turned him down flat. Even from across an ocean she'd managed to throw a bucket of cold water on his attempts to ask her out. And get her back in his bed. Because he still wanted her. As foolish as it was, as different and unsuitable for one another as they were—he couldn't stop thinking about her.

She knew that. She knew they were from different worlds. She'd accused him of thinking she was an easy mark and that was why he wanted her. But it wasn't that. He wanted her because she stirred him like no other woman ever had. From her crazy beautiful hair to her curvy body and her sassy mouth, Daniel had never known a woman like her. He might not like her...but he wanted her. And it was as inconvenient as hell.

"So what do you want, then?"

Daniel's back straightened. She didn't hold back. She clearly didn't think she had anything to gain by being friendly or even civil. It wasn't a tactic he was used to. She'd called him a spoiled, pampered and arrogant snob, and although he didn't agree with that assumption, it was exactly how she treated him.

"To talk," he replied. "Seems we've got plenty to talk about."

"Do you think?" she shot back. "Since you don't believe

that this baby is yours, I can't see what's so important that you felt compelled to come back so soon."

Daniel took a breath. "I guess I deserve that."

"Yeah," she said and plucked the glasses off her nose. "I guess you do."

He managed a tight smile. "I would like to talk with you. Would coffee be too much trouble?"

She placed the soldering iron on the bench. "I guess not."

As she walked past him and through the door to the kitchen it occurred to Daniel that she swayed when she moved. The kitchen seemed small with both of them in it, and he stayed on the outside of the counter.

"That's quite a collection your friend has up there," he remarked and pointed to the cooking pots hanging from an old window shutter frame that was suspended from the ceiling.

"Audrey likes pans," she said without looking at him. "I don't know why."

"She doesn't need a reason," he said and pulled out a chair. "I collect old books."

She glanced up. "Old books?"

"First editions," he explained. "Poetry and classic literature."

One of her eyebrows rose subtly. "I didn't peg you as a reader. Except perhaps the *Financial Times*."

Daniel grinned a little. "I didn't say I read them."

"Then why collect them?"

He half shrugged. "They're often unique. You know, rare."

"Valuable?" she asked, saying the word almost as an insult. "Does everything in your life have a dollar sign attached to it?"

As digs went between them, it was pretty mild, but it still irked him. "Everything? No."

"Good," she said, and held up a small sugar pot. When he shook his head, she continued speaking. "Because I have no intention of allowing my baby to become caught up in your old family money or your sense of self-entitlement."

Daniel stilled. "What does that mean?"

"It means that people like you have a kind of overconfident belief that money fixes everything."

"People like me?" Daniel walked across the small room and moved around the countertop. "Like me?" he asked again, trying to hold on to the annoyance sneaking across his skin. "Like me, how…exactly?"

She stepped back. "You're rich and successful. You can snap your fingers and have any number of minions willing to do whatever you need done."

He laughed humorlessly. "Really? I must try that next time I want someone to bring me my slippers."

Her green eyes glittered brilliantly. "Did you just make a joke? I didn't realize you had it in you."

Daniel's shoulders twitched. "Perhaps I'm not quite the *uptight, overachieving, supercilious snob* you think I am."

"Oh, I wouldn't go that far," she said and pushed the mug along the countertop. "There's milk in the fridge."

"This is fine." Daniel took the mug and leaned a hip against the counter. "Thank you."

"No problem. And you *are* uptight, Daniel. Everything about you screams order and control."

"Because I don't live in chaos?" he asked, deliberately waving a hand around the untidy room. "That doesn't necessarily equate to being a control freak."

She crossed her arms. "Chaos? So now you think I'm a slob?"

He drank some coffee and placed the mug on the

counter. "What I think is that it's interesting that you express every opinion you have without considering the consequences."

"Oh, have I offended your sensibilities?"

"Have I offended yours?"

She shrugged. "I'd have to care what you thought, wouldn't I?"

In all his life he'd never met anyone who tried so hard to antagonize him. Or anyone with whom he'd been compelled to do the same. Mary-Jayne got under his skin in ways he could barely rationalize. They were all wrong for one another and they both knew it.

And now there was a baby coming...

His baby.

Daniel glanced at her belly and then met her gaze.

"Mary-Jayne." He said her name quietly, and the mood between them changed almost immediately. "Are you... are you sure?"

She nodded slowly. "Am I sure the baby is yours? Yes, I'm certain."

Resistance lingered in his blood. "But we—"

"I may be a lot of things, Daniel...but I'm not a liar." She drew in a long breath. "The contraception we used obviously failed. Despite what you think of me, I've been single for over twelve months and I haven't slept with anyone since...except you."

A stupid, egotistical part of him was glad to hear it. One part wanted to believe her. And the other...the other could only think about what it meant for them both if what she said was true.

"I need to be sure," he said.

"I understand," she replied. "You can have your proof when he or she is born."

Guilt niggled its way through his blood. "I appreciate you agreeing to a paternity test."

She shrugged lightly. "There's little point in being at odds over this. Be assured that I don't want anything from you, and once you have your proof of paternity you can decide how much or how little time you invest in this."

As she spoke she certainly didn't come across as flighty as she appeared. She sounded like a woman who knew exactly what she wanted. Which was her child…and no interference from him.

Which of course wasn't going to happen.

If the baby *was* his, then he would be very involved. He'd have no choice. The child would be an Anderson and have the right to claim the legacy that went with the name. Only, he wasn't sure how he'd get Mary-Jayne to see it that way.

"If this child is mine, then I won't dodge my responsibility."

She looked less than impressed by the idea. "If you're talking about money, I think I've made it pretty clear I'm not interested."

"You can't raise a child on good intentions, Mary-Jayne. Be sensible."

Her mouth thinned and she looked ready for an argument, but she seemed to change her mind. Some battles, he figured, were about defense, not attack…and she knew that as well as he did.

"We'll see what happens," she said casually as she crossed the small kitchen and stood in front of the refrigerator. She waited for him to stand aside and then opened the door. "I'm heating up lasagna. Are you staying for dinner?"

Daniel raised a brow. "Am I invited?"

She shrugged, as if she couldn't care either way. But

he knew she probably wanted to tell him to take a hike in some of her more colorful language.

"Sure," he said, and grabbed the coffee mug as he stepped out of her way. "That would be good."

He caught a tiny smile on her mouth and watched as she removed several items from the refrigerator and began preparing food on the countertop. She placed a casserole dish in the microwave and began making a salad. And Daniel couldn't take his eyes off her. She was fascinating to watch. Her glorious hair shone like ebony beneath the kitchen light, and she chewed her bottom lip as she completed the task. And of course thinking about her lips made him remember their night together. And kissing her. And making love to her. She had a remarkable effect on his libido, and he wondered if it was because they *were* so different that he was so achingly attracted to her. She was all challenge. All resistance. And since very little challenged him these days, Daniel knew her very determination to avoid him had a magnetic pull all of its own.

And he had no idea what he was going to do about it.

Or if he could do actually do anything at all.

Chapter Four

Mary-Jayne finished preparing dinner, uncomfortably conscious of the gorgeous man standing by the kitchen table. There was such blistering intensity in his gaze she could barely concentrate on what she was doing. She hated that he could do that to her. If she had her way she'd never see him again.

But the baby she carried bound them together.

He wouldn't, she was certain, simply disappear from her life.

She had five months until the baby came, and she had to figure out how to get through those months with Daniel in the background. Or worse. He wasn't the kind of man who'd simply go away until the baby came…regardless of how much she might wish for things to go that way.

"How long are you staying at the resort?" she asked, hoping he'd say not too long at all. Best he leave quickly.

"I'd planned to only be here a week to visit with my

grandmother," he replied, and shrugged slightly. "But now I'm not sure."

She frowned. "Don't you have a company to run or something?"

"Yes."

"Isn't it hard to do that from here? You live mostly in San Francisco, right?"

He placed the mug on the dining table and crossed his arms. "Most of the time. Anderson's corporate offices are there. And the Bay Area resort is the largest."

"Well, I'm sure they need you back."

His mouth twitched. "Eager to see me gone, Mary-Jayne?"

"If I said no I'd be lying," she replied, and brought plates and cutlery to the table. "And as I've repeatedly said, I don't lie. So if you're thinking of extending your stay on my account, there's really no need. The birth is five months away and there's nothing you can do until then."

Mary-Jayne brought the food to the table and gestured for him to take a seat. When he was sitting she did the same and took the lids off the salad and lasagna. She didn't bother to ask what he wanted and quickly piled a scoop of pasta on his plate. Once she'd filled her own plate she picked up the utensils and speared some lettuce and cucumber with a fork.

"What…is…that?"

She looked up and smirked when she saw how Daniel was staring at his food. "Lasagna. With mushroom, spinach, shredded zucchini flowers and goat cheese."

He looked as if she'd asked him to chew broken glass. He took a breath and met her gaze. "You're a vegetarian?"

"Of course."

Mary-Jayne knew his parents were strict vegans. She

also knew he and his brothers had made a point from his early teens of *not* following in their footsteps.

"Of course," he repeated with more than a touch of irony. "Looks...delicious."

"I'm not much of a cook," she said frankly. "So don't hold your breath."

"Thanks for the warning."

She smiled to herself as they began to eat. He was being good-humored about her attempts to wind him up and it surprised her. Maybe he wasn't quite as straitlaced and up-tight as she'd believed. Which didn't mean anything. He could be nice. He could be the most charming and agreeable man on the planet and it wouldn't change the one significant fact—they were like oil and water and would never mix. Despite the fact that they'd made a baby together and were now bound by parenthood. They were in different leagues, and she had to remember that every time she was tempted to think about his sexy voice and broad shoulders.

"I have an ultrasound appointment on Tuesday at ten-thirty," she said, and speared some pasta. "My doctor gave me a referral to a medical center in Cairns."

The regional city was forty miles south of Port Douglas. "And?"

"And you're welcome to come along if you want to," she replied flatly.

He didn't really look as though he wanted to. But he did nod. "I'll pick you up."

"I can drive myself."

He raised a brow. "I'll pick you up."

She was about to argue, but stopped herself. Battling with Daniel over the small stuff was pointless. "Okay," she said, and didn't miss the flash of surprise in his eyes.

For a while the only sound in the room was the clicking of cutlery. He seemed happy not to talk and Mary-Jayne was content to eat her food and not think about how intimate the situation was. Once dinner was done he offered to help wash up, and before she had a chance to refuse his assistance he was out of the chair and in the kitchen, rinsing the plates with one hand while he opened the dishwasher with the other.

"You know your way around a kitchen," she said, surprised.

He shrugged. "Bernie made sure my brothers and I knew how to cook and clean up."

"That's your mother?"

"Stepmother," he replied, and began stacking the dishwasher. "She married my dad when I was two."

Her insides contracted. "Solana told me your mother passed away just after you were born."

"That's right."

Mary-Jayne moved into the kitchen. "You were born in Australia, weren't you?"

"That's right. My dad moved to California when he married Bernie and the twins were born there. They moved back here about ten years ago."

"I like your dad."

He glanced sideways. "I didn't realize you were acquainted."

"He came here to visit your grandmother and Caleb a few weeks ago. I was with Solana at the time and she introduced me to him. He had a very relaxed sense of self, if that makes sense. He was very charismatic and friendly," she said, and smiled a little.

"Not like me, you mean?"

Mary-Jayne grabbed a tea towel. "I'm sure you could be the same if you put your mind to it."

He turned and faced her. "And ruin my image of being an uptight bore?"

She laughed softly. "One thing you're not, Daniel, is boring."

"Just uptight?" he asked.

Mary-Jayne shrugged lightly. "I guess it goes with the territory. Solana told me how you took over the business when you were in your early twenties. That must have been quite a responsibility to shoulder. Duty above all else, right?"

He didn't move. "My grandfather was dead. My father had tried his hand at the business and bailed when he realized he was happier growing organic vegetables and pursuing his art. So yes, being drafted into the business that young had its challenges. But I wasn't about to let my family down. Or the people who rely on Anderson's for their livelihood. I did what I had to do... If that made me an uptight bore in the process, then I guess I'll simply have to live with it."

She took a deep breath. There was something so seductive about his deep voice it was impossible to move. She could have easily moved closer to him. The heat that had been between them from the start was as vibrant and scorching as it had ever been.

It's just sex...

Of course she knew that. Sex and lust and some kind of manic chemical reaction that had her hormones running riot. She had to get them under control. And fast.

"So I'll see you Tuesday. Around nine o'clock."

His gaze darkened. "Are you kicking me out?"

Mary-Jayne took a tentative step backward. "I guess so."

He laughed. "You know, I've never met anyone quite like you. There are no punches pulled with you, Mary-Jayne—you say exactly what you think."

"Blame it on my middle-class upbringing."

"I'm not criticizing you," he said, and folded his arms. "On the contrary, I find it intriguing. And incredibly sexy."

She stepped back again. "If you're flirting with me, stop right now. Your *charm* has got us into enough trouble already."

He laughed again. "Good night, Mary-Jayne."

"Good night," she whispered as she followed him up the hall, and she didn't take a breath until she closed the front door behind him.

After a restless night spent staring mostly at the ceiling, Daniel went for a long run along the beach around ten o'clock on Sunday morning. He stayed out for over an hour, and when he returned to his villa, took a shower and dressed and was about to head for his grandmother's when there was a tap on his door.

It was Caleb.

His brother walked across the threshold and dropped a set of keys onto the narrow hall table. "The keys to my Jeep," Caleb said and grinned. "In case you want to visit the folks."

Caleb never failed to remind him or Blake about the importance of family.

"Thanks," he said, and walked down the hallway.

His brother followed, and they each dropped into one of the two leather sofas in the living room. "Have you heard from Audrey?" Daniel asked the one question he knew his brother wouldn't want to answer.

Caleb shook his head. "I screwed up, and she's not about to forgive me anytime soon."

"You did what you thought was right."

"I moved my ex-girlfriend and her child into my house without thinking about what it would mean to my *current* girlfriend. I mean, I know Audrey and I had only been together a couple of months…but still…" The regretful look on his brother's face spoke volumes. "I should have done things differently. I shouldn't have taken Nikki's word that he was my kid without getting tested. I should have known Audrey was going to end up bailing. Hell, I probably would have done the same thing had the situation been reversed. When her mother got sick she had just the out she needed to get away from the resort for a while…and from me."

Which had been the catalyst for Mary-Jayne coming to the resort. Daniel was certain that his brother was in love with Mary-Jayne's friend Audrey. But when his ex-girlfriend had arrived on his doorstep, holding a baby she'd claimed was his, Caleb had reacted instinctively and moved them into his home.

"She's coming back in two weeks."

"Audrey?" Caleb's gaze narrowed. "How do you know that?"

He shrugged. "Gran must have mentioned it."

"Gran did?" His brother raised both brows. "You sure about that?"

"I don't know what—"

"Less than twenty-four hours, hey?" Caleb laughed. "I take it you've seen her?"

Her.

He'd told Caleb about spending the night with Mary-Jayne. He hadn't been able to avoid it since his brother had spotted her leaving his villa early that morning. "Yes, I've seen her."

"You still hung up on her?"

Daniel shrugged one shoulder. Caleb knew him well enough to sniff out a lie. "Things are a little more complicated."

"Complicated?"

He didn't flinch. "She's pregnant."

His brother's eyes bulged. "Hell! And it's yours?"

"So she says."

Caleb let out a long breath. "Do you believe her?"

"Do I have doubts?" He shrugged again. "Of course. But Mary-Jayne isn't like—"

"Like Nikki?" Caleb suggested, cutting him off. "Yeah, you're right. She seems like a real straight shooter. I know Audrey trusted her to run the store in her absence without hesitation. You gonna marry her?"

Daniel's back straightened. "Don't be stupid. I hardly know her."

Caleb grinned. "Well, you'll have plenty of opportunity to get to know her once you start raising a child together."

Raising a child together...

Daniel knew it wouldn't be that simple. She lived in Crystal Point. He lived in San Francisco. There was a hell of a lot of geography separating them. Which would make him what? A once-a-year father? Summer-vacation time or less? He was looking down the barrel at an impossible situation.

"We'll see what happens."

His brother's expression turned serious. "Tell me you're getting a paternity test?"

"Once the child is born," he said, and explained about the risks of doing the test during the second trimester.

Caleb nodded slowly. "And what do you plan to do until then?"

He shrugged a little. "It's not really up to me."

His brother made a disagreeable sound. "I can see that attitude lasting about two days," he said, and smiled. "Until the shock really hits you."

Caleb knew him well. The idea of doing nothing until the baby came sat like a lead weight in his gut. But what choice did he have? Mary-Jayne wasn't the kind of woman to take easily to being watched or hovered over. She was obviously fiercely independent and made it clear she didn't need him for anything.

Which should have put him it at ease.

Instead his insides churned. He was torn between wanting to believe her child was his and knowing it would be much better for them both if it wasn't true. But he had no real reason to disbelieve her. Sure, he thought she was a bit of a flake. But according to Solana she was honest and forthright and exactly as she seemed—a free, independent spirit who answered to no one but herself. Not the kind of woman to claim paternity when she wanted nothing in return.

"I thought I'd visit Gran," Daniel said, and sprang from the sofa. "Feel like joining me?"

Caleb shook his head and grinned as he stood. "I'm not on vacation like you. I have a business to run. And don't forget to go and see the folks this week."

"I won't," Daniel promised, and walked his brother down the hall.

Once Caleb left he locked up the villa, grabbed the keys on the hall stand and headed out. He walked around the grounds for a few minutes, and instead of going directly to Solana's villa made his way to the western side of the resort where the condos were smaller and home to many of the employees. He tapped on Mary-Jayne's door and ignored the interested looks from a few people in corporate shirts who passed him on the pathway that separated the apartments.

The door swung back and she stood in front of him. "Oh…hi."

She sounded breathless, and he was immediately concerned. "Are you okay?"

"Fine," she replied and took a deep breath. "I've been doing Pilates."

Daniel looked her over. Her hair was tied up in a haphazard ponytail and she wore black leggings and a hot pink racer-back tank top that clung to her curves. Her belly looked like it had popped out a little more overnight and he fought the unexpected urge to place his hand on her stomach. Her cheeks were flushed and her lips looked plump and red. There was something wholly healthy and attractive about her that warmed his blood.

"Pilates?" he echoed, and curled his fingers into his palms to stop himself from reaching out to touch her.

"It's good for the baby," she replied. "And me. So did you want something?"

"Only to see how you are feeling today."

"I'm fine," she said, her hand positioned on the door like she couldn't wait to close it. "How are you?"

"Okay," he said.

"Well, thanks for stopping by."

Daniel shifted on his feet. "I thought… I wondered if you would like to have lunch."

Her brows arched. "Lunch? With you? Where?"

He shrugged a little. "There are four restaurants at this resort…take your pick."

Her brows stayed high. "Beneath the prying eyes of wait staff and various employees? Isn't that a little risky? People might start thinking you've been consorting with the help."

Daniel's jaw clenched. She was an argumentative and provocative pain in the neck. And he wanted her anyway.

"First, I don't care what anyone thinks. And second, you are not *the help*, Mary-Jayne. Are you going to be difficult and refuse every request I make? Or accept that you need to eat and since you're a lousy cook anyway, it would—"

"I'm not a *lousy* cook," she retorted and a tiny smile

curved her mouth. "Just not a good cook. And while I appreciate your invitation, I'm hardly dressed for anything other than a cheese sandwich in front of the TV."

He looked her over again and his libido twitched. "I'll come back in half an hour. Unless you need help getting out of your clothes?"

For a second he thought she might slam the door in his face. But to his surprise she laughed softly. "I'm sure I can manage. Okay, see you in thirty minutes."

Then she did close the door and Daniel turned on his heels. And as he walked back down the path he realized he was grinning foolishly.

Lunch.
Great idea.
Not...

As she slipped into a knee-length white denim sundress, Mary-Jayne cursed herself repeatedly for being so agreeable and for finding Daniel Anderson charming and attractive and so darn sexy he could ask her to jet to the moon and she probably would.

She had to get a handle on the chemistry between them. There was no other option.

He tapped on her door exactly thirty minutes later and Mary-Jayne scowled as she moved down the short hallway. He was the punctual type. It figured. Everything about him screamed order and control.

She opened the door and faced him. "I'm ready."

"So I see," he said, and stood aside to let her pass.

Mary-Jayne closed the door and dropped the key into the tote draped over her left shoulder. "Where are we going?" she asked.

"Your choice," he replied. "Like I said."

Mary-Jayne took a deep breath. There were four restaurants at the resort: two bistros designed for families, a trendy Japanese teppanyaki bar and an exclusive à la carte restaurant named after his grandmother that Mary-Jayne had never been in because the menu was way out of her price range, even though Solana had offered to take her there several times.

She smiled sweetly. "Solana's. Think you'll be able to get a table at such short notice?"

His mouth turned up a little. "I'm sure they will be able to accommodate us."

Mary-Jayne looked up at him. "No one would dare defy you, would they?"

"Oh, I could think of someone who would."

He was smiling now and it made her smile back. *Keep your head.* The warning voice at the back of her mind told her to ignore the way her insides fluttered. She didn't want to *flutter* around him. She didn't want to have any kind of reaction. He was her baby's father—that was all. Besides, he didn't actually believe he had fathered her baby, so she should keep being madder than hell and resentful that he thought her so deceptive.

"Well, there's no point in going through life thinking you can have everything your own way, is there?" she replied, and started walking down the path.

He caught up with her in a few strides. "Or thinking you can say whatever you like."

Mary-Jayne stopped in her tracks. "Is that a nice way of saying I have a big mouth?"

"Actually," he said as he came to a halt beside her, "you have a very…lovely mouth."

There was something so flagrantly suggestive about his words that heat quickly travelled up her legs, belly and chest and then hit her directly in her cheeks. Memories banged around in her head. Memories of his touch.

His kiss. His possession. It was too easy to recall the crazy chemistry they shared and the night they'd spent together.

"I wish you wouldn't…"

Her words trailed off as she met his steely gaze. He had a hypnotic power that was uniquely his and it was something she'd never experienced before. She didn't *like* him. She didn't *want* him in her life. But Daniel had a way of invading her thoughts and plaguing her dreams.

"You wish I wouldn't…what?"

She sucked in a shallow breath and stepped sideways. "Stand so close," she said and crossed her arms.

A grin tugged at his mouth. As if he knew just how profoundly he affected her. And as if it pleased him no end.

"Not everything has to be a battle, Mary-Jayne."

And she wished he'd stop saying her name like that… kind of silky and smooth and sexy and impossible to ignore.

He was wrong. Everything did have to be a battle. It was the only way she'd remain unscathed. "Sure," she said and started walking again.

He stopped to make a phone call and was by the main entrance when he caught up with her. Without saying another word she followed him inside, across the foyer and then toward the elevator. The looks and stares from staff as they passed didn't go unnoticed, and Mary-Jayne suspected she'd quickly be the subject of whispers and conjecture. Since she'd arrived at the resort she'd kept to herself. She hadn't socialized with the staff or other store owners. She managed Audrey's store during the day and worked on her jewelry in the evenings. After Solana's birthday party she'd kept her head down and minded her own business, figuring others would do the same in regard to her. And mostly the staff did. Of course everyone knew about Audrey's disastrous affair with Caleb and speculation was rife that her friend had bailed simply to get away from the resort and him and avoid further humiliation. Only Mary-Jayne knew the truth. Sure, Audrey's mother was unwell…but it *was* exactly the excuse Audrey had needed to salvage her pride and put serious miles between herself and the man who'd hurt her so badly.

Mary-Jayne certainly didn't want to trade one scandal for another.

And she certainly didn't want anyone thinking she was sleeping with the boss!

"Everything all right?"

She glanced sideways and pulled her tote close to her belly. "Peachy."

"Worried what people might think?"

Her mouth tightened. He was too intuitive for her liking. "Couldn't care less."

She stepped into the elevator and he moved in behind her. He stared at her for a second before raising one dark brow. "Perhaps you're not as free-spirited as I thought."

She shrugged. "Maybe not."

The door opened, and Mary-Jayne was about to step out when she realized they weren't on the restaurant level. They were one floor up on the conference suites and boardroom level.

He touched her back and gently urged her forward. "Come on."

"Why are we here? I thought we were—"

"This way," he replied, and kept her moving down the short corridor.

A door opened at the end of the hall and a young man in white chef's gear greeted them. Mary-Jayne had seen him around the resort a few times. Daniel greeted him by name and they were shown directly into a private dining area. It was luxury personified. There were half a dozen tables covered in crisp white linen and the finest dinnerware and crystal. A long panel of windows overlooked the pool area and also offered an incredible view of the ocean.

A waiter emerged from another door and pulled out a seat at a table by the window.

Mary-Jayne rocked back on her heels and looked at Daniel. "Nice view."

"Shall we sit?"

His words were more request than question, and she fought the urge to turn around and leave. Instead she smiled a little and sat down. The waiter offered her some sparkling water, and she gave a grateful nod and only spoke again when the young man and the chef left the room.

She dropped her tote to her feet, stared out the window for a moment before resting her elbows on the table and turning her gaze toward the man sitting opposite. "Clearly I'm not the only one concerned about what people think."

He stilled. "What?"

She waved a hand vaguely. "Up the back elevator and into a secret room?"

"Private," he clarified. "Not secret. I thought you might prefer it. Personally I couldn't care less what people think."

She wondered if that were true. Daniel possessed a kind of confidence she suspected was born from arrogance. He was used to getting his own way. Used to telling people what to do. He called the shots...and she couldn't imagine him tolerating speculation from anyone in his employ.

"Well, they'll be *thinking* plenty once my belly really pops out."

His mouth curled at the edges. "They can think what they like. I should have realized you were pregnant when I first saw you yesterday," he said quietly. "It suits you."

She smirked a little. "Am I glowing?"

He nodded. "Yes."

It was a nice compliment, and her skin warmed. "I'll probably end up the size of a house, though," she said and laughed. "All the women in my family have looked like they've swallowed an elephant when they were pregnant."

His mouth curled at the sides, and it was incredibly sexy. "Tell me about them."

"My family?" She shrugged. "There's not much to tell. We all live in Crystal Point. My parents are both retired. My older brother, Noah, is married to Callie and they have four kids. He builds boats and she's a horse-riding instructor. Then there's my sister Evie, who's an artist and runs a bed-and-breakfast. She's married to Scott—who's actually Callie's brother. He's a firefighter and they have two kids. Then there's Grace, who is married to Noah's best friend Cameron. He's a cop, she's a finance broker and they had their first baby two months ago. And then there's little-old-knocked-up me."

He smiled at her words. "No...not much to tell at all."

Mary-Jayne laughed again. It occurred to her that despite how much he aggravated her, she smiled a lot around Daniel. "They're good people."

"I don't doubt it. I imagine you had a very happy childhood."

"Mostly," she admitted. "Of course it was fraught with the usual teenage-girl angst and rebellion, I suppose. I'm the youngest and therefore it's expected that I would be the most troublesome."

He grinned a little. "What kind of trouble?"

"Oh...crushes on inappropriate boys, late nights, the wrong company...and I got my tattoo at fourteen."

He grimaced. "Brave girl."

"Getting a tattoo? Brave or foolish, you mean, because basically I'm marked for life."

"I mean the pain thing."

"Pain?"

"They use needles...right?"

Mary-Jayne tilted her head. "Well...yes."

"I don't like needles."

She laughed loudly. "Chicken."

"You're mocking me," he said, his mouth twisting a little. "That's something of a habit of yours."

The waiter returned with their drinks and placed a menu on the table. Once the young man left, she returned her attention to Daniel.

"I imagine your ego is healthy enough to take it."

He grinned again. "You're probably right. So..." he said and pushed the glass around the table. "Is there any chance your father is going to come after me with a shotgun?"

She laughed loudly. "Not one. My brother, Noah, on the other hand, is very protective of his sisters." She took a long breath. "Seriously...my family let me live my own life. I'm fully prepared to raise this baby alone, Daniel. Be involved or don't. It's that simple."

His brows rose fractionally. "With me in San Francisco and you in Crystal Point? That's not simple. That's about as complicated as it gets, Mary-Jayne. Because I'm not about to avoid my legal and moral responsibility...no matter how much it seems you would like me to."

She frowned and touched her belly. "If I wanted that I would never have told you I was pregnant. Frankly, I just don't want you to get hung up on what you think you *have* to do. Sure, I'd like my baby to have a father who's involved in his or her life, but I don't want this to turn into some kind of parenting battleground with you on one side and me on the other and our child stuck in the middle."

"Nice speech. Is it meant to put me in my place?"

She shrugged. "Take it how you want. It's all rather

moot, anyhow…isn't it? Since you don't actually believe this baby is yours."

His eyes darkened and she was quickly drawn into them. Something passed between them, a kind of relentless energy that warmed her blood.

"It's not that…it's…"

"It's what?" Mary-Jayne asked, and met his gaze and asked the question hovering on her lips. "Is it because of your wife?"

Chapter Five

Daniel stilled. It was the first time the subject had been mentioned since Mary-Jayne had told him she was pregnant. Had he spared Simone more than a fleeting thought in the past twelve hours? The past twenty-four? He'd become so consumed by Mary-Jayne and the idea she was carrying his baby that he could barely think of anything else.

"I gather my grandmother told you what happened?"

She shrugged lightly. "Solana told me she was killed in a car wreck a few years ago."

"Four years," he corrected. "Four years, four months and three weeks."

Her eyes shone. "She was pregnant, wasn't she?"

He nodded slowly as his throat tightened. "Yes. Five months."

"I'm so sorry." Her hand moved across the table and connected with his for a moment before she quickly pulled it back. "It must have been devastating."

"It was the single worst day of my life."

She gathered her hands together in her lap and opened her mouth to speak when the waiter returned. Daniel watched as she studied the menu for a few seconds and then ordered one of the three vegetarian options he'd insisted be included. When she was done he ordered the swordfish, and when the waiter left he grabbed his glass and took a drink.

He put the glass down and spoke. "If you want to ask me about it, go ahead."

Her eyes widened. "You don't mind?"

He shrugged one shoulder.

"How did it happen?"

Daniel closed his eyes for a second as memories banged around in his head. He'd gone over that day countless times in his mind and the pain never lessened. "Simone was driving home from a doctor's appointment and stopped off at the mall to get a birthday gift. She pulled out of the parking lot and into the flow of traffic and a vehicle coming in the opposite direction slammed into her car. The brake line had snapped on the other car and the inexperienced driver panicked, hit the accelerator and crossed over the road."

"Was she killed instantly?"

He shook his head, almost admiring Mary-Jayne's blunt questioning. There was no false pity in her expression. Only curiosity and genuine concern.

"She died in hospital. The doctors tried to save her but her injuries were too severe."

"And the baby?"

"Our daughter died within minutes of Simone passing away."

"That's so sad. Did you have a name picked out for her?"

Daniel pushed down the heat clawing up his throat.

"We'd planned on naming her Lana, after my grandmother."

She was quiet for a moment, her gaze lowered, clearly absorbing what he'd said. When she looked up her eyes were bright, almost glistening. He watched as she bit down on her bottom lip as moisture quickly filled her eyes. He'd observed many emotions cross her face in the time they'd known one another—anger, dislike, humor, passion—but this was something else. Sadness. Acute and heartfelt. He didn't like how it made him feel. Dealing with the combative, argumentative Mary-Jayne was easy compared to seeing her in tears.

"I'm sorry," she said, and grabbed the napkin to dab at her eyes. "I didn't mean to…" Her words trailed and she swallowed hard. "It's the baby hormones. They get me at the most unexpected times. Anyway," she said, her voice a little stronger, "thank you for telling me."

"It's not a secret. I'm sure my grandmother or Caleb would have told you the same thing had you asked them. It was an accident…and like all accidents, it was simply a series of events that merged into one terrible outcome."

She looked at him with silent intensity. "You mean, if she'd lingered at the mall a little longer, or if she had taken another exit from the parking lot, or the other driver had gotten out of bed ten minutes later that morning things would have turned out differently?"

"Exactly."

"You said she was buying a birthday gift. Who was it for?"

Daniel hesitated for a moment. "My grandmother."

It took a moment, but her eyes widened as realization dawned. "So…that night…the night of Solana's birthday party…it was the…the…"

"The anniversary of their deaths? Yes, it was."

The waiter returned with their meals before she had a chance to respond, and Daniel watched with keen interest as she took a long breath and stared into her plate. Once the waiter left them she looked up.

"Is that why you...why you..."

"Why I what?" he asked.

"The party, you know...and how we..." Her words trailed and she shrugged lightly.

"We had sex, you mean?"

Sex. He wasn't going to call it anything else. He wasn't going to suggest they'd made love because it would have been a lie. He used to make love to his wife. There was love and heart and passion between them. They'd been friends since college and started dating when Simone had finished law school. What he felt for Mary-Jayne wasn't grounded in that kind of friendship or any measure of deep emotion. It was base and instinctual and fuelled by attraction and sexual desire. And he intended for it to stay that way. She might be under his skin, but he wasn't about to let her get into his heart.

"I thought there might be a connection," she said and arched one brow. "Like you were wanting...to forget about..."

"I could never forget my wife," he said quietly.

She flinched a little. "I didn't mean that. I was thinking perhaps you needed a distraction that night and that's why you were interested in me."

"I was *interested* in you from the moment I saw you in the store window."

He knew she wouldn't be surprised by his admission. There had been heat between them from that first glance. Daniel wasn't conceited, but he knew the attraction he felt for Mary-Jayne was very much reciprocated.

"Oh...okay."

"The fact it was my grandmother's birthday was a co-incidence," he said, stretching the truth to avoid her questions or her censure. He wasn't about to admit that the hollow feeling that had haunted him since Simone's death had been amplified that night. Or that for a few incredible hours he'd found solace in the arms of a woman he barely knew. "So have you been well other than the nausea?" he asked, shifting the subject.

"Mostly," she replied. "Both my sisters suffered from gestational diabetes when they were pregnant, so my doctor is keeping watch on my sugar levels. But I feel fine at the moment."

Concern tightened his chest. "Does that mean this pregnancy holds risks for you? Is there something we should talk to your doctor about? Perhaps a second opinion is needed to ensure you get the best possible care. I can arrange an appointment with a specialist if—"

"I'm fine," she said sharply, interrupting him as she picked up the cutlery. "The nausea and appetite issues are a normal part of being pregnant. And I like my current doctor just fine, thank you. Stop interfering."

He bit back a grin at her impatience. "Don't mistake concern for control, Mary-Jayne."

She flashed him an annoyed look. "I don't."

"Oh, I think you do. I think you're so desperate to stay in control here that anything I say will be like waving a red flag at a bull."

She looked as if she wanted to jab him in the forehead with her fork. "You really do love to hear the sound of your own voice."

He laughed. "Hit a nerve, did I?"

"By implying that I value my independence?" she shot back. "Not a nerve...a fact. I'm not about to be lorded over like some spineless minion."

"That's a favorite insult of yours," he said and watched her. "Despite what you've conjured in your colorful imagination, I don't live in a house filled with servants. I cook my own meals, launder my own clothes and even tie my own shoes."

Her green eyes flashed. "Doesn't stop you from being a condescending horse's ass, does it?"

He laughed again. They had a way of pushing each other's buttons, and watching her fiery expression quickly stirred his blood and libido. "We have five months to get through until the baby comes, and I'd prefer it if we could manage that time without constantly goading one another, wouldn't you?"

She shrugged as if she couldn't have cared less. But Daniel wasn't fooled. She was as wound up as he was. "Since you'll be in San Francisco and I'll be in Crystal Point, what difference does it make?"

An ocean. Thousands of miles. A different life. There would be so many things between them. Between him and the child she carried. The child she said was his. Most of the shock had worn off overnight. Sure, he wanted a paternity test, but there were months ahead where he either had to accept the child was his, or not. And, despite everything between them, he realized that he believed Mary-Jayne. His grandmother knew her, trusted her... and although some old cynical instincts banged around in his head, Daniel realized he trusted her, too.

"You could come to San Francisco."

She looked up and made a scoffing sound. "Yeah... right."

Maybe not. "What about here?"

Her gaze sharpened. "Here? At the resort?"

"Yes."

"I can't do that, either," she said, and put down her fork.

"Why not?" he shot back. "Your jewelry business is mostly done online, so you could do that anywhere...San Francisco or here."

"This isn't my home, that's why not. I live in Crystal Point... I've lived there all my life. It's where I was born and it's where my baby will be born."

"Our baby."

Her jaw dropped slightly. "You believe me?"

He took a breath and nodded. "I believe you."

She looked wary. "Why the sudden change of heart?"

"Because *not* believing you essentially means I forfeit any rights to be part of this experience."

Mary-Jayne stilled. Rights? What did he mean by that? He wanted rights? He believed her? It should have put her at ease. Instead her entire body was suddenly on red alert. What had she expected? That once she told him about her pregnancy then he would quietly go away and leave her to raise her child alone?

Naive idiot.

The urge to get up and leave suddenly overwhelmed her, and it took all her strength to remain in her seat. She slowly met his unwavering gaze. "I'll be leaving in less than two weeks," she said. "As soon as Audrey returns I'm going home. My home," she reiterated. "Where I belong."

"Then I'll go with you," he said, so casually that her blood simmered. "We need to tell your folks, anyhow."

"I'll tell *my* family when *I* choose," she said, and pushed back her chair a fraction. "Stop bossing me about."

"Stop acting like a child."

It was the kind of verbal gridlock she expected when she was near him. They didn't like one another. They never would. They had sexual chemistry and nothing more. Fatigue and a sudden surge of queasiness shortened her patience and she pushed the seat back.

"Thanks for lunch," she said, and stood. "I'll see my own way out."

"My case in point," he said as he got up. "Run when you don't like what you hear. That's a child's way out, Mary-Jayne."

Her rage sought release. "Go to hell."

His mouth quirked fractionally. "I'll see you Tuesday morning, at nine, for the ultrasound appointment."

"I'd rather—"

"At nine," he insisted, cutting her off.

She didn't respond. Instead she grabbed her tote, thrust back her shoulders and left the room with a pounding heart, more determined than ever to keep him at arm's length.

Back in her condo she calmed down a little, took a shower and called Audrey. Her friend didn't answer her phone so she left a brief message. She spent the remainder of the day staring at her phone, hoping Audrey would call and watching an old movie on the television. By the time she dropped into bed her head was thumping and her rage was festering.

How dare he call her childish? He was an arrogant, pompous jerk! The sooner she was away from him, the better.

On Monday Mary-Jayne lay low. She opened the store and kept away from the front window as much as possible, in case *he* walked by. Or watched her. Or stalked her. But thankfully he didn't show up at the store and didn't call. And since Caleb didn't do his usual midmorning drop in either, Mary-Jayne knew Daniel had told his brother to steer clear.

Puppet master...

Controlling everything and everyone around him.

It made her mad, and got her blood boiling.

On Tuesday morning she set her alarm an hour early, showered and forced herself to eat breakfast. She dressed in a knee-length button-up blue floral dress and tied her hair up in a ponytail. Then she waited on the sofa for him to arrive, hands clasped together. He tapped on the door at nine o'clock with his usual annoying promptness.

He looked so good in jeans and a collared black T-shirt she could barely croak out a greeting when her level gaze met the broad expanse of his chest. She stupidly wished she were taller, more slender, more elegant…and able to meet his eyes without having to look up.

"Good morning."

Mary-Jayne forced out a smile. "Are you always on time for everything?"

"Always."

"It's an annoying trait of yours."

He grinned and motioned for her to pass. Once he pulled the door shut he placed a hand into the small of her back and ushered her forward. "Well, I guess it's one of those things you'll have to get used to."

Not when there's an ocean between us I won't…

By the time they were in his car she was so worked up her teeth chattered. He asked for the address and she replied quietly, staying silent as he punched the information into his GPS. Once they were on their way she dropped her tote to her feet and stared out the side window. But his nearness still rattled her. He was so close and had a kind of hypnotic power she'd never experienced before. Any man she'd ever known paled beside him. Any attraction she'd had in the past seemed lukewarm compared to the heat that simmered between them. The arguments didn't mask anything. It only amplified the undercurrent of desire and made her remember the passion and pleasure they'd shared that night four months ago.

She turned her head to glance at his profile. "Have you ever done that before?"

"Done what?"

"Sleep with someone you hardly know."

His mouth curved, but he looked straight ahead. "I don't recall either of us getting a whole lot of sleep that night."

Her cheeks heated. "You know what I mean." She swallowed hard. "I… It's just that I… Despite how I *seem*… I'm not like that…usually."

"Usually?"

She let out a heavy breath. "I don't sleep around…okay. I might come across as free-spirited and all that…but when it comes to sex I'm not easy. I've had three serious relationships including my high school boyfriend and I've never had a one-night stand before."

"Are you asking how many relationships I've had? Or one-night stands?" He glanced at her for a moment. "Does it really matter?"

His reticence irritated her and she frowned. "Is the subject off-limits for some reason?"

His jaw tightened. "My wife died over four years ago. Have I remained celibate since then? No. Have I had a committed relationship since then? No. Is that enough of an answer, Mary-Jayne?"

She got the message. She was one in a long line of meaningless one-night stands.

Just as well she didn't like him in the least, or she might have been offended by his admission. "I don't have any kind of ulterior motive for asking," she said and stared directly ahead. "I was curious, that's all."

"Well, if your curiosity has you imagining I have a

different woman in my bed every night, you'll be disappointed."

She didn't want to think about any woman in his bed, different or otherwise. "I'd have to care to feel disappointment, wouldn't I?"

"I guess you would," he said quietly. "But in case you've been having sleepless nights over it—my bed has been empty since you left it so quickly in the small hours of the morning all those months ago."

It was a dig. She'd snuck out of his villa, all right, and he clearly didn't appreciate her efforts to avoid any uncomfortable morning-after postmortems. Obviously he'd been stung by her disappearing act. And it took her a moment to realize what he'd said about his empty bed.

"No one since? Have you already nailed every woman in San Francisco? Is that the problem?"

He laughed humorlessly. "You're the problem."

"Me?" She almost squeaked the word out. "I can't imagine why."

"One night didn't really do us justice, did it? Not with that kind of instant attraction."

She knew what he meant. The store window. The resort foyer. The beach. Solana's party. Every time they'd met the heat had ramped up a notch. Until it had become so explosive the outcome was unavoidable.

"So you want…you still want…"

He chuckled. "You know, you really are a fascinating contradiction. For such a *free-spirited* woman, you can be equally shy and self-conscious."

"Because I think sex should mean something? Because I think one-night stands are empty and pointless and of little importance?"

His profile was unmoving. "Since our night together

resulted in this pregnancy, I'd say it's about as important as it gets, wouldn't you?"

She frowned. "You're twisting my words. I meant the sex wasn't important…not the baby."

There was insult in her words, and she was surprised that he stayed silent.

Silent and seething.

He was mad. Perhaps his ego wasn't as rock solid as she thought?

"That's not a complaint, by the way," she said, and pushed the tote around with her feet. "The sex was very… nice."

"It wasn't *nice*, Mary-Jayne. It was hot and incredibly erotic and about as good as it gets."

He was right. They both knew it.

"That, too," she admitted. "And the reason I left," she said, and figured she may as well tell him the truth, "is I didn't want any morning-after awkwardness. I thought it would be easier to bail and forget the whole thing. I mean, it was never going to be any more than one night. I think we both knew that."

"If I believed that I wouldn't have repeatedly asked you out."

It was true. He *had* pursued her. And she'd refused him every time. Because they were too different. As clichéd as oil and water. He wanted her in his bed and he got what he wanted. Only a fool would imagine he was looking for anything more.

"To get me into bed again, right? Which means we would have been back to square one. The point I'm making is men and women generally think about sex differently. I'm not saying I'm after a picket fence quite yet, but I'm not foolish enough to waste time on something or someone where it wouldn't be on the table ever."

"That's quite a judgment."

"Can you deny it?" she asked. "Let's face it, Daniel, you and I are polar opposites in every way. Sure, we have chemistry, but that's all. Most of the time we barely seem to tolerate one another. That's not a recipe for romance. It's a recipe for disaster."

She turned back to look out the side window with a heavy sigh, and they didn't say another word to one another until they'd reached Cairns. With a population of over one hundred thousand, the bustling regional city was a popular tourist spot and served as a starting point for people wanting to visit the Great Barrier Reef.

Within minutes they were pulling into the car park in front of the medical center. She got out of the Jeep, grabbed her tote and waited for him to come around to the passenger side.

"If you like, we can look around town when we're done," he suggested and locked the vehicle. "Maybe have lunch."

"The way you keep trying to feed me, anyone would think I need fattening up."

His brows narrowed. "Well, I have noticed you don't eat enough."

Mary-Jayne put her hands on her thickening waist. "I eat plenty. Have you seen my ever-expanding middle? I told you how the women in my family look when they're pregnant."

"You hardly touched your food the other day."

Mary-Jayne looked up at him. "I was too mad to eat."

"Too hot headed, you mean."

"You were being a bossy, arrogant jerk. It annoyed me."

"Everything I do appears to annoy you," he said and ushered her toward the steps that led into the building. "Perhaps you should consider why that is."

"I know why," she said, and moved up the steps. "Because you're a bossy, arrogant jerk."

He laughed softly and grasped her hand, stopping her before they reached the door. Mary-Jayne looked up and met his gaze. His gray eyes were dark and intense, and for a second she couldn't do anything but stare at him. The pulse in his cheek throbbed and she fought the urge to touch the spot.

He threaded their fingers and drew her closer. "How about you let me off the hook for a little while, hmm?"

Don't do it...

"I can't..."

"Sure you can," he said, and rubbed his thumb inside her palm. "I'm not your enemy, Mary-Jayne...except perhaps in your lively imagination."

"Daniel..."

"Come on," he said, and gently led her inside. "Let's go and meet this baby."

It took about twenty minutes to find the correct office, see reception and be shown to a small room when she was instructed to lie on the bed and wait for the doctor. A nurse appeared and wheeled the imaging machine close to the bed and told them the doctor would be in soon.

"Are you okay?" he asked from the chair he sat on from across the room.

Mary-Jayne lay back on the table and wiggled. "Fine. Peachy. Never better."

"You look nervous."

She shrugged. "Well, I've never done this before, so of course I'm a little nervous."

As she said the words it occurred to her that Daniel probably *had* done this before. With Simone. With the wife he'd loved and the baby they'd lost. It must have been hard for him to come into the room with her, a woman he hardly knew, and potentially have the same experience he'd shared with his wife.

Shame hit her square between the shoulders.

All morning she'd been thinking of herself and hadn't spared a thought for his feelings. *What's happened to me? When did I become so self-absorbed?*

"I'm sorry."

He looked at her. "For what?"

"For not considering how difficult it must be for you to do this."

His gaze didn't waver. "It's not difficult. Just...different. Simone and I had planned everything, from conception to her due date. She'd had endometriosis for several years and had trouble getting pregnant. Eventually we used IVF and she got pregnant after three attempts. It was all rather clinical and organized and more about the treatments and processes rather than the baby...at least in the beginning. So, yes, this is different."

There was heat in her throat. "Okay," she said, and smiled a little. "You're off the hook."

The doctor came into the room then and Daniel got to his feet. Mary-Jayne lay back and tried to relax. He moved beside her and touched her shoulder.

"So," Doctor Stewart said once she'd introduced herself and perched on a stool at the side of the bed. "Would you like to know your baby's sex?"

Mary-Jayne looked at Daniel.

He shrugged lightly. "It's up to you."

She swallowed hard. "I think... Yes...I'd like to know."

She glanced at him again and thought he looked relieved.

The doctor got her to unbutton her dress, and Mary-Jayne tried not to be self-conscious of Daniel's presence in the chair at her side as her belly was bared. A cool gel was placed on her stomach and she shivered a little. Daniel took hold of her hand and squeezed gently.

Once the ultrasound started she was riveted to the image on the small screen. It didn't look like anything at first, until the doctor pointed out an arm and the baby's head. Emotion welled inside her and she bit back a sob.

Hi there, peanut... I'm your mother...and I love you more than I thought possible.

"And there's your baby," the doctor said, and rolled the device lower. "You have a perfectly lovely boy."

She looked at Daniel and noticed he stared directly at the screen, clearly absorbed by what they saw. He'd never looked more attractive to her, and in that moment an unexpected surge of longing rushed through her entire body.

Longing and desire and something else...something she couldn't quite fathom.

Something she didn't want to think about.

"Oh..."

The doctor's voice quickly cut through her thoughts.

"What is it?"

Daniel's voice now. Deep and smooth and quicker than usual. It gave her comfort. If something was wrong, he was there, holding her hand, giving her strength. He glanced at her and squeezed her fingers.

Doctor Stewart looked at them both. "Well...I see."

"What?" he asked again, firmer this time. "Is something wrong?" It was the question she was too afraid to ask.

"Nothing's wrong," the doctor said, and smiled broadly. "It's just...there are two of them."

Mary-Jayne stared at the screen. "What do you mean?"

The doctor smiled. "Congratulations to you both... you're having twin boys."

Chapter Six

Someone could have told him that he was going to live on the moon for the next fifty years and he wouldn't have been more shocked.

Twin boys...

"You're sure?" he asked the doctor, and noticed how Mary-Jayne hadn't moved. He squeezed her hand reassuringly. "And they're fine?"

The doctor nodded. "Fine. Big, strong and healthy. Would you like to listen to their heartbeats?"

Daniel didn't recall saying yes. But within seconds he had small earphones on and heard the incredible sound of his sons' hearts. Emotion rose up and hit him directly in the solar plexus, polarizing him for a moment. He swallowed hard, fighting the heat in his eyes and throat. Nothing he ever heard again would match the sound of the two tiny heartbeats pounding almost in unison. Longing, absolute and raw, filled his chest with such force he grabbed the side of the chair for support.

The doctor said something about having a picture done for them, but he barely heard. He took off the earphones and gently placed them over Mary-Jayne's head. Watching her expression shift from shock to wonderment was incredible. Her face radiated with a joy so acute it was blinding in its intensity. She'd never looked more beautiful.

The doctor stood. "I'll arrange for a picture and come back in a little while," she said, and quickly left the room.

Daniel tightened his grip on Mary-Jayne's hand. "Are you okay?"

She dropped the earphones onto the bed. "Um…I think so."

"Not what you were expecting, huh?"

She sighed. "Not exactly. But…" Her words trailed off for a moment. "I'm happy." She glanced at the now-blank screen. "I can't quite believe it."

"Are there many twins in your family?" he asked, and rubbed her fingertips. She shrugged. "Not really. I know there are in yours, though."

He nodded and grinned. "Yes. My brothers are twins. My grandfather was a twin, and I have two sets of cousins who are twins. It's like an epidemic in my family."

"This is all your doing, then?" she said and smiled.

"I don't think there's actually a genetic link on the father's side, but I'll happily take the credit if you want," he said softly. "Are you okay with this?"

"I'm happy, like I said. And a little scared. I wasn't expecting two." She looked down at her naked stomach. "I wonder if the nurse will come back to get this goo off my belly."

Daniel released her hand and got up. He found a box of tissues on the counter and came back to her side. "This should do it," he said as he sat down and began wiping the gel off her skin.

It was the most intimate thing they'd done in months, and even though he acted as perfunctory as he could, it didn't stop a surge of desire from climbing up his spine. She lay still, perfectly composed. Until he met her gaze and saw that she was watching him with scorching intensity. When he was done her hand came up and she grabbed his fingertips and then gently laid his palm against her belly. She placed her hand on top of his, connecting them in a way that was mesmerizing. Feeling her, feeling their babies, Daniel had no answer for the sensation banging around in his head.

He'd never wanted to feel this again. Not after Simone.

But it was inevitable. They were his children. His sons. They were part of him. How could he not get drawn into feeling such acute and blinding love for them? He couldn't. And he wanted them. He wanted to be part of their lives. Full-time. A real parent.

A real father.

He looked at Mary-Jayne. Her eyes were bright. Luminous. She chewed on her bottom lip and his gaze immediately went to her mouth. He touched her forehead with his other hand and felt the connection down deep. Soul-deep.

In that moment he could nothing else but kiss her.

And her lips, as new as they were familiar, softened beneath his instantly. Daniel's pulse quickened as the kiss quickly deepened. Her breath was warm, her tongue accepting when he sought it with his own. She sighed deep in her throat, and a powerful surge of desire wound through his blood. He touched her hair, twirling the glorious strands between his fingertips. Her hand came up to his chest and he felt the connection through to his bones. And he kissed her again. And again. With each kiss his need for her grew. As did the knowledge he had one option. One way to make things right.

"Mary-Jayne," he said against her lips, trailing his mouth down her cheek to the sensitive spot by her earlobe. A spot he knew made her quiver. "We should get married."

She stilled instantly. Her mouth drew in a tight line and she pushed his hand off her belly. "What?"

Daniel pulled back and stared into her face. "Married," he said again. "We should get married."

She put a hand on his shoulder and gave him a shove. "Don't be ridiculous."

He straightened and got to his feet. "It's the only solution."

"To what?" she said, and pulled her dress closed over her stomach as she swung her legs off the bed. "Since there's no problem, we don't need a solution." She swiftly buttoned up her dress.

He crossed his arms. "There *is* a problem. We're having two children together and we live on opposite sides of the world."

"I said you can see the baby…I mean, babies, as much as you want. But I'm not interested in a loveless marriage, Daniel. Not with you or anyone else."

The doctor returned before he had an opportunity to say anything more. She gave them the photo of the twins and advised Mary-Jayne to make another appointment with her obstetrician in the next few weeks. Daniel listened while she briefly explained how she was returning home to Crystal Point in the next fortnight and how she would see her family doctor once she was back home.

Home…

He almost envied the way she spoke about the tiny town where she'd lived all her life. Nowhere felt like home to Daniel. Not Port Douglas. Not San Francisco.

They left a few minutes later and Mary-Jayne didn't

say a word as they made their way out of the building to-ward their vehicle.

"Are you hungry?" he asked as he opened the passen-ger door. "We could stop somewhere for—"

"I'd prefer to just go back to the resort," she said, cut-ting him off. "I'm a little tired."

Daniel didn't argue. He nodded and closed the door once she was inside. They were soon back on the road, and he made a quick stop to refuel and grab a couple of bottles of water. She took the water with a nod and tucked it by the seat. Fifteen minutes into their return trip he'd had enough of her unusual silence and spoke.

"Avoiding the subject isn't going to make it go away, Mary-Jayne."

"What subject?"

"My proposal."

She glanced sideways. "I thought you must have been joking."

"I'm perfectly serious. Once you calm down you'll re-alize it's the only thing we can do."

She huffed. "I'm perfectly calm. And marrying you is the *last* thing I want to do."

"Why not?" he asked, ignoring how much disdain she had in her voice.

"Because I'm not in the market for someone like you."

"Like me?" He smiled at her relentless insults. "Straight, healthy and financially secure?"

"Arrogant, judgmental and a pain in the—"

"Don't you think our children deserve two parents?"

"Our children *will* have two parents," she said, her knuckles white where she clasped her hands together. "Two parents who live in different countries. Two parents who have too much good sense to marry because it's expected they should." She turned her head. "Be honest, Daniel. You don't want to marry me, you just think you *have* to. But you don't. You're off the hook here. So please, don't mention it again."

He pushed down his irritation. She wound him up like no one else ever had. "I take it you're not opposed to marriage entirely...just marriage to me?"

"I'm opposed to marrying someone I don't love," she said bluntly. "And someone who doesn't love me. The thing is, I believe in love...and I want it. I want to be with someone who wants *me* above all others. Who wants only me and sees only me and who carries only me close to his heart."

It was foolish and romantic nonsense. "How can that matter when there are children involved?"

"Because it does," she insisted. "You've had some attack of conscience since you saw them on that screen and think marriage will somehow uncomplicate this...but it won't. We're too different to be tied to one another for life. And I'm not criticizing your motives, I'm simply trying to do what's best for everyone involved...including you."

Daniel wasn't convinced. His father and stepmother had married because Bernie was pregnant, and their marriage had turned out fine. They'd scraped a family together despite their differences. And if he was going to have any chance of being a hands-on father to his sons, Daniel knew he had to do the same.

But he knew Mary-Jayne well enough to recognize she wasn't prepared to discuss it any further. At least for now.

"We'll talk about it later."

"No, we won't," she reaffirmed. "And what was with that kiss?"

"It was a kiss. People kiss, Mary-Jayne."

She pointed to him and then herself. "Well, not *these* people. Don't do it again."

Had he lost his mind?

Marriage? As if she'd ever agree to that? Couldn't he see it was madness? He'd married for love once…how could he be prepared to settle for anything less? He could still be a father to their children. Sure, it would be challenging, considering the miles between them. But they could make it work. Plenty of people did the same. He was simply being bullheaded about it. Wanting his own way. Trying to control her.

Well, she wasn't about to be maneuvered into a loveless marriage.

She didn't care how much chemistry they had.

And he better not try to kiss her again, either!

"I'd like to stop and see my parents and tell them the news, if that's okay with you?"

Mary-Jayne turned her head. "Sure. Whatever."

It was a small detour, but she didn't mind. She liked Miles and figured they had to start telling people about the babies at some point. It took about half an hour to reach their small hobby farm, and Mary-Jayne sat up straight as he turned off into a narrow driveway and drove half a mile down the bumpy road until they reached the house. She saw the lovely timber home with wide verandas and noticed a small structure built in replica.

"My dad's studio," Daniel explained.

She turned her head. He watched her with such intensity for a moment her breath stuck in her throat. There was something riveting about his gaze, and she turned hot all over. She foolishly thought about the kiss again. It had been sweet and hot and had stirred her libido.

People kiss...

His words fluttered around in her head. Of course she knew it had been a spur-of-the-moment thing—they were looking at their babies for the first time, he'd helped remove the gel from her belly... No wonder she'd kissed him back so eagerly. She was only human. But he had an agenda. He'd decided what he wanted and would use whatever method he could to achieve that goal—which included seducing her!

She stared at him. "Please, Daniel...don't..."

"Don't what?" A smile creased the corners of his mouth. "What have I done now?"

"You know what," she said, pretty sure she sounded like a petulant child but not caring. "You kissed me."

"You kissed me back."

Color spotted her cheeks. "Well, I'm not going to be swept up in a whole lot of sex stuff...if that's what you're thinking."

He laughed as though he thought her hilarious. "I guess time will tell."

She seethed. "Just because you got me into bed once doesn't mean you will again. That night was out of character for me. I don't even *like* you."

Daniel sat back and turned the engine off. "Is this your usual mode of defense, Mary-Jayne? Attack first?"

She made a scoffing sound. "That's rich, coming from you. You're the corporate shark, not me."

"What is it exactly that you think I do for a living—steamroll over whoever gets in my way? I hate to disappoint you, but I'm not that mercenary. I'm the CEO of a large business that employs several thousand people around the globe. I'm not sure what it is you find so disagreeable about that or me."

"Everything," she replied. "Your arrogance for one..."

like right now when you think I'm loopy because I dare to admit that I don't like you."

"I think you're scared," he said quietly. "Not loopy. And I think your emotions are heightened because you're pregnant."

Logically, she knew he was right. But he wound her up in a way that fueled every rebellious streak she possessed. And she was fairly certain he knew it.

"It's not baby brain," she shot back. "This is *me*. Emotional and loopy."

He made an exasperated sound. "Can we put a hold on this conversation? My dad is on his way over."

Sure enough, Miles Anderson was walking toward them from his studio, one strap of his shabby overalls flapping in the breeze. At sixty, he was still handsome and fit, and Mary-Jayne got a snapshot of what Daniel would be like in thirty years. The notion made her insides flutter. *Stupid*. She had to concentrate on now, not some time in the unknown future.

Daniel got out of the vehicle and Mary-Jayne remained where she was for the moment, watching as the two men greeted one another and shook hands. No embrace. No obvious display of affection. It saddened her a little. Would Daniel be like that with his own sons? He spoke to his father for a moment and then turned back toward the Jeep. Mary-Jayne was half out by the time he met her at the door. Miles wasn't far behind, and he watched as his son helped her out of the car.

"Lovely to see you again M.J.," Miles said cheerfully.

"Mary-Jayne," Daniel corrected, as though his father had committed the crime of the century.

She grabbed her tote and looked up at him. "No one really calls me that," she said quietly as he closed the door. "Except my folks…and you."

His mouth twitched. "It's your name."

"It's an old-fashioned mouthful."

"I think it's very pretty," Miles said, and took her arm. "Let's get up to the house. Bernie will be delighted you're here."

She could feel Daniel behind her as they walked toward the house. Mary-Jayne made a comment about how lovely the gardens were and Miles began chatting about the vegetable patch, the chickens and the new milking goat he'd recently bought who kept getting into the yard and eating the zucchini flowers.

Once they reached the veranda Miles spoke again. "My wife has a client in half an hour, but we have time for coffee and some of her pecan cookies."

Mary-Jayne noticed a door to the left of the main door and the shingle that hung to one side—Homeopath, Masseuse and Acupuncturist. Daniel's stepmother came through the open doorway, wearing a blue-and-gold tunic over white trousers, her blond hair flowing. She rushed toward him with a happy squeal and gave him a long hug.

"I'm so glad to see you," she said, all breathless energy, as they pulled apart. "Your brother told us you were back. Four months in between visits is too long."

He is loved.

It was all Mary-Jayne could think of. And then she realized how lucky her babies would be to have two such lovely people as grandparents. Her hand moved instinctively to her belly, and she noticed how Bernie's gaze immediately shifted toward the movement. She looked as though she was about to say something when Daniel stepped back and introduced them.

"It's lovely to meet you," Bernie said, smiling broadly. "Solana has told me all about you, of course. You've made quite an impression on my mother-in-law, and she's the best judge of character I know."

Mary-Jayne returned the smile. "Thank you."

Bernie tapped her husband's shoulder. "Why don't you take Daniel to the studio and show him the piece you're working on for the Phuket renovation, and Mary-Jayne and I will make coffee," she suggested, and then looked back toward Mary-Jayne. "My talented husband is sculpting an incredible bronze for the resort's foyer," she explained animatedly. "It's a dolphin pod diving through a wave." She sighed and smiled. "Just breathtaking."

Mary-Jayne grinned at the other woman's enthusiasm. She liked her immensely. "How lovely," she said, and noticed Miles looked faintly embarrassed by the praise. Daniel stood beside her, unmoving. She tapped his shoulder lightly, trying not to think about how her fingertips tingled at the connection. "You go, I'll be fine."

"Of course she will be," Bernie said, and linked their arms.

They headed inside and into the huge red cedar kitchen in the center of the house. Mary-Jayne noticed the dream catchers in nearly every window and smiled. A large pebbled water feature took up almost an entire wall, and the sound of the water slipping gently over the rocks created a charming ambience and feeling throughout the house.

"You have a lovely home," she said and perched onto a stool behind the wide kitchen counter.

"Thank you. We've been here for nearly ten years. We wanted somewhere where Miles could work without disturbing the neighbors," she said and grinned as she fiddled with the coffee machine. "Sometimes the soldering and battering goes on for hours. But we love it here and we wanted a place where our boys could call home. You know, for when they get married and have families of their own."

The innuendo wasn't missed and she dropped her gaze, took a breath and then met the other woman's inquisitive look head-on. "Yes, I'm pregnant. And yes, Daniel is the father. And we just learned we're having twin boys."

Bernie's beaming smile was infectious, and she came around the counter and hugged her close for a few seconds. "I'm so delighted. He deserves some happiness in his life after what he's been through."

Mary-Jayne was pretty sure Daniel wouldn't consider her a tonic for unhappiness.

"He loved his wife a lot, didn't he?" she asked quietly when the other woman moved back around the bench.

Bernie shrugged a little. "Simone? Well, she was easy to love. She was a nice woman, very kind and good-hearted. She was a lawyer, you know, very successful one, too, from all accounts."

As the other woman made coffee for the men and tea for them, Mary-Jayne fiddled with the silver ring on her right hand. She wasn't sure how she felt knowing Daniel had loved his wife so much. Not jealous—that would be plain stupid. Because it would mean she had feelings invested in him. Which she didn't. But displaced. As though she didn't quite belong. She wasn't someone whom Daniel would *choose* to bring home to meet his parents. Or choose to marry. She was there because she was carrying his babies. If she hadn't gotten pregnant that night they spent together then they probably would never have seen one another again.

"I'm sure she was lovely," she said and smiled.

"Daniel doesn't talk much about her," Bernie remarked, and grabbed four mugs. "He's always been a little closed off from his feelings. When Simone and their unborn baby died he kind of turned inward. The only person he really opens up to is Solana—they're very close. He never knew his real mother," she said and sighed. "I've always treated him like my own, of course. He was just a toddler when the twins were born. But I think losing his mother had a profound impact on him. And Miles grieved for a long time," she said candidly. "Even after we married and had our sons he was still mourning her death. I tried not to take it personally. I still don't on those times when he mentions her."

Mary-Jayne didn't miss the message in the other woman's words. But the situations weren't the same. She was sure Miles Anderson loved Bernadette, even if he had still grieved the wife he lost. Whereas Daniel didn't even *like* her. He might want her in his bed, but that was all it was.

"Thanks for the talk," Mary-Jayne said and smiled. "And the support."

"Anytime," Bernie said just as the men walked in through the back door.

Mary-Jayne swiveled on the stool and looked at Daniel. "How's the sculpture look?"

"Good."

Miles clapped a hand onto his son's shoulder. "Why don't you take her to the studio and show her?" he suggested, then winked at Mary-Jayne. "I should've guessed a brilliantly creative girl like you might want to critique my work. Go easy on this old man, though. My fragile artistic ego can't take too much criticism."

Mary-Jayne laughed. She genuinely liked Miles and understood his self-effacing humor. "Of course," she said and slid off the stool.

Daniel watched the interaction in silence and only moved when she took a few steps toward the door. "Coming?" she asked.

She was through the door and down the back steps quickly and didn't wait for him to catch up as she headed across the yard toward the studio. She was already inside and staring at the huge bronze sculpture when he came up behind her.

"Wow," she said as she stepped around the piece and admired the effort and imagination that had gone into its creation. "This is incredible."

Daniel came beside her. "He'll be delighted you approve."

She looked up and raised a brow. "I suppose you told him, then."

"About the babies?" He nodded. "Yes. He's delighted about that, too. Told me it was about time I settled down and raised a family."

"I hope you set him straight?"

"You mean did I tell him you've turned down my proposal? No, I thought I'd try my luck again before I admitted that."

Mary-Jayne offered a wry smile. "One marriage proposal in a day is enough, thanks very much."

"Even if I get down on my knee this time?" he asked, his eyes glittering. "Or get you a ring?"

"You're too uptight to get your kneecap dirty," she shot back, saccharine sweet. "And I want to design my own ring when I *eventually* get married."

He laughed, and she liked the sound way too much. "So, how'd Bernie take the news?"

"Very well. Tell me something, why do you call her Bernie? She's the only mother you've known, right?"

"I call her Mom sometimes," he said, looking just a little uncomfortable. "And stop cross-examining me."

"Gotta take the chance when I can. They're very nice," she said and moved around the sculpture some more. "And they love you."

"I know that," he said, and came closer again. "We just live different lives."

"But you had a happy childhood?"

He shrugged loosely. "I guess. Although there were times when I wished they'd stop moving the furniture around the house to accommodate their feng shui beliefs or eat a steak and fries instead of tofu burgers. Or have an aspirin for a headache instead of Bernie's acupuncture jabs to the temple."

Mary-Jayne stilled and looked up at him. "Is that why you don't like needles?"

"Well, I—"

She was mortified when she realized what it meant. "They stuck needles into their child?"

"They thought they were doing the right thing," he said and moved around behind her.

She turned to face him and looked up. "But that's why you don't like needles?"

"I guess," he said and shrugged again. "Seems foolish to make that kind of connection, though. It was a long time ago and it wasn't as if it was some kind of deliberate torture. Bernie's well qualified in her field and she thought she was helping. They were good parents."

"I know. And we'll be good, too," she assured him. "We've had good role models."

"Good parents who live in two different countries?" He reached out and touched a lock of her hair, twirling it between his fingertips. "I want to be their father, Mary-Jayne. All I'm asking for is a chance to do that."

Her heart tugged, and she pushed back a sudden swell of emotion "I can't. It wouldn't work," she implored. "Look, I'm not saying it's going to be easy doing this with the situation being what it is. We both know there will be challenges, especially as the children get older. But I can't and won't commit to a loveless marriage. I want what my parents have, and I want to raise my children in the town I've lived in all my life." She moved back fractionally and his hand dropped. "And I know you think that's all a load of overly romantic hogwash, but I can't change who I am and what I believe any more than you can. I've never really been in love. But I want to be."

"Yeah," he said, and shook his head. "And you want some romantic sap to carry you next to his heart... I heard all that the other day."

"But did you listen? Love isn't an illusion, Daniel. You loved your wife, right? Bernie said she was smart and beautiful and how everyone adored her. So if love was good enough for you back then, why do you think I'm so foolish for wanting the same thing?"

"Because it doesn't last."

"It does," she refuted. "Our parents are testament to that."

"So maybe sometimes it does last. But when it doesn't... When it's gone it's about as bad as it gets."

There was real pain in his voice, and she unconsciously reached out and grasped his upper arm. The muscles were tight and bunched with tension, and she met his gaze head on.

"You're still hurting," she whispered, fighting the need to comfort him.

He looked down into her face, his expression unmoving. The pulse in his cheek throbbed, and his gray eyes were as dark as polished slate. Her fingers tingled where she touched him, and when he reached up and cupped her cheek Mary-Jayne's knees wobbled.

"Most days...most days I'm just...numb."

Every compassionate and caring instinct she possessed was quickly on red alert. "It was an accident, Daniel. A terrible accident. And she wouldn't want you to feel this way, would she?"

"No," he said and traced her cheek with his thumb. "She'd want me to marry you and raise our sons together. And that's what we're going to do, Mary-Jayne. We have to get married. For the sake of our sons. All you need to do is say yes."

Chapter Seven

She didn't say yes. She didn't say anything. Instead she pulled away from him and headed back inside. They stayed for another twenty minutes, and when Bernie's client showed up they said their goodbyes and Daniel promised to return to see them in a couple of days. Being around his family made her long for her own, and Mary-Jayne stayed quiet on the trip back to the resort.

All you need to do is say yes...

As if it was so easy.

She almost admired his perseverance. Almost. He was relentless when he wanted something. No wonder he was so successful professionally. Solana had told her that he'd pretty much singlehandedly turned the chain of Sandwhisper Resorts into a flourishing enterprise around the globe. When his grandfather had been at the helm, Anderson's had only recently ventured into the new direction after spending years in copper and ore mining. Most of that was sold off now and the business focused on the resorts. While other empires had failed, Daniel had kept Anderson's afloat by using natural business acumen and innate tenacity. She remembered how he'd told her how so many people relied on the company for their livelihood and that was what made him determined to keep the organization growing.

Once they got back to the resort, he walked her to her door and lingered for a moment. "Can I see you tonight?"

Mary-Jayne shook her head. "I don't think so."

His eyes flashed. "You can't avoid me. I'm not going away, and neither is this situation."

"I'm tired, that's all. It's been a long day. And eventful," she said, and waved the envelope that held the picture of their babies.

He nodded. "All right, Mary-Jayne, I'll back off for tonight. But we have to get this sorted out."

"Yes," she said, and sighed heavily. "And we will. Just not today."

He left her reluctantly, and once he was gone she moved into the living room and slumped into the sofa. She was more confused than ever. *Daniel* confused her. Confounded her. He was relentless about the marriage thing. But she wouldn't change her mind. She couldn't. It would be a complete disaster.

She wanted love...not duty. Maybe he wasn't quite the closed-off corporate shark she'd first thought him to be; maybe there were moments when she enjoyed his company and liked the way they verbally sparred. And maybe there *was* a constant undercurrent of attraction and desire between them that made her head spin. But it still wasn't enough. And it never would be. Attraction alone wasn't enough. And those few unexpected moments where she relaxed around him were unreliable.

She hung around the condo for the remainder of the afternoon and at five o'clock was about to call Audrey again when there was a knock on her door. She groaned, loathing the thought of going another round with Daniel when all she wanted to do was talk to her friend and then curl into bed.

But it wasn't Daniel at her door. It was his grandmother.

"Can I come in?" Solana asked.

Mary-Jayne stepped back and opened the door wider. "Of course."

Once they were both settled in the living room, Solana spoke again.

"My grandson came to see me," she said and smiled. "He told me you were expecting twin boys."

Mary-Jayne wasn't surprised. It was the last thing he'd said to her when he'd walked her to her door earlier that day. He'd announced how he planned telling his grandmother about her pregnancy.

She nodded. "Yes, I am."

"And are you happy about it?"

"Very," she admitted. "I'm sorry I haven't told you earlier. Things were a little complicated and I—"

"You don't need to explain yourself. Daniel told me what happened."

She was relieved Solana understood. "Thank you. I know it must be something of a shock."

The older woman smiled. "Well, I was lining you up for Caleb...but now I think about it, you are definitely much better suited to Daniel. He needs someone who won't let him rule the roost. Caleb is way too easygoing. Whereas Daniel," Solana grinned widely, "is as wound up as a spring. You'll be good for him, I'm sure of it."

Mary-Jayne perched on the edge of the sofa. "Oh, it's not like that. We're not together or anything," she explained, coloring hotly. "I mean, we were *together*…just that once…but not now."

Solana's brows raised. "He said you've refused his marriage proposal."

"I did," she replied. "I had to. Please try to understand."

"I do," Solana said gently. "You want to fall in love and be swept off your feet. You want roses and moonlight and real romance."

"Yes," she admitted. "Exactly."

"And my grandson is too sensible and pragmatic for all that, right?"

Mary-Jayne shrugged. "We're not in love. We never would be. It would be a catastrophe."

Solana got up and moved to sit beside her on the sofa. "My son Miles married his first wife after dating her for two years. They were more in love than I'd ever seen two people in love. When she died so soon after Daniel was born Miles was heartbroken. And then along came Bernie and a few months later she was pregnant. It wasn't a love match at first…but they've made a good marriage together and raised three boys into the finest men I know."

She ignored the heavy thump behind her ribs. It was a nice story. But it's wasn't hers and Daniel's. "I know you want to see your grandson happy, but believe me, I could never be the person to do that. We don't even *like* one another."

Solana's hand came out and she briefly touched her stomach. "Oh, I'd say you liked one another well enough."

"That's not love…that's…"

"It's a place to start, that's all," Solana said. "Don't make a rash decision because you're scared of the future. Work on the present and let the future take care of itself."

It was a nice idea. But Mary-Jayne wasn't convinced.

Once the other woman left, she returned to her pacing.

She wasn't about to marry a man she didn't love. She might want him. She might even like him a little bit. Maybe more than a little bit. Maybe she liked him a lot. But it wasn't enough. It would never be enough. And she wasn't about to be railroaded into something she didn't want.

The phone rang and she snatched it up. It was Audrey.

"Thank God," she said, and quickly explained what was happening to her concerned friend.

Fourteen hours later Mary-Jayne was on a flight home.

She was gone.

Gone...

Again.

Daniel's mood shifted between concern and rage and in varying degrees.

How could she leave without a word?

Damn it, they were his children, too. His flesh. His blood.

He'd knocked on her door on Wednesday afternoon after Caleb had called and told him the store was closed again. He knocked and waited, and when she didn't respond he called her cell. It went to message and he hung up. On Thursday morning Audrey Cooper answered the door. And he knew instantly that she'd bailed. Her friend was of little help and regarded him with barely concealed contempt. The pretty redhead stood in the doorway, arms crossed, defiant and clearly willing to go into battle for her friend.

"Is she back in Crystal Point with her family?" he asked, his rage simmering, his patience frayed.

Audrey pushed back her hair, clearly unimpressed. "I'm not saying. But wherever she is, there's no point in going after her. I think it's fairly clear she doesn't want to see or hear from you."

"She said that?"

Audrey, who evidently had as much contempt for him as she did for Caleb, nodded slowly. "If you go after her she'll spook and disappear."

It sounded a little melodramatic. Mary-Jayne wouldn't do that. She wouldn't put their babies at risk. Not for anything. He knew her well enough to realize that. "That doesn't make sense."

Audrey's brows rose sharply. "I know M.J. way better than you do. She doesn't like to be hemmed in, and if you push her she'll react and run. She's got friends all over the place and they and her family would do anything for her…and that includes helping her avoid you at all costs. Just leave her alone."

Run? Jesus…she wouldn't… Would she?

Audrey grabbed the door and closed it a little. "Since you own this place, I should tell you I'm looking for someone to take over the lease on the store. If I can't find anyone in a week I'm closing up and leaving. So if you want to sue me for breach of contract, go right ahead. And tell that lousy brother of yours to stay out of my way."

Then she closed the door in his face.

Daniel was furious by the time he reached Caleb's office. His brother was sitting at his desk, punching numbers into the computer.

"Your redhead is back," he said when the door was shut.

Caleb almost jumped out of his chair. "Audrey?"

"Yeah."

"Is she still…"

"Angry?" Daniel nodded. "She hates you as much as ever and me by association, which is why she wouldn't confirm that Mary-Jayne has gone home."

His brother grabbed his jacket off the back of the chair. "I'm going to see her. Is she at the—"

Daniel pulled the jacket from his brother's hands and tossed it on the desk. "You'd better not. She's leaving the resort, closing up the store if she can't find someone to take on her lease."

Clearly agitated, Caleb grabbed the jacket again. "She can't do that. She signed a contract. We'll get the lawyers to make sure she—"

"Stop being such a hothead," Daniel said, and took the jacket, throwing it onto the sofa by the door. "And leave the lawyers out of it. She's angry and hurt and has every reason to hate you, so if she wants to leave and break the lease agreement then she can do just that…without any interference from you, understand?"

Caleb glared at him. "When did you get so sentimental?"

"When I realized that Audrey has probably already contacted Mary-Jayne and told her I'm looking for her."

His brother's temper calmed a little. "Okay, I get the point. You're concerned Mary-Jayne might do something rash."

"Actually," he said, calmer now, "I think she'll do whatever is best for the babies. Which in her eyes is going home to be around her family."

"And that's where you're going?"

He shrugged. "I have to make this right."

Caleb raised an eyebrow. "You sure you want to make a commitment to a woman you don't love? Hell, you don't even know for sure if those babies are yours."

"I do know," he said. He wound back the irritation he felt toward his brother and tapped his hand to his chest. "I feel it…in here."

And that, he figured, was all that mattered.

Mary-Jayne had been holed up in her small house for four days. Her family knew she was back, but she'd insisted she had a bad head cold and said she needed some time to recover. Her mother had tutted and pleaded to bring her some soup and parental comfort, but Mary-Jayne wasn't prepared for them quite yet. Her sisters called every day and her friend Lauren did the same. Her dog, Pricilla, and parrot, Elvis, were happy she was home and gave her all the company she needed. While she waited for Daniel to turn up. Which she knew he would.

He wasn't the kind of man to give up when he wanted something.

Mary-Jayne had no illusions… His proposal was only about their children. He didn't want to marry *her*. And she didn't want to marry him. He was single-minded in his intent… He wanted the babies. He'd take her, too, if it meant getting full-time custody of their sons.

She wondered what his next move would be. And made herself sick to the stomach thinking about the possibilities. Since she'd refused his outrageous proposal, would he try another tack? Was he thinking about sole custody? Would he fight her in court to get what he wanted? He had money and power, and that equated to influence. He could afford the finest lawyers in the country and they'd certainly be out to prove she was less capable of giving their children the best possible life. Maybe the courts would see it that way, too.

By Sunday morning she was so wound up she wanted to scream. And cry. And run.

But she wouldn't do any of those things. She needed to stay strong and focus on growing two healthy babies. She'd fight the fight she needed to when she faced it head on. Until then, her sons were all that mattered.

When Evie and Grace arrived at her door late on Sunday afternoon she was almost relieved. She hated lying to her sisters, even if it was only by omission.

One look at her and Evie squealed. "Oh, my God, you're pregnant!"

"Well, don't tell the whole neighborhood," she said, and ushered them both inside.

Grace, who was easily the most beautiful woman Mary-Jayne had ever known, was a little less animated. She'd also had her first child two months earlier. But Evie, ever the nurturer, who had a seventeen-year-old son and a toddler daughter, was still chattering as Mary-Jayne closed the door and ushered them down the hallway.

"Tell us everything," Evie insisted as the trio dropped onto the big chintz sofa. "And first the part about how you've managed to keep from spilling the beans about this."

"Forget that," Grace said and smiled. "First, tell us who the baby's father is?"

"Babies," Mary-Jayne said and waited a microsecond before her sisters realized what she meant.

There were more shrieks and laughter and a load of questions before Mary-Jayne had an opportunity to explain. It took several minutes, and when she was done each of her sisters had a hold of her hands.

"And he wants to marry you?" Grace asked.

She shrugged. "That's what he says."

Evie squeezed her fingers. "But you don't want to marry him, M.J.?"

She screwed up her face. "Definitely not."

"Is he that awful?"

She opened her mouth to respond, but quickly stopped herself. She couldn't, in good conscience, make out as if he was some kind of ogre. Once he'd settled into the idea that he was the father he'd been incredibly supportive. And she couldn't forget his caring behavior when she'd had the ultrasound.

And then there was that kiss.

Don't forget the kiss...

Of course she needed to forget the kiss. It shouldn't have happened. It had only confused her. "He's not awful," she said and sat back in the chair. "Most of the time he's quite...nice."

Grace frowned. "Most?"

"Well, he can also be an arrogant jerk," she replied. "You know, all that old money and entitlement."

"Is he tall, dark and handsome to go along with all that old money?" Evie asked and grinned.

"Oh, yeah. He's all that. And more."

"And you *still* don't want to marry him?"

"I want to marry for love," she said and sighed. "Like you both did. I don't want to settle for a man who looks at me as some kind of incubator. We might have a whole lot of chemistry now, but when that goes what's left? An empty shell disguised as a marriage? No, thanks."

"That's a fairly pessimistic view of things," Grace remarked. "And not like you at all."

"I'm tired of being the eternal optimist," she said, feeling stronger. "Being pregnant has changed my thinking. I want to build a good life for my babies—one that's honest and authentic. And if I married Daniel I would be living a lie. Despite how much I..." She stopped and let her words trail.

"Despite how much you *like* him, you mean?" Evie prompted.

She shrugged again. "Sure, I like him. But I dislike him, too, and that's where it gets complicated."

"Maybe you're making it more complicated than it needs to be," Grace suggested. "I mean, you don't really know him very well. Perhaps over time you will change your mind."

"I doubt it," she said. "I live here and he lives in San Francisco. There's a whole lot of ocean in between. Look, I'm happy for him to see his sons and have a relationship with them. I *want* them to have a father. But when I get married I want it to be with someone who wants *me*...and not just because I'm the mother of his children."

She was about to get to her feet when the doorbell rang.

"That's probably the folks," Evie said and smiled. "They've been worried about you. Which might have something to do with the fake head cold you said you had to keep us all at bay."

"Not that it did any good," Mary-Jayne said and grinned.

"Want me to get it?" Grace asked.

"Nah," she said and pulled herself out of the soft sofa. "I got it."

She walked down the hall and opened the front door, half expecting her mother to be standing there with a big pot of chicken soup. But it wasn't either of her parents.

It was Daniel.

He looked so good. So familiar. In jeans and a blue shirt, everything about him screamed sexy and wholly masculine. She wished she was immune. She wished he didn't set her blood and skin on fire. His steely gaze traveled over her slowly until he finally met her eyes with his own and spoke.

"So you didn't run too far after all?"

"Run?"

Daniel had expected her to slam the door. But she didn't look all that surprised to see him on her doorstep.

"Your friend said you might be tempted to run to get away from me."

"Audrey did?" She laughed loudly. "I'm afraid she's got a vivid imagination and a flair for the dramatic."

"Speaking of which," Daniel said pointedly, "taking off without a word was a little theatrical, don't you think?"

She shrugged and her T-shirt slipped off her shoulder. "I needed some breathing space."

"I wasn't exactly smothering you."

"Maybe not to you," she flipped back.

He grinned a little, even though his insides churned. She had a way of doing that—a way of mixing up his emotions. He was as mad as hell with her for taking off without a word, but he wouldn't show her that. Daniel turned to briefly look at the two cars in her driveway. "You have company?"

She nodded. "My sisters."

His gaze dropped to her belly. "You told them?"

"They told me," she said, and pulled the T-shirt over her middle a fraction. "Hard to hide this from the world now."

"You shouldn't," he said quietly. "You look good."

She shrugged. "So…I guess I'll see you around."

Daniel laughed lightly. "Oh, no, Mary-Jayne, you don't get out of it that easy."

Her gaze narrowed. "You plan on camping on my doorstep?"

"If I have to," he replied. "Or you could invite me in."

His eyes widened. "You want to meet my sisters, is that it?"

"Absolutely."

She exhaled heavily and stepped back. "Okay. Best you come inside."

Daniel crossed the threshold of her small cottage and followed her down the hall. Her house was filled with old furniture and bric-a-brac and was as muddled as he'd expected. The Preston sisters regarded him curiously when he entered the living room and as Mary-Jayne introduced him. They were similar, all with the same dark curling hair and wide green eyes. Evie was down to earth and friendly, while Grace had a kind of ethereal beauty that made her look as though she'd stepped off the set of a Hollywood movie.

The eldest, Evie, asked him if he'd had a good trip and began chatting about flying and vacations, which he figured she was doing to break the ice a little. The other sister was more serious and content to stand back and watch Mary-Jayne and him interact. It didn't bother him. All he cared about was Mary-Jayne.

He cared...

Damn.

He didn't want to think about that. But he couldn't get the vision of her staring up at him in his dad's studio, her hand gently rubbing his arm, all wide-eyed and lovely. In that moment he realized she was kind and considerate, despite the bouts of exuberant bravado.

Her siblings were nice women who were clearly curious about him but were too polite to say too much. They stayed for a few minutes, and he asked about Evie's art and mentioned how his father was an artist, and she said she knew his work. Both women talked about Crystal Point and how much they loved the small town. Daniel hadn't taken much notice as he'd driven along the waterfront. His mind was set on seeing Mary-Jayne, not the beach. Evie suggested he drop by her bed-and-breakfast, and he noticed how Mary-Jayne scowled at her sister. Maybe he had an ally in the Preston sisters? Maybe they agreed that she should marry him? He wasn't averse to using whatever leverage he could if it meant he'd have the chance to be a full-time father to his sons.

Once they left, Mary-Jayne propped her hands on her hips and glared at him.

"I suppose you'd like coffee?"

He smiled. "If it's not too much trouble."

She tossed her incredible hair. "Oh, it is...not that it would make one damn bit of difference to you. And by the way," she said as she walked down the hall, "don't think you can sway me by charming my family. I've already told my sisters what a jerk you are."

He laughed and walked after her. "I don't think they quite believed you, Mary-Jayne."

When he reached the kitchen he stood by the counter for a moment, looking around at the crowded room with its cluttered cabinets, colorful drapes and assortment of pots hanging from hooks above the stove top. But as untidy and overdone as it was, there was something oddly welcoming about the room. With its mismatched table and chairs and the wrought iron stand in the corner jammed with an array of ceramic vases containing a variety of overgrown herbs, it was far removed from the huge ultra-modern kitchen in his San Francisco apartment. He never used it these days. Even when he was married, Simone had worked long hours like he did and they preferred to dine out most evenings. But Mary-Jayne's kitchen suited her. It was easy to imagine her sitting at the round scrubbed table, sipping tea from one of the patterned china cups from the collection on the dresser.

"Yes," she said, still scowling. "I'm a slob, remember?"

"Did I say that?"

"Words to the effect. One of my many flaws."

He chuckled and watched her pull a pair of ceramic mugs from the cupboard. She looked so beautiful with her scowl, all fired up and ready to do battle with him. One thing was for sure, life with Mary-Jayne Preston sure wasn't dull!

Daniel came around the counter and stood beside her.

She turned and rested her hip against the bench, arms crossed.

"Yes?"

"Nothing," he said and reached for her, curling his hand gently around her neck.

"Don't you dare," she said, but didn't move.

"What are you so afraid of?" he asked, urging her closer. "That I'm going to kiss you? Or that you'll like it?"

"Neither," she said on a shallow breath. "Both."

"You never have to be afraid of me, Mary-Jayne," he said quietly, bringing her against him. The feel of her belly and breasts instantly spiked his libido. "I'd never hurt you. Or make you to do something you didn't want to do."

"Then, stop asking me to marry you," she said, still breathless as she looked up into his face.

"I can't. When I want something I'm—"

"Relentless," she said, cutting off his words. "Yeah, I know. I'm not used to someone like you," she admitted, her mouth trembling a little. "My last boyfriend was—"

"An unemployed musician," he finished for her, not in the mood to hear about the man she'd once dated. "Yes, I had you investigated, remember?"

She frowned and wriggled against him. "Jerk."

Daniel moved his other arm around her waist and gently held her. "Me or him?"

"You."

He chuckled. "You know, I don't think you really mean that."

"Sure I do," she said, and wriggled some more. "And kissing me isn't going to get me to change my mind."

"Maybe not," he said and dipped his head. "But it sure beats arguing about it."

Her lips were soft when he claimed them. Soft and sweet and familiar. Her hands crept up his chest and reached his shoulders and she clung on to him. Daniel pressed closer and she moaned softly. The sweet vanilla scent that was uniquely hers assailed his senses, and he tilted her head a fraction. Their tongues met and danced. And he was pretty sure she knew exactly the effect she had on him and his libido. His hand moved down to her hip, and he urged her closer. Heat flared between them, and suddenly kissing wasn't enough. Her fingertips dug into his shoulders and she arched her back, drawing them closer together.

"Mary-Jayne," he whispered against her mouth and trailed his lips down her cheek and throat. "Let me stay with you tonight."

She shivered in his arms. "I can't," she said on a shallow breath. "Tomorrow…"

"Forget tomorrow," he said, and pushed the T-shirt off her shoulder. Her creamy skin was like tonic for the desire that churned through his blood. "Forget everything but right now."

It was what he wanted. What he needed. Her skin, her mouth, her tender touch. He'd shut off from truly feeling anything for so long, but Mary-Jayne made him feel in ways he could barely understand. They fought; they battled with words and with ideals. But underneath the conflict simmered an attraction and a pull that was the most powerful of his life.

And it also had the power to undo him.

Chapter Eight

She didn't let him stay. She couldn't. If he'd stayed and they'd made love she wasn't sure she would have had the strength to refuse his marriage proposal. He'd use sex to confuse and manipulate her, even if that wasn't his intention. She was like putty in his arms. One kiss, one touch and being with him was all she could think about.

Idiot...

Mary-Jayne garnered all her strength and sent him packing. And tried to convince herself she couldn't care less where he went. There were plenty of quality hotels in the nearby town of Bellandale. It was barely a twenty-minute drive from Crystal Point. He had a GPS. He'd be fine. She didn't feel bad at all.

She had a shower, made soup and toast and curled up on the sofa to watch TV with Pricilla and pretended she'd put Daniel out of her mind once and for all.

Her dreams, however, were something else altogether.

He invaded them. She couldn't keep him out. His touch was like a brand against her skin, and she could still feel the heat of his body pressed against her for hours later. And his kiss... It was like no other. She remembered his comment about her ex-boyfriend. *An unemployed musician?* Toby had been exactly that. He wasn't even much of a musician. They'd dated off and on for two years and she often wondered if she'd brought home a tattooed, frequently pierced, dreadlocked boyfriend simply because that was what everyone expected of her. Her teenage willfulness made her rebel against what she'd considered the average or mundane. After she'd left home she'd saved her money and quickly headed overseas. She'd returned feeling even more independent and more determined to live her own life.

And Toby was the end result. A deadbeat, she realized now. Someone who took advantage of her generous nature and swindled her out of her money and her pride. She'd been left with a debt for a car he crashed and a guitar he'd taken with him when he walked out the door. He had no goals, no ambition and no integrity. She'd had one serious relationship since with a man who ended up complaining about her spending too much time worrying about her career. He'd had no ambition, either—except the desire to sit in front of his computer all day playing games. She'd foolishly believed she chose men who were free-spirited and artistic. Now they simply seemed lazy and immature.

She tossed and turned all night and woke up feeling nauseated and unable to stomach the dry crackers and green tea that usually helped most when morning sickness came upon her.

She changed into her favorite overalls and grinned when she discovered she had to leave two of the three side buttons undone to accommodate her rapidly expanding middle. Her workshop needed a cleanup before she got to work on the few back orders she had, so she headed outside and began decluttering the counters. It was midmorning before she took a break and snacked on some apple slices and a cup of tea.

At eleven Daniel rocked up.

In dark jeans and a navy polo shirt he looked effortlessly handsome, and her stomach flipped with familiar awareness. He looked her over and smiled.

"Cute outfit."

Her overalls were paint splattered and had holes in each knee. But they were comfy, and she could care less what he thought about her clothes. "Thanks. Did you want something?" she asked, pushing the memory of his kisses from her mind.

"We're going out."

Bossy, as usual. "Are we? Am I allowed to ask where we're going?"

"To see your parents," he said swiftly. "It's about time they were told they're about to become grandparents again."

"I'd rather tell them myself."

"*We'll* tell them," he said, firmer this time. "Stop being stubborn."

Mary-Jayne turned and sashayed down the hall. "I'd really prefer to do it some other time. Please try to understand."

"Well, I don't. We're in this together," he said, and followed her into the house. "We told my parents together… and now we'll tell yours…together. That's how things are going to be, Mary-Jayne. They have a right to know, don't you think?"

When she reached the living room she turned and

propped her hands on her hips. "Of course. I just don't want you to meet them right now."

His brows shot up. "Why the hell not?"

"Because," she said, and dragged out a long breath, "you don't know them. One look at you and they'll get all...thingy."

He stilled. *"Thingy?"*

Her patience frayed. "Excited, okay? Thrilled. Happy. They'll feel as though they've won the lottery in the potential son-in-law department."

He laughed. "They want you to nab a rich husband?"

"No," she corrected. "That's not it. It's just that you're different from anyone I've ever...you know...dated. You're not an *unemployed musician*," she explained, coloring hotly. "Or a beach bum or a lazy good-for-nothing, as my dad would say. You're...*normal*... You're successful and hardworking and come from a nice family. Once they know that, they'll get all worked up and start pressuring me to...to..."

"Marry me?"

"Well, yeah," she admitted. "Probably."

"I thought you said they let you lead your own life?"

"They do," she replied. "But they're still my parents. They still want what's best for me. Once they clap eyes on you, I'll be done for."

His mouth twitched at the edges. "Best you get changed so we can get going."

Mary-Jayne frowned. "Didn't you hear what I said?"

"Every word," he said, and dropped into the sofa. "Hurry up, *dear*."

Impatience snaked up her spine. "You are the most infuriating and—"

"Want me to kiss you again?" he asked as he grabbed a

magazine from the coffee table and opened it at a random page. "If not, go and get changed."

Irritated, she turned on her heels and stomped to her bedroom. He was an ass. He didn't give a hoot what she wanted. Or care about how she felt. By the time she'd dressed, Mary-Jayne was so mad she could have slugged his smug face.

Once they were out of the house she pointed to her car. "I'll drive," she said and rattled her keys. "I know the way."

Daniel stopped midstride and looked at the battered VW in the driveway. "In that hunk of junk? I don't think so." He gestured to the top-of-the-range Ford sedan parked alongside the curb. "We'll take my rental car."

"Snob."

He laughed and gently grasped her elbow. "Come on."

"Sometimes I really don't like you much at all."

He laughed again. "And other times?"

She quickstepped it to the car and waited by the passenger door. It was hard to stay mad at him when he was being so nice to her. "No comment."

Once they were in the car she gave him the address. The trip took only minutes, and by the time they pulled into the driveway her temper had lost its momentum.

"You're something of a hothead, aren't you?" he asked as he unclipped his seat belt.

"Around you?" She raised a brow and smiled a little. "Yeah."

He seemed to find that idea amusing and was still chuckling by the time he was out of the car and had come around to her side. "It's one of the things I find captivating about you, Mary-Jayne."

Captivating? That was quite an admission. He usually didn't admit to anything, not when it came to feelings. Oh, sure, she knew he wanted her in his bed, but anything else seemed off his agenda. He'd said he felt numb. The very idea pained her deep down. He'd lost the woman he'd loved and didn't want to love again… That was clear enough.

"What are you thinking about?" he asked as he took her hand.

I'm thinking about how it must feel to be loved by you…

Mary-Jayne's fingers tingled at the connection with his. She didn't want to be so vulnerable to his touch, but her attraction for him had a will of its own. She simply couldn't help herself. That was why she'd become so caught up in the heat and passion between them the night of Solana's birthday party. It was heady and powerful and drove her beyond coherent thought. It was more than attraction. More than anything she'd felt before.

And the very idea scared her senseless.

Her parents, as expected, were delighted, if not a little shocked at their news. Once the shock settled, her mother had countless questions for Daniel and he answered every one without faltering. He was as resilient as the devil when under intense scrutiny. Barbara Preston skirted around the question about marriage and Mary-Jayne was relieved that Daniel didn't mention that she'd refused his proposal. There was time for that revelation later. Her father, she realized, looked as pleased as she'd ever seen him. Bill Preston approved. Daniel was a hit. Her parents were clearly delighted, even with her out-of-wedlock pregnancy. Her mother was all hugs and tears when they explained she was expecting twins.

Over a jug of iced tea her father spoke. "What do you think of our little town, son?"

Son?

Her dad was already calling Daniel "son"?

Great.

"I haven't had a chance to see much of it yet," Daniel

replied. "But I'm hoping Mary-Jayne will show me around sometime today."

She smiled sweetly and nodded, and then noticed how her mother seemed to approve wholeheartedly about the way Daniel used her full name. He could clearly do no wrong.

I'm doomed.

They stayed for two hours, and Daniel answered every probing question her parents asked. He talked about his career, his family and even his wife and the baby they had lost. Before they left her father ushered him off to his garage to inspect the Chevrolet Impala that he was restoring, and Mary-Jayne was left to endure her mother's scrutiny.

"Now," Barbara said, hugging her closely once the men had left the room. "What don't I know?"

"Nothing," she replied and began collecting the mugs from the table. "The babies are doing fine and I feel okay other than a little morning sickness."

"I meant with the two of you," Barbara said and raised a brow. "He's awfully handsome, isn't he? And such nice manners."

Mary-Jayne smiled. "I know he isn't what you've imagined I'd bring home to meet you."

"Well, your track record hasn't exactly given us confidence."

"I know. And you're right—he's handsome and nice and has good manners."

"Are you in love with him?"

Love...

She'd not considered the word in regard to him. Falling in love with Daniel was out of the question. He'd never love her back. *He was numb.* There was nothing left in his heart. He'd love their sons and that was all.

"No," she said and heard the hesitation in her own voice. "Definitely not."

Barbara smiled. "It wouldn't be the end of the world, you know... I mean, if you did fall in love with a man like Daniel."

"It would," she corrected, suddenly hurting deep in her chest. "He still loves his wife. And she was very different from me. She was smart and successful and everything I'm not."

There...I said it out loud.

Her mother's expression softened some more. "You're smart, and your dad and I have every faith that your business will be a success one day. And sometimes being *different* is a good thing," Barbara added gently.

"Not in this," she said, her heart suddenly and inexplicably heavy. "I know you only want to see me happy, and I am happy about the babies. Really happy. Even though it's been something of a shock I'm looking forward to being a mother."

Barbara rubbed her arm comfortingly. "You'll be a good one, too, I'm sure of it."

"I hope so," she said. "Although I'm sure some people will think having twin boys is my medicine for being such a difficult child myself."

Her mother smiled. "You were spirited, not difficult."

"That's sweet of you to say so, but I know I caused you and Dad some major headaches over the years. Remember when I ditched school for three days to follow that carnival that had arrived in town?"

Barbara laughed. "Every kid dreams of running away and joining the circus at some point. Especially a strong-willed eleven-year-old."

Mary-Jayne giggled. "I had visions of being a trapeze artist."

They chatted for a few more minutes about her childhood escapades, and by the time her father and Daniel returned her mood was much improved. Daniel looked his usual self-satisfied self and her dad looked pleased as punch. Whatever had transpired in the garage, she was sure it had something to do her father giving Daniel his blessing and full support.

Typical...

Once they were back in the car, she strapped on the seat belt and pasted on a smile.

"Take a left at the end of the street," she instructed.

"Because?"

"You wanted to see my town, my home, right?"

"Well...yes."

"So we'll go to the beach."

He frowned a little. "We're not exactly dressed for the beach."

Mary-Jayne laughed. "Does everything always have to be done to order with you? Live dangerously, Daniel," she said and laughed again. "You might surprise yourself and enjoy it."

His mouth tightened. "You know, despite what you think, I'm not some overworked killjoy."

"Prove it," she challenged. "Get those extrastarched clothes of yours crumpled for a moment."

"Extrastarched?" he echoed as he started the ignition.

She chuckled. "Oh, come on, even you have to admit that you're a neat freak. You even folded your clothes that night we spent together." It was something of an exaggeration...but she had a point to prove. "My dress got twisted amongst the bedsheets and your suit was perfectly placed over the chair."

"I don't remember it that way."

"Hah," she scoffed. "You have a selective memory."

"I remember everything about that night," he said and drove down the street. "Left, you said?"

"Left," she repeated. "We'll drive past my sister's bed-and-breakfast."

"I know where that is already."

Her brows came up. "You do?"

He nodded. "Of course. I stayed there last night."

Daniel knew it would make her nuts. But he'd thought it was a good idea at the time and Evie Jones seemed to agree. After Mary-Jayne had kicked him out of her house the evening before, he'd driven around the small town for a while and come across Dunn Inn by chance. The big A-framed house stood silhouetted amongst a nest of Norfolk pines and the shingle out front had told him exactly who the place belonged to. So he'd tapped on the door and was met by Evie's much younger husband, Scott, and within minutes Evie herself was insisting he stay at the bed-and-breakfast while he was in Crystal Point.

"You stayed at my sister's place?"

She was all outraged, and it made him grin a little. "Sure. Something wrong with that?"

"Something? Everything! Of all the manipulative and conniving things I could imagine you—"

"I needed somewhere to stay," he said quickly. "You told me to leave, remember?"

"Ever heard of a thing called a hotel?" she shot back. "There are many of them in Bellandale."

"I wanted to stay in Crystal Point."

"Why?"

He glanced at her belly. "You have to ask?"

She glared at him. "Don't use the twins as a way of getting around this. How long do you intend on staying?"

"As long as I need to."

"You could stay for a lifetime and nothing would change. I will not marry you. Not now and not ever."

"We'll see," he said, with way more confidence than he felt.

The truth was, he was tired of arguing with her about it. She was as stubborn as a mule. Last night he could have stayed with her. He'd wanted to. A part of him had needed to. He'd wanted to spend the night making love to her. And her rejection had stung like a bucket of ice water over his skin.

"What about your job?" she asked. "You can't just pack that in for an indeterminable length of time."

"Sure I can," he said, and flipped a lazy smile and drove toward the beach. "I'm the boss, remember? I can do what I want."

She was clearly fuming. "Solana told me you never take vacations."

"This isn't a vacation," he said, and pulled the car into the parking area.

"No," she said, opening the door. "It's a hunting expedition…and I'm the prey."

Daniel got out of the car, ignoring the niggling pain in his temple. "Such drama. Let's just forget my marriage proposal for the moment, shall we?"

"It's all I can think about," she muttered.

"Well, that's something, at least." He locked the car. "So this beach?"

She crossed her arms and stormed off down the pathway. Daniel had to admit the beach was spectacular. The white sand spanned for several hundred meters until it met the pristine river mouth. No wonder she loved this place so much. It was early winter and a weekday, so there was no one about other than them and a lone dog walker playing chase with his pet. He watched as Mary-Jayne flipped off her sandals and strode across the sand until she reached the water. Daniel looked down at his shoes. They were Italian leather and not designed for the beach. He perched on a rock and took them off, stuffing the socks into the loafers. She'd called him an uptight neat freak on several occasions. Maybe she was right. When he was young he'd been impulsive and adventurous. Now he rarely did anything without considering the consequences. Taking over the helm of Anderson's from his grandfather had changed him. He felt the weight of responsibility press heavily on his shoulders 24/7. The most impulsive thing he'd done recently was go after Mary-Jayne. And even that he did with a tempered spirit. What he really wanted to do was haul her in his arms and kiss her senseless.

By the time he stepped onto the sand she was twenty meters in front of him. He quickened his steps and watched her as she walked, mesmerized by the way her hips swayed. She had a sensuality that affected him in a way that blurred the lines between desire and something else. Something more. He couldn't define it. Couldn't articulate in his mind what it was about Mary-Jayne that caused such an intense reaction in him. It wasn't simply attraction. He'd felt that before and it had always waned quickly. No, this was something he'd never experienced before. Not even with Simone. His wife hadn't driven him crazy. Loving her had been easy. She had never challenged him, insulted him or made him accountable for his beliefs. But Mary-Jayne did at every opportunity. She questioned everything and anything.

She made him think.

Feel...

It was a kind of heady mix of torture and pleasure.

Which was why making love with her had been so intense. They had chemistry and more. A connection that went beyond physical attraction. A mental attraction that defied logic.

Yeah, loving Simone had been easy. But loving Mary-Jayne… There would be nothing easy about that. Which was why he wouldn't. Why he'd keep it clear in his head what he wanted. His sons. A family. But where? It could never be here, he thought as he walked along the sand. Sure, it was a nice town. Peaceful and safe… Exactly the kind of place to raise children. The kind of place a person could call home. But not him. For one, Mary-Jayne would never agree to it. And he had his life in San Francisco.

She was walking at a leisurely pace now and stopped to pick something up, perhaps a shell. Daniel caught up with her and matched her slow strides.

"It's a beautiful spot."

She glanced sideways. "It's the prettiest beach along this part of the coastline."

"You're fortunate to have grown up in a place like this. To have made it your home."

She shrugged and tossed the shell in the shallow water. "What about you?" she asked. "Where's home for you?"

Daniel rubbed the back of his neck to ease the tension creeping up his spine. "San Francisco."

"That's where you live," she said quietly. "Where's home?"

He shrugged loosely. "When my grandfather was alive he and Solana had a place in the Napa Valley, and I used to go there for school vacations. Miles and Bernie moved around a lot, so my brothers and I always welcomed the stability of my grandparents' small vineyard. But when Gramps died things changed. Gran wasn't interested in the business end of things and decided to sell the place. Solana likes the warmer weather and divides her time between Port Douglas and San Francisco."

She stopped walking and faced him, her hair flipping around her face from the breeze. "So...nowhere?"

"I guess so," he replied, and started walking again.

She caught up with him quickly. "I don't want that for my babies. I want them to be settled. I want them to have a place they can always call home."

"So do I," he said, and stopped to look out over the water. "What's that called?" he asked, pointing to a land mass separated from the shore by an expanse of water that fed from the mouth of the river.

"Jays Island," she replied. "Years ago they used to bring sugarcane ferries up the river, so this was quite a busy spot. Now they use trains and trucks to transport the sugar so the river doesn't get dredged anymore. The sand banks built up and the island came about. Birds nest over there and at a really low tide you can wade through the shallows to get over there. When I was young I used to swim over there at high tide and come back when the tide went out." She laughed and the sound flittered across the wind. "Much to my parents' despair. But I loved sitting on that patch of rock," she said, and pointed to a ragged rock outcrop on the island. "I used to sit there for ages and just let the wind hit my face. It was the kind of place where a person could dream big and no one was around to make judgment. Where *I* could sit without worrying about other people's opinion."

"You mean your family?"

She shrugged. "My family are the best."

"But?"

Her green eyes glittered. "But everyone has a role, you know... My brother, my sisters. Noah took over the family business, Evie's the successful artist, Grace is the supersmart financial whiz who once worked on Wall Street."

"And you?"

Her shoulders lifted again. "I'm just the youngest. The one who got away with everything as a kid. I guess I have the role of being the one who hasn't amounted to anything."

Surely she didn't believe that. "A college education and a big bank balance don't equate to a person's value, Mary-Jayne. There's greatness in simply being yourself."

She offered a wry smile. "Is that why you've worked so hard to climb the corporate ladder? Because you believe it's enough to live a simple life?"

"An authentic life," he corrected, doing his best to ignore the growing throb in his head. "But I didn't really have a choice when I was drafted into the company. My dad wasn't interested, and my grandfather had a lot of health issues. I either joined or the company folded. Too many people were invested in Anderson's... I couldn't let it go down without a fight. So I made a few changes to the company's structure, sold off most of the mining interests and concentrated on the part that I enjoyed. Ten years later the resorts are now some of the most successful in the world."

"And if you hadn't joined the family business, what would you have done?"

"I'm not sure. Maybe law."

She laughed. "Oh, yes, I can see you as a lawyer. You do pose a good argument."

He reached out and grabbed her left hand, and then gently rubbed her ring finger with his thumb. "Not good enough, obviously. This is still bare."

She went to pull away but he held on. "You know why I won't."

"Because you hate me."

She shook her head. "I don't hate you, Daniel."

"No?" he queried as he turned her hand over and stroked her palm. "But you don't like me."

"I don't *dislike* you," she said quietly. "The truth is, I'm very confused about how I do feel about you. And it's not something I'm used to. Normally I know exactly how I feel about everything. I have an opinion and I usually express it. But around you..." Her words trailed. "Around you all I seem to do is dig myself into this hole and say things I don't mean. And I'm not like that. It's not a reaction I'm particularly proud of."

"So I wind you up," he said, still holding her, even though the pain in his head gained momentum. "We wind one another up. What's wrong with that? It'll keep things interesting."

"What things? A marriage where we're always fighting, always at each other's throats? That's not something I want our children to witness." She pulled away and crossed her arms tightly around her waist. "Because if you do, that's about as selfish and self-destructive as it gets."

Selfish? Selfish because he wanted to give his sons his name and the legacy that went along with it. She was the one being selfish—thinking only of herself. Like a spoiled brat.

"If you had any consideration for their future, for what they deserve, then you would see that I'm right," he said stiffly. "But right now you're acting like a petulant child, Mary-Jayne. Maybe this isn't what either of us planned. And maybe you're right, maybe we would never have seen one another again after that night if you hadn't gotten pregnant. But you did, and we are and I'll be damned if I'm going to let you dictate the kind of father I'm allowed to be. This might be a shock to you, but you're *not* the center of the universe, and right now the only thing that matters is the welfare of our sons."

She glared at him. "You're calling *me* self-absorbed? When you think you can simply snap your fingers and get what you want?"

Annoyance swept over his skin. He tried to keep his cool. Tried to get her to show some sense. But be damned if she wasn't the most infuriating woman on the planet!

In that moment a flashing light appeared out of the corner of his eye. And another. A dreaded and familiar ache clutched the back of his head. He recognized what was coming.

"We have to get back. I'll take you home."

And he knew, as he turned and walked back up the sand, that he was in for one hell of a headache.

Chapter Nine

Two days later Mary-Jayne got a call from her sister Evie. She'd had a peaceful two days. No Daniel. No marriage proposals. No insults. It gave her time to seethe and think and work.

"I think you should get over here."

She ground her teeth together. She didn't want to see him. She was still mad at him for calling her a petulant child. And she certainly didn't want her sister interfering or trying to play matchmaker. "What for?"

"He's been holed up in his room for forty-eight hours. No food or coffee or anything. I don't want to pry…but I thought you should know."

Mary-Jayne pushed down the concern battering around in her head. "He's a big boy. I'm sure he's fine."

"Well, I'm not so sure. And I have an obligation to my guests to ensure their welfare while they stay here."

"Good… You go and check on him."

"M.J.," Evie said, sterner this time. "Whatever is going on between the two of you, put it aside for a moment. *I* need your help."

Unable to refuse her sister's plea, Mary-Jayne quickly got dressed and headed over to the B and B. Evie looked genuinely concerned when she met her by the side door.

"So what's the big emergency?" she asked as she walked into the house and dropped her tote on the kitchen counter. "Maybe he's gone out."

"He's here," Evie said. "His rental car is outside."

"Maybe he's asleep."

"For two days?" her sister shot back. "Something's not right, and since you're the soon-to-be mother of his babies, it's your responsibility to find out what's wrong."

"I think you're under the illusion that Daniel and I have some kind of real relationship. We don't," Mary-Jayne informed her. "We barely tolerate one another."

Evie placed a key in her palm, touched her shoulders and gave her a little sisterly shove. "Go and find out. He's in the brown room."

There were four guest rooms at the B and B, each one styled in a particular color. Mary-Jayne left the family residence area and headed into the bigger section of the house. She lingered outside the door for a moment and finally tapped. Nothing. She tapped again.

She was about to bail when she heard a faint sound. Like a moan.

Did he have a woman in there?

The very idea made her sick to the stomach. He wouldn't...surely.

She stared at the key in her hand. What if she opened the door and found him doing who knows what with some random woman? She wouldn't be able to bear it.

Suck it up...

She pushed the key in the lock and slowly opened the door. The room was in darkness. The heavy drapes were shut and she couldn't hear a sound. There was someone on the bed, lying facedown.

"Daniel?"

She said his name so softly she wasn't surprised he didn't respond. She closed the door and stepped closer. He was naked from the waist up and had a pillow draped over his head. She said his name again and the pillow moved.

"What?"

His voice was hoarse. Groggy. Nothing like she'd heard before. She squinted to accustom her eyes to the darkness and spotted an empty bottle of aspirin on the bedside table. She took notice of everything, and a thought popped into her head.

"Are you drunk?"

He groaned softly. "Go away."

"You're hungover?"

He rolled slightly and took the pillow with him, facing away from her. "Leave me alone, Mary-Jayne."

She walked around the bed and looked at him. "Daniel, I was only wondering if—"

"I'm not drunk," he said raggedly, clearly exasperated. "I've got a headache. Now go away."

She glanced around the room. Total darkness. He hadn't eaten for two days. Empty painkiller bottle. She got to the edge of the bed and dropped to her haunches.

"Daniel," she said gently, and tried to move the pillow. "Do you have a migraine headache?"

He moaned and his hold on the pillow tightened. "Yes. Get out of here."

She got to her feet and headed into the bathroom, emerging a minute later with a cold, wet washcloth. He hadn't moved. She sat on the edge of the bed.

"Here," she said, and pried the pillow off him. "This will help." She gently rolled him onto his back and placed the cloth across his forehead.

"Stop fussing," he said croakily.

She pressed the cloth around his temples. "Let me help you."

"You can't."

"I can," she said and touched his hair. "My mother gets migraines. I know what I'm doing." She glanced at the empty medicine bottle. "When did you last take a pain-killer?"

He shrugged and then moaned, as though the movement took all his effort. "This morning. Last night. I can't remember."

She stroked his head. "Okay. I'll be back soon. Keep the cloth on your forehead."

Mary-Jayne was back in a matter of minutes. Evie had what she needed, and when she returned to his room she noticed he was still lying on his back and had his hand over his eyes. She fetched a glass of water from the bathroom and sat on the bed again.

"Take these for now," she instructed, and pressed a couple of aspirin into his hand. "And I have some paracetamol you can take in two hours."

"Would you stop—"

"Take the pills, okay?" she said, holding on to her patience. "You'll feel better for it." He grumbled again but finally did as she requested. Mary-Jayne took the glass and placed it on the bedside table. "It's important that you take in plenty of fluids."

"Yes, nurse."

"And drop the attitude for a while."

He didn't respond. Instead he rolled over and buried his face into the pillow. Mary-Jayne got up and pushed the drapes together as close as they would go. She knew many migraine sufferers had sensitivity to light. Countless times she'd watched her mother battle for days on end with the nausea and blinding pain.

She stayed with him for the next few hours. She gave him water and made him take some more medication. When she thought he could handle it, she sat on the bed and gently massaged lavender oil into his temples. There was a strong level of intimacy in what she did, but she couldn't let him suffer.

By late afternoon there was significant improvement in his pain level, and she left for a while to make him a sandwich and peppermint tea.

"How's the patient?" Evie asked when she came into the kitchen.

Mary-Jayne looked up from her task. "A little better. He's hungry, so that's a good sign."

Evie nodded and grinned. "Yeah... You were right—you two don't have a relationship at all. What was I thinking?"

"I'm helping someone who's in pain, that's all."

"That someone is the father of your babies. It's a bond, M.J. A strong bond that will forever keep you and Daniel in each other's life."

"I know it will," she said, heavyhearted. "I just don't know why he keeps insisting that we get married."

Evie raised her brows in dramatic fashion. "He lost a child once... I think it's easy to understand why he doesn't want to lose his sons, too."

"Lose them to what?" she shot back.

"Geography," Evie replied. "An ocean between you is a big incentive. Or the idea you might meet someone else one day and get married."

She wasn't about to admit she'd deliberately avoided considering any of that before.

"Marriage without love could never work."

"Are you sure about that?" Evie queried. "I mean, are you sure there's no love there? Looks to me as if you're behaving exactly like a woman in love would act."

She stilled instantly. Her sister's words rattled around in her head.

No, it wasn't true. She didn't. She couldn't.

"I'm not," she said, defiant.

Evie smiled gently. "I've never known you to be afraid of anything. What is it about loving this man that scares you so much?"

Nothing. Everything. Her sister was way too intuitive. "He's out of my league."

"Why? Because he has short hair and a job?"

The reference to her ex-boyfriend didn't go unmissed. "We're too different. And he'll want to shuffle me off to San Francisco. I don't want to live there. I want to live here. But he'll do and say whatever he has to in order to get his own way. I know he's handsome and can be charming and ticks all the boxes. But I know him… He's a control freak."

"So are you, in your own way," Evie remarked. "So maybe you're not so different after all."

Was that it? Was it their similarities and not their differences that spooked her? He'd called her a hothead. She'd called him arrogant. Were they both guilty of those traits?

Mary-Jayne ignored the idea for the moment and grabbed the tray. "I have to get back in there."

Evie smiled. "See you a little later."

When she returned to his room the bed was empty. The curtains were still drawn and there was a sliver of light beaming from beneath the closed bathroom door. He came out moments later, naked except for a towel draped around his hips, another towel in his hand that he used to dry his hair.

She pushed down the rush of blood in her veins. But his shoulders were so wide, his chest broad and dusted with a smattering of hair and his stomach as flat as a washboard that the picture was wholly masculine. A deep surge of longing flowed through her.

"You're back."

She swallowed hard and tried to not look at his smooth skin. "I'm back," she said, and placed the tray on the small table by the window. "How are you feeling?"

"Weary," he said, and smiled fractionally as he came toward her. "It takes me a few days to come good after."

Mary-Jayne poured some tea and made a determined effort to stop looking at him as if he was a tasty meal. "Have you always suffered from migraines?" she asked, eyes downcast.

He nodded. "Since I was a kid. They're less frequent now, but when one hits I usually just lock myself in my apartment with some aspirin for a couple of days and try to sleep it off."

"Have you tried stronger medication? Perhaps an injection of—"

"No needles," he said, and moved beside her.

He smelled so good. Like soap and some musky deodorant. She swallowed hard and glanced sideways. The towel hitched around his hips had slipped a little. "I should let you have some privacy and—"

"Shy?" he queried, reading her thoughts effortlessly. "It's nothing you haven't seen before."

Mary-Jayne swallowed hard. He was right. She'd seen every part of him. Touched every part of him. Been with him in the most intimate way possible. And still there was something unknown about him, something inviting and extraordinarily sexy. There was nothing overt about Daniel. He wasn't one of those constantly charming men who flirted and manipulated. He was sexually confident but not obvious. It was one of the reasons why she found him so blindingly attractive. He could have her as putty in his hands if he wanted to, but he didn't try to sway her with sex. For sure, he'd kissed her a couple of times, but even then he'd held back. When they'd been kissing in her kitchen days earlier and she'd told him to go, he hadn't lingered. He hadn't tried to persuade her or coerce. Because he possessed, she realized, bucketloads of integrity.

"You know," she said bluntly as she stirred the tea, "if you kissed me right now you'd probably have me in that bed in less than two seconds."

He chuckled. "I know."

"Except for your migraine, of course."

"I wouldn't let a lousy headache get in the way."

His words made her insides jump. She poured a second mug of tea and sat down. "Shall I open the curtains?" she asked, noticing that the only light in the room was coming from the direction of the open bathroom door. "Or are you still too sensitive?"

"I'm okay now."

She pushed the drapes aside a little. "My mother can't bear light when she has an attack. My dad usually bundles her in the car and takes her to the doctor for a painkiller injection."

He flinched. "Bernie used to try acupuncture rather than meds when I was young to combat the worst of the pain."

"Did it work?"

He shrugged loosely and sat in the chair opposite. "At times. Thank you for the tea and...everything else today."

"No problem. Glad I could help."

He sniffed the air. "I can smell flowers."

She grinned. "It's lavender oil," she explained. "I massaged some of it into your temples. It's something my dad does for my mother."

He rubbed his forehead. "Oh...well, thanks. It helped."

She sipped her tea and pushed the sandwich toward him. "You really should eat something."

He nodded and picked up the bread. "How are *you* feeling? Any nausea today?"

"No," she replied. "I've been okay for the past couple of days." She rubbed her belly and smiled. "And it's a small price to pay for having these two growing inside me."

He regarded her thoughtfully. "You're really happy about being pregnant, aren't you?"

"Ecstatic," she said and smiled. "I mean, it's not what I'd planned...but then again, I don't ever really plan anything. My work, my travels... It's always been a little ad hoc. But now I can feel them, I know I couldn't be happier."

"Except for the fact that I'm their father?" he queried, one brow raised.

Mary-Jayne met his gaze. "I've never wished for it to be any different. I think you'll be a really great dad." She sighed heavily. "And I get it, you know...about why you want to get married. You didn't get a chance, last time, to be a father. That was taken away from you. But I would never do anything to keep you from your sons, Daniel. They're a part of you, just like they're a part of me."

His gray eyes smoldered. "So you think all that, and you still won't marry me."

"No."

He tossed the untouched sandwich back onto the tray. "Okay. I won't ask you again."

It was what she wanted. No more proposals. No more pursuit. But somehow, in the back of her mind, she felt a strange sensation. Like…like disappointment. But she managed a tight smile. "Thank you."

"And custody?"

"We can share it. Of course, I'm going to live here and you'll be in San Francisco…but you can see them whenever you want."

"Don't you think that will confuse them?" he asked quietly. "Me randomly turning up to play daddy."

"At first," she said, and gritted her back teeth. "But it's going to be impossible to share custody when we live in two different countries."

"They could live here for six months and then in San Francisco for six months."

Fear snaked up her spine. "You wouldn't?"

"I wouldn't what?"

Mary-Jayne perched herself on the edge of the chair. "Try to get fifty percent custody. I couldn't bear to be away from them for six months at a time. I know you've got money enough to get the best lawyers, but I really couldn't—"

"You misunderstand, Mary-Jayne," he said, cutting her off. "I meant you and the twins could live in San Francisco for six months. Look, I know you love this town and don't want to be away from it permanently, but perhaps we could meet in the middle, metaphorically speaking. I'll buy you a house near where I live and you could settle there every six months."

"You'll *buy* me a house? Just like that?"

He shrugged. "Sure."

"And fly me and the twins back and forth every six months?"

"Yes."

Meet in the middle? Perhaps that was the only way to settle the tension between them. And as much as she protested, she knew she'd do whatever she had to do if it meant retaining full custody of her babies. "We'll see what happens. Anyhow," she said and got to her feet, "you should rest for a while. You look like you need it."

"Can I see you later?"

"No," she replied. "You need to get some sleep. And I have some work to do. I'm making some pieces for a friend of Solana's and I need to concentrate."

"My grandmother is very fond of you," he said, and got to his feet. The towel slipped a little more and she averted her gaze. It wasn't good for her self-control to keep staring at his bare chest.

"I'm fond of her, too."

"I know," he said, and then added more soberly, "and I apologize if I might have suggested you were not pure in your motives when you got to know her. She told me you turned down her offer to finance your business. I should trust her judgment… She knows people way better than I do."

Heat crawled up her neck. He was paying her a compliment. It shouldn't have embarrassed her, but it did. "I understand you only wanted to protect her. But I genuinely like Solana and would never take advantage of her in any way."

"I know that, Mary-Jayne. But if you need help getting your business off the ground, then I would be more than—"

"No," she said and raised a hand. "My business is mediocre because I'm not all that ambitious… I never have been. I like designing and crafting the pieces, but that's where my interest ends. I started selling them online almost by mistake. My friends Lauren and Cassie persuaded me to start a website showcasing the things I'd made and then all of a sudden I had orders coming in. I do it because

I have to make a living doing something, and why not earn money doing what I enjoy creatively."

He nodded as if he understood. She'd expected him to try to sway her some more, but to his credit he accepted her explanation. "I'll see you soon, then."

"Okay," she said, and shrugged lightly, even though the idea of spending more time with him tied her insides into knots. She liked him. A lot. And that made it increasingly difficult to keep him at arm's length. "I hope you feel better."

It took another two days for Daniel to get back to his normal self. He conference called his brothers to keep up with business and spoke to his grandmother. Solana was keen to know the details of his visit with Mary-Jayne, but he didn't tell her much. He certainly wasn't going to admit she'd turned him down again and again.

On Friday morning he headed to the kitchen and found Evie elbow-deep in some kind of baking.

"Good morning," she greeted, and smiled. "Coffee?"

He nodded and helped himself to a mug and half filled it with coffee. "Cooking for the masses?" he asked as he looked over the large bowls in front of her before he perched himself on a stool by the counter.

"For the fire station," she said cheerfully. "My husband, Scott, is a fireman. He's on night shift at the moment and I usually bake a few dozen cupcakes to keep him and the rest of the crew going."

It was a nice gesture, he thought. A loving gesture. "He's a lucky guy."

She smiled. "I'm the lucky one. He moved here, you know, from California. He'd come here for his sister's wedding to my older brother and we fell in love, but he left a few weeks after he arrived. When I discovered I was pregnant he came back and stayed. He knew I could never leave here... I had a teenage son and my family. So he changed his life for me. It was a very selfless gesture."

Daniel didn't miss the meaning of her words.

But live in Crystal Point permanently? He couldn't. It wasn't the place for him. He had a business to run. He couldn't do that from a tiny town that was barely a spot on the map. Plus, he had a life in San Francisco. Friends. Routine. A past. He'd known Simone there. Loved her there. Grieved her there. To leave would be like abandoning those feelings. And Mary-Jayne had made her thoughts abundantly clear. He was pretty sure she didn't want him anywhere near her precious town. That was why he'd suggested she come to San Francisco for six months of the year. It was a sensible compromise. The only way around the situation.

"I'm glad it worked out for you," he said, and drank some coffee.

One of her eyebrows came up. "Things have a way of doing that, you know."

"Or they don't."

She smiled. "I like to believe that anything is possible... if you want it enough."

It was a nice idea, but he didn't really agree. He'd wanted his wife and daughter to be safe. But fate had other plans. Things happened. Bad things. Good things. Sometimes it was simply a matter of timing.

"She's always been headstrong," Evie said, and smiled again. "Don't let that bravado fool you though. Underneath she's as vulnerable as the next person."

"I know she is. She's also stubborn."

"Perhaps that's because she thinks you shouldn't always get your own way?" Evie suggested.

He laughed a little. "You might be right. But I'm not out to change her. I only want to be a father to my children."

"Maybe that's where you're going wrong," Evie said. "Maybe you need to concentrate on her first and foremost."

"Nice idea," he said ruefully. "Have you met your sister? She's not exactly giving me an opportunity."

"She's scared of you."

Daniel straightened. "Of me? Why? I'd never harm her or—"

"Of course you wouldn't," Evie said quickly. "I mean she's scared of what you represent. You're...normal... You know...not a—"

"Unemployed musician?" he finished for her. "Yeah, we've already had the ex-boyfriend discussion. She's anti-wealth, antisuccess, anti-anything that gives her a reason to keep me out of the little bubble she's wrapped in."

"It's protection, that's all. Her first boyfriend was a deadbeat who stole her money. The one after that was a lazy so-and-so. If she's with you, it's as if she's admitting that she's not who everyone thinks she is. That all the other guys were just a phase...an aberration. That she isn't really a free spirit who does what she wants. It means that she's as vulnerable to a perfectly respectable and nice man as the rest of womankind is."

Daniel laughed. "So you're saying she won't marry me because I'm not a deadbeat?"

"Precisely."

He was still thinking of Evie's words when he was in town later that morning. Bellandale was a big regional town and had sufficient offerings to get what he needed done. By the afternoon he was back in Crystal Point and pulled up outside Mary-Jayne's house around five o'clock. She was in the front garden, crouched down and pulling weeds from an overgrown herb garden. She wore bright pink overalls that showed off her lovely curves and the popped-out belly. He watched her for a moment, marveling at her effortless beauty. His insides were jumping all over the place. No one had ever confounded him as much as Mary-Jayne Preston.

She stood up when she realized there was a car by the curb. She dropped the gloves and small garden fork in her hand and came down the driveway. Her crazily beautiful hair whipped around her face.

Daniel got out of the car and closed the door. "Good afternoon."

"You look better," she said as she approached. "Headache all gone?"

"Yes. How are you feeling?"

"I'm good," she said, and came beside the car. "Nice wheels. It doesn't look like a rental."

Daniel glanced at the white BMW and rattled the keys. "It's not."

Her eyes widened. "You bought a car?"

He nodded. "I did. Do you like it?"

She shrugged. "It's nice, I suppose. Very…highbrow."

A smile tugged at his mouth. "It's a sensible family car."

She looked it over and nodded. "I suppose it is. Since you had the rental, I didn't realize you needed a car."

"I don't," he said and grabbed her hand. "I still have the rental." He opened her fingers and rested the key in her palm. "It's yours."

Her eyes instantly bulged and she stepped back. "Mine?"

He nodded. "That's right."

The moment it registered her expression sharpened. "You bought me a car?"

"I did. I thought you—"

"I have a car," she said stiffly. "And it works just fine."

Daniel glanced at the beat-up, rusted yellow Volkswagen in the driveway. "Your car is old and not roadworthy."

Her hands propped onto her hips. "How do you know that? Have you taken it for a spin around the block?"

"I don't need to," he replied. "Take a look at it."

"I like it." She stepped forward and put the key back in his hand. "And I don't need another."

Daniel let out an exasperated breath. "Does everything have to be a battle between us? So I bought you a car. Sue me."

"I can't be bought."

Annoyance surged through his blood. "I'm not trying to buy you. I bought something *for* you. There's a significant difference."

"Not to me," she shot back. "First it's a car and then what…a house? Maybe one to match the house in San Francisco you want to buy? What then? A boat? What about a racehorse? Don't forget the jewels. I'll probably need a private jet, too."

"You're being ridiculous. It's just a car."

"Stop trying to justify this. Take it back. I don't want it."

He kept a lid on his simmering rage. "I want my sons to be safe, and they won't be in that jalopy," he said, and hooked a thumb in the direction of her old VW. "Be sensible, Mary-Jayne."

"I am sensible. And they'll be perfectly safe," she said hotly. "I would never put them at risk. But I won't let you tell me what to do. Not now, not ever."

He shook his head. "This isn't a multiple-choice exercise, Mary-Jayne. And I won't compromise on this issue. The car is yours." He took a few steps and dropped the key on top of the letterbox. "I want you to have it."

"I don't care what you want!"

Daniel stilled and looked at her. Her cheeks were ablaze,

her hair framing her face, her chest heaving. A thousand conflicting emotions banged around in his head. And he knew there was no reasoning with her. No middle road.

"No," he said wearily. "I guess you don't."

Then he turned around and walked down the street.

Chapter Ten

Bossy. Arrogant. Know-it-all.

Mary-Jayne had a dozen names for him and none of them were flattering.

He'd bought her a car. A car! Without discussing it with her first. Without any kind of consultation. He really did think he could do whatever he liked.

On Saturday afternoon she headed to her parents' place for lunch. The whole family got together once a month for a day of catch-up that included lunch, dinner and plenty of conversation and games with the kids. It was a Preston tradition, and since she'd missed the get-togethers while she'd been away, Mary-Jayne looked forward to spending time with them. Her father was manning the barbecue with her brother, Noah, while her brothers-in-law, Scott and Cameron, played pool in the games room, as Noah's wife, Callie, kept their kids entertained. Evie's toddler and Grace's newborn were the center of attention in the kitchen

while her mother fussed around making her famous potato salad. Her best friend Lauren was there, too, with her
fiancé and her own parents. Lauren was Cameron's sister
and her fiancé, Gabe, was Scott and Callie's cousin. It was
a close-knit group. The blood ties alone made it a mam-
moth exercise to remember who was related to whom. She
cared for them all, but as she sat at the kitchen table, one
hand draped over her abdomen and the other curled around
a glass of diet soda, she experienced an inexplicable empty
feeling deep down, almost through to her bones.

She couldn't define it. She should he happy. Elated. She
had her babies growing in her belly and her whole family around her. But something was amiss. Something was
missing. *Someone was missing.*

She quickly put the idea from her head.

"Where's Daniel today?"

Her mother's cheerful voice interrupted her thoughts.
She shrugged. "I have no idea."

Barbara frowned a little. "I thought he might have liked
to come and meet everyone."

"I didn't invite him."

The room fell silent, and she looked up to see her mother's frown.

"I did," Evie added quickly. "But he said he wouldn't
come unless you asked him to be here."

Shame niggled between her shoulders. "Good. He's finally showing some sense."

Evie sighed. "What's he done now?"

Mary-Jayne couldn't miss the disapproval in her eldest sister's voice. It irritated her down to her teeth. "He
bought me a car," she said tartly. "A brand-spanking-new
BMW with all the trimmings." She laughed humorlessly.
"Imagine me driving around town in that."

The three women stared at her. It was Grace who spoke next.

"That was very thoughtful of him, don't you think? Considering how old and unreliable your current car is."

Mary-Jayne's jaw tightened. "I know it's old. And I know it's unreliable. But it's mine by choice because it's what I can afford. And he wasn't being thoughtful... He was being controlling."

Evie tutted. "Have you considered that perhaps he only wants you and the babies to be safe while you're driving?"

"That's what he said," she replied impatiently. "But I know Daniel and he—"

"Didn't his wife and baby die in a car accident?" Grace again, equally disapproving as Evie and their mother.

"Yes, they did," Evie supplied.

"And wasn't the other car involved an *old and unreliable* vehicle that had a major brake failure?"

"Yes," Evie said, looking directly at Mary-Jayne.

She sat up straight in the chair.

I don't care what you want...

Her careless words banged around in her head. Simone and their baby had died because the car that struck them had a broken brake line. She realized what he must have thought when he saw her old car—that history might repeat itself. That their sons' lives might be at risk.

It wasn't control that had motivated him to buy her a car. It was fear.

She stood up, her hands shaking. "I have to go out for a while." She looked toward Grace. "I'm parked behind you. Can you ask Cameron to move your car?"

Evie pointed to a set of keys on the counter. "Take mine," her sister suggested pointedly. "He's there alone, in case you're wondering, working in the office. My other guests left yesterday."

Mary-Jayne nodded, grabbed the keys and left.

The trip took just minutes, and she pulled the Honda Civic into the driveway. The gardens at Dunn Inn were like something out of a fairy tale, and she walked up the cobbled pathway, past the wishing well and headed up the steps to the porch. A couple of the French-style doors were open, and she slid the insect screen back. Her sister's artwork graced most walls, and the furnishings were well matched and of good quality. Evie had a style all of her own. There was a small office off the living room and when she reached the doorway she came to a halt.

Daniel sat in the chair, earphones on, tapping on the computer keys. She came behind him and touched his shoulder. He flinched and turned, tossing the earphones aside.

"Hi," she said, and dropped her tote.

He wore jeans and a blue shirt that looked as though it had been tailored to fit his gorgeous frame. His gray eyes scanned her face, his expression unreadable.

"I thought you had a family thing to go to?"

"I did," she said. "I do."

"Then, what are you doing here?"

"I left." She shrugged one shoulder. "I wanted to see you."

He swiveled the chair around and sat back. "So you're seeing me. What?"

Mary-Jayne swallowed hard. "You're working. I'm probably interrupting and—"

"What do you want, Mary-Jayne?" he asked impatiently.

She let out a long breath. "To apologize."

He stood up immediately and folded his arms. "Consider it done."

"I was wrong, okay," she said when she noticed his expression was still unmoved. "I shouldn't have reacted the way I did. I shouldn't have *overreacted*. I didn't stop to think about why it was so important to you that I have a new car." She rubbed her belly gently. "But I get it now... I understand that you need to know that our sons are safe because of what happened to your wife and daughter... You know, how the other car was old and had brake failure." Her throat thickened as she said the words. She looked at him and tried to read what he was thinking. But she couldn't. She wished she knew him better. And wished she understood the emotions behind his gray eyes.

The shutters were still up, so she pressed on.

"And I shouldn't have said that I didn't care what you wanted. I didn't mean it," she admitted.

His jaw was achingly tight. "I can't bear the thought of you driving around in that old car."

"I know," she said softly. "And I understand why you feel that way. I should have been more considerate of your feelings. But sometimes, when I'm with you, I react before I think about the consequences. It's not a conscious thing." She waved her hands. "But between you and me there's all this...tension. And getting mad at you is kind of like a release valve for that."

The mood between them suddenly altered. There *was* tension between them. Built on a blinding, blistering physical attraction that had never been truly sated. One night would never be enough for that kind of pull. Daniel had known it all along. She realized that as she stared up at him, breathing hard, chest heaving. That was why he'd pursued her for a month after Solana's birthday party. And that was why she'd refused him. She was scared of those feelings. Terrified of the way he made her feel. Because she still wanted him.

"Daniel..."

She said his name on a wispy breath. His eyes were

dark, burning and filled with desire. It was heady and commanding. It made her shake with longing and fear. Of course she wasn't afraid of him, only the hypnotic power he had over her.

He groaned, as though he knew he was about to do something he probably shouldn't. But Mary-Jayne didn't care. In that moment, with nothing between but barely a foot of space, all she wanted was to be in his arms.

"I'm trying so hard to fight this."

"I know. But it's me you're fighting," he said softly. "Not this."

He was right. She fought him. In her heart she felt she had to. But in that moment all her fight disappeared.

"Make love to me," she whispered and reached out to touch his chest.

He flinched against her touch as though it was poker hot. "Are you sure that's what you want?"

She shrugged lightly. "The only thing I'm sure about is that I'm not sure about anything anymore."

He reached for her shoulders and molded them with his hands. He fisted a handful of her hair and gently tilted her head back. "You drive me crazy, do you know that?"

She nodded a little. "I don't mean to."

"You can trust me, you know," he said and lowered his head toward her face. "I'm not your enemy. Even if it does feel as though most of the time we're at war with each other."

He kissed her then. Not gently. Not softly. But long and deep and fueled with heated possession. Mary-Jayne kissed him back and wrapped her arms around his waist. "Do you have any idea how sexy you are?" he whispered against her lips.

"No," she said, and smiled as she trailed her lips along

his jaw. "We've got the place to ourselves… Let's not waste any time."

He got her to his room in ten seconds flat. He closed the door and locked it.

They stood opposite one another by the bed. Last time there'd been no thinking, nothing but desire and pure instinct. This was different. This was conscious and planned and fueled by more than simple attraction.

"Do you know what I thought the first time I saw you?" he asked quietly.

Mary-Jayne shook her head.

"I thought," he said as he reached for her, "that I had never seen a woman with such beautiful hair in all my life."

He kissed her again, and she shuddered and tossed her head. When he pulled back she was breathing so hard she thought her lungs might explode. He slipped her T-shirt off one shoulder and trailed his mouth along her collarbone. There was such blistering intensity in his touch that it thrilled her to the soles of her feet. He kept kissing her, making her sigh and moan until finally she begged him to take her to the bed.

"What's the hurry?" he muttered against her neck.

Mary-Jayne ran her hands over his chest. His heart beat furiously behind his ribs and her hand hovered there for a moment. Last time they'd made love as if there was no time to waste. But now he seemed in no rush to get her naked and between the sheets. He was taking his time exploring her mouth with his own and gently smoothing his hands across her back and shoulders. They stood kissing like that for minutes. Or was it hours? She couldn't tell. She was too overwhelmed by the narcotic pleasure thrumming through her body at the seductive tone of his skilled touch. By the time they worked their way to the side of the bed she was a wriggling mass of need.

He stripped the T-shirt over her head and Mary-Jayne watched, fascinated as he slowly undressed her. It was intensely erotic and made her long for him with such urgency she could barely breathe. When she was naked, when her shirt was on the floor and her bra dispensed with, he hooked his thumbs under the band of her briefs and slowly skimmed them down over her bottom and legs. Then he was on his knees in front of her, touching her belly, pressing kisses across the curved, tightened skin. She'd never experienced anything more intimate or soul reaching in her entire life. He reached up to cup her breasts, and they felt heavy in his hands. As he gently toyed with her nipples, every part of her body felt more alive, more sensitive to his touch than ever before.

She whispered his name, and he looked up to meet her gaze. He was still fully dressed and she wanted nothing more than to feel his skin against her, to wrap herself in his embrace and feel his body deep within hers. Mary-Jayne curled her fingers around his shirt collar and found the top button. She flicked it open with eager hands.

"Take this off," she instructed with way more bravado than she felt.

He smiled, urged her to sit, and once she was settled on the bed he shrugged out of his shirt. Shoes and socks and jeans followed, and once he was naked he sat beside her.

"Better?" he asked, reaching for her again, kissing her neck and shoulders.

Mary-Jayne sighed heavily. "Much."

He palmed her rounded belly. "Pregnancy has made you even more beautiful, if that were possible."

It was a lovely thought. She'd never considered herself all that beautiful. Not like her sister Grace. Or Evie, with her dancing eyes and seductive curves. She was pretty at best. Not even particularly sexy. But beneath Daniel's glittering gaze she felt more beautiful than she ever had in her life.

She placed a hand on her belly. "Are we going to be able to do this?" she asked, smiling a little. "My middle is expanding at an alarming rate."

Daniel grasped her hand and spanned his own across her stomach. "I'm sure we'll manage just fine, darling."

Darling...

It was the first endearment he'd said to her. And it sounded so lovely coming from his lips that emotion unexpectedly gathered at the back of her eyes. She wanted that and more. Despite every argument and every rational part of her brain telling her it was madness—she wanted to be the woman he called darling every day of his life.

Because...

Because she loved him.

She'd fallen in love with the father of her babies. Wholly and completely. Even knowing that he didn't love her back and that he was all wrong for her and she for him. None of that mattered. Her heart had decided.

"What are you thinking?" he asked.

Mary-Jayne shook her head. "Nothing... Just...kiss me."

He smiled and found her mouth again. His kiss was long and slow and everything she wanted. She kissed him back with every ounce of feeling in her heart. He lowered her onto the bed and began to make love to her with such excruciating sweetness she could barely stop herself from calling out his name. He touched her, stroked her and worshipped her breasts with his mouth and hands until she was quivering in his arms. By the time he moved his hand between her legs to caress her she was so fueled with passion she rose up and over and found release almost immediately. It was wondrously intense, and when she came back to earth and the stars had stopped exploding behind her eyes she saw that he was staring down into her face.

"What's wrong?" she asked tremulously, pushing air into her lungs.

"Not a thing," he replied, and kissed her again. "So I guess we don't have to be too concerned about birth control?"

She grinned and stretched. "The horse has already bolted on that one."

Daniel laughed and rolled over, positioning himself between her legs. She relaxed her thighs and waited, so consumed with love for him in that moment that if he'd asked her for the moon she would had flown into the sky to catch it for him.

When they were together, when she couldn't tell when she began and he ended, Mary-Jayne let out a contented moan. He moved against her with such acute tenderness her heart literally ached. Nothing had ever felt so good. And she'd never been more connected to anyone than she was with him as he hovered above her, taking most of his weight on his strong arms, ensuring she was comfortable and relaxed. Release came to her again, slow and languorous and fulfilling, and when he shuddered above her she held on, gripping him tighter, longer and with more feeling than she ever had before in her life.

When he moved and rolled over onto his back, they were both breathing madly. Mary-Jayne closed her eyes and sighed. When her breathing returned with some normalcy she shifted onto her side and looked at him. His chest rose and fell, and he had his eyes closed. He reached for her hand and linked their fingers.

"You know," he said, and sighed, "we should do it down on the beach."

"Do what?" she asked, and kissed his shoulder. "This?"

"Get married. What else?"

Mary-Jayne stilled. A little voice at the back of her mind chanted that she should grab his idea with both hands and say a resounding *yes*. But she couldn't. He didn't love her. He never would. Sure, the sex was incredible and she had his babies growing inside her, but not even that was enough to sustain a lifetime relationship. He had to know that. Only a fool would believe otherwise. She loved him. But she wasn't about to become strapped to a one-side marriage.

"You said you wouldn't ask again," she reminded him.

He shrugged. "I can't help it. I want what I want."

"I can't."

"Or won't?" he asked.

"Both," she admitted, and rolled onto her back. "Can't we just get to know one another a little, Daniel? I mean, I hardly know anything about you and—"

"Because you've never asked," he said a little more harshly. "Okay—I'm thirty-four and recently had a birth-day. My favorite color is yellow and I loathe brussels sprouts. When I was fifteen I chipped my two front teeth and now I have veneers. I was seventeen the first time I had sex and since my wife died I've slept with just over half a dozen women. I like imported beer but rarely drink. I haven't had a meaningful conversation with my dad in years and I still think it sucks that I never knew my real mom." He pulled himself up and draped the sheet across his hips. "Satisfied?"

Mary-Jayne sat up and covered her bare breasts with her arms. "That's not what I meant. I'm talking about time. We need time to get to know one another."

"We don't have it," he said flatly. "You live here. I live in San Francisco. I need an answer, Mary-Jayne."

She pulled herself across the bed and got to her feet. "Then, it's no."

* * *

No. Again.

Was there a bigger sucker than him?

Daniel sprang out of the bed and watched her as she snatched up her clothes. "You're being rash…as usual."

"I'm being honest," she said, and pulled on her underwear. "And sure, I'm impulsive and over the years it has gotten me into trouble every now and then. But in this I'm not being rash. I'm using my head," she said, and looked him over with deliberate emphasis. "And not the part of my anatomy that you are if you think having great sex is enough of a reason to get married."

"They're the reason," he said, and pulled on his jeans as he motioned to her belly. "Our children. The great sex is a bonus."

She tossed a shoe at him. And then another.

The first one hit him in the shoulder and the second sandal he caught midair. There was so much fire and spirit in her, so much passion. Daniel was inexplicably drawn to her like a moth to a flame. He liked that she wasn't a pushover, even though it drove him to distraction. "Stop throwing things at me."

"Well, you stop doing what you're doing and I will."

Daniel dropped the shoe and shrugged, holding out his hands. "What have I done now?"

"You know exactly what," she said on a rush of breath. "You know how I feel, Daniel. I don't want to get married and live somewhere else. I want to live here, in Crystal Point. I want our children to grow up in a home, not a house. And I want my family around me while I raise them."

"While *you* raise them?" he said flatly. "Which is exactly my point. *We* need to raise them, Mary-Jayne, together. And I think today proved that we can. We have a connection that's—"

"We had sex," she corrected. "But it's not enough. The truth is, you confuse me when you kiss me and touch me, and then I can't get any of this straight in my mind. I won't let you use sex as a way of—"

"*You* came here today, remember?" he reminded her, cutting her off. "*You* asked me to make love to *you*, remember? Not the other way around. I've left you alone these past few days…just as you asked."

She stilled. "But…"

Her words trailed and she glared at him, her eyes glittering with a kind of fiery rage. She was brash and argumentative and generally on the attack…but caught out, and she was as meek as a lamb. She was a fascinating contradiction. And he craved her more than he'd ever wanted any woman in his life.

"You came here today looking for me. For this," he said and gestured to the bed. "Because we have an insane attraction for one another that neither of us expected."

She sucked in a long breath. "I came here today because I felt bad for what I said the other day. I felt guilty, okay?"

"So today was about sympathy? Throw a crumb to the lonely widower whose wife and baby died?"

"No," she said quickly. "Of course not. I just thought we could…talk, that's all."

"Talk about what?" he asked. "You and me? There is no you and me, right? Or do you want to know about Simone? Or our daughter? What do you want to know? How long I sat in hospital the night my wife died? Eight hours," he said, feeling the memory of those hours through to the marrow in his bones. "Do you also want to know that I never got to say goodbye to her? I never got a chance to tell her what she meant to me—hell, I never even said it enough when she was alive. And yes, I held my daughter's lifeless body for a few moments before they took her away. Do you want to know if I cried? Once, after the wake when everyone had left and I realized for the rest of my life I'd be living with the fact that my daughter's birthday was the same day she and her mom died."

He stopped speaking and looked at Mary-Jayne. Her eyes brimmed with tears, and he immediately felt bad. He didn't want to upset her. He wanted to do the exact opposite, if she'd only let him.

"I'm so sorry…"

"You can't have it both ways," he said as he retrieved her skirt and T-shirt and passed them to her. "Yes, my wife and baby died. And yes, sometimes I feel alone *and* lonely because of that. Who the hell doesn't feel alone at times? But if you want to be here, then really be here, Mary-Jayne. Stop making excuses."

"I'm not," she said, wiping her eyes before she quickly slipped into her clothes.

"You are," he said, suddenly impatient. "And the next time you turn up on my door and ask me to make love to you, it'll only happen if my ring is on your finger."

"Then it will never happen again."

He shrugged, pretty sure she didn't believe that any more than he did. "You should get back to your party."

She shoved her feet into her shoes. "Would you like to come with me?"

He cocked one brow. "Are you sure that's what you want?"

"What I want is for us to get along for the sake of our children." She planted her hands on her hips and spoke in a quiet voice. "I'm trying to be rational and realistic. I don't want to be trapped in a loveless and empty marriage. And if you're honest with yourself, if you can think of only that and not about custody of the babies or how challenging it's going to be to raise them together when we live on opposite sides of the world, you'd realize that you don't want that, either. Especially after the way you loved your wife."

A loveless and empty marriage? Was that what she truly thought it would be? Were her feelings for him that hollow? He did his best to ignore the way that idea made him feel.

"I want," he said with deliberate emphasis, "my family."

"So do I," she said quietly. "But *my* family is here, Daniel. In Crystal Point. I like living a few streets away from my parents and having my sisters and brother close by. I don't come from a family where we greet one another with a handshake and live in different parts of the world. I like knowing that 'I love you' is the last thing I hear from my mother when I hang up the phone after I speak to her, and I like knowing that my dad would be there for me in a heartbeat if I needed him. And maybe that sounds like a silly TV movie to you, but it's what I want for my children."

For a second he envied her. It didn't sound silly at all. It sounded real and authentic and exactly what he'd hoped he'd have for his own children one day. Being around Mary-Jayne and her family had only amplified that need. He wanted to tell her that. But he held back.

I don't want to be trapped in a loveless and empty marriage.

That was what she imagined they'd have. Not a marriage like her siblings' or her parents'. But something less, something that would never measure up to the standards she witnessed in her life. It would never be enough. They would never be enough.

"We should get going," he said, and grabbed his shirt. "I would like to see your parents again."

She nodded and made her way across the room.

They drove separate cars to her parents' home. Him in his rental. She in her sister's Honda. He knew the BMW still sat outside her house. She hadn't driven it once, he was sure. She was stubborn and infuriating. When they arrived at the Preston house, he got out and met her by her car door, not saying a word about the old VW he spotted in the driveway, even though he hated the idea of her driving something so unreliable and potentially dangerous.

"I'm sorry about before," he said, and took her elbow. "I didn't mean to make you cry."

She sniffed. "Okay...sure."

He rubbed her skin. "I don't enjoy seeing you upset."

She nodded, eyes still glistening. "I know that. I don't mean to upset you, either. I just don't seem to be able to help myself sometimes."

Inside, he was welcomed by her family with the warmth he'd come to expect from them. They were good people, and it made him think about the dig she'd made about handshakes and living on opposite sides of the world. She was right. He was close to his brothers but not in the way she was with her siblings. And his relationship with Miles and Bernadette had been taxing most of his life.

He was by the pool talking to her brother and enduring a moderate kind of grilling about his intentions when his phone rang. He excused himself and picked up the call on the fifth ring.

It was Caleb.

Daniel listened to his brother's concerned voice, and once he ended the call went looking for Mary-Jayne. She was inside, in the kitchen with her mother and sister-in-law.

"I need to talk to you," he said, and ignored the thunder behind his ribs.

She must have picked up on his mood, because she

complied immediately and ushered him into the front living room.

"What is it?" she asked once they were alone.

"I have to leave."

"Oh, okay. I'll see you Monday, then. Remember I have an appointment with my OB at ten."

"I'm leaving Crystal Point," he said again, firmer. "Caleb just called me—Bernie's in the hospital in Cairns. She had a massive heart attack a couple of hours ago."

Mary-Jayne gasped and gripped his arm. "Oh, how awful. Is there anything I can do?"

Marry me and stay by my side...

He reached out and touched her belly, felt the movement of his babies beneath his palm and experienced such an acute sensation in his chest he could barely breathe. The connection was mesmerizing. Her green eyes glittered brilliantly, and he got so caught up in her gaze he was rooted to the spot.

"I could... I could..." Her voice trailed off.

"What?" he asked.

She shrugged a little. "I'm not sure... I just thought perhaps I could..."

She could what? Come with him? A part of him wanted that more than anything. But that couldn't be what she meant. She'd have to care one way or another. Daniel swallowed hard. "Take care of yourself, Mary-Jayne."

"You, too," she whispered. "Give your dad and Bernie my love."

But not you...

He got the message loud and clear.

"I'll talk to you soon."

"Please let me know how she is."

Daniel nodded, suddenly numb all over. "Sure." He

shrugged off her touch and walked to the door, but something stopped him. Then he turned and looked at her.

"What?" she asked softly.

"I've just realized that you're a fraud, Mary-Jayne," he said. "You walk and talk like some restless free spirit who can take on the world, but underneath all that talk is someone who's afraid to truly be who she is."

She frowned. "That doesn't make sense."

"Doesn't it? You've wrapped yourself up in this image of being a certain kind of person and it's as though you've locked yourself in a cage. Admit it, if I was some unemployed, tattooed and unsuccessful guitarist things would be very different. You'd have nothing to hide behind. You say you don't want to be trapped in a loveless marriage—but that's not it. You just don't want to marry *me*. Because if you did it would mean that everything you've ever stood for is a great big lie. It would mean that you've settled for the safe road, and then everyone around you would know that your boldness and bluster is just an act and that you're as mainstream and sensible as the rest of us. And that's what scares you—being like everyone else. That's why your last boyfriend was a deadbeat and why your business fails to get off the ground. You think that makes you a free spirit? You're wrong… All that makes you is a coward."

Then he turned on his heel and left.

Chapter Eleven

"Are you still feeling unwell?" Evie's voice cut through her thoughts.

Mary-Jayne battened down the nausea she'd been battling for a week. She'd spent the morning babysitting her niece while Evie and Scott attended an art show in Bellandale. She loved looking after Rebecca and considered it good practice for when her babies arrived.

"On and off. The crackers help a little, but yesterday I spent an hour bent over the toilet bowl. I saw my doctor the other day and we discussed some medication I can take to alleviate the nausea if it gets much worse. I just don't want to do anything that might harm my babies. But after yesterday I think I'm going to have to take his advice. I've got another doctor's appointment tomorrow at three."

Evie grimaced. "That's not much fun. Other than that, is everything going okay?"

"With the pregnancy? Yes, no problems. Except I'm getting as big as a house."

"You look lovely as always," Evie assured her. "Heard from Daniel?"

"Nope."

Evie's brows furrowed. "Everything okay on that front?"

"Nope," she said and sighed. "We sort of had a fight before he left."

"Just a fight? Anything else?"

Her sister was way too intuitive. Mary-Jayne shrugged. She wasn't about to admit he'd called her a coward, or that it was exactly how she felt. "Sex isn't enough to sustain a marriage...no matter how good it is."

Evie came around the kitchen counter and rested her hands on the back of a dining chair. "Why didn't you go with him?"

She shrugged, hurting all over. "He didn't ask me."

"Maybe he thought you'd say no."

She shrugged again, still hurting, and more confused than ever. She wasn't about to admit to her sister that she missed him like crazy. "I'm not part of his life in that way."

"But you're lovers?"

Heat crept over her skin. She could never lie to Evie. "I guess. Does one night and one afternoon together make us lovers? I'm not sure what that makes us. All it makes me is confused."

"But you're in love with him, right?"

"It doesn't matter what I am," she insisted. "I can love him until the cows come home and it won't change the fact that he doesn't love me back."

"Are you sure?"

"Positive," she replied, aching deep down. She pressed her hands to her belly and rubbed her babies as they moved inside her. "He's all one-eyed about what he thinks we should do. Which is get married and raise our children in San Francisco."

"He said that?" she asked. "He said he wants you to move there?"

She nodded. "Well, he offered to buy me a house so I can live there for six months of the year."

Evie tilted her head. "I thought he might have decided he liked it here."

Mary-Jayne's eyes popped wide. "Daniel live here? In Crystal Point?" She laughed shrilly. "Not likely. Too hometown for him. He's all business and logic. He'd be bored out of his mind in a place like this."

Her sister smiled. "Really? He looked pretty comfortable here to me. And since when did you get all stuck on Crystal Point as a be-all and end-all? You spent a good part of the past ten years away from here, traveling from one place to the next." Her brows came back up. "I can remember a certain nineteen-year-old telling me in no uncertain terms that it was the most boring, uneventful spot on the map before you hopped on a plane for Morocco. I think the folks thought you'd closed your eyes and pointed to a spot on an atlas and thought, 'Why not go there?' And then there was Thailand, and Cambodia, and after that it was Mexico. And wasn't it you who spent three months back-packing through Greece and working transient jobs and peddling your jewelry to patrons in sidewalk cafés to make ends meet? And didn't you recently leave here to bail out your old school friend in Port Douglas with only a day's notice?" Evie smiled. "What's happened, M.J.? Have you lost your restless spirit? Have you realized that this little town is not such a bad place after all?"

"I never thought it was bad. I love this town. I've just

always loved traveling and experiencing new places, that's all."

"New places except San Francisco?"

Mary-Jayne stilled. Evie had a point. "You think I should do it? You think I should marry him and move to another country?"

"I think you should do whatever your heart tells you is right."

"That's what I'm doing," she insisted.

"Your heart," Evie said pointedly. "Not your head."

But my heart will get pummeled, for sure...

"I can't." She stood and grabbed her bag. "I have to get going."

Her sister nodded. "Okay. Thank you for babysitting. Rebecca loves spending time with you."

Mary-Jayne smiled broadly. "It's mutual."

Evie reached out and hugged her tight. "By the way, I see you're driving the Beamer."

Mary-Jayne wondered how long it would take for her sister to remark about the car parked along the front curb. She shrugged. "Seemed silly to let it sit there, that's all."

"Smart move. Is it good to drive?"

"Like a dream," she admitted, and grinned. "And two baby seats arrived for it yesterday."

Evie's smiled widened. "He thought of everything, didn't he?"

"Pretty much," she replied, ignoring the jab of pain in her chest. "Anyway, I have to run."

"Let me know how things go at the doctor's."

"Will do," she said as she left.

By the time she got home it was after four. She fed the dog and parrot and took a shower and then changed into baggy sweats and flaked out on the sofa. She flicked channels on the television and stared absently at the screen for an hour. Later, she ate a grilled-cheese sandwich and attempted to do some work on a new bracelet for one of Solana's friends. But she couldn't concentrate. Her mind was filled with thoughts of Daniel and his parting words.

Four days after Daniel left, Mary-Jayne got a text from Audrey informing her that Bernie was finally off the critical list but still in intensive care. There was no word from Daniel. It had been a long, lonely week. Part of her was glad. Part of her never wanted to see him again. Another part missed him so much she ached inside.

Coward...

The word had resonated in her head for days. No one had ever called her that before. No one would ever dare. But not Daniel. He called it how it was. He made her accountable for her convictions. For the first time in her life Mary-Jayne felt as though she had met her match. Her *perfect* match.

If only he loved her...

But he didn't. He thought that physical attraction was enough to sustain a marriage. But in her heart she knew it wasn't. He was kidding himself. Sure, maybe for the first few years everything would be okay. They'd be busy raising their children and there wouldn't be time to think about how loveless their marriage was. But later, once the children were older and there was only them, their differences would be evident and insurmountable. It was an impossible situation. And she wouldn't do it. She couldn't. She owed her babies more than a life where their parents were together for the wrong reasons.

As much as she appreciated her sister's support, Evie didn't really understand. She'd fallen madly in love with Scott and he'd loved her in return. He'd wooed her and fought for her and laid his heart on the line as if nothing else mattered. But Daniel... There was no heart in his proposal. Only logic and his desire to share custody of their sons.

And that would never be enough.

Five days after arriving back in Port Douglas, Daniel and his brothers were still maintaining a rotating vigil outside Bernie's hospital room. Their father hadn't left his wife's side, and at seven o'clock on Thursday evening, Daniel headed for the small hospital cafeteria and returned with two double-shot espressos. Bernie had finally been taken off the critical list, and Blake and Caleb had gone back to the resort to get some much-needed rest while Daniel stayed with his father, ensuring Miles at least ate and drank something.

"Here," he said, and passed his father a take-out cup as he sat in one of the uncomfortable chairs outside the intensive care ward. "And don't let it get cold like the last one I gave you."

Miles managed a grin and then nodded. "Thanks."

His father's pain was palpable. "She's out of danger, Dad. That's good news."

"I know," Miles said, and sighed. "I don't think I could have taken another night of wondering if she was going to make it."

"You heard what the doctor said a few hours ago," he assured his father. "She's going to pull through and be back to her old self in no time."

His dad sighed again. "Who would have thought this might happen? I mean, she's always been so health conscious... I never would have guessed she had a weak heart."

"No one can predict the future, Dad."

His words felt hollow as they left his mouth. How often had he thought that? When his grandfather passed away?

When Simone and their baby died? When Mary-Jayne told him she was pregnant?

"Yeah, I know," his dad said, and tapped him on the shoulder. "Thanks for being here this week. It's meant a lot to me."

"I wouldn't be anywhere else."

Miles shrugged a little. "I know you've got a lot going on."

Daniel drank some coffee and stared at the wall ahead.

"You should go back," Miles said quietly. "You need to sort it out."

"Actually, I think a little time apart might be what we both need."

He wasn't about to admit that he missed Mary-Jayne more than he'd believed possible. But he hadn't called her, even though he craved the sound of her voice. And he was right about thinking they needed some time out.

"Nonsense," his dad said gently. "Time apart serves no purpose. Because one day you might find you have no time left, right?"

Daniel looked at his father. Miles had one of his serious expressions on his face, and as much as Daniel wanted to fob the other man off, he resisted. He'd seen that look once before, right after his grandfather had died and Daniel was preparing to step into the role of CEO. Miles had tried to talk him out of it. At the time, Daniel was convinced his father lacked vision and ambition and simply wanted to sell the company. And it had taken years for that idea to fade. It wasn't until the wake after Simone's death that he'd realized that there was more to life than business. More to life than seventy-hour weeks and meetings and racing to catch flights from one corner of the globe to the other. But still, he hadn't changed. He'd kept on doing the same things. He'd drowned himself in work to avoid thinking about all he'd lost.

"How about we concentrate on Bernie getting better and—"

"I'm very proud of you, you know," Miles said, uncharacteristically cutting him off. "I'm very proud of the man you have become."

Daniel's throat thickened. "Dad, I—"

"And I know I never say it enough." His father shrugged. "I guess I'm not sure if that matters to you."

"It matters," he said quietly. "The talking thing… It goes both ways."

Miles smiled. "Your mom was always telling me I needed to talk more to my own father. When you were born I promised myself I'd be a better father than Mike Anderson…but I'm not sure I have been. When your mom died I fell apart. Thankfully Bernie came along and picked up the pieces, even though she had every reason to run a mile. I was a grieving man with a baby, and I had so much emotional baggage it's a wonder she was able to see through all that and still give me a shot."

"She loved you," Daniel said, and drank some coffee.

"Not at first, she didn't," Miles said. "Some days I think she might have hated me. But we worked it out." His father nodded and grinned a little. "And you will, too."

Daniel didn't share his dad's optimism. Mary-Jayne opposed him at every opportunity. And he couldn't see a way out of it. He wanted her, sure. And sometimes…sometimes it felt as though he needed her like he needed air in his lungs. But it wasn't anything more than that. How could it be? They hardly knew one another. She was dreaming about some silly romantic notion that simply didn't exist. So maybe he did think about her 24/7. And maybe he did long for her in ways he'd never longed for anyone before.

But that was just desire and attraction. Add in the fact that he wanted the chance to be a full-time father to his sons…and of course it might seem like something else. Something more.

"I loved your mom," Miles said quietly. "But I love Bernie, too. It's not more, it's not less… It's simply a different kind of same."

A different kind of same…

He was still thinking about his father's words for hours afterward. And still when he tried to sleep later that night. His dreams were plagued by images of Mary-Jayne. He dreamed of holding her, of making love to her, of waking up with her hair fanned out on the pillow beside him. He awoke restless and missing her more than he'd imagined he could. And in the cold light of morning he realized one irrefutable fact.

He was in love with her.

And their relationship had just become a whole lot more complicated.

On Monday, with the nausea and lack of appetite still lingering, she went back to her doctor to discuss some medication and get her blood pressure checked. She was waiting for the doctor to come into the room when Julie, an old school friend and now the receptionist from the front desk, popped her head around the door.

"M.J.," she said and made a face. "There's someone out here who wants to see you. Who *insists* on seeing you."

She perched herself on the edge of the chair. "Who?"

Julie's eyes widened dramatically. "He says he's your fiancé."

The blood left her face. There could only be one possibility. "Oh…okay," she said, trying not to have a reaction that Julie would see through and then question. "Tall, dark hair, handsome, gray eyes?"

Julie nodded. "Oh, yeah, that's him."

She managed a smile. "You should probably send him through."

"Okay, sure."

She disappeared, and barely seconds later the door opened and Daniel strode into the room. Mary-Jayne looked him over. He seemed so familiar and yet like such a stranger. He wore dark chinos and a creaseless pale blue shirt. Her heart skipped a beat. She'd never found any man as attractive as him. And doubted she ever would. And deep down, in that place she'd come to harbor all her feelings for him, she was happy to see him. More than happy. Right then, in that moment, she didn't feel alone.

She took a breath and met his gaze. "Fiancé?"

He shrugged loosely. "Got me in the room, didn't it?"

She didn't flinch. "What are you doing here? How did you—"

"Your sister told me I'd find you here."

She nodded. "So you're back?"

"I'm back." He moved across the room and sat beside her.

"How's your mother?"

He rested back in the seat a little. "Out of intensive care. She had major bypass surgery for two blocked arteries. She's doing okay now. She'll be in the hospital for another week, though. So why are you here? Checkup?"

Mary-Jayne tried to ignore how her insides fluttered from being so close to him. "I haven't been feeling well and—"

"You're sick?" he asked and jackknifed up straight. "What's wrong? Is it the babies?" he asked and reached out to touch her abdomen.

She flinched a little from his touch, and he noticed immediately because he snatched his hand away. "Just nausea again. And I've lost my appetite."

He frowned. "Why didn't you call me? I would have come back sooner."

She pressed her shoulders back. "You needed to be with your family. It was important for your parents."

"I need to be here for you," he said with emphasis. "That's important, too."

"I'm fine," she insisted, feeling like a fool for thinking his concern must mean he cared. Well, of course he cared. She was carrying his babies. But caring wasn't love. And love was all she'd accept.

He inspected her face with his smoky gaze. "You look pale."

"Stop fussing," she said and frowned. "I'm fine, like I said. Just tired and not all that hungry because of the nausea. But I'm sure it will pass soon."

The doctor entered then, and she was glad for the reprieve. Until Daniel started barking out questions about her fatigue, her blood pressure and the likelihood of risks associated with the antinausea medication the doctor suggested she take if the symptoms didn't abate soon. She gave Daniel a death stare—which he ignored completely.

The doctor, a mild-mannered man in his fifties, just nodded and answered the questions in a patient voice. When he said he was going to draw some blood, Daniel almost rocketed out of his seat.

"Why? What's wrong?" he asked. "If you think there's a risk to her health then I insist we—"

"It's okay," she assured him and grasped his arm. "It's just a blood test. Remember how I told you that my sisters had gestational diabetes? It's only precautionary."

She thought he might pass out when the nurse came

in and took the blood. To his credit he sat in the chair and watched the entire thing, unflinching. When it was over and the doctor passed her a note with some more vitamins he wanted her to take, Daniel got to his feet and wobbled a little. She grabbed his hand and held on. Once they were in the corridor she slowed down and looked up at him, smiling.

"My hero."

He frowned. "It's not funny."

"Sure it is. Big, strong fella like you afraid of a little old needle… Who would have thought it possible?"

"I'm not afraid of them," he said, and grasped her fingers, entwining them with his own until their palms were flat against each other. "I simply don't like them. And just because you aren't afraid of anything, Mary-Jayne, doesn't mean you should make fun of people who are."

She grinned, despite the fact she was shaking inside. Holding his hand, making jokes and simply *being* with him shouldn't have made her so happy. But it did. Even though in her heart she knew it wasn't real. When they were outside he looked around.

"Where's your car?"

She took a second and then pointed to the BMW parked a few spots from the entrance. "Over there."

He glanced at the car and then to her. "Good to see you're coming to your senses."

She shrugged. "I hate waste, that's all. The car seats arrived, too… That was very thoughtful of you."

He gave her a wry smile. "Oh, you know me, an arrogant, entitled jerk and all that."

Mary-Jayne blew out a flustered breath. "Okay…so you're not all bad."

"Not all bad?" he echoed. "That's quite a compliment."

"All right, I'm an ungrateful coward who has been determined to see the worst in you from the moment we met. Satisfied?"

He smiled. "I shouldn't have called you that. I was frustrated and annoyed and worried about my mom and took it out on you. I missed you, by the way, in case you were wondering."

She nodded as emotion tightened her throat. "I might have missed you a little, too."

"I should have taken you with me."

She ached to tell him that was what she'd hoped for. But she didn't say it. "Well, I'm glad she's going to get well."

"Me, too," he said, and grinned. "So, truce?"

She smiled back at him. "I guess. Where are you staying this time? The B and B?"

He shrugged. "I'm not sure. I didn't get the chance to talk to your sister about it. Once she told me where you were I bailed and headed here."

"Would you like to stay for dinner tonight?" she asked.

He nodded. "I would. But I'll cook."

She gave him a colorful glare. "Are you suggesting that my cooking is below par?"

"I'm saying your cooking is woeful." He grabbed her hand and squeezed her fingers gently. "I'll stop at the supermarket and get what we need, and then I'll see you at home."

Home...

It sounded so nice the way he said it. The fluttering she'd had in her belly since he'd first walked into the doctor's office increased tenfold. "Okay, see you a little later."

And then he kissed her. Softly, sweetly. Like a man kissed a woman he cared about. Mary-Jayne's leaping heart almost came through her chest. And if she'd had any doubts that she'd fallen in love with him, they quickly disappeared.

* * *

Daniel pulled up outside Mary-Jayne's house a little over an hour later. He'd been all wound up in knots earlier in the morning at the thought of seeing her again, but the moment he'd opened the door and spotted her in the chair in her doctor's office, hands clasped together and her beautiful hair framing her face, all the anxiety had disappeared. She hadn't looked unhappy to see him. She'd looked…relieved. As if she welcomed him there. As if she wanted him there. Which was more than he deserved after the insensitive words he'd left her with, right before he'd returned to Port Douglas to be with his family.

He'd had a lot of time to think about their relationship in the past week. Sitting in the hospital waiting room with his father had been incredibly humbling and at times fraught with emotion. Memories of his own wife had bombarded him. Of the night they'd brought Simone into emergency and he'd arrived too late. She was already unconscious. Already too far gone for the doctors to try to save her. And then he'd waited while they'd delivered their baby and hoped that a miracle would happen and their daughter would survive. But she hadn't, and he'd lost them both.

And while he'd waited at the hospital after Bernie's surgery he'd really talked to his dad for the first time since forever. About Bernie, about his own mother, about Simone and their baby. And about Mary-Jayne. Miles had been strong, more resilient than he'd imagined. He'd wanted to comfort his dad, and in the end it happened the other way around. He was ashamed to remember how he'd always considered his father as weak. As a kind man, but one driven by his emotions. Daniel had mistaken Miles's lack of ambition as a failing. But he was wrong. His father's ambitions were simply different from his own. And yet, in some ways, very much the same. Because Miles had endeavored to be a worthy, caring dad to his sons, and Daniel was determined to emulate that ambition. He wanted to be around his sons and watch them grow into children and then teens and finally into adulthood. He wanted to share their lives and be the best man he could be for them. And for Mary-Jayne, too. He cared about her too much to simply let her be only the mother of his sons. He wanted more. He *needed* more.

And since he'd screwed up big time in the courtship department, he had to go back to square one and start all over again. Like he should have done in the beginning, on that first time they'd met. Instead of making that stupid, off-the-cuff comment about how they'd end up in his condo at some point, he should have asked her out. He should have wooed her and courted her like she deserved. He should have gone to see her while she was in South Dakota at her friend's wedding and pursued her properly, and not asked her to meet him on his turf as though all he was interested in was getting her into bed. No wonder she'd turned him down flat. And since then they'd been at war—arguing and insulting one another. She'd called him arrogant and she was right. He'd come out fighting on every occasion and hadn't let her really get to know him at all.

She wants romance and all the trimmings…

Well, he could do that if it meant she would eventually agree to marry him.

He walked up the path and saw that her old car had a for-sale sign propped inside the back window. It pleased him, and by the time he reached her door he was grinning like a fool.

"Oh, hi," she said, breathless and beautiful in a white floaty dress that came to her knees and buttoned down the front. Her belly had popped out more and she looked so beautiful he couldn't do anything other than stare at her. "Come inside."

He crossed the threshold and walked down the hall. Her little dog came yapping around his ankles, and he made a point of patting the animal for a moment before he entered the kitchen.

"So what are you making?" she asked when he put the bags on the counter.

He started unpacking the bags. "Vegetarian tagine… Spiced carrots…amongst other things."

Her green eyes widened. "Moroccan?" She laughed and the sound rushed over his skin and through his blood. "My favorite."

"Want to help?"

She nodded and tossed an apron at him. "Only if you wear this."

He opened up the garment and read the words *Kiss The Cook*. "Really?"

She shrugged. "You never know your luck."

He popped it over his head. "I already feel lucky."

She came around the counter and methodically tied it around the back. "You mean because of your mother? You must be so relieved that she's out of danger."

"We all are," he said, thinking how he was imagining he'd get to kiss her again and that was why he felt lucky. "My dad couldn't bear to lose her."

"I can imagine," she said, and pulled a couple of cutting boards from a drawer. "I mean, he already lost your mother, so to lose Bernie, too… I mean, I know your mother was the love of his life because Solana told me… but he loves Bernie dearly, you can tell by the way he looks at her."

Daniel stopped what he was doing and stared at her. Her green eyes shimmered so brilliantly it was impossible to look anywhere else. The awareness between them amplified tenfold, and he fought the urge to reach for her and take her in his arms. Instead he met her gaze and spoke. "Just because he loved my mom didn't mean he had less of himself to give to someone else."

She inhaled sharply. "I...I suppose so... I mean, if he was willing to open his heart."

"He was," Daniel said quietly. "He did."

The meaning was not lost on either of them. "And they've had a good marriage, Mary-Jayne. They got married quickly and didn't really know one another very well. But it worked. It *can* work."

She started to nod and then stopped. "But they love one another."

"They do now. They got married, had children, made a life together. So perhaps it did start out a little unorthodox...but in the end it's how it plays out that's important."

She didn't look completely convinced and as much as he wanted to keep pushing, he backed off and returned his attention to the grocery bags on the counter. They chatted about mundane things, like her new car and the weather. She asked after his grandmother and was clearly delighted when he told her Solana wanted to come to Crystal Point for a visit.

"She'd like it here," he said when the food was cooking. He stood by the stove, stirring the pot. "Once Bernie is assured of a full recovery, I'm sure my grandmother will come."

"I'd like that," she said as she grabbed plates and cutlery and took them to the table. "Um...how long are you staying for this time?"

He kept stirring. "I'm not sure. I have to get back to

work at some point. I need to go to Phuket for the reopening once the renovation is complete in a couple of weeks."

She nodded, eyed the salad he'd made and sniffed the air appreciatively. "That smells good. You really do know how to cook."

He grinned. "Told you," he said, and then more seriously, "There's a lot you don't know about me, Mary-Jayne. But I'd like to change that. You said we should take some time and you were right. But I don't want to pressure you. So if you want slow, then we'll go slow."

She stopped what she was doing and looked at him. "Honestly, I don't know what I want."

"How about you take some time to figure it out?"

"You said we didn't have time."

He shrugged loosely. "I was mad at you when I said that. We have time."

She nodded a little and took a couple of sodas out of the fridge. "I don't have any of that imported beer you like," she said, and placed the cans on the counter. "But I can get some."

"This is fine," he said, and cranked both lids. "I don't drink much."

They ate a leisurely dinner and she entertained him with stories of her youth, and when she was laughing hard and out of breath he did the same. It was interesting to learn they had both been rebellious as children and teenagers.

"I guess you had to rein in all that when you took over the company from your grandfather? Can't have a respectable CEO wreaking havoc, right?" she asked and laughed.

Daniel grinned. "I guess not. Although I wasn't quite the wayward teen that you were. No tattoos...so I was nowhere near as hardcore as you."

She laughed again. "That's only because you're scared of needles."

"No need to rub it in. I'm well aware of my weakness."

She rested her elbows on the table and sighed. "You don't have a weak bone in your body."

He met her gaze. "I have a weakness for you."

"That's not weakness," she said. "That's desire. Attraction. Lust."

Daniel pushed his plate aside. "Maybe it's more than that."

"More?"

He reached across the table and grasped her hand. "I care about you."

"Because I'm having your babies," she said, and went to move her hand.

Daniel's grip tightened. "That's only part of it."

She looked at him, her eyes suddenly all suspicious as she pulled her hand free. "What are you saying?"

He met her gaze. "Can't you guess?"

"I don't understand. Are you saying that you're… That you have feelings for me…?"

"Yes," he replied. "That's precisely what I'm saying."

Her gaze widened. "Are you saying that…that you're in love with me?"

Daniel nodded. That was exactly what he was saying. He *did* love her. The empty feeling he had inside when he was away from her was love. That was why he couldn't wait to return to Crystal Point. He wanted her. He craved her and ached thinking about it. She was the mother of his babies. And she was vivacious and fun and as sexy as anything.

He'd loved Simone. It had made sense. Loving Mary-Jayne made no sense at all. And yet, in the past few days it had become a clear and undeniable truth.

"Would it be so hard to believe?"

"Yes. Impossible," she said with a scowl and pushed the chair back. "I think you should leave."

Daniel got to his feet the same time she did. "Why are you angry?"

She glared at him. "Because you're lying to me. Because you'll say and do anything to get what you want and all of a sudden you seem to think that making some big statement about love will make me change my mind about getting married."

"I haven't mentioned marriage," he reminded her.

"It's on the agenda, though, right?"

"Eventually," he replied. "That's generally the result of a relationship between two people who fall in love."

"But *two* people haven't fallen in love."

Right. So she didn't love him. Didn't care. That was plain enough. His heart sank. Maybe she would… someday? If he tried hard enough to earn that love.

"We could try to make this work."

"Like your parents did?" she asked. "Maybe it worked for them because they actually liked one another to start with. I'll bet they didn't call one another names and look for the worst in each other."

Daniel expelled an impatient breath. "I apologized for what I said the last time I was here."

"You mean when you called me a fraud who had locked herself in a cage?" she enquired, brows up, temper on alert. "Don't be… You were right. I have been in a cage, Daniel. But as of this moment I'm out of it. And do you know what…I'm not going to trade one cage for another. Because being married to you would put me right back inside."

"I don't want to keep you caged, Mary-Jayne. I love your spirit and your—"

"Can you hear yourself? Three weeks ago you were calling me a flake and a gold digger and now you've miraculously fallen in love with me. I'm not stupid. I know when I'm being played. So you can come here with your sexy smile and make dinner and act all interested in my childhood and this town, but it doesn't change one undeniable fact—you want me to marry you because it suits you and your arrogant assumption that you can simply take whatever you want. Well, you can't take me."

He took a step toward her, but she moved backward. "What do I have to say to convince you that I'm serious about my feelings for you?"

"Say?" she echoed. "Nothing. Words are empty. It's actions that matter."

He waved an arm. "I'm here, aren't I? I came back. I feel as if I've been pursuing you for months."

"You first chased me because you wanted to get me into bed," she said hotly. "And now you're chasing me because you want your sons."

"I'm chasing you because I love you."

There… It was out on the table…for her and her alone.

She laughed, but it sounded hollow. "You're chasing me because you think it's a means to an end. Well, forget it. What I want for my life I can't get from you."

Pain ripped through his chest. "How do you know that? Just tell me what you want."

"I've told you in half a dozen ways. I want a man who carries me here," she said and put her hand against her breast. "In his heart. Over his heart. On his heart. Forever. And it might sound sentimental and foolish to you, but I don't care. I think I really know that for the first time in my life. And I have you to thank for it. You've shown me what I want…and what I don't."

"And what you don't want…that's me?" he asked, aching through to his bones.

"Yes," she said quietly. "Exactly."

He moved closer and grasped her shoulders, gripping her firmly. And then he kissed her. Long and hot and loaded with pain and guilt and resentment. When he was done he lifted his head and stared down into her face. She was breathing hard and her eyes were filled with confusion and rage.

He ran a possessive hand down her shoulder and breast and then down to her belly. "Nothing will change the fact that a part of me is growing inside you. Love me or hate me, we're bound together. And we always will be."

Chapter Twelve

The following Saturday, it was her niece's second birthday and Mary-Jayne didn't have the strength of mind to go, or to excuse herself. She'd exiled herself in her little house for five days, working on new pieces, revamping her website, thinking of her work, her babies and little else. She didn't spare a thought for Daniel. Not one. Not a single, solitary thought.

Big, fat liar...

He was in her dreams. She couldn't keep him out.

He'd said he loved her. It should have made her day. It should have...but didn't. It only made her angry. And achingly sad.

He hadn't contacted her. She knew from Evie that he wasn't staying at the B and B, and could only assume that he was at a hotel somewhere in Bellandale. It suited her just fine. She didn't want to see him. Not yet. She was still reeling from his declaration of love. Still hating him for it. And still loving him more than she had imagined she could ever love anyone.

Jerk...

Plus, her belly was getting bigger every day and now she waddled rather than walked. She went shopping for baby clothes with her sisters and cried all the way home because she felt as though part of her was missing. She considered buying furniture for the nursery and then put the idea on hold. The spare room needed significant work. In fact, she wondered how she was supposed to raise two babies in such a small house. Once she put two cribs, a change table and a cupboard in the spare room there wouldn't be much space for anything else. What she needed was a bigger house. With a large yard. With a swing set that the twins would be able to play on when they were old enough.

She felt a sense of loneliness so acute it physically pained her. And nothing abated it. Not her parents or her sisters. Not talking to her long-distance friends or cuddling with her dog on the lounge. Only her babies growing peacefully in her belly gave her comfort.

On the afternoon of the party she laid her dress on the bed, flicked off her flip-flops and started getting ready. The dress was a maternity smock in bright colored silk that tied in a knot at her nape, and the outrageously red sandals were low heeled and comfortable. Or at least they would have been, had she been able to get them on. Her body simply wouldn't bend like it used to. She twisted and turned herself inside out and still the darn sandals wouldn't clasp.

Frustration crept over her skin as she kept trying. And failing. Fifteen minutes later and she was ready to toss the shoes at the wall. Until the tears came. Great racking sobs that made her chest hurt. After a few minutes she couldn't actually remember why she was crying. Which only made her more emotional. More fraught. More miserable.

She considered calling Evie and then quickly changed her mind. Her sister had enough to do organizing the party. And Grace had a newborn and would be too busy. She thought about calling her brother, but once he saw she'd been crying he'd be all concerned and want to know why she was upset and then act all macho when she told him how much she hated and loved Daniel. He'd probably want to go and punch him in the nose. It would serve Daniel right, too. Although she was pretty sure he'd throw a punch as good as he got.

Not that she wanted to see him hurt. That was the last thing she wanted.

She sat on the edge of the bed and cried some more. And thought about how ridiculously she was behaving. And then cried again. She gave the shoes another try and gave up when her aching back and swollen feet wouldn't do what she wanted.

She flopped back on the bed and grabbed her phone. The battery signal beeped. She'd forgotten to charge it overnight. Typical. She flicked through the numbers and reached the one she wanted. After a few unanswered rings it went straight to message service.

"It's me," she said, and hiccupped. "Can you come over?"

Then she buried her head in the pillow and sobbed.

Daniel had been in the shower when Mary-Jayne called. He tried to call her back several times but it went to message. Unable to reach her back, he was dressed and out the door of his hotel in about two minutes flat. He drove to Crystal Point as speedily as he could without breaking the law. Pulling up outside her house, he jumped out and raced to the front door. No one answered when he knocked. He heard the little dog barking behind the door and panic set in behind his ribs. What if she was hurt? Perhaps she'd fallen over trying to lift something heavy? Or worse. He rattled the door but it was locked, and then saw that the front window was open. He pushed the screen in and climbed through, not caring if the neighbors thought he was an intruder. They could call the cops for all he cared. He just needed to know she was safe.

Once he was in the living room he called her name. Still nothing.

He got to her bedroom door and stilled in his tracks. She was on the bed, curled up.

He'd never moved so fast in his life. He was beside the bed in seconds. He said her name softly and touched her bare shoulder. Her red-rimmed eyes flicked open.

"Hey," he said and stroked her cheek. "What's wrong?"

She shook her head. "Nothing."

"You left a message on my cell."

"I know," she whispered. "I didn't know who else to call. And then you didn't call back and then my phone went dead and..." Her voice trailed off.

Daniel's stomach churned. He grasped her shoulders. "Mary-Jayne, what's wrong? Are you sick? Is it the babies?"

"I'm not sick," she said. "I'm fine. The babies are fine."

She didn't look fine. She looked as if she'd been crying for a week. But she'd called him. She'd reached out when he'd feared she never would. It was enough to give him hope. To make him believe that she did care. "You've been crying?"

She nodded as tears welled in her eyes. She hiccupped. "I couldn't..."

"You couldn't what?" he prompted.

"I couldn't get my shoes on!"

And then she sobbed. Racking, shuddering sobs that reached him deep down. He folded her in his arms and held her gently. "It's okay, darling," he assured her.

"I'm as fat as a house."

"You're beautiful."

"I'm not," she cried, tears running down her face again. "And my ankles are so swollen that my shoes don't fit. I tried to put them on but my belly got in the way."

Daniel relaxed his grip and reached for her chin. He tilted her head back. "Would you like me to put them on for you?"

She nodded, and he moved off the bed and found her shoes by the wall. He crouched by the bed and reached for her legs. He slipped the shoes on and strapped each sandal at the ankle. "See...they fit just fine," he said, and ran a palm down her smooth calf.

She hiccupped and some fire returned to her eyes. "Why are you being nice to me?"

"That's my job," he said, and sat beside her. "Isn't that why you called me?"

She shrugged helplessly. "I just called a number... Any number..."

He grasped her chin again and made her look at him. "You called *me* because you wanted me here."

She sighed. "I don't know why. Probably because I was dreaming about you and—"

"Good," he said, feeling possessive and frustrated. "I want you to dream about me. I ache to be in your dreams, Mary-Jayne," he rasped, and pulled her close. "I won't be kept out of them."

"I couldn't keep you out if I tried," she admitted, and then relaxed against him, despite her better judgment, he suspected. "I don't know what's wrong with me. I feel so—"

"You're pregnant," he said, and gently spread a hand over her stomach. "Your hormones are running riot. Don't beat yourself up about being emotional. It's perfectly normal."

Her eyes flashed. "Aren't you Mr. Sensitive all of a sudden?"

Daniel's mouth curled at the edges. "With you, absolutely."

"Only to get what you want," she said and sniffed. "Now who's the fraud?"

He tilted her chin again and inched his mouth closer to hers. "I really did screw up, didn't I, for you to have such a low opinion of me? I generally think of myself as a good sort of person, Mary-Jayne... Give me half a chance and you might, too."

She harrumphed. "Manipulative jerk," she whispered, but then moved her lips closer.

He kissed her gently. "I'm not manipulating you. I love you."

She moaned. "Don't say things you don't mean."

Daniel swept her hair back from her face. "I mean it. And I'll tell you every day for the rest of my life."

"I won't listen," she retorted, and tried to evade his mouth. "And one day I'll find someone who really does—"

"Don't do that," he said painfully, cutting through her words. "That would just about break me."

"I'll do what I want," she said and pulled back. "You don't own me."

Daniel held her still. "Oh, darling...I do. And you own me. You've owned me since the first time I saw you in that store window. And I'm not going anywhere, Mary-Jayne."

"You'll have to at some point," she remarked, all eyes

and fiery beauty in her stare. "You don't live here. You live in San Francisco. Then I'll be free of you."

"We'll never be free of one another. That's why you called me today. Admit it," he said, firmer this time. "You could have called any one of half a dozen people and they all would have been here in a matter of minutes. But you didn't," he reminded her. "You called me."

"It was the first number I pressed. It was random, and then my battery died. Don't read anything into it."

He chuckled, delighted and spurred on by her reticence. "Admit it… You're in love with me."

"I am not!" she denied, and pulled herself from his arms. "I don't love you. I never will. I'd have to be stark raving mad to fall in love with you. And you're only saying all this to get what you want."

"I am? Really?" He stood up and propped his hands on his hips. "Have I asked for anything? I've given you space. I've left you alone. I've holed myself up in a damn hotel room for a week, even though all I want to do is be here with you every day and hold you in my arms every night. I haven't sent you flowers or bought anything for the babies even though I want to because I know you'd accuse me of trying to manipulate you. I haven't gone to see your parents and explain to them what you mean to me and assure them I'll do whatever is in my power to do to make you happy even though my instincts tell me I should. I'm *trying*, Mary-Jayne… I'm trying to do this your way. Just… just try to meet me in the middle somewhere, okay?" He placed a hand over his chest. "Because this is killing me."

"So he's still in town?"

Mary-Jayne looked at Evie. Her sisters had come over to cheer her up and bring her some gifts for the babies. The tiny pair of matching baseball caps Grace gave her was so incredibly cute that she cried a little. Which seemed to have become a habit of hers in the past few weeks.

Crying… Ugh!

She had become a sentimental sap.

"I guess so."

"You've seen him?" Grace asked.

"Not for a week. Why?"

Her sisters both shrugged and smiled. It was Evie who spoke next. "It's only that…well… In the past few days he's come to see all of us and told us…"

"Told you all what?" Mary-Jayne asked, pushing up on her seat.

"That he's in love with you," Grace supplied. "That he wants to marry you."

Mary-Jayne saw red. "That no-good, sneaky—"

"It's kinda romantic," Evie said and grinned.

"It's *not* romantic," Mary-Jayne said hotly. "It's deceitful and underhanded. And do you know what else he did? He bought all this baby stuff and had it delivered. The garage is full of boxes and toys and baby furniture and—"

"Oh, how awful for you," Evie said and grinned. "Such a terrible man."

Mary-Jayne scowled. "You're on his side, then?"

"We're on your side," Grace said and smiled gently. "You seem unhappy, that's all."

"I'll be happier when he's gone."

"I don't think he's going anywhere any time soon," Evie said. "He told Scott he's going to buy a house here."

The color bled from her face. "I don't believe it. He wouldn't. He's got a business to run and he can't do that from here."

"Maybe he's found something more important than business," Grace said pointedly.

"Yeah—his heirs. He wants his children. Don't be blinded by the good looks and money."

"We could say the same thing to you."

Mary-Jayne stilled. Her sister's words resonated loud and clear. Was that how she appeared—as a judgmental and narrow-minded snob—and exactly what she'd accused him of being?

She'd resented his money and success without good reason. On one hand, she recognized his honesty and integrity. And yet, when he'd told her the very thing she wanted to hear, she hadn't believed him. She'd accused him of trying to manipulate and confuse her. But what proof did she have that he'd ever done that? None. He hadn't manipulated her to get her into bed. Their attraction had been hot and intense from the start. Not one-sided. She'd craved him and he'd made it abundantly clear that he wanted her. And then she'd convinced herself he was all bad, all arrogance and self-entitlement.

To protect herself.

Because he was nothing like any man she'd previously dated she regarded him as an aberration…someone to avoid…someone to battle. And she had at every opportunity. She'd fought and insulted and pushed him away time and time again. Because loving Daniel meant she would be redefined. He was rich and successful and all that she had professed to loathe. He'd asked her to marry him. He'd said he loved her. And still she let her prejudice blind her.

His parting words a week earlier still echoed in her mind. *This is killing me.* Real pain. Real anguish. And she'd done that to him. She'd hurt him. She'd hurt the one person she loved most in the world. She felt the shame of it through to her bones. He'd asked her to meet him in the middle.

But she could do better than that.

"You look as though the proverbial penny just dropped," Evie said.

Both her sisters were staring at her. "I think it just did. He asked me to marry him. He said he was in love with me."

"That's what he told us, too."

Tears filled her eyes. "I never imagined that I'd fall in love with someone like him. I thought that one day I'd meet someone like myself... Someone who wasn't so... conventional, if you know what I mean."

Evie came and sat beside her and grabbed her hand. "You know, just because he's not a bohemian poet, it doesn't make him wrong for you. If anyone had told me a few years ago that I would fall in love with a man nearly ten years younger than me I wouldn't have believed them."

"Same here," Grace said, and sat on the other side. "I never intended to fall in love with our brother's best friend. But I did. When you love, you simply love. That's the thing that's important, M.J. Not how successful or wealthy he is."

"He's a good man," Evie said quietly. "Give him a chance to prove it."

"What if he's changed his mind?" she asked, thinking of the terrible way they'd parted and how she'd told him she didn't love him and never would. "I said some pretty awful things to him the last time we were together. What if he doesn't want to see me?"

"You need a plan," Grace suggested.

"Leave that to me," Evie said, and she grabbed her phone from her bag.

Three hours later Mary-Jayne was at the B and B, sitting in the garden on a bench by the wishing well. She smoothed down the skirt on her white dress and then fluffed her hair. She'd always loved this spot. Through the vine-covered hedge she saw a car pull up to the curb.

Minutes later he was walking up the path, all purposeful and tight limbed. He wore jeans and a polo shirt and looked so good it stole her breath. When he spotted her he came to a halt midstride.

"Hi," she said, and smiled.

His expression was unreadable. "I didn't expect you to be here."

"I didn't expect me to be here up until a couple of hours ago."

His gaze narrowed. "Are you all right? No problems with the babies?"

She touched her abdomen gently. "No… Everything is fine. I feel good. The nausea is gone for the moment. I haven't seen you for a while… Where have you been?"

"I was under the impression you had no interest in seeing me." He took a step closer. "I had a call from your sister. Is she here?"

"No…just me."

His brows drew together. "Subterfuge?"

"Kind of," she admitted. "I wasn't sure if *you'd* see *me* after the last time."

"If you had called me, I would be here. Always. I've told you that before. What's this about, Mary-Jayne?"

He looked so good. So familiar. And she ached to be in his arms. "I'm sorry about what I said the last time we were together."

"Which part? When you said you didn't love me and never would?" he quizzed.

She nodded. "All of it. You came over to help me and I was thoughtless and ungrateful."

"Yes, you were."

She ignored a hot niggle of impatience that crept up her spine. "I hear you're looking at real estate?"

He shrugged loosely. "Do you disapprove of that, as well?"

God, he was impossible. "Of course not. I understand that you'll want to be close to the babies when they are born."

He nodded. "So anything else?"

Mary-Jayne sighed and grabbed the shopping bag by the bench. She stood up and extracted the two tiny baseballs caps. "I thought you might like these. They're cute, don't you think?"

He took the caps and examined them. "Cute. Yes. Is that it? You got me here to give me a couple of baseball caps?"

"I wanted to see you."

"Why now? Nothing's changed."

"Everything's changed."

His mouth flattened. "What?"

Her cheeks grew hotter by the second. "Me. This. Us. A week ago you told me you loved me."

"I know what I said," he shot back. "I also know what you said."

She took a breath. "Shall we go inside? I'd like to talk to you."

"So when you want to talk, we talk? Is that how this plays out? I don't seem to be able to get it right with you, do I?"

Mary-Jayne let her impatience rise up. "I'm going inside. You can stay out here in the garden and sulk if you want to."

She turned on her heels and walked up to the house as quickly as she could. He was about four steps behind her. Once she was through the French doors and in the living room she spun around.

He was barely a foot away, chest heaving. "Sulk?"

She shrugged. "Sure. Isn't that what you've been doing

this week? So I said something mean and unkind. I'm sorry. But you said yourself that I'm running on hormones because of my pregnancy. I should think it's about time you started making allowances for that."

"Allowances," he echoed incredulously. "Are you serious? I've done nothing *but* make allowances since the moment you told me you were pregnant. Nothing I do is right. Nothing I say makes any difference. You trust me, you don't. You need me, you don't. You want me, you don't. Which is it? I'm so damned confused I can barely think straight. I'm neglecting my business, my family, my friends…everything, because I'm so caught up in this *thing* I have with you."

Mary-Jayne watched him, fascinated by the heat and fire in his words. There was so much passion in him. She'd been so wrong, thinking he was some sort of cold fish who didn't feel deeply. He did. He just didn't show that side of himself to the world.

"I do trust you," she said, and moved toward him. "And I do need you," she said, and touched his chest. When he winced and stepped back she was immediately concerned. "What's wrong? Are you in pain? Have you had another migraine?"

"No. Stop this, Mary-Jayne. Tell me what I'm doing here and—"

"I'm trying," she said frantically. "But I need to know if you meant what you said."

He frowned. "What I said?"

"You…you said you loved me," she said, suddenly breathless. "Did you mean it?"

"Do I strike you as someone who says things I don't mean?"

"No," she replied, and blinked back the tears in her eyes. "It's just that…what you said about me being in a cage and about how things would have been different from the start if you hadn't been…well…*you*. If you'd been a dreadlocked, unemployed musician, I wouldn't have been so determined to keep my distance. Because that's what I thought I wanted. What I knew, if that makes sense. All that stuff you said, you were right." She touched his arm, gripped tightly and felt his muscles hard beneath her palm. "For as long as I can remember I've craved freedom and independence. But now I feel as if I've lived a life that isn't authentic. I left home at seventeen, but only moved three streets away from my parents. Some independence, huh? So you're right, I'm a fraud. I'm tied to this little town. I'm not a free spirit at all." She took a breath, not caring about the tears on her cheeks. "And you…you saw through that and through me. What you said about marriage makes sense. Each one starts out differently, like your dad and Bernie. And if this…" she said, and touched her stomach gently. "If this is what we start with, just these two precious babies bringing us together, then that's okay. Because if you do want me, and if you do love me, even a little bit, that will be enough."

He stared at her, holding her gaze captive. "But it's not enough for me, Mary-Jayne."

She froze. "I don't understand…"

"We both deserve more than some half-baked attempt at a relationship."

"But you said you wanted to get married and be a family," she reminded him, crumbling inside.

"I do," he said, and grabbed her hand. "But I want *all* of you, every beautiful, spirited, intoxicating piece. I had a good marriage once. But I want more than that this time. I don't want to leave at six in the morning and arrive home at eight. I don't want to eat out five nights out of seven because work always comes first. I don't want to miss family gatherings because I'm too busy landing some deal or flying from one country to the next. I've lived that life and I was never truly happy. I want us to raise our children together, like *they* deserve."

Tears wet her cheeks again. "I want that, too. You really... You really do love me?"

He grasped her chin and looked directly into her eyes. "I really do love you, Mary-Jayne. And I know they're only words, but they are what I feel."

"Words are enough," she said, happiness surging through her blood. "I love you, too."

"Words will never be enough," he said, and kissed her gently. "Which is why I did this."

"What?" she muttered against his mouth.

"This," he said, and stepped back a little. He tugged at the collar of his T-shirt and showed her what he meant.

Her name, in small but strikingly dark scrolled script, was now written on the left side of his chest. The ink was new and still healing, but she could see through all that to the beauty of what he had done.

"You got a tattoo?" she asked, crying. "I can't believe you did that. The needles... You hate needles."

He shrugged one shoulder. "I love you more than I hate needles." He grasped her hand and held it against his chest. "In my heart. Over my heart. On my heart. Forever."

They were the most beautiful words she had ever heard.

She reached up and touched his face. "I'm so much in love with you, Daniel. And I'm sorry I kept pushing you away."

He held her in his arms. "You had more sense than me. We needed to get to know one another. You knew that. I just arrogantly thought I knew how to fix things."

"At least you wanted to try," she said, and settled against

his shoulder. "I've been fighting this and you since the very beginning."

"I know," he said, and laughter rumbled in his chest. "You took off as if your feet were on fire after Solana's birthday party."

"I was in shock," she admitted. "I'd never had an experience like that before."

"Me, either," he said. "Making love with you is like nothing on earth." He kissed her nape. "But you never have to run from me again, Mary-Jayne."

"I promise I won't."

Seconds later they were settled on one of the sofas and he wrapped her in his arms. "There's something about you that draws me. You have this incredible energy…a life force all your own. I love that about you. And I love that our sons are going to have that, too."

She sighed, happy and content and so in love her head was spinning. "So where are we going to live? Here or San Francisco?"

He reached for her chin and tilted her face toward his own. "Darling, do you think I would ever ask you to leave here? This is your home."

"But San Francisco is *your* home."

"It's where I live," he said and kissed her gently. "I don't think I've ever considered anywhere as really home. Until now. Even when I was married to Simone and we had our apartment, most times it was simply a place to sleep."

She couldn't believe what he was saying. "Do you mean we can stay here permanently? I was imagining we'd do some time here and some over there."

He shook his head. "Your family is here. Your roots are here. And I like this town and I want to raise our sons here. If they turn out half as good as you then I'll be a happy man."

"But your business? How can you—"

"I need to let go a little," he admitted. "I need to trust Blake and Caleb more. They have just as must invested in Anderson's as I do… I think it's about time I lessened the reins. You see," he said, and grinned, "I'm learning to not be so much of a control freak."

"Don't change too much," she said, and pressed against him. "I like you just as you are."

He kissed her, long and sweet, and when he finally lifted his head he stared into her eyes. "You know something…I think it's time I proposed properly."

"What a great idea," she said, and laughed, so happy she thought she might burst.

Daniel grabbed her hand and brought it to his lips. "Mary-Jayne, I'm lost without you… Marry me?"

"Yes," she said, laughing, crying and loving him more than she had believed possible. "Absolutely, positively, yes!"

Epilogue

Three and a half months later...

At seven o'clock at night on a Monday, Mary-Jayne's water broke. Daniel was walking into the bedroom when she hovered in the bathroom doorway.

"What is it?" he asked immediately.

She grimaced. "It's time."

Panic flittered across his face. "You're in labor?"

"Yep," she said, and grinned.

He strode toward her. "But there's still nearly three weeks to go."

"We were told I'd probably go into labor early," she said and touched his arm. "Stop worrying."

"I'm not worried," he assured her. "How do you feel?"

"Better now I know what the niggling backache I had all day is about."

"You were in pain and you didn't tell—"

"Stop worrying," she said again, and ushered him out the doorway. "I'm fine." She rubbed her huge belly. "We're fine. Is my bag still in the car?"

He'd insisted they have her baby bag ready for when she went into labor. He'd also insisted on a trial run in the car and had organized Evie to be the backup driver just in case he wasn't around when the time came. Of course she knew that was never going to happen.

In the past few months so much had changed. Since their wedding two months earlier, he'd taken some much-needed time off from Anderson's. His brother Blake had taken on more global accountability, and general managers had been put in place in some of the resorts to alleviate the workload. Caleb was still recovering from an unexpected and serious boating accident and had been recuperating from his busted leg with Miles and Bernie for the past eight weeks. It had been a fraught time for the entire family, but since Bernie's heart attack, the family had become closer and they all rallied around to ensure Caleb had all the support he needed.

Despite all that, she knew Daniel had never been happier. She still marveled at how well he'd adjusted to not having such tight control over the company anymore. He'd learned to trust his brothers and share the responsibility. Of course, with Caleb out of action for a while, there were times when he was needed to fly back to San Francisco or one of the other locations, but he was never gone for more than a few days. And Mary-Jayne didn't mind.

He'd bought a house in Crystal Point just four doors down from Dunn Inn, and she loved the big low-set brick-and-tile home with its floating timber floors, racked ceilings, wide doorways and sprawling front deck that offered an incredible view of the ocean. She surprised herself by how much fun she had purchasing new furnishings. He was generous to a fault, and they had a wonderful time working on the nursery and getting the room ready for the babies.

Their relationship was amazing. *He* was amazing, and she'd never been happier.

The drive to the hospital took twenty minutes, and another five to find a vacant car space and get her into the emergency ward. She was quickly transported to maternity, and by the time she was settled in a room her contractions were coming thick and fast.

It was an arduous twelve hours later that her doctor recommended a caesarean birth. Mary-Jayne cried a little, and then agreed to do what best for their babes. William and Flynn Anderson were born a minute apart, both pink and screaming and perfect in every way.

Still groggy from the surgery, it was another few hours before she had a chance to nurse her sons. Daniel remained by her side, strong and resilient and giving her every ounce of support she needed. And when he held their sons for the first time, there were tears in his eyes. And he didn't seem to care one bit. Watching him, seeing the emotion and pure love in his expression made her fall in love with him even more.

"They really are beautiful," she remarked as William settled against her breast to nurse and Daniel sat in the chair by her bed and held Flynn against his chest.

Daniel looked at his son, marveling at the perfect beauty in the little boy's face, and smiled. When he returned his gaze to his wife he saw she was watching him. "You did an amazing job, Mrs. Anderson."

She smiled. "You, too. But then again, you do everything well, and I knew this wouldn't be any different."

Daniel reached for her hand and rubbed her fingers. "You know, we're going to have to start letting the masses in at some point. Your sisters are keen to spend some time with you. And Solana has been circling the waiting area with your parents for the past two hours. She's very excited about meeting her great-grandsons."

"I know," she said, and sighed. "I just selfishly want our babies and you to myself for as long as I can."

Daniel stood and gently placed their sleeping son into his mother's arm, watching, fascinated, as she held them both. It was the most beautiful thing he had ever seen. His wife. His sons. They were a gift more precious than anything he could have ever imagined. Love, the purest and most intense he'd ever experienced, surged through his blood.

"I love you," he said, and bent down to kiss her sweet mouth. "And, my darling, you have me to yourself for the rest of our lives."

Tears welled in her beautiful green eyes. "I never intended to love anyone this much, you know," she said, and batted her lashes. "I never thought it was possible."

"Neither did I."

"It's actually all Audrey and Caleb's doing," she said, beaming. "If they didn't have such a dysfunctional relationship we would never have met."

"Oh, I don't know about that," he said, and chuckled. "Audrey would have returned to Crystal Point eventually and Caleb would have eventually followed her, and since my brother is a hothead without any sense I would have had to come here and sort things out. So I'm pretty sure our paths would have crossed."

Mary-Jayne glanced at the twins. "Maybe you're right. Now they're here I can't imagine a world without these two in it." She looked up and smiled gently. "Speaking of Caleb and Audrey...any news?"

Daniel shrugged. "You know Caleb. He's refusing to get the marriage annulled."

They had all been shocked to learn that Caleb and Audrey were in fact married, and had been just a month after they'd met.

She sighed. "Well, I'm glad we don't have all that drama in our relationship."

Daniel smiled, remembering their own fraught beginnings. "Nah...we were a piece of cake."

She laughed, and the lovely sound echoed around the room.

"Shall I let them in?" he asked, kissing her again.

"You bet."

And he was, he realized as he opened the door, just about the happiest man on the planet. Because he had Mary-Jayne's love and their beautiful sons. He truly did have it all.

* * * * *

FROM PARADISE...
TO PREGNANT!

KANDY SHEPHERD

To my husband James for the trip to Bali
and the answers to my endless questions
about 'The Beautiful Game'.

CHAPTER ONE

ZOE SUMMERS KNEW she wasn't beautiful. The evidence of her mirror proved that. *Plain* was the label she'd been tagged with from an early age. She wasn't *ugly*—in fact ugly could be interesting. It was just that her particular combination of unruly black hair, angular face, regulation brown eyes and a nose with a slight bump in the middle added up to pass-under-the-radar plain.

After a particularly harrowing time in her life, spent at the basement level of the high school pecking order, she'd decided to do something about her unremarkable looks. Not a makeover, as such—rather, she'd aimed to make the best of herself and establish her own style. Now, at the age of twenty-seven, Zoe Summers was known as striking, stylish and smart. She couldn't ask for more than that.

As a consequence of her devotion to good grooming she'd spent some time every day of her vacation on the beautiful tropical island of Bali in the spa of her luxury villa hotel.

Back home, fitting in beauty treatments around running her own accountancy and taxation business could be problematic for a self-confessed workaholic. Here, a programme that included facials, exfoliation, waxing, manicure and pedicure fitted right in with her mission to relax and replenish. And all for less than half the price of what it would cost in Sydney.

Late on the fourth and final afternoon of her vacation, she lay face-down on a massage table in the spa and let the masseuse work her skilled magic on the tight knots of tension in her shoulders. *Bliss.*

As she breathed in the soothing scents of sandalwood, frangipani and lemongrass her thoughts started to drift. She diverted them from anything to do with her business and the decisions she still had to make. Or from the very real concern that her cat had gone on hunger strike at the cat boarding place.

Instead she pondered how soon after her massage she could take a languorous swim in the cool turquoise waters of the hotel's lagoon pool. What to choose for dinner at one of the many restaurants in Seminyak. Should she buy that lovely batik print sundress in the nearby boutique? Or the bikini? Or both? The price tags bore an astonishing number of Indonesian rupiah, but in Australian dollars they were as cheap as chips.

She sighed a deep sigh of contentment and relaxed into that delicious state somewhere between consciousness and sleep.

When the massage table began to vibrate she thought at first, through her blissed-out brain, that it was part of the treatment. But then the windows rattled and the glass bottles of scented oils and lotions started to jiggle and clank. When the bottles crashed to the stone floor she jumped up from the table in alarm.

She knew before her masseuse's cry of, 'Earthquake!' what was happening.

It was an effort to stay on her feet when the floor moved beneath them like the deck of a boat on choppy waters. No use trying to hold on to the walls, because they seemed to flex inward. The masseuse darted under the protection of the wooden table. Zoe did the same.

She cowered with her knees scrunched up to her chest, heart pounding, swallowing against a great lump of fear, her hand gripping tightly to the girl's—she didn't know who'd grabbed whose hand first, but she was grateful for the comfort. The room shuddered around them for what seemed like for ever but was probably seconds, stopped, then shuddered again.

Finally everything went still. Cautiously, Zoe inched out from under the table. She nearly gagged on the combined scent of spilled aromatherapy oils. When the masseuse told her they had to head to an emergency meeting point she nodded, too choked with anxiety to actually reply.

She wanted to get out into the open ASAP. But she was naked—save for the flimsy paper panties she'd donned for the massage to protect her modesty—and her clothes and sandals were in an inaccessible closet. She snatched up the white towel that had covered her on the massage table and with clumsy, trembling fingers wrapped it around her, tucking it in as securely as she could. In bare feet, she picked her way around the shards of broken bottles on the floor, grabbed her handbag and followed the masseuse outside.

Still reeling with shock, Zoe hurried along the tropical plant-lined pathway that led from the spa to the main building and pool area of the hotel. To her intense relief there didn't appear to be a lot of damage. But her fear didn't dissipate. Once before disaster had struck from nowhere, changing her life for ever. Who knew what she could expect here?

During her stay she hadn't taken much notice of the other guests. Each villa was completely private, with high walls around it and its own lap pool. Now she was surprised at the number of people gathered for an emergency briefing in the open courtyard outside the reception area. She was the only one in the crowd to be clad in just a towel, but other people were in swimwear or wearing assorted hastily donned garments.

Could she get to her room? If she was going to die she didn't want it to be in a white standard-issue hotel towel.

The other guests were terrified too. She could see it in their grim faces, hear their concern in the murmur of conversation in several different languages.

The hotel manager took the floor to reassure them that the tremor was low on the Richter Scale of seismic activity. He told his guests that electricity had been knocked out but that the hotel emergency generators would soon kick in and it would be business as usual. There was no need to panic.

But what if there were aftershocks?

The manager's reassuring words did little to make Zoe's rapid heartbeat subside or her hands less clammy. It was time to get out of here, before any other disaster might strike. She'd seen the sights. She'd wound down. She'd been pampered from head to toe. Now she was anxious to get home.

She was just about to ask the manager if the airport was open when a man spoke from several rows of people behind her.

'Is there a tsunami warning?' he asked.

The word 'tsunami' was enough to strike renewed fear into Zoe's heart. But it wasn't the thought of an imminent tidal wave that kick-started her heartbeat into overdrive, it was the man's voice. Deep, confident, immediately familiar.

Mitch Bailey.

But it couldn't be. There must be lots of Australian-accented male voices in Seminyak. The west coast town was a popular vacation playground for Australians. Besides, it was ten years since she'd last heard that voice. She must be mistaken.

'No tsunami warning,' the manager replied to the man. 'There's no danger.'

'What about aftershocks?' The man asked the question she was too paralysed by fear to ask herself.

It sounded so like him.

'Not likely now,' said the manager. 'It was a small tremor.'

Zoe risked a quick glance behind her to identify the owner of the voice.

And froze.

It was Mitch Bailey, all right—right up at the back of the room. He was instantly recognisable: green eyes, dark blond hair, wearing a pair of blue checked board shorts and nothing else. His tanned, well-honed chest was bare. The blood drained from her face and her mouth went dry.

He was as handsome as he'd been at seventeen. *More handsome.* His face was more chiselled, more lived in, and his dark blond hair was cut spikily short—much shorter than when she had known him. He was tall, broad-shouldered, but lean, with well defined muscles. Then he'd been a suburban high school heart-throb. Now he was an international soccer star, who regularly topped magazine lists of 'The Sexiest Men Alive'.

She quickly turned back and ducked her head. *Dear heaven, don't let him recognise her.* He was part of a past she had chosen to put well behind her. She couldn't let him see her.

Zoe thought back to the first day she'd met him. Grieving over the death of her parents, in an accident that had also injured her, she'd been removed from her inner city home and her laid-back, no-uniform high school and dumped mid-term by her disapproving grandmother—her father's mother—into an outer suburbs school where she'd known no one and no one had seemed to want to know her. The uniform had been scratchy, uncomfortable and hideous—which was just how she'd felt during her time at Northside High.

Her first sight of Mitch Bailey had been of him surrounded by girls, with his girlfriend Lara—blonde and beautiful, of course—hanging possessively onto his arm. Zoe had kept her head down and walked past. But a burst of chatter had made her lift her head and she'd caught his eye. He'd smiled. A friendly, open smile born of his place as kingpin of his social group. He'd been a jock, a sports star—the most popular of the popular boys.

He hadn't needed to smile at nerdy *her*. But he had, and it had warmed the chill of her frozen heart even though she'd been unable to manage more than a polite stretching of her lips in return.

Later they'd become sort of friends, when he'd had a problem she'd been able to help him with. But the last time she'd seen him he'd been so unforgivably hurtful she'd shrivelled back into her shell and stayed there until she'd got out of that school. Now she had no desire to make contact again with anyone from that place—least of all with him.

She tensed, her eyes darting around for an escape route, then realised her panic was for nothing. No way would he recognise her. She looked completely different from the unhappy seventeen-year-old he'd befriended all those years ago. But she kept her eyes to the ground anyway.

She wanted to ask the manager about the airport as she was due to fly back to Sydney the next morning. But she didn't want to draw attention to herself. If she'd recognised his voice, Mitch might recognise hers. It was unlikely, but possible. She kept her mouth shut just in case.

The manager had said it was okay for the guests to return to their villas. That was where she was headed—pronto.

As other people started to ask more questions Zoe inched to the edge of the group. Not meeting anyone's gaze, and as unobtrusively as she could, she edged away towards the pathway that led to her private villa. Once there she could order room service for the rest of her stay, to make sure she didn't bump into Mitch Bailey.

Please, please don't let him be anywhere around when she checked out.

She quickened her pace as she got near the pathway.

'Zoe?'

His voice came from behind her and she started. She denied the reflex that would have had her turning around. Instead she kept her head down and kept walking, hoping against hope that he wouldn't call her name again. *Let him think he'd been mistaken.*

Mitch had noticed the dark-haired girl wrapped in a white towel as soon as she'd come into the courtyard. What red-blooded male wouldn't? The skimpy towel barely covered a sensational body.

It was knotted between high, round breasts and fell just to the top of slender, tanned thighs. Might it fall off at any moment? And, if so, was she wearing anything underneath? He'd been lying by his pool when the earth-quake had hit. What had *she* been doing to be clad only in a towel?

But he'd thought no more about it as the girl had found a place near the front of the group of guests who had gathered to hear the charming Balinese hotel manager explain the ramifications of the earth tremor.

Mitch had been to Bali before, and knew small tremors like this weren't uncommon. He'd appreciated the manager's well-meant reassurances. But still, he'd asked the question about the tsunami because it didn't pay to ignore possible danger. Mitch was the kind of guy who liked to anticipate and prepare for the next move—'reading the play', they called it in soccer. There was a prominent sign on the beach warning people what to do if there was a tsunami warning. Therefore he'd needed to ask about it.

At his second enquiry the girl in the towel had turned briefly, to see who was asking the scary questions. Recognition had flashed just briefly before she had hastily turned back round.

He was used to that these days. Strangers recognised him as being an international soccer player. Or from the endorsements for designer menswear and upscale watches he'd posed for—the advertisements were on billboards even here in Bali. This woman might be a young mum who wanted him to sign her child's soccer ball. Or a fan with much more than signing on her mind.

He narrowed his eyes. The thing was, she had also seemed familiar to him. Her eyes had only caught his for a split second but there had been something about the expression in them—anxious, in a pale, drawn face—that had tugged at his memory. He'd met so many people over the last years, but he couldn't place her. He'd dredged his memory with no luck.

But then she'd hotfooted it away from the group of guests. He'd admired her shapely behind, swaying in that tightly drawn towel as she'd headed for the pathway that led to the private villas. Once she was gone he'd probably never see her again, and would be left wondering who she could possibly have been.

Then he'd noticed the slight, almost imperceptible limp as she'd favoured her right leg. It was enough to trigger memories of a girl he'd known for a short time in high school.

'Zoe!' he'd called.

She'd paused for a moment, her shoulders set rigidly. Then continued to walk away.

Now he pushed his way to the edge of the row of people and took a few strides towards her to catch up.

'Zoe Summers?' he asked, raising his voice.

This time she stopped and turned to face him. For a long moment their gazes met. Mitch was shocked to realise she had recognised him and yet had chosen to walk away. He was swept by conflicting feelings—the most predominant being shame. It was what he deserved after the way he'd treated her all those years ago.

'Mitch Bailey,' she said, head tilted, no trace of a welcoming smile. 'After all this time.'

'I knew it was you,' he said.

Her expression told him a kiss on the cheek, a hug, even a handshake would not be welcome. He kept his hands to his sides.

She looked much the same. More grown-up, of course. But the same sharp, intelligent face. The same black hair— only shorter now, and all tousled around her face. The piercings she'd sported so defiantly at school had gone, leaving tiny telltale holes along the top of her right eyebrow and in her nose, and there was just one pair of discreet gold studs in her ears instead of multiple hoops.

There was something indefinably different about her. Perhaps it was her air of assuredness. He didn't remember that. Back then she'd emanated a miasma of misery that had made other adolescents uncomfortable around her. The 'keep away' glower hadn't helped either. He'd considered himself privileged to have discovered the amazing person behind it all. Until he'd blown their friendship.

'I didn't think you'd recognise me,' she said.

He'd forgotten what an appealing voice she had: mellow, slightly husky.

'You mean you hoped I wouldn't.' He'd intended his words to sound light-hearted, but they came out flat.

She shrugged. 'I didn't say that. It's been years.'

He swallowed uncomfortably. 'Strange way to meet again. In an earthquake.'

'A "tremor" the management called it,' she said with a wry twist to her lips. 'Playing it down so as not to freak out the tourists.'

'Whatever name you give it, it scared the daylights out of me.'

She reacted with a raising of her perfectly shaped black eyebrows. 'Me too,' she said, with the shadow of a smile. 'I thought my end had come. Still think it's a possibility.'

'Where were you when the quake struck?'

'Having a body massage down at the spa.'

Where she must have been naked. So that was why she had only a towel wrapped around her.

Mitch willed his eyes to stay above her neck. Before today he'd only ever seen Zoe in a shapeless school uniform. He hadn't taken much notice of her body back then—it was her brain that had interested him. Besides, he'd had a girlfriend. Now he realised what great shape Zoe was in—in her own quiet way she was hot.

'Where were *you* when it hit?' she asked.

'Just about to dive into my lap pool. Then I noticed the surface of the water shimmering, which was kind of weird.'

'That must have been scary.' She shuddered as she spoke.

'Yeah. It was.'

'So much for relaxing in a tropical paradise,' she said, with a bravado that didn't hide the shadow of unease in her eyes.

She clutched her towel tighter to her. Mitch refused to let himself imagine what might happen if it slid off.

An awkward silence fell between them. Zoe was the first to break it. 'I'm going to head back to my villa,' she said.

'How about I come with you? Who knows what we'll find when we get back to our rooms.'

Her response was more of a cynical twist than a smile, but it was nonetheless attractive. 'Thank you, but I don't need a big strong man to protect me. I'm quite capable of looking after myself.'

'I'm sure you are,' he said. 'But I... Well, I don't really want to be on my own if we get any aftershocks.'

He wasn't afraid to admit to vulnerability. Just never on a football pitch.

'Oh,' she said.

For the first time she seemed flustered.

'You're not...you're not with someone?'

'You mean a girlfriend? No. What about you? Are you on your own?'

'Yes,' she said, with no further explanation.

He glanced down at her hand. No wedding ring. Though that didn't necessarily mean no man in her life. 'I'd like to catch up, Zoe. Find out what you've been doing in the last ten years.'

She paused. 'I don't need to ask what you've done since we last met,' she said. 'You're quite the sporting hero. The media loves you.'

He shrugged. 'Yeah... That... Don't believe everything they dish up about me. But seriously, Zoe, I'd really like to spend some time with you.'

Zoe looked up at him and her heart gave a flip of awareness. Mitch Bailey. Still the same: so handsome, so unselfconscious, standing before her in just a pair of swim shorts that did nothing to hide the athletic perfection of his body. So full of the innate confidence that came with the knowledge that he had always been liked, admired, wanted. So sure she'd want to spend time with him.

And she'd be lying to herself if she said she didn't.

He was the best-looking man she'd ever met. Had been then—still was now. She couldn't deny that. But all those years ago she'd seen a more vulnerable side of Mitch that had endeared him to her before he'd pushed her out of his life. Had it survived his stardom? It was difficult to resist the chance to find out.

'I'd like to catch up too,' she said lightly. 'After all, it isn't every day an earthquake brings long-lost school buddies together.'

He didn't seem to remember the circumstances of their last meeting. It had been a long time ago. Devastating to her at the time. Insignificant, it seemed, to him.

Had she had a crush on him back then? Of course she had. A deeply hidden, secret, impossible crush. He'd been so out of her league she would have been relentlessly mocked if anyone had found out.

'Great,' he said with a smile.

If she didn't know better, she'd think it was tinged with relief.

'The manager said it was business as usual. We can order drinks. I don't know about you, but I could do with a beer.'

'Me too,' she said.

And the first thing she'd do before she spent any more time alone with Mitch Bailey would be to put on some clothes.

CHAPTER TWO

ZOE'S VILLA HAD suffered minimal damage from the tremor—just a few glasses she'd left out had smashed to the tiled floor. Still, it was a shock—a reminder of how much worse it could have been. Might yet be.

She wanted to clear up the broken glass. But she felt awkward dressed only in the towel and she still felt very shaky. For every piece she picked up, she dropped another.

Mitch insisted he do it for her. Thanking him, she escaped into her bedroom and pulled closed the door that divided the room from the living area. The villa was like a roomy one-bedroom apartment, with all the external doors folding back to access the enclosed courtyard and private lap pool.

Her heart was thumping like crazy. Residual fear from the earthquake? More likely the effect of being in close proximity to Mitch Bailey.

She hadn't *stalked* him over the years. Not that. But when a boy she'd gone to school with had shot to fame she wouldn't have been human if she hadn't read the magazine stories, watched the television interviews, cheered for him when he'd been the youngest ever player in the Australian Socceroos team for the World Cup.

All the while she'd been getting on with her life—first

studying, then working, dating, and only ever thinking about him when the media brought him to her attention.

Now he'd been thrust into her life again. And she was clad in a towel, with no make-up on and her hair all mussed up with massage oil.

Hastily she pulled on a sleekly cut black bikini, then slid into a simple sleeveless dress in an abstract black-and-white print. It fell to just above her knees. The humid tropical heat made anything else uncomfortable. She pulled a brush through her hair and slicked on a natural toned lipstick.

Did she want to look her best for Mitch? Her 'best' involved twenty minutes in front of a mirror with a make-up kit and heated hair tongs. She shouldn't be worried about how she looked now; he'd seen her at her worst ten years ago. She shuddered at the memory of what she'd looked like back then. The mono-brow. The bushy hair. The prone-to-eruption skin.

But still, she wished today she could look her usual polished, poised self. Her best self. There was no denying she'd feel more confident with straightened hair and more make-up. But she didn't want to waste time fussing over her appearance when she could be catching up with Mitch. Who knew when she'd see him again—if ever?

He'd switched on the television in the living area and was watching the screen when she came back out of her bedroom.

'The manager was right—there's minimal disruption,' he said. 'Seems like Bali gets small tremors like this quite often. But the risk of aftershocks is real.'

Aftershocks. She knuckled her hand against her mouth to suppress a gasp; she didn't want to appear too fearful. Not when Mitch seemed so laid back about the risk.

He switched off the TV and turned to face her. Had he

grown taller since she'd last stood so near to him? They were both in their bare feet. He seemed to stand about six-foot-one to her five-foot-five.

Six-foot-one of total hotness.

Mitch was an elite sportsman in his prime, and he had celebrity status with as many fans as any actor or musician.

Her proximity to his bare chest was doing nothing to slow down her revved-up heartbeat. If she'd had a T-shirt big enough to stretch over all those muscles, she would have offered to lend it to him. But wouldn't it be a crime to cover that expanse of buff body?

She wanted to take a step back, but didn't want to signal how disconcerted she felt by said buff body being so close to her. Instead she stood her ground and forced her voice to sound controlled and conversational.

'So this region sometimes gets harmless tremors? That didn't stop it from being frightening, though, did it?' she said. 'I huddled under the massage table, making all sorts of bargains with myself about what I'd do if I got out safely.'

'What kind of bargains?' he asked.

'Spend more time with friends and less at work. Give more to charity.' She shrugged. 'Stuff that wouldn't interest you.'

His eyes were as green as she remembered them, and now they looked intently into hers. 'How do you know they wouldn't interest me?' he said, in a voice that seemed to have got an octave deeper.

A shiver of awareness tingled through her. *Sexiest man alive, all right.*

'Our lives are so different. It's like we inhabit different spaces on the planet,' she said.

'What do you think is my space on the planet?'

'Spain? I believe you play for one of the top Spanish teams. I've never been to Spain.'

'I live in Madrid.'

'There you go. I still live in Sydney. Fact is, the air you breathe is way more rarefied than mine.'

'I don't know if that's true or not. We're both staying in the same hotel.'

'My booking was a last-minute bargain on the internet. Yours?'

He smiled. The same appealing, slightly uneven smile he'd had at the age of seventeen. 'Maybe not.'

'That's just my point. You're famous. Not just for being a brilliant football player but for being handsome, wealthy, and photographed with a different gorgeous woman on your arm every time you're seen in public.'

And they were all tall, blonde and beautiful clones of Lara, back in high school.

'That's where you have an unfair advantage over me,' he said. 'You've read about me in the media—seen me on TV, perhaps. That's not to say what you've seen is the truth. But I know nothing about what's happened to you since we were at Northside High.'

'Because we occupy different space on the planet,' she repeated, determined to make her point. 'I went to another school after Northside, but I was still in Sydney. Away from school I hung out in the same clubs and went to the same concerts as other kids our age. But our paths never crossed again.'

'Until now,' he said.

'Yes. It took an earthquake to shake us back into the same space.'

He laughed, and she had to smile in response.

'You've still got a quirky way of putting things. Seriously, Zoe, I want to know all about you,' he said.

His words were flattering, seductive. Not seductive in a sexual way, but in a way that tempted her to open up and confide in him because he sounded as though her answer was important to him. That *she* was important to him. Even aged seventeen he'd had that gift of being totally focussed on the person he was addressing.

She realised it was highly unlikely she'd see Mitch again after today. He would go home to Madrid; she would fly back to Sydney. There was also a chance that a bigger earthquake might hit and the whole resort area would be wiped out. It was unnerving in one way—liberating in another.

'How about we get that beer and then we can talk?' she said.

'About you?'

'And you too,' she said, finding it impossible not to feel flattered. 'I'd like to hear about your life behind those media reports.'

'If that's what you want.'

'I'm warning you: my life story will be quite mundane compared to yours.'

'Let me be the judge of that,' he said.

'There are beers in the mini-bar,' she said. 'I've been on an alcohol-free detox since I've been in Bali and sticking with mineral water. Not that I drink a lot,' she hastened to add.

'I think getting out of an earthquake unscathed is reason enough to break your fast,' he said, heading towards the fridge.

He brought out two bottles of the local Indonesian beer, took off the caps and handed one to her.

'Let's take them out near the pool,' she said, picking up one of the remaining glasses to take with her. The ceiling fans were circulating air around the rooms, but the air-conditioning didn't appear to be back on yet. Besides, it felt too intimate to be alone in here with Mitch, and the king-sized bed was too clearly in view.

It was only a few steps out to the rectangular lap pool, which was edged on three sides with plantings of broad-leaved tropical greenery. Two smart, comfortable wooden sun loungers with blue-striped mattresses sat side by side in the shade of a frangipani tree. A myriad of pink flowers had been shaken off the tree by the quake onto the loungers and into the water. The petals floated on the turquoise surface of the pool in picture-perfect contrast.

In different circumstances Zoe would have taken a photo of how pretty they looked. Instead she placed the beer bottle and the glass on the small wooden table between the two loungers. She flicked off the flowers that had settled on one lounger before she sat down, her back supported, her legs stretched out in front of her. Thank heaven for all that waxing, moisturising and toenail-painting that had gone on in the spa yesterday.

She felt very conscious of Mitch settling into the lounger on her right. His legs were lean, with tightly defined muscles, his classic six-pack belly hard and flat. Even she knew soccer players trained for strength, speed and agility rather than for bulky muscle. Come to think of it, she might know that from hearing him being interviewed on the subject at some stage…

These villas were often booked by honeymooners, she knew. The loungers were set as close as they could be, with only that narrow little table separating them. Loved-up couples could easily touch in complete privacy.

She had never touched Mitch, she realised. Not a hug. Not even a handshake. Certainly not a kiss. Not even a chaste, platonic kiss on the cheek. It just hadn't been appropriate back then. Now she had to resist the urge to reach out and put her hand on his arm. Not in a sexual way, or even a friendly way. Just to reassure herself that he was real, he was here, that they were both alive.

She and Mitch Bailey.

He swigged his beer straight from the bottle. The way he tilted back his head, the arch of his neck, made the simple act of drinking a beer look as if he was doing it for one of those advertisements he starred in.

He was graceful. That was what it was. Graceful in a strong, sleek, utterly masculine way. She didn't remember that from the last time she'd seen him. Off the football field he'd been more gauche than graceful. At seventeen he hadn't quite grown into his long limbs and big feet. Since then he'd trained with the best sports trainers in the world.

Yes, he inhabited not just a different space but a different planet from her. But for this time—maybe an hour, maybe a few hours—their planets had found themselves in the same orbit.

Mitch put down his beer. 'So, where did you go when you left our school?' he asked. 'You just seemed to disappear.'

Zoe felt a stab of pain that he didn't seem to remember their last meeting. But if he wasn't going to mention it she certainly wasn't. Even now dragging it out of the recesses where her hurts were hidden was painful.

She poured beer into her glass. Took a tentative sip. Cold. Refreshing. Maybe it would give her the Dutch courage she so sorely needed to mine her uncomfortable memories of the past. She considered herself to be a private person. She didn't spill her soul easily.

'I won a scholarship to a private girls' boarding school in the eastern suburbs. I started there for the next term.'

'You always were a brainiac,' he said, with what seemed to be genuine admiration.

Zoe didn't deny it. She'd excelled academically and had been proud of her top grades—not only in maths and science but also in languages and music. But if there'd been such a thing as a social report card for her short time at Northside she would have scored a big, fat fail. She'd had good friends at her old inner city school, an hour's train ride away, but her grandmother had thwarted her efforts to see them. The only person who had come anywhere near to being a friend at Northside had been Mitch.

'I had to get away from my grandmother. Getting the scholarship was the only way I could do it.'

'How did she react?'

'Furious I'd gone behind her back. But glad to get rid of me.'

Mitch frowned. 'You talk as though she hated you?'

'She did.' It was a truth she didn't like to drag out into the sunlight too often.

'Surely not? She was your *grandma.*'

Mitch came from a big, loving family. No wonder he found it difficult to comprehend the aridity of her relationship with her grandmother.

'She blamed me for the death of my father.'

Mitch was obviously too shocked to speak for a long moment. 'But you weren't driving the car. Or the truck that smashed into it.'

He remembered.

She was stunned that Mitch recalled her telling him about the accident that had killed her parents and injured her leg so badly she still walked with a slight limp when she was very tired or stressed. They'd been heading north to a music festival in Queensland; just her and the mother and father she'd adored. A truck-driver had fallen asleep at the wheel and veered onto their side of a notoriously bad stretch of the Pacific Highway.

'No. I was in the back seat. I...I'm surprised you remember.'

He slowly shook his head. 'How could I forget? It seemed the most terrible thing to have happened to a kid. I loved my family. I couldn't have managed without them.'

Zoe shifted in her seat. She hated people pitying her. 'You felt sorry for me?'

'Yes. And sad for you too.'

There was genuine compassion on his handsome famous face, and she acknowledged the kindness of his words with a slight silent nod. As a teenager she'd sensed a core of decency behind his popular boy image. It was why she'd been so shocked at the way he'd treated her at the end.

As she'd watched his meteoric rise she'd wondered if fame and the kind of adulation he got these days had changed him. Who was the real Mitch?

Here, now, in the aftermath of an earthquake, maybe she had been given the chance to find out.

CHAPTER THREE

WERE THERE ELEPHANTS in Bali? There were lots of monkeys; Mitch knew that from his visit to the Ubud area in the highlands.

He'd heard there were elephants indigenous to the neighbouring Indonesian island of Sumatra that had been trained to play soccer. But he would rather see elephants in their natural habitat, dignified and not trained to do party tricks.

Whether or not there were elephants on Bali, there was an elephant in the room with him and Zoe. Or rather, an elephant in the pool. A large metaphorical elephant, wallowing in the turquoise depths, spraying water through its trunk in an effort to get their attention.

Metaphorical.

Zoe had taught him how to use that term.

The elephant was that last day they'd seen each other, ten years ago. He'd behaved badly. Lashed out at her. Humiliated her. Hadn't defended her against Lara's cattiness. He'd felt rotten about it once he'd cooled down. But he had never got the chance to apologise. He owed her that. He also owed her thanks for the events that had followed.

Zoe hadn't said anything, but he'd bet she remembered the incident. He could still see her face as it had crumpled with shock and hurt. He mightn't have been great with words when it came to essays, but his words to her had wounded; the way he'd allowed her to be mocked by Lara had been like an assault.

Now Zoe sat back on the lounger next to him, her slim, toned legs stretched out in front of her. He didn't remember her being a sporty girl at school. But she must exercise regularly to keep in such great shape. It seemed she hadn't just changed in appearance. Zoe was self-possessed, composed—in spite of the fact they'd just experienced an earthquake. Though he suspected a fear of further tremors lay just below her self-contained surface.

'I want to clear the air,' he said.

'What...what do you mean?' she said.

But the expression in her dark brown eyes told him she knew exactly what he meant. Knew and hadn't forgotten a moment of it.

'About what a stupid young idiot I was that last day. Honest. I didn't know that would be the last time I'd see you.'

Mitch was the youngest of four sons in a family of high achievers. His brothers had excelled academically; he'd excelled at sport. That had been his slot in the family. His parents hadn't worried about his mediocre grades at school. The other boys were to be a lawyer, an accountant and a doctor respectively. Mitch had been the sportsman. They could boast about him—they hadn't expected more from him.

But Mitch had expected more of himself. He'd been extremely competitive. Driven to excel. If his anointed role was to be the sportsman, he'd be the *best* sportsman.

The trouble was, the school had expected him to do more than concentrate on soccer in winter and basketball in summer. With minimal effort he'd done okay in maths, science and geography—not top grades, but not the lowest either. It had been English he couldn't get his head around. And English had been a compulsory subject for the final Higher School Certificate.

His teenage brain hadn't seen the point of studying long-dead authors and playwrights. Of not just reading contemporary novels but having to analyse the heck out of them. And then there was poetry. He hadn't been able to get it. He hadn't wanted to get it. It had been bad enough having to study it. He sure as hell hadn't been going to write the poem required as part of his term assessment. He *couldn't* write a poem.

Zoe Summers hadn't been in his English class. No way. The new girl nerd was in the top classes for everything. But during a study period in the library she'd been sitting near him when he'd flung his poetry book down on the floor, accompanied by a string of curses that had drawn down the wrath of the supervising librarian.

The other kids had egged him on and laughed. He'd laughed too. But it hadn't been a joke. If he didn't keep up a decent grade average for English he wasn't going to be allowed to go to a week-long soccer training camp that cut into the school term by a couple of days. He'd been determined to get to that camp.

The teenage Zoe had caught his eye when he had leaned down to pick up his book from the floor. She'd smiled a shy smile and murmured, 'Can I help? I'm such a nerd I actually *like* poetry.'

Help? No one had actually offered to help him before. And he'd had too much testosterone-charged teenage pride to ask for it.

'I'll be right here in the library after school,' she'd said. 'Meet me here if you want me to help.'

He'd hesitated. He couldn't meet her in public. Not the jock and the nerd. A meeting between them would mean unwanted attention. Mockery. Insults. Possible spiteful retaliation from Lara. He could handle all that, but he had doubted Zoe could.

His hesitation must have told her that.

'Or you could meet me at my house after school,' she'd said, in such a low tone only he could have heard it.

She'd scribbled something on a piece of paper and passed it unobtrusively to him. He'd taken it. Nodded. Then turned back to his mates. Continued to crack jokes and be generally disruptive until he'd been kicked out of the library.

But he had still needed to pass that poetry assignment. He had decided to take Zoe up on her offer of help. No matter the consequences.

Her house had been just two streets away from his, in the leafy, upmarket northern suburb of Wahroonga. Their houses had looked similar from the outside, set in large, well-tended gardens. Inside, they couldn't have been more different.

His house had been home to four boys: he still at school, the others at universities in Sydney. There'd been a blackboard in the well-used family room, where all family members had chalked up their whereabouts. The house had rung with lots of shouting and boisterous ribbing by the brothers and their various friends.

Zoe's house had been immaculate to the point of sterility. Straight away he'd been able to tell she was nervous when she'd greeted him at the front door. He'd soon seen why. An older woman she'd introduced as her grandmother had hovered behind her, mouth pinched, eyes cold. He'd never felt more unwelcome.

The grandma had told Zoe to entertain her visitor in the dining room, with the door open at all times. Mitch had felt unnerved—ready to bolt back the way he'd come.

But then Zoe had rolled her eyes behind her grandmother's back and pulled a comical face.

They'd established a connection. And in the days that had followed he'd got to like and respect Zoe as she had helped him tackle his dreaded poetry assignment.

'I want to explain what happened back then,' he said now.

Zoe shrugged. 'Does it matter after all this time?' she said, her voice tight, not meeting his eyes.

It did to him. She had helped him. He had let her down.

'Do you remember how hard you worked to help me get my head around poetry?' he asked.

'You were the one doing all the work. I just guided you in the right direction.'

He slammed down his hand on the edge of the lounger in remembered anger. 'That's exactly right. You made me use my own words—not yours. It was unfair.'

'What…what exactly happened in the classroom that day?'

'The teacher had had the assignment for a week. So I was on edge, waiting to see if I'd passed or not. By then it had become something more than just wanting to go to the soccer camp. She handed out the marked essays, desk by desk. She saved mine for last.'

'You should have easily passed. By that time we'd spent so much time on it—you really understood it.'

'I thought I'd understood it, too. She got to my desk. Held up the paper for everyone to see the great big "Fail" scrawled across it. Told the class I was a cheat. Read out my grade and added her comments for maximum humiliation.'

The look on that teacher's face was still seared into his memory.

Before he'd studied with Zoe he would have made a

joke of it. Clowned around. Annoyed the teacher until she'd kicked him out of the classroom. But not that time. He'd deserved better.

'What happened?'

'I snatched the paper from the teacher's hand and stormed out.'

'To find me lurking outside in the corridor. Pretending I was waiting for a class to start in the next room. Ready to congratulate you on a brilliant pass. Instead I got in your way.'

He noticed how tightly she was gripping on to her glass. No wonder. He'd vented all his outraged adolescent anger and humiliation on her. It couldn't be a pleasant memory.

'Instead I behaved like a total jerk.'

'Yeah. You did. You...you thrust the paper in my face. I can still see that word written so big in red ink: "Plagiarism".'

'She thought I was too stupid to write such a good essay. And I took it out on you.'

He'd yelled at her that it was *her* fault. Told her to get out of his way. Never talk to him again. Had he actually shoved her? He didn't think so. His words had been as effective as any physical blow.

He'd seen her face crumple in disbelief, then pain, then schooled indifference as she'd walked away. She'd muttered that she was sorry—she'd only been trying to help. And he'd let her go.

Worse, a half-hour later he'd encountered Zoe again. This time he'd been hanging near the canteen, with his crowd of close friends and his girlfriend, Lara. Zoe had obviously been startled to see them. Startled and, he'd realised afterwards, alarmed. She'd immediately started to turn away, eyes cast down, shoulders hunched. But that hadn't been enough for Lara, who hadn't liked him study-ing with another girl one little bit.

'Buzz off, geek-girl,' Lara had sneered. 'Mitch doesn't need *your* kind of help. Not when he's got *me*.'

Then Lara had pulled his face to hers and given him a provocatively deep kiss. Her girlfriends had started to laugh and his mates had joined in, their laughter echoing through the corridors of the school.

He'd just kept on kissing Lara. When he'd finally pulled away Zoe had gone. It was only later that he'd realised how he'd betrayed her by his silence and inaction.

That had been ten years ago. Now she smiled that wry smile that was already becoming familiar. 'Teenage angst. Who'd go back there?'

'Teenage angst or not, I behaved badly. And after ten years I want to take this opportunity to say sorry. To see if there is any way I could make it up to you.'

Digging deep into feelings she'd rather were kept buried made Zoe feel uncomfortable. She found it impossible to meet Mitch's gaze. To gain herself a moment before she had to reply, she put her glass down onto the table and tugged her dress down over her thighs.

'We were just kids,' she said.

Though Lara's spite had been only too grown up. And the pain she'd felt when Mitch had ignored her hadn't been the pain of a child.

Truth was, the episode was a reminder of a particularly unhappy time in her life. She'd rather not be reminded of how she'd felt back then. That was why she had tried to avoid Mitch earlier on, when she'd first recognised him.

'I was old enough to know better,' he said.

Now she turned to face him. 'Seriously, if you hadn't

always been popping up in the media I would have forgotten all about what happened. I'm cool with it.'

He persisted. 'I'm *not* cool with it. I want to make amends.'

She wished he would drop it. 'If it makes you feel any better, my experiences at Northside made me stronger—determined to change. No way was I going to be that miserable at my new school. I decided to do whatever it took to fit in.'

'Your piercings? Which, by the way, I used to think were kinda cute.'

'Gone. I wore the uniform straight up—exactly as prescribed. Put the "anything goes" lifestyle I'd enjoyed with my parents behind me. Played the private school game by their rules. I watched, learned and conformed.'

And it had worked. At the new academically elite school she hadn't climbed up the pecking order to roost with the 'popular' girls, but neither had she been one of the shunned.

'Was it the right move?'

Again she was conscious of his intent focus on her. As if he were really interested in her reply.

'Yes. I was happy there—did well, made some good friends.'

One in particular had taken the new girl under her wing and helped transform the caterpillar. Not into a gaudy butterfly, more an elegantly patterned moth who fitted perfectly into her surroundings.

'I'm glad to hear that. But I want you to know I feel bad about what happened. I want to right the wrong.'

Zoe shrugged, pretended indifference, but secretly she was chuffed. Mitch Bailey apologising? Mitch Bailey maybe even grovelling a tad? It was good. It was healing. It was—she couldn't deny it—*satisfying*.

'Consider it righted,' she said firmly. 'Apology accepted. You were young and disappointed and you took it out on the first person who crossed your path.'

'I tried to find you,' he said.

'You did?' she said, startled. That he'd remembered the incident at all in such detail was mind-boggling.

'After the soccer training camp I went away on vacation with my family. When I got back to school you weren't there. I went around to your house. Your grandmother told me you didn't live there any more. I thought she was going to slam the door in my face.'

'Sounds like my grandmother.'

'Remember how she always made you leave the door open and patrolled outside it? I felt like a criminal. Did she think I was going to steal the silver?'

'She was terrified you'd get me pregnant.'

Mitch nearly choked on his beer. He stared at her for a long, astounded moment. *'What?'*

Zoe waited for him to stop spluttering, resisting the temptation to pat him on that broad, muscular back. She probably shouldn't have shared that particular detail of her dysfunctional relationship with her grandmother.

She felt her cheeks flush pink as she explained. 'I told her we were just friends. I told her you had a girlfriend. That the only thing going on in that room was studying.'

Not to mention that Mitch Bailey wouldn't have looked at her as girlfriend material in a million years.

'Why the hell did she think—?'

'She wasn't going to let me—' Zoe made quote marks in the air with her fingers '—"get pregnant and ruin the future of some fine young man" the way my mother had ruined my father's. You counted as one of those fine young men. She knew of your family.'

How many times had her grandmother harangued her

about that, over and over again, until she'd had to put her fingers in her ears to block out the hateful words?

Mitch frowned. 'What? I don't get it.'

Thank heaven back then her grandmother hadn't said anything to Mitch about the pregnancy thing. She would have been mortified beyond redemption.

'It sounds warped, doesn't it? I didn't get it either when I was seventeen. I thought she was insane. I'd adored my parents. They'd adored each other. But Mum was only nineteen when I was born. Because my father dropped out of his law degree my grandmother blamed my mother for seducing him, getting pregnant on purpose and ruining his life.'

'Whoa. You said your life story was *mundane.*' He paused, narrowed his eyes. 'And she transferred the blame to you, right?'

'Yep. If I hadn't come along her son would have got to be a lawyer.'

'And he wouldn't have died?'

'Correct.'

'That's irrational.'

'You could say that.'

'Yet she gave you a home?'

'Reluctantly. She couldn't even bear to look at me. I look like my dad, you see. A constant reminder of what she had lost. But she felt she had to do the right thing by her granddaughter.' In spite of herself a note of bitterness crept into her voice. 'After all, what would her golfing friends have thought?'

'Did you have any other family you could have gone to?'

'My mother's brother, whom I love to pieces. But as he has a propensity to dress in frocks sometimes the courts didn't approve of him as guardian to a minor.'

Mitch laughed. 'The lawyers must have had fun with

that one.' He sobered. 'No wonder you were so miserable back then.'

The rejection by her grandmother had hurt. There had been no shared grief. No comfort. Just blame and bitterness. 'I did something about it, though,' she said.

'What could a kid of seventeen have done?'

'My new best friend at school—who incidentally is still my best friend—had a mother who was a top lawyer. She helped me get legal emancipation from my grandmother. There was compensation and insurance money from the accident that got signed over to me. I was able to support myself.'

He whistled. 'That was a tough thing to do. Brave too.'

She shrugged. 'My new life started then.'

'You had worse things going on than a teenage me ranting at you…'

She met his gaze. 'What happened with you hurt me. I won't deny it. I…I valued our friendship. It was a beacon in the darkness of those days.'

Mitch swore low and fluently.

She waited for him to finish. 'It's history now. I appreciate your apology. And I don't want to hear one more word about it.'

'Just a few more words,' he said, with that engaging grin.

'I can't imagine what more there is to be said,' she said, her lips twitching into a smile in response. 'But okay. Your final words. Fire away.'

'I was sent to the principal to be punished for my plagiarism. She was new that year and didn't know me. When I explained she listened. Turns out I had a mild form of dyslexia that had never been diagnosed. I got help. My grades picked up. Not just in English, but all my subjects. I could have gone to university on my Higher School Certificate results if I hadn't chosen to play soccer instead.'

'Mitch, that's wonderful news!'

Her instinct was to reach out and hug him. With every fibre of her being she resisted it. She could not trust herself to touch him.

But while *she* thought touching was not on the agenda, Mitch obviously thought otherwise. He reached out and put his hand on her shoulder. 'I have a lot to thank you for, Zoe,' he said.

His hand was warm and firm on her bare skin and she had to force herself not to tremble with the pleasure of it.

She had to clear her throat before she could reply. 'Not me. The principal. Yourself. That's who you should thank.'

He let his hand drop from her shoulder and she felt immediately bereft of his touch. That attraction she'd felt for him at seventeen was still there, simmering below the surface.

'I'm determined to thank you, whether you acknowledge your role in the outcome or not,' he said. 'The least I can do is buy you dinner.' He looked at his watch. 'An early dinner?'

That threw her. She'd assumed once they'd sorted out the problems of the past he'd be on his way. 'Here? Now?'

'I don't think it would be a good idea to go into Seminyak so soon after the quake. Too dangerous.'

'I…I was going to order room service,' she blurted out.

'I was going to suggest the hotel restaurant. But I might get recognised. And I don't want anyone else intruding on our reunion celebration. Room service is a great idea. Your villa or mine?'

'Uh… H-Here would be good,' she stammered. *Reunion celebration?*

Had the earthquake knocked her off that massage table

and she'd hit her head? Was she hallucinating? Or in some some kind of coma?

Her and Mitch Bailey, having dinner *tête-à-tête* in the seclusion of a luxurious private villa in Bali? Maybe she'd wake up and find herself back in the spa, sprawled amid the debris with a big fat headache.

But if it *was* a dream, or a long-ago fantasy come true, she was going to enjoy every second of being with Mitch. Who knew what tomorrow might bring?

She swung her legs off the side of the lounger. 'I'll go get the room service menu.'

CHAPTER FOUR

MITCH RECLINED ON HIS lounger and watched Zoe as she walked into the living area. He couldn't keep his eyes off the way her hips swayed enticingly under the body-hugging dress. Somehow he doubted that seductive sway was intentional. He'd seen enough of the type of woman who turned on the sex appeal with seduction in mind to know the difference.

No. Zoe had a natural, unconscious sensuality. The fact that she seemed unaware of it made her only more appealing. *Zoe Summers. Who would have thought it?*

He couldn't get over the difference in her. It wasn't that he'd found her unattractive as a teenager. There'd been something quirky and rebellious about her that he'd liked. But now...now she was sexy as hell. Sparky and feisty too. He was finding it fascinating to discover the woman she'd become. Was grateful to the twist of destiny that had flung them together.

She headed back towards the pool, waving a cardboard folder. 'I had to hunt for it, but I've got the room service menu.'

Mitch swung his legs from the lounger so he sat on the edge. 'Let's take a look.'

'It's the same food as the restaurant. I've eaten there a few times. It's good.'

Menu in hand, she hesitated near his lounger. He patted the seat next to him. Cautiously she sat down, being so careful to keep a distance between them that it made him smile. Again she tugged down her dress to cover her thighs. But that only meant the neckline of her dress slid down, revealing more than a tantalising glimpse of the swell of her breasts.

Surely he would have noticed if she'd had a body like that back at school?

'What's for dinner?' he asked, shuffling a little closer to her until her scent filled his senses. 'Any recommendations?'

'I don't know what you like,' she said.

Of course she wouldn't. Despite that briefly opened window on a shared past, he and Zoe were strangers.

'What are *you* going to order?' he asked.

'Something not too spicy,' she said. 'The curries don't agree with me.'

'Bali belly, huh?' he said. 'Happens to the best of us. But you survived?'

Zoe pulled a face. 'I'll spare you the details,' she said. 'I seem to be over it now, but don't want to risk a relapse.' She handed over the menu. 'I'm going to stick with the *ayam bakar*—I've had it before with no…uh…ill effects.'

Mitch read out the description of her chosen dish. 'Organic chicken pieces marinated in a special blend of Indonesian spices, grilled, and served with a lemongrass salsa. Sounds good.'

'It's absolutely delicious. I want to learn how to make it when I get home.'

'You like cooking?'

She nodded. 'I wanted to have cooking lessons while I was in Bali but I've run out of days.'

'Next time,' he said.

She bit her lip and paled at his words, paused for a long moment. 'Yes,' she said finally. 'Next time.'

Mitch cursed himself for his insensitivity; he'd already suspected she was only masking her fear.

Would there be a next time? Or another earthquake? Maybe a tsunami?

Despite the manager's reassuring words Mitch knew there was a risk the entire resort would be wiped out by breakfast. But he tended towards optimism in his view of life. Not so Zoe, he suspected.

She'd lost her whole family when disaster had hit from nowhere. No wonder she was frightened. He wanted to take her in his arms and reassure her that there was a low statistical risk of any more serious danger. But he sensed she wouldn't welcome it. He sensed a 'hands off' shield around her.

'Y'know, I'm not really that hungry,' she said in a diminished voice.

She twisted her hands together. To stop them trembling, he guessed.

'You do realise it's highly unlikely anything else is going to happen?' he said gently.

Her chin rose. 'I know that.'

'There's no need to be frightened.'

'Who said I was frightened?'

'I thought that was why you'd lost your appetite?'

'No. I...' She met his gaze. 'Maybe I *am* a little frightened,' she admitted.

'Let's order for you anyway. You might get hungry later.' He scanned the menu. 'I'm hungry right now.'

'You were always hungry,' she said, with a weak smile that tugged at the corner of her mouth.

Her lovely, lovely mouth.

'Back then, I mean.'

'Your granny mightn't have been so nice, but she made good cookies.'

Zoe nodded. 'Baking cookies with her is one of the few nice memories I have of her. She liked having a boy to cook for. I realise that now.'

'Is she still around?'

Her lips tightened. 'I guess so. I don't know and I don't care.'

'I don't blame you,' he said. Not after the way she'd been treated by someone who should have cared for her. Hearing about the old woman's pregnancy fear for Zoe had given him the creeps.

She nodded and quickly changed the subject. 'Anything on the menu appeal?'

This was the first time he'd eaten at the hotel apart from breakfast. He'd spent most evenings with friends who owned the most fashionable beachfront nightclub in Seminyak. 'I'm going for the Balinese mixed seafood.'

Zoe had to shift a little closer to him to read the menu. Her scent was fresh, tangy, with an underlying sweetness. Much like her personality, he suspected.

'That looks good,' she said. 'Healthy.' She looked up at him. 'I guess you have to watch everything you eat?'

'All the time. When I'm training or before a game I carb-load. On vacation I stick with lean protein and veg-etables.'

'I eat healthily too,' she said. 'But as I'm far from a pro-fessional athlete I also make room for chocolate.'

'I can't remember when I last ate chocolate.'

From the time when he'd first started playing for Syd-ney soccer clubs his diet had been overseen by a nutri-tionist. It was all about discipline. Discipline and constant self-denial.

'You want to order dessert?' he said, flipping the menu to the appropriate page.

'Why not? The mini chocolate lava pudding with lychee ice cream might be good for my nerves.'

He liked her self-deprecating attitude to her fears. 'That's as good an excuse as any,' he said. 'Fruit salad for me. I've spent a season on the sidelines. I have to be at my peak when I start intense training again.'

She glanced at his right knee. So she knew about the incident when two opposing players had slammed into him and his anterior cruciate ligament had snapped.

'Australia's most famous knee...' she said.

Mitch found it disconcerting that Zoe was so aware of the details of his life while he knew so little about hers. He doubted he'd ever get used to the scrutiny he endured as a celebrity athlete. Even his knee had become public property.

'I wouldn't say "most *famous* knee",' he said, laughing it off.

'How about most notorious knee?' she said, her head tilted to one side, teasing.

'Notorious knee? I like that.'

Most painful knee was more like it. Both in terms of the actual injury and also in the way it had lost him a season of play. The memory of being carried off the field came flooding back. The agony. The terror that he wouldn't be able to play again. The months of rehabilitation and physiotherapy that had followed. The effort to get himself back to peak fitness after the weeks on crutches.

'I don't see a scar,' she said, her eyes narrowed.

'No scar,' he said. 'Three small incisions for keyhole surgery have left tiny marks. That's all.'

For a moment he was tempted to place Zoe's hand on

his knee and let her feel the punctures. Not a good idea. He found her way too attractive to be able to trust himself.

'Is it healed now?' she asked.

'Good as new.' He wouldn't admit to anyone his niggling fear that once he was back in the game his knee would betray him again. His sporting life would be over if it did.

'There was talk that your injury might force you to retire,' she said.

'No way,' he said vehemently.

This exact injury had brought other great players' careers to a skidding halt. He wasn't going to let it end *his*.

It would take something more catastrophic than a cruciate ligament repair for his manager, his fans *or* himself to allow him to consider giving up. At the age of twenty-seven he was in his football prime. He cursed the six months it had taken him to achieve full recovery. Now he had to get back out there on the field and prove he could play better than ever.

Soccer was his life.

Zoe drew her dark brows together. 'So, why are you in Bali?'

'I was visiting family in Sydney, then decided to have a break here on the way back to Madrid. I met up with a mate who has a surf gear business. Another runs a big nightclub.'

'When do you go back?'

'Who knows how the earthquake has affected the airlines? But I'm scheduled to fly to Singapore then back to Madrid the day after tomorrow.'

It was May. He would hurl himself into intense training immediately he got back. Pre-season games started at the end of June. He needed those 'friendly' games to test his knee and get back into top form before the season proper commenced. The first games for La Liga—the Spanish league—started at the end of August.

'What about your flight?' he asked Zoe.

'I fly out tomorrow morning, if all goes well.' She crossed her fingers.

'I guess the airlines will keep us informed,' he said.

If all goes well.

He didn't repeat her words—didn't want to bring her fear to the fore again.

There was an awkward pause that she rushed to fill. 'Do you like living in Madrid?'

'Madrid rocks. An Aussie boy from the north shore of Sydney living in one of Europe's great cities never tires.'

All true. But he hadn't admitted to anyone how lonely he could get there, despite the buzz of playing for one of the world's best teams. He had friends on the team, of course, but there were also some big egos to deal with—and the truth was they were in competition with each other as well as the opposing teams.

He wasn't about to admit to that downside now. Zoe had flitted into his life again and he was very careful of what he said to people except his family and his closest friends—careful of who he let in to his private world. You never knew who would talk to the press. Or misrepresent his words on social media. Or post a compromising selfie.

'Do you speak Spanish?' she asked.

'Enough to get by.'

Mitch decided the conversation had centred too much around him. He was way more interested in her.

'Me muero de hambre.'

Zoe laughed—a low, husky laugh that hadn't changed at all since she was a teenager. She'd grown into that sensual, adult laugh.

'You're dying of hunger. Did I get that right?'

'You speak Spanish?' He knew so little about her—wanted to know more in this accelerated getting-to-know-you situation they found themselves in.

'Hablo un poco de español,' she said, with an appropriately expressive shrug.

'You speak a little Spanish,' he translated.

'And a little French, and a little Italian, and a few phrases in Indonesian that I've learned in the last few days.'

'You've travelled a lot?'

'So far most of my travel has been of the armchair variety. I'd *like* to travel a lot. I'd love to be fluent in different languages. I'll study more some day—when I'm not so busy working.'

Of course she would. Zoe had been so smart at school. And she'd grown up into a formidable woman. Formidable and sexy. How very different from the women he usually dated. From nowhere came the thought that Zoe Summers would be a challenge. The kind of challenge it would be pleasurable to meet.

'I have no idea what work you do,' he said.

'I have my own accountancy and taxation advice company.' She paused. 'Yeah. I know. *Boring.*'

'I didn't say that,' he said.

She pulled a face. 'I can see the thought bubbles wafting around your head.' She made a series of little quote marks in the air as she sang the words in a clear contralto. '"Boring. Boring. Boring."'

He laughed. 'Wrong. My thought bubbles are "Clever Zoe" and "Intelligent" and "Entrepreneurial".'

'Oh,' she said. 'They…they're great thought bubbles.'

'But don't ask me to sing them as I'm totally tone deaf.'

She laughed. 'I'm grateful—both for the thought bubbles and for sparing me the singing.'

'You couldn't call it singing. There isn't a musical bone in my body.'

'Not a singer and not a poet?' She smiled. 'Seriously, though, my clients are anything but boring—'

'And neither are you boring,' he said.

She flushed pink, high on her cheekbones. He would have liked to trace the path of colour with his fingers, then move down to her mouth. Her lovely mouth, with the top lip slightly narrower than the bottom lip, giving it an enticing sensuality.

'That's nice,' she said simply.

'Tell me about your clients,' he said. 'I'm intrigued.'

'I specialise in working with creative people.' Her face softened. 'People like my parents, who were hopeless money-managers. Charming. Talented. My father played guitar. My mother's instrument was her voice. But they were feckless with money.'

She stopped.

'That was way more information than you wanted.'

He leaned closer to her. 'No, it wasn't. Tell me more. I'm interested in what you do.'

She backed away—so slightly he might have thought he'd imagined it if he hadn't been so focused on her. He found it intriguing to have her nervous of him. He was used to women who were unabashed—blatant, even—in expressing their desire for him.

'Shall we order the food first, if you're so hungry?' she said, her words tumbling out in a rush. 'I know the manager said it was business as usual, but the kitchen might not be up to speed after the quake.'

Mitch's empty belly told him that was a very good idea. But he wasn't going to let her get away for long with changing the subject. He was fascinated by her—wanted to make the most of the hours they were fated to spend together.

'Okay,' he said.

She got up from the lounger. 'I'll phone it through.'

Mitch got up too, and took the menu from her. 'No. I'll order. They can bill the meal to my room.'

She went to snatch it back. 'It can be billed to my room.'

He held on firmly to the menu. When she tried to take it he held it above his head. 'In the rarefied space where I dwell, I pay for dinner.'

Zoe bristled at his comment. She liked to be independent. 'Please at least let me pay for my own meal,' she said.

'No,' he said, in a firm, forceful way that brooked no argument.

It was a gracious gesture on his part, and it would be crass of her to argue. 'Okay. Thank you. I'll—'

She was going to say she'd pay next time, but of course it was highly unlikely she'd be having dinner again with Mitch Bailey. Further earthquakes or not.

Mitch headed to the phone to order the meal. His back view was breathtaking: broad shoulders tapered to a swoon-worthy butt, then long, strong legs. No wonder his fans went crazy over him. Lost in admiration, she felt a tad light-headed herself.

She observed the way he walked, with the confident easy strength of a man at the peak of physical perfection. There wasn't the slightest indication that he favoured his right knee in his athletic stride. She prayed the knee was now strong enough to help him soar right back to the heights of the success he craved.

'You were right—the meal will be around an hour,' he said when he returned.

'Lucky we ordered when we did, then.'

Mitch didn't sit back down on the lounger. 'It's hot. How about cooling down in your pool?'

It *was* hot—and humid—and suddenly Zoe wanted more than anything to dive into the water. Perspiration prickled on her brow and her dress clung stickily to her back. But the pool wasn't very large. It seemed too intimate to be sharing it with him. Maybe she'd spent too long admiring his rear view. Then again, sitting outside was starting to get uncomfortable—despite the shade of the frangipani tree.

Mitch didn't hesitate. He strode to the edge of the pool and dived in with an arrow-perfect dive and barely a splash.

He swam the length of the pool underwater, his tanned, perfect body spearing through the turquoise depths. When he emerged his hair sat sleek and dark against his head, and his broad shoulders and chest glistened with drops of water caught in the late-afternoon sun. Zoe caught her breath at how handsome he looked.

'Come on in!' he called with the engaging grin that had appealed to her so much all those years ago.

Still she hesitated. Usually she wouldn't think twice about slipping off her dress and diving in. But the very act of taking off her dress in front of Mitch paralysed her. It seemed like... Well, it seemed like a striptease—as if she were displaying her body for his delectation. But it would seem ridiculous to go inside when she already had her bikini on underneath.

She compromised and turned away, angling her body for minimum exposure to Mitch. Then slid her dress up and over her head, tossing it onto the lounger.

She was aware of Mitch's gaze on her. Of the admiration in his eyes. It disconcerted her. She wasn't afraid to be seen in a bikini. She worked hard to stay slim and strong. And her fashionable bikini was quite modestly cut, in a retro style reminiscent of a swimsuit from the nineteen-fifties. But she was suddenly aware of how its very design drew attention to her breasts, her hips. In the past Mitch had seen her as a nerd, a geek. She doubted he'd even noticed she was female. Not with tall, curvy Lara always in tow, staking her claim on Mitch at any opportunity. Not that she'd needed to—Mitch had only had eyes for his blonde girlfriend.

But now... Now Mitch had noticed she was female. It was in his narrowed eyes, in the way his head was tilted to the side as he watched her.

And she liked it.

CHAPTER FIVE

ZOE LIKED THE way Mitch didn't hide his appreciation of the woman she'd become. She liked the easy way she could talk with him. She liked having him back in her life, even if only for these few hours. No way would she let that be ruined by feeling awkward or self-conscious. That kind of negativity had been left far behind her, in the corridors of Northside High.

He was the most beautiful man she was ever likely to meet—and not just in appearance. Scratch the surface of the mega sports star, the billboard model, the oestrogen magnet who had female hearts in a flurry all around the world, and the Mitch she'd liked so much when she was seventeen was still there. Even more confident and self-assured, but still Mitch.

Thanks to a random shifting of the tectonic plates beneath the earth's crust she'd been gifted this time before they each went back to their lives on opposite sides of the world.

She took a few swift steps to the edge of the water and waded in. Although a more than competent swimmer, she didn't want to risk an embarrassing belly flop in front of one of the world's elite athletes.

Zoe gasped and squealed at the initial coolness of the water, then welcomed it. With slow, easy strokes she swam from one end of the pool to the other. On her return lap she found herself very close to Mitch—so close their bodies actually nudged in the water: thigh against thigh, hip against hip. His body was strong, hard, muscular.

A shiver of pleasure ran through her at the contact. Had he noticed? Hastily she pushed away through the water to swim another lap.

He must be so used to women fawning all over him. That would *not* be her. She was determined to seem friendly, but not too friendly. No groupie-like grasping for attention from Mr Sexiest Man Alive for her. Much as she might yearn for it.

Her laps completed, she stood facing him in the shallow end of the pool, the water up to her waist

'That was a good idea. So refreshing.'

'It's not a huge pool, but it works,' he said.

No doubt he was staying in one of the larger, more luxurious villas the size of a house at the other end of the resort.

'This pool's only meant for two,' she said, breathless more from her proximity to him than from the vigour of her swimming. 'These villas are popular with honeymooners, I believe.'

She was suddenly heart-stoppingly aware of the utter privacy afforded by the high wall and the tropical trees and shrubs that grew above it, the solid, ornately carved wooden gate. A couple could frolic without a stitch on in this pool and no one would know.

'I booked in to this place because I wanted privacy,' Mitch said. He looked down to the bare third finger of her left hand. 'Why are you here on your own?'

'Because I want to be,' she said, careful to keep her voice matter-of-fact. 'May is a good time to take a break before all the end-of-financial-year mayhem in the final weeks of June.'

No need to mention that she'd needed to get away on her own to escape the fallout of a relationship break-up.

'That wasn't what I meant,' Mitch said with a slow grin. 'I wanted to know if there was a man in your life.'

'Oh,' she said. It was a reasonable question but she felt flustered by it. As if he'd been reading her mind. 'No,' she said. 'Not...not any more.'

'That surprises me,' he said.

She was aware of his appreciative gaze taking in the swell of her breasts over the top of her bikini bra, her bare shoulders and arms. She sucked in her stomach.

'There was someone. But...but I broke up with him a month ago.'

'Were you meant to come here with him?' He gestured around him. 'To this "couples' paradise"?'

'We were talking about Thailand. This was a last-minute booking.'

He nodded. 'Yeah, you said.' Mitch's green eyes narrowed. 'So you came to Bali to nurse a broken heart?'

'No.' She sighed, looked down at the water where it rippled around them. 'More likely I...I broke *his* heart.'

'I didn't take you for the heartbreaker type,' Mitch said.

Zoe slowly shook her head. 'I didn't think I was the heartbreaker type either. I've had my share of dating hurt, but it's not pleasant to be the one dishing it out. I'm not proud of it. He was a wonderful guy.'

'But not wonderful enough to go on vacation with?'

She met his gaze. 'Not wonderful enough to marry. We were talking about taking a vacation together. Then he turned it around to talk of a honeymoon.'

'And you ran scared?' Mitch said.

'I don't know about being scared. I just didn't feel the same way he did.'

She was beginning to wonder if there was something

wrong with her that at the age of twenty-seven she still didn't want to commit to a man. This recent proposal was the second one she'd turned down. But she wasn't going to share that with Mitch.

'You're not interested in marriage?' he asked.

'Of course I am. One day. And I'd like to have a family. But not now. Not to him—nice as he was. I didn't feel strongly enough to make that kind of commitment.'

The conversation was taking on a more personal slant than she cared for. But the shock of the earthquake, the surprise of seeing Mitch again, had loosened her inhibitions about talking about her love-life—or lack of it.

'Fair enough,' he said.

'I won't compromise. When I get married it will be because I'm head over heels in love and know it will last for ever.'

His brow raised. 'Okay…'

She laughed. 'You're looking at me as if you can't believe I said that.'

'I was surprised,' he admitted. 'I took you more for the practical, pragmatic type.'

'Because I'm an accountant with a business degree?'

'Who knew that underneath the number-crunching and the bean-counting there beats the heart of a romantic?'

Zoe tried not to sound defensive. 'Maybe it *is* ridiculously romantic of me, but I want the kind of love my parents had. They adored each other. I won't settle for less.'

'Admirable,' he said.

'But over-idealistic?'

'I didn't say that.'

'Just raised your eyebrows and let me think it?'

He grinned. 'I didn't realise my eyebrows were so expressive.

'You'd be surprised what your eyebrows reveal about you,' she said.

Mitch waggled his eyebrows. 'What are my eyebrows saying now?'

Zoe paused to think up a sassy reply—only to be hit by a splash of expertly aimed pool water.

'Hey!' she spluttered, wiping water from her eyes with the back of her hand. 'What was that for?'

His eyes crinkled in amusement. 'You didn't read my eyebrows quickly enough, did you? They were challenging you to a water fight.'

'Challenge accepted,' she said without further hesitation. 'This is war.'

Laughing, she angled around him, shooting sprays of water with the edge of her hand as she struck the surface. Laughing too, he retaliated faster, harder, until the spray was constant between them. Defence became attack; attack became defence.

As Mitch pulled his arm way back, for a powerful splash she couldn't hope to deflect, Zoe ducked and swam underwater to the other end of the pool before resurfacing.

'Hah! Retreating from the battlefield,' said Mitch.

'A tactical move to regroup my energies,' Zoe said breathless, laughing, pushing back her wet hair from her eyes.

Mitch raised his hands above his head. 'I surrender,' he said, with that big, endearing grin that had made him the darling of the women's magazines.

It wouldn't take much for her to surrender to him.

With just a few strokes of his strong, sinewy arms he had reached her. He wasn't the slightest bit out of breath.

'Why don't I trust that surrender one little bit?' she said, moving back in the water so she could feel the edge of the pool at her spine.

'Because I learned the game fighting dirty with my three brothers in our backyard pool,' he said, stopping just a pace from her.

'Let's call it a draw, then, shall we?' she said. Her heart was pounding—not from exertion, but from his closeness: the muscled breadth of his chest, the washboard abs.

The utter male perfection of him.

'I'm a competitive guy. I don't give in too easily.'

She didn't know whether the towering conquest in his stance was real or part of the game. Her heartbeat skipped up a further gear.

She met his gaze for a long moment before replying. 'I'm a diplomatic woman. I'm thinking of ways we can end this peacefully.'

Oh, she could think of several ways that she'd never dare put voice to.

He laughed. 'Seriously? How can I argue against that? I really am conceding.'

'Can I trust you?' she asked playfully.

He held out his hands, palms up in supplication. 'You can trust me, Zoe,' he said.

Other words unspoken hung in the air. Trust had been an issue in their brief, shared past. But he had redeemed himself by apologising for the incident that had ended their youthful friendship.

This was just a game.

The silence was broken by the loud crowing of a rooster coming from a few buildings away.

'The final word comes from Mr Rooster,' Zoe said.

Mitch scowled. 'Darn bird. He crows morning, noon and night.'

'He must have quite the harem of hens to keep happy.'

'It's not a sound I hear in the heart of old Madrid.'

'Or me in Balmain, in inner Sydney.'

'You live in Balmain?'

She nodded. 'In a converted warehouse on the waterfront, overlooking Mort Bay.'

'I played the Balmain Tigers in junior club. They were a good team. Beat 'em, of course.'

'You really are competitive, aren't you?'

'Only winners are grinners,' he said, and although he was smiling his words rang true. 'In my game you can't afford to be anything else.'

'An attacking midfielder. That's what I've seen you described as. It sounds aggressive.'

Zoe had seen him play on screen: swift, superbly balanced, relentless and graceful all at the same time. No other player had caught her attention. She'd thrilled at the TV commentator's praise for Mitch. While she didn't know a lot about soccer, she'd got what the commentator had meant when he'd said Mitch had the vision to split a defence with unerringly accurate passes perfectly weighted to gift his teammates with scoring opportunities. No wonder his team wanted him back.

His jaw set. 'You have to be aggressive to win, Zoe. Tactical and ruthless.'

'And you're all about winning?'

'The game is *everything*.' He emphasised the word so there was no missing his message.

'And in your personal life?'

'What personal life?' he joked, but his eyes were shadowed and serious.

He had quizzed her about *her* love-life; she had a few questions of her own.

'You were with Lara for a long time,' she said.

Again, she didn't want him to think she'd been stalking him. But Mitch's hometown girlfriend had attracted lots of media attention—both in Australia and overseas. Lara had only got blonder and more glamorous as she'd grown up. The golden couple had been all over the media, and Lara had become the queen bee of the contingent of foot-ballers' wives and girlfriends the media nicknamed WAGs.

'We had our ups and downs,' Mitch muttered.

Zoe wouldn't have been human if she hadn't felt a small degree of satisfaction when she'd seen Mitch had finally split with Lara. Much as she'd put that incident at school behind her, Lara's maliciousness had been impossible to forget. She'd been the meanest of the mean girls. *Mitch deserved better.*

'I'm sorry,' she said, willing her voice to sound sincere.

Mitch shrugged and water slicked off his broad shoul-ders. 'Don't be. We broke up and got back together so many times. It was never going to work.'

From his carefully schooled expression and even tone of voice Zoe sensed there was more to it than Mitch was saying. That was okay. It was none of her business.

'No one special since?' She thought of the parade of Lara look-alikes who'd featured briefly on Mitch's arm.

He turned to scoop up a palm frond that had fallen into the water and tossed it out onto the courtyard, his back rippling with sculpted muscle. 'I don't have time for some-one special. Date someone more than a few times and they start thinking it's more than a casual thing.'

Who could blame the poor girls for wanting more with a man like Mitch?

'You must get women flinging themselves at you all the time.' *But what a way to get your heart broken.*

He shifted and looked uncomfortable. 'Football group-ies and over-eager fans come with the territory,' he said. 'What's more difficult is meeting genuine women not blinded by money and fame.'

'I can see that, but—'

He cut across her. 'But that's irrelevant right now. My personal life is on hold. Indefinitely. I've got something to prove. There's no room in my life for relationships. Not now. Not for years.'

'You're focusing on success and nothing is going to distract you?'

'That's exactly right,' he said. 'I'm glad you understand. Women usually think they can change my mind.'

'The hopes of all those fans shattered!' she said with mock mournfulness.

'And you breaking hearts all the way, let me remind you.'

'If you put it like that…'

'Putting it like that makes us both single,' he said, his deep voice a tone deeper.

'Yes,' she murmured through a suddenly choked throat.

For a long, still moment their eyes held. The intensity of his gaze reminded her of Mitch as a student, determined to understand the subject she was helping him to master. Back then he'd been reading a page in a poetry book; right now it felt as if he was reading her face as his gaze searched her eyes, her mouth.

In turn she explored *his* face. His chiselled face. His strong jaw. The knowing glint in his green eyes framed by those too-expressive eyebrows. And his mouth, lifted to a half-smile that gave a promise of pleasure that made her own lips part in anticipation, her breath quicken.

Her eyes locked with his and a thrill of anticipation tingled through her.

Mitch Bailey was about to kiss her. And she was going to kiss him right back.

CHAPTER SIX

MITCH HAD BEEN aching to kiss Zoe ever since she'd joined him in the pool. But just as his lips grazed hers, just as her lips parted under his, just as she uttered a delicious little moan of surprise and need, an Oriental-sounding chime came from the carved gate to the villa.

'Room service!' called a cheerful voice with a lilting Balinese accent.

Mitch stilled. Zoe looked up into his eyes. He saw echoed in hers the same frustration he was feeling at being thwarted in their first kiss.

For a long moment they stood motionless in the water, his mouth still claiming hers, her hands resting on his shoulders in silent agreement to pretend they weren't there.

The doorbell chimed again.

Mitch muttered a curse under his breath. Then he pulled Zoe closer and kissed her hard. She wound her arms around his neck and kissed him back with equal passion. Heat ignited between them so fast he was surprised steam wasn't rising from the water.

Damn the room service timing.

With regret he let her go, then pulled her back for a final swift kiss. If she could see his thought bubble now it would give her the promise torn from him. *Later.*

'Come in,' he called to the waiter on the other side of the gate, his voice hoarse.

Reluctantly he let Zoe go, supporting her when she seemed to stagger in the water. When she'd regained her balance he swam to the edge of the pool, then turned back to check she was okay.

The sight of her wading out of the water made him suck in a gasp of admiration. *She was awesome.* With both hands she pushed her wet hair from her face, so it was slicked behind her ears and flat to her head. The severe hairstyle emphasised the angular, unconventional beauty of her face. That black bikini concealed more than it revealed, yet he found the very subtlety of it tantalising. Zoe was smart, fun, *different.* He couldn't remember when he'd last bantered and laughed like that with a woman.

He flung a blue-striped beach towel around his shoulders and handed her one as she got out of the pool. 'It's an improvement on the white one,' he said in a low voice.

'Anything would be an improvement on that,' she said, her voice not quite steady as she wrapped the towel around her.

The smiling young waiter, dressed in the version of traditional garb that formed the staff's uniform, carried in a large silver tray. He placed the tray on the outdoor table and, with a flourish, lifted the lids that covered the plates.

'*Terima kasih*—thank you,' Zoe said to the waiter with her vibrant smile.

Her teeth were perfect—even and white. Had she worn braces at school? Mitch couldn't be sure. He was racking his brains to try and remember everything about her back then.

Their dinner was presented with simple Asian elegance. No one would know it had come from a kitchen suffering the after-effects of an earthquake. Deliciously spicy smells wafted from the tray and Mitch's stomach rumbled. But hunger of a different kind was foremost in his mind.

He echoed Zoe's thanks to the waiter, tipped him generously, and watched impatiently for the high, ornate gate to close behind him.

Finally he was alone again with Zoe, in the total privacy of the villa. It seemed suddenly very quiet. He was aware of the faint lapping of the water against the sides of the pool; the rustle of birds settling for the night in the surrounding trees. He swore he could even hear the fizzing of the bubbles in the mineral water Zoe had ordered. A faint smell of incense wafted across from the nearby Hindu temple, to mingle with the aromas of their dinner and the sweetness of frangipani blossom.

Mitch found he had to clear his throat to speak. 'Dinner is served,' he said, with a mock bow.

'So I see. It smells amazing. I...I'm suddenly hungry again.'

There was an edge to her voice—as if she were trying too hard to make conversation. She tugged at the knot that kept the beach towel secure between her breasts.

'The waiter has gone,' he said. 'You can ditch the towel.'

'I'd rather keep it on,' she said.

'Because it's so cold?'

Although it was starting to get dark, it was still hot, the air thick and humid.

'I feel more comfortable covered up,' she said, not meeting his eyes.

'Zoe—'

'Mitch—' she said at the same time.

'Back then—'

'In...in the pool—' she stuttered.

'When we—'

She raised her eyes to meet his. 'I don't think it should happen again. The…the kiss, I mean.'

'I didn't think you meant the water fight,' Mitch quipped.

She smiled and her shoulders visibly relaxed. 'I enjoyed the water fight.' She flushed high on her cheekbones. 'I…I enjoyed the kiss.'

'I'm glad to hear that.' He couldn't keep the irony from his tone.

'But…'

With a sinking feeling, Mitch had known there was a *but* coming.

'But, considering the circumstances, I think we should stick to…to being friends.'

Mitch felt intense disappointment with an overlay of relief. He suspected Zoe wasn't the kind of girl for a one-night fling. And right now that was all he could offer with his life the way it was. He'd hurt her in the past. He certainly had no wish to hurt her now.

'You're right,' he said through gritted teeth.

Of course she was right—much as he might wish otherwise, much as he ached for her to continue that kiss.

'Just friends.'

'Thank you,' she murmured.

But he wanted her.

This urgent desire for her had come from left field. He hadn't looked at Zoe in that way when they'd been teenagers, much as he'd liked her. He'd been with Lara, and he'd prided himself on being faithful even then.

But now he was single, and the sway of Zoe's hips, the swell of her breasts, her lovely mouth and her husky laughter was driving him crazy with want. However, he knew it would be better for her if he held back and didn't act on that desire. Better for him too. He didn't want to carry another burden of guilt away with him when they said goodbye.

'So we'll treat that kiss as the spoils of our water battle in the swimming pool?' he said, forcing his voice to sound light-hearted.

'In which both sides triumphed,' she said, with a sigh that sounded halfway between relief and regret. Which only made him want her more.

Oh, yes, a kiss from Mitch was a prize indeed.

Zoe's head was still spinning from the impact of Mitch's brief but passionate possession of her mouth. His lips had only been on hers for such a short time, but the joy of it had been seared into her soul.

If a kiss felt like that what would making love with him be like?

She pushed the thought far, far away into the deepest recesses of her heart.

Had she always wanted this? Her body pulled close to his? The taste of him? the touch of him? The sheer bliss of being with him?

That teenage crush had never gone away.

It was only one kiss. But it had awakened a desire for him so powerful it would have led to more than a kiss. And she couldn't deal with that. Not when he'd made it so clear that there was no room for a woman in his life. Not when, once this brief alignment of their planets was over, they'd go back to their different worlds. *She would probably never see him again.* Her desire for him was as impossible as that deeply buried crush had been so long ago.

'No need to look so woeful,' he said.

He pulled her into a hug. She hesitated at first, then relaxed into his arms. Her head rested on his shoulder and he stroked her hair. She closed her eyes, the better to savour the utter pleasure of his hands on her.

'It's not our time, not our place,' he said. 'But I'm glad we met up again, Zoe Summers. I'm pleased to count you as a friend.'

'Me too,' she said, wishing she could stay in his arms longer, knowing it wasn't a good idea. Her in a bikini, him in his swim shorts—full-body, bare skin contact. While her mind was telling her to pull away her body was clamouring for more.

'Let's enjoy our dinner,' he said. 'Then I'll go back to my villa. Because I can't guarantee I won't kiss you again.'

Zoe blinked down hard on a sudden smarting of tears. 'Good idea. I...I mean bad idea. I mean *wise* idea.'

She pulled away from his hug, feeling bereft of his warmth, his strength, and forced her voice to sound cheerful and matter-of-fact when inside she was a churning mess of conflict.

It would be only too easy to tell him to stay. But then, when they went their separate ways, she would have to live with it—and that might throw her right back into those high school feelings of unworthiness she'd worked so hard to shake off. Her life was settled, steady, sure—dull compared to his.

She could never be part of Mitch's world.

She tucked the beach towel around her a little more firmly. *'Usted debe ser hambre,'* she said in her best Spanish accent.

'Now that you mention it, yes, I am starving,' he said. He took her hand and led her to where the waiter had set up their dinner table, with two chairs facing opposite each other. 'Let's make the most of this meal.'

Zoe did her best. The *ayam bakar* with lemongrass salsa was one of the best chicken dishes Zoe had ever enjoyed.

But she managed only a few half-hearted bites, pushing it around her plate. Mitch, on the contrary, ate heartily. By not eating was she trying to postpone the moment dinner was over? If so, what did that mean *he* was doing?

He pushed his plate away with a satisfied sigh. 'The food in Madrid is amazing, but this fish is up there with the best meal ever.'

'It looked really good,' she said, struggling to make polite conversation.

'But you've hardly touched yours,' he said.

'I'm not really hungry,' she murmured, the knot in her stomach tightening.

'Why don't we wait a while before we eat dessert?' he said.

'Good idea,' she said.

Anything to postpone the time when they had to say goodbye.

Darkness had fallen, but the sensor-driven lights hidden in the greenery and at the edge of the pool had been switched on. The scene was peaceful and beautiful.

'This time last night I was watching the sunset on the beach,' Mitch said.

'Me too,' she said.

She wished he hadn't evoked the memory of it. Standing on the endless stretch of the dark Seminyak sand, watching the magnificence of the sun sinking into the sea, had been the only times she'd felt lonely on this solitary vacation. To know Mitch had been somewhere on the same beach somehow made it worse.

He got up from his chair.

'Let's sit over here,' he said, heading towards the loungers.

He dragged away the small table from in between and pushed the loungers together. When he'd sat down he patted the lounger next to him. It was an invitation she could not resist.

Mitch put a friendly arm around her. She relaxed against his shoulder, breathing in the clean, male scent of him, storing up the memory of it to relive next time she saw him on television, playing the game he loved so much on some international soccer pitch, where tens of thousands of spectators watched him in the flesh.

How would she be able to bear it?

At that precise moment the rooster chose the occasion for another of his raucous, triumphant cries, which lifted her from her maudlin thoughts.

'Trust him to have the last word,' she said.

Both she and Mitch laughed.

But the laughter froze in her throat as she noticed the still turquoise surface of the swimming pool start to shimmer—as if a giant hand had picked up the concrete edge and shaken it.

CHAPTER SEVEN

LAUGHING AND FOOLING AROUND with Mitch had distracted Zoe from the danger of a possible aftershock. Now her fear came rushing back as powerfully as a possible tsunami.

The loungers she and Mitch were reclining on started to shake. The plates, knives and forks and glasses from their unfinished feast clattered together. Zoe shrank against Mitch, paralysed with terror. The whimpering that echoed in her ears came from her.

'Under the table—now,' Mitch urged, and he helped her roll off the lounger and crawl to the table. He pushed her under first, then squeezed in with her, putting his arm around her to pull her tight to him.

Was this it—the big one?

Every so often she had nightmares about being in the car when the truck had hit them. Of struggling in and out of consciousness with an agonising pain in her leg. Paramedics talking to her in soothing tones with an edge of pity they hadn't been able to suppress. No one answering her questions about her parents. The eventual dreadful knowledge that she would never see them again.

She was usually successful at pushing thoughts of her loss to the dark shadows at the back of her mind. Not so now.

Earlier today something with the potential to wipe out

her world had again come from nowhere, completely out of her control. Now it was threatening her again.

She burrowed her face against Mitch's shoulder, grateful for his comfort, his strength, for the soothing reassuring sounds he was making as he stroked her back.

'You'll be okay. I think it's only a tiny tremor,' he repeated.

As it happened, he was right. It was probably only seconds rather than minutes before the tremor subsided.

For a few long moments she stayed in Mitch's protective embrace as the resort settled again.

'Do you think there'll be another tremor?' she asked, her voice muffled.

'Difficult to say,' he said. 'If anything catastrophic had happened—like a tsunami warning—we would have heard alarms by now.'

'That...that wasn't too bad.' She lifted her head to meet his gaze but was reluctant to move out of the comforting circle of his arms, the illusion of safety under the table.

'I think it's safe to come out now,' he said with that disarming smile, but he made no effort to move away from her.

'Thank you,' she said, mildly ashamed of her reaction. 'I never thought I'd dive under a table twice in one day.'

She'd always prided herself on her level-headedness. *But she had been afraid.*

She eased away from his arms and crawled out from under the table while Mitch did the same, then stood next to him as they looked around them. Except for a further scattering of frangipani blossoms and a new palm frond on the surface of the pool, now still again, there had been no damage. The rooster was going crazy—but then he did tend to sound off at this time of evening.

But what if it hadn't been that way?

What if she and Mitch had been injured? What if she'd never seen him again not because he'd gone back to Madrid but because he…?

She couldn't bear even to think through the rest.

Or what if another quake came during the night and…?

You could never be certain of tomorrow.

'You okay?' he said.

She nodded. 'You?'

'Fine. It was nothing compared to the last one. Though it did jolt me.'

'I'm glad you didn't go back to your villa.'

'Me too,' he said. 'I would have been in a state without you to hold on to.'

He was being kind, uttering the self-deprecating words for her sake. She knew that. It was she who had fallen to pieces. Not him. He hadn't been afraid. Not for a moment. He was just trying to make her feel better.

That seemed to be Mitch all round. Sexiest man alive. Star athlete. Fun. And kind. In short, the most wonderful man she had ever met or was ever likely to meet. *Mitch was unique.* And not just because of the way he looked or his skill with a ball.

The earthquake had dropped him into her life again and shaken the way she thought to its very foundations. Nothing could be the same.

Suddenly everything became very clear. She did not want to be plagued with regrets. This might be the only chance she ever had to be with Mitch.

She couldn't let him go back to his villa.

She turned to face him and clutched his arm so hard he winced. Her heart was thudding so loudly she was surprised he couldn't hear it, and her mouth was dry.

'Don't go tonight, Mitch. Stay with me.'

His eyes seemed to darken to a deeper shade of green. 'Zoe, are you sure?'

She tilted her face to his, twined her arms around his neck and kissed him. He seemed surprised, and paused for just a second before he kissed her back. His lips were warm and firm and exciting beneath hers and she explored the way he tasted, the way he felt. Mitch hugged her to him as he deepened the kiss so it escalated into a passionate meeting of mouths, tongues, teeth.

Desire for him rushed through her—urgent, demanding, insistent. *She wanted him and she wanted him now.*

It wasn't about the earthquake—that was just a facilitator. It was about *him.* If she'd bumped into him at sunset on the beach she would have wanted him. If she'd chanced upon him in a bar in Seminyak and they'd got chatting she would have wanted him.

She was realistic. Mitch obviously went for stunningly beautiful girls like Lara—blonde and glamorous. She, Zoe, hitting average on the looks scale, was never likely to capture Mitch Bailey's attention. But here, now, she had.

She'd wanted him at seventeen and hadn't been able to have him. Now she was going to take what she wanted. Even if it was for only one night.

She broke the kiss and pulled away, panting and breathless. 'I...I think we should go inside.'

'It's completely private here—look at the height of those walls.'

'Wh...what about helicopters?'

Mitch's brow rose, bemused. 'Helicopters? Why would you worry about *helicopters*?'

She felt a little foolish. 'I don't know. Your world is so different to mine. But I thought—'

Mitch laughed, but it was laughter free of mockery.

'I'm not so famous that I'm harassed by paparazzi buzzing overhead in helicopters.'

'Just being sure,' she said. 'I would hate to see a blurry photo of us on the internet, with a reference to myself as the "mystery brunette" seen making out with Mitch Bailey in his luxurious Bali villa.'

'Not going to happen,' he said.

'You're sure of that?' she said, with more than a touch of worry.

Mitch trailed a finger along the curve of her jaw, sending a jolt of awareness through every pleasure receptor in her body. 'What happens in your villa stays in your villa,' he said. 'I don't want publicity either.'

'I'd still be happier if we went inside,' she said.

The walls were high, but she *would* prefer to be behind closed doors with Mitch, safe from any curious eyes.

'Just one thing before we go,' he said.

He picked up a frangipani blossom and tucked in behind her ear, making it a caress.

The gesture undid her. Who knew Mitch could be so romantic?

'Thank you,' she said with a slow smile. 'I love the scent.'

'And a second thing...'

He reached over and undid the knot that secured her beach towel so it fell to the ground.

Zoe in his arms. Zoe kissing him. Zoe wanting him to stay with her.

There was nothing he wanted more.

But, much as he ached to pick her up and carry her into her bedroom, Mitch knew he had to slow things down.

For all Zoe's sassiness and smarts, Mitch sensed a vulnerability about her that had not lessened since he'd known her as a recently bereaved seventeen-year-old. The foundations of her life had been yanked out from underneath her. This earthquake had shaken them some more—and he didn't just mean literally.

He wanted to take up her invitation. But he wanted her to be sure what she was letting herself in for. He could not damage her further.

As soon as they got inside the villa Zoe tilted her face to his. Her flawless skin was flushed, her brown eyes luminous with desire, and her lips were parted on a half-smile that was so seductive he caught his breath. Laughing that low, husky laugh, as though she knew her power over him, she pulled him to her for another urgent kiss.

When the kiss threatened to get out of control he broke away, smoothed her hair—drying now into a dark mass of waves—from around from her face, and secured the flower behind her ear. He liked the way it looked there—exotic, sensual. Then he cupped her face in his hands, looked deep into her eyes.

He had to clear his throat to speak. 'Before we go any further we have to be sure. This is all there can be for us. Tonight.'

She laughed a husky, strangled laugh. 'Tonight might be all we ever have. We could wake up to find ourselves floating out to sea.'

'There's that,' he said. 'But—'

She put a finger to his lips to silence him.

He moved it away, then slipped his fingers through hers and firmly held her hand by her side.

'This has to be said.'

He was trying to be the sensible one here, when all he could think of was how much he wanted Zoe.

She made a pretend pout, which astounded him, and had him fighting the temptation to kiss her again.

'I don't want to waste any more time talking,' she murmured.

He groaned. Did she know what she was doing to him? He gave in to temptation and planted a quick kiss on her lovely mouth. But that was it until they'd got this sorted. He wanted her—but he did not want her hurt.

'You're amazing, Zoe. Gorgeous. Fun. Smart as ever. A surprise. But there's no room for a serious relationship in my life. Not for years. Not until I'm thirty. Maybe thirty-five. I was at the top of my game when I got injured. I have to prove myself all over again. I can't afford...emotional entanglements.'

She shook her head and made a little murmur of impatience. 'Can't you see I'm not looking beyond tonight? The world as we know it could be wiped out—I want to take the chance for us to be together while we can. You were wonderful when you were a teenager and you've grown into a wonderful man. All the qualities you had then are still there, and more. I want to spend this night with you. No matter what tomorrow might bring.'

'Thank you,' he said, moved by her words.

Back then, he realised, she had seen potential in him that others hadn't; only Zoe had recognised him as more than a good-looking jock.

'I could say the same about you.'

There was a wistful edge to her smile. 'Thank you. But, as I said earlier, we live on different planets. I'm not expecting more from you than this one night.'

He started to say something but she put her finger across his mouth again.

'I want you. But I wouldn't want a relationship with someone in the public eye—a man who belongs to his fans, not one hundred per cent to me. I'd be miserable with someone who travels the world while I'm left at home, torturing myself with thoughts about the women who might be throwing themselves at him. I'm a private person. I don't want the world to know me because of the man I'm with. I...I could never be a WAG.'

Though her words made absolute sense, he found them more than a touch insulting. That *was* his life. And it was the best life a guy could have. *It was all he wanted.* For him it wasn't about the kudos, the fame, the money. It was about the game.

'That's a lot about what you *don't* want,' he said. 'Now let's hear what you *do* want, Zoe.'

She pulled one of those faces he found so appealing. 'We've established it's ridiculously romantic of me, but one day I want a real, for ever kind of love.'

'Like your parents had?'

She nodded. 'Not just for me, but for my children. I had the happiest childhood you can imagine. It was erratic. We moved from one shared household to another. From one failed venture to another. And at the age of ten I knew how to lie to a debt collector. But I was secure in the love my parents had for each other and for me. I want to love and be loved on that scale. I...I think I value it so much because it was wrenched away from me.'

'And that happened not long before I first knew you.' He felt a surge of anger against his younger self, who had hurt her at a time when she hadn't needed more hurt added to her burden.

'When you first knew me I was like a...like a creature who had been wrenched from its cocoon way too soon and thrown into the harsh reality of life with a grandmother who resented me.'

Mitch realised his parents also had a good marriage. They argued. There was noise and fireworks. But they were happy, and they'd raised well-balanced, successful sons. It was a fine goal to aspire to. *Just not yet.* Marriage right now would seem like a trap.

'I guess that's what I want too, one day. But not now.'

He'd made a lot of sacrifices to get where he was. Since he'd left school he hadn't had what most people would call a 'normal' life. Giving up any thought of a permanent relationship was another sacrifice he was more than happy to make. But if he could have Zoe for tonight—for one night—that would be something very special.

She looked up to him. 'Mitch, you asked me what I really want...'

'Yes. And you told me.'

'I told you what I want for the future. Ask me what I want for *now*.'

'I'm asking you,' he said, his voice hoarse with need.

Her eyes were huge and her mouth quivered. 'I want *you*, Mitch. Just you.'

He could not resist her any longer.

With a groan, he lifted her up to sit on the edge of the countertop. She wound her arms around his neck, her thighs gripping his waist as he held her to him. He kissed her mouth, deep and demanding, then pressed urgent, hungry kisses down the smooth column of her throat as she arched her body to his.

He hoped his kisses would transmit everything he couldn't say about how glad he was to be with her on this night, when they didn't know what they might wake up to the next hour, the next day. He kissed her and kissed her and kissed her—until kissing was no longer enough.

Zoe was woken by the soft, insistent buzzing of her mobile phone to let her know there was a text message for her.

For a moment she didn't know where she was. She blinked against the early-morning light filtering in through the louvered doors. Heard that noisy rooster greeting the dawn.

She was in Bali. Still alive. With Mitch.

Mitch.

He lay beside her on his back, the sheets rumpled around his hips, his arms flung above his head in total relaxation. Her breath caught at how beautiful he was. *Beautiful* wasn't a word she'd normally use to describe a man, but it fitted Mitch. His smooth skin was gilded by the sunlight, his face rough with golden stubble she wanted to reach over and stroke. But she didn't want to risk waking him.

Her heart gave a huge, painful lurch at the thought that she would most likely never see him again. But if she'd woken up alone this morning she would have always regretted it.

Cautiously, so as not to disturb him, she reached over to her phone and slid the buzzer off. It was a message from the airline. Her plane back to Sydney was on schedule. She needed to be at the airport in two hours. That just gave her time to have breakfast with Mitch. To say goodbye.

No.

She couldn't bear that.

This kind of situation was a first for her. She could only imagine how awkward and embarrassing it would be to face him. Last night with Mitch had been perfect. She wanted to keep its perfection encapsulated in her mind for ever. Not sullied by awkward goodbyes, murmured promises they both knew would never be fulfilled.

Besides, she rationalised, the Ngurah Rai International Airport at Denpasar was sure to be bedlam because of the earthquake and its aftershock. She wanted to make sure she got on that plane and out of here; she didn't think she could cope with another tremor.

She looked back at Mitch, breathing deeply and evenly in her bed. They'd both got what they'd needed from each other at a time of threat and uncertainty. Comfort. Reassurance. *Sex*.

Oh, yes. Sex such as she'd never imagined. Sex that had seen her soaring to unimaginable heights of pleasure with Mitch. Again and again. Then again, when they'd woken some time after midnight, turned into each other's arms, laughed at the fact that they could still want each other after all the satisfaction they'd already given each other, and once more made love.

Afterwards they'd crept outside to the courtyard in the moonlight and polished off their abandoned desserts—even her melted ice cream—whispering and stifling their laughter when Mitch had threatened to crow out loud like a rooster.

They'd finally gone to sleep entwined in each other's arms.

Now, she supported herself on her elbow as she admired him for the last time—his handsome face, his finely honed athlete's body. In repose, his features looked much as when she'd first met him as a teenager, but layered now with the strength and character of a successful man.

For a fleeting, heart-wrenching moment she wished that things could be different.

She could so easily fall in love with Mitch.

She acknowledged the thought before she pummelled it, vanquished it, shoved it away into the furthest corner of her heart, never to be acknowledged again.

She slid out from the sheets as silently as she could. Mitch murmured in his sleep, threw out an arm across her abandoned pillow. She stilled. Held her breath. Waited a heartbeat, then another. But he didn't wake up.

She crept to the bathroom, then haphazardly flung her

stuff into the wheeled carry-on bag that was her only luggage. She regretted the lack of the batik bikini; she should have bought it when she saw it. She tugged a brush through her hair...decided to put on her make-up at the airport.

As quietly as she could she checked the closet, the bathroom, the hooks behind the bathroom door for anything she might have left behind. Before she slid on her shoes she tiptoed into the bedroom for a final silent farewell to the special man who had brought her body alive with so much pleasure last night.

She could not resist bringing her face to his and pressing a butterfly-light kiss on his beard-roughened cheek.

'Thank you,' she whispered.

Her heart caught at his sleepy murmur in response, at his faint smile. But he was still asleep.

She filled her memories with one final look at him. Then she turned and walked out through her hotel room, past the still waters of the pool, where three pink frangipani blossoms floated on the surface, and through the ornately carved wooden gate that led to the outside without looking back.

Mitch woke to bright sunlight that made him screw his eyes up against it. *Zoe.* Memories of the night he'd spent with her came flooding back.

'Stay with me,' he murmured, still half asleep.

He rolled over, seeking her, wanting to pull her close. He could smell her scent on his pillow, on *him.* But he was alone in Zoe's king-size hotel bed, the sheets next to him crumpled and cold.

Fully awake now, he strained to hear if she was in the shower. But the door to the adjoining bathroom was open and no one was in there.

'Zoe?' he called.

He swung himself out of the bed.

'Are you there?' His voice echoed in the empty stillness of the room.

Then he noticed the closet door, ajar so he could see where a row of empty hangers swung. A drawer had been left slightly open.

Naked, he padded out into the living area. He looked through the sliding glass doors to the empty pool area. Plates and glasses lay haphazardly on the round table where they'd left them after their post-midnight snack.

Then he noticed the stack of Indonesian rupiah near the telephone. *'For the maid—thank you,'* was written in a bold, slanted hand on a piece of hotel notepaper.

She was gone.

He sank onto the sofa, stabbed by a feeling he couldn't put a name to. Loss. Regret. *Loneliness.*

The pain of it made him double over, his elbows on his knees, his head cradled in his hands. *Zoe.* What an amazing woman. Last night had been like nothing he'd ever experienced before. Her lithe, slender body. Her generous mouth. Her laughter. Her warmth. Her wit. The thoughtfulness and tenderness that was innate to her.

Zoe.

He wanted to roar out her name so she could hear him wherever she was—at the airport, on the plane. Hear him and come back to him.

But that couldn't be.

He had a difficult road ahead of him. Starting over. Fighting for his place in every game. Proving to the naysayers that his knee injury had not relegated him to the status of a once great player.

He could not be distracted by a woman. And Zoe would be a major distraction. She was a for ever kind of woman—

and for ever was a long way away from him. She deserved more than what he had to give.

The game. *The Beautiful Game*. That was the important thing.

A woman he could love—that had to come later.

CHAPTER EIGHT

Two months later

ZOE WAS STANDING by her desk, checking that all the documents she needed for that morning's important meeting in the city were loaded on her tablet. She was concentrating hard, but at the back of her mind she was aware of her senior accountant, Louise, chatting with someone at the external door to the office.

Her business—The Right Note: Accountancy and Tax—occupied the ground floor of a converted warehouse, part of a complex in Balmain. Zoe's living space was on the mezzanine level above.

She hoped the person at the door wasn't a client, hoping for an unscheduled appointment. That was the trouble with a client base drawn from musicians, writers, artists and entertainers—their idea of time didn't always match hers.

A glance at her watch told her she had time to catch the 9:15 a.m. ferry for the twenty-minute ride from Balmain into the city—but not a lot to spare.

She'd come to a crossroads with her business, and today's meeting with a potential buyer might help her decide which path to take. She needed to be at her most alert for the appointment—not flustered from being late. Louise would have to deal with the client.

Then Louise was by her side, her face flushed with excitement. 'Zoe, you've got no idea who's at the door, wanting to see you. *Mitch Bailey.*'

Zoe was too taken aback to do anything but stare at Louise.

'You know—the soccer player—the really hot one,' Louise added, her intonation implying that any red-blooded woman who didn't know who Mitch Bailey was needed her head read.

Zoe felt the blood drain from her face. Her heart started to hammer and a wave of nausea threatened to overwhelm her. Her hand went suddenly nerveless and her tablet started to slip from her grasp.

Louise caught the tablet and placed it on Zoe's desk. 'That's how I'd react if Mitch Bailey came to see me,' she said in a low, excited tone. 'He's even better-looking in person. Those eyes really are the most amazing green. And his smile… *Wow!*' Louise paused when she didn't get any reaction. 'Are you okay, Zoe?'

Zoe nodded. Cleared her throat. 'Of course I'm okay,' she choked out, in a reasonable facsimile of her normal speaking voice.

Mitch was here?

Louise nattered on. 'Do you think he's come to see us as a client? Someone might have recommended us to him. He wouldn't say. Just wants to see you. He's in the waiting area.'

Zoe cleared her throat. 'I…I'll see him.' She dragged in some deep, steadying breaths.

Mitch.

What was he doing in Sydney? What was he doing *here*?

As far as she knew Mitch was in Madrid, but her information wasn't up to date. On her return from Bali she'd found it impossible to stop thinking about him. Reliving over and over again the magical hours they'd shared at the villa. Every day she'd scoured the press for mentions of him, checked his official social media pages.

Ultimately she'd found it too distracting, too painful.

One night—that was all it was ever going to be. Mitch had made it very clear that there would be nothing more than that between them. An interlude with no future.

After a week she'd made a conscious decision—for her sanity's sake—not to check up on him, never to read the sports pages of the newspapers or watch the sports reports on television.

For all that, she hadn't been able to stop the dreams of him, of them together, that came to haunt her sleep. But she had nearly succeeded in putting him behind her—their time in Bali had been relegated to a bittersweet memory. And now he was here. It hardly seemed real.

Her hand went automatically to smooth her hair, and she pressed her lips together to ensure her lipstick was smooth.

'Don't worry about that. You look great,' whispered Louise, her eyes alight with curiosity.

Zoe hadn't confided in Louise or any other friend what had happened between her and Mitch in Bali.

'I wasn't worrying—' Zoe started to say, then stopped. Of *course* she was worrying about how she looked. *Mitch was here.*

Zoe wanted to sprint into the waiting area but forced herself to a sedate pace. She shouldn't read anything into this. Not after two months. Maybe Mitch was seeking some help with a double tax agreement with Spain. Or some other accountant-type advice.

She pasted a professional smile to her face. But her smile froze in stupefied admiration when she saw him. Mitch. Wearing a stylish tailored charcoal suit that emphasised his broad shoulders and strong, graceful body. He looked as if he'd stepped down off one of his billboards. The sexiest man alive was here in the waiting area of her company. And after the night they'd spent together she knew only too well how much he deserved that label.

Warm colour rushed into her cheeks when she realised it was the first time she'd seen him with clothes on—or more clothes than a pair of checked swim shorts.

Mitch seemed to freeze too, and she was conscious of him taking in every detail of her appearance. Thank heaven she'd taken extra trouble to look her best for the meeting. She was wearing a fitted deep pink designer suit—on sale at a bargain basement price but still designer—with slick black accessories. And she'd been up at the crack of dawn to make sure her hair and make-up were perfect.

She thought she'd got close to the image she wanted to portray to the management of the bigger firm—professional, but with a creative edge. To Mitch she hoped she appeared self-assured and independent. The kind of woman who took it completely in her stride when she was suddenly confronted by a man she had made love with two months ago. Without any communication whatsoever in between times. A woman who never cried into her pillow when she woke from her dreams of him.

She started to speak but had to clear her throat in order for the words to come out. In truth, she wasn't sure what to say. The last words she'd spoken to Mitch had been interspersed with sighs and murmurs of pleasure as they'd made love.

'Mitch—this is a surprise,' was all she could manage. 'Zoe.'

He took a few steps towards her and halted. She realised with a start that he seemed uncertain of his reception from her.

Her first impulse was to fling herself into his arms—that was where she wanted to be more than anything. But

she wasn't a person who generally acted on impulse—
unless an earthquake prompted her to do so, that was.

Instead she greeted him with a polite kiss on the cheek.

He held her briefly to him. Even that close contact was
enough to send her senses skittering into hyper-awareness.
Of his scent. His hard strength. The warmth of his body.

As he released her she stepped back and almost tripped
on her stiletto heels. So much for seeming nonchalant, as
if his presence didn't bother her at all.

'I was in Sydney and decided to look you up,' he said.

'How did you—?'

'Know where to find you? It didn't take advanced de-
tective work to find an accountancy firm in a converted
warehouse at Balmain.'

'Clever you,' she said, glad beyond measure that he
had taken the trouble to track her down, uncertain as to
his reason for doing so. 'But *why* are you in Sydney? Is
it your knee?'

Mitch shook his head. 'My father had an accident.'

Zoe's hand flew to her mouth. 'I'm so sorry. Is he—?'

'He's fine. But I had to fly out to make sure for myself.
I got here yesterday.'

He'd been in Sydney a day and she'd felt no awareness of him, had no 'Spidey-sense' knowledge that he was
nearby. But then why should she? He was a one-time friend
who'd become a one-time lover. That was all.

She was aching to ask him why he had come to see her,
but instead took refuge in polite conversation.

'What happened to your dad?'

'He took up cycling—became a MAMIL.'

'You mean a Middle-Aged Man in Lycra?'

'That's the one. He went head over heels over his handle-
bars. Thankfully not in the path of any traffic. But he dislocated his collarbone, broke an arm and cracked a few ribs.'

'Ouch.' She shuddered in sympathy for the man she'd never met. 'Poor guy. Is he in hospital?'

'He's back home now. Complaining about having to stay in bed and making my mother's life hell.'

'But she must be so glad he's okay?'

His eyes crinkled in fond amusement. 'Of course she is.'

'Do your parents still live in Wahroonga?'

He nodded. 'In the same house I grew up in.'

The Bailey house was just a few streets away from her grandmother's house, where she'd spent such a miserable time. Since her return from Bali, Zoe had checked up on her grandmother. She was still alive, also still living in Wahroonga. But Zoe felt no desire to get in touch. Her life there seemed such a long time ago. The only good thing about that time had been Mitch.

'How long are you in Sydney for?' she asked, and immediately wished she could drag back the words. She didn't want him to think she was fishing for a chance to see him. But then again, he'd sought her out...

'I fly out tomorrow.'

'A short visit?' Her carefully modulated words masked her disappointment.

'Enough time to take you out to dinner.'

She swallowed hard. 'You mean tonight?'

'Are you free?'

Her pride didn't want him to think she was immediately available for a last-minute date. But she didn't want to play games. Especially not when the prize was an evening with Mitch. She couldn't lie to herself. Pride lost the battle.

'Of course I'm free,' she said.

Back in Madrid, Mitch hadn't been able to get Zoe out of his head. Her laughter, her passion, her vivacious face and gorgeous body had kept invading his thoughts.

He'd thrown himself into training. But still he'd thought of her. He'd dated other women. But each date had been hours wasted as in his mind he compared the poor woman—no matter how beautiful and charming—unfavourably with Zoe.

It had irked him. He didn't *want* to be distracted by thoughts of her. He didn't know why she'd slipped so thoroughly under his skin. Was it because *she'd* left *him* that morning two months ago? Left him and not made any effort to get in touch?

Yes, they'd agreed not to contact each other. But women had a tendency not to believe him when he told them he couldn't get involved. He'd had a few holiday flings before. With beautiful women who had recognised him and wanted to take whatever Mitch Bailey had to offer. He had always been the one to leave them to wake alone in their hotel room. And, when they'd tried to get in touch, to politely make it obvious that they were wasting their time.

Not Zoe. She'd left a note for the maid, but not for him. Was it a sense of unfinished business that bothered him? That made him unable to forget her?

He'd had no intention of seeing her when he'd unexpectedly come to Sydney. But he'd found himself looking her up—just out of interest, he'd told himself.

This morning he'd been on his way to a meeting with his Australian agent in the eastern suburbs. Somehow he'd detoured west to Balmain and down the narrow streets to this complex of converted warehouses. Now he'd asked Zoe out to dinner.

It was insanity. He should not be nudging open a door that should be kept firmly shut. Nothing had changed since Bali. There was still no room for Zoe or any other woman in his meticulously planned life. Yet here he was. And regretting it already.

Because the polished businesswoman standing before him wasn't the Zoe he remembered from their time together in Bali. That uninhibited Zoe had had tousled hair, worn no make-up, and had looked quite at home in nothing but a plain white towel—or nothing at all.

This Zoe—Corporate Zoe—was strikingly attractive in a very different way. The tailored, form-fitting suit and high heels, the shorter hair cut in an artfully layered style, the perfect make-up—all screamed candidate for Businesswoman of the Year. Not the girl who'd given as good as she'd got in a no-holds-barred water fight. Or in a big bed among tangled sheets under the slow flick of a ceiling fan on a steamy tropical night.

'Dinner tonight it is,' he said.

Though now he'd seen her he wondered if it was such a good idea.

In Madrid, he'd kept thinking about the connection they'd shared. A connection that had gone way beyond the physical and was like none he'd ever felt with a woman. But had it just been a holiday fling spiced by peril, the urgency of danger? Would they now struggle to find common ground?

'I'll look forward to it,' she said in her characteristic husky voice.

In any other woman he would find that voice an affectation. But Zoe's voice had had the same deep timbre at seventeen. Then it had seemed at odds with her schoolgirl persona. Now she'd grown into it—a sensual adult voice that sent awareness of her as a woman throbbing through him.

'Have you got anywhere in mind?'

He didn't. It had been a spur-of-the-moment decision to track her down. It would make him late for his meeting with his agent. Not that the agent would care. He made enough from his cut of Mitch's local earnings to put up with tardiness from his star client. Still, Mitch had called ahead to alert him. He believed in professional behaviour at all times.

He hadn't got as far as thinking about a restaurant. To see Zoe again, to see if she was still the woman who'd haunted his thoughts for two months, was all he had thought about.

'I'm going to be flat out all day so I'll look forward to dinner,' she said. 'I have a really important meeting with a company that—' She squealed. 'The ferry! I'm going to miss it! Be late for the meeting!'

Her face was screwed up in panic. Suddenly she looked more approachable. More like the Zoe he knew—or thought he knew.

'Let me drive you,' he said. 'To the city?'

'No. I mean yes. The meeting *is* in the city. But peak-hour morning traffic will be too heavy; I'll still be late. A ride to the ferry stop would be helpful, though.'

'Can do,' he said. 'I'm parked in your car park.'

'How did you get past the security guard?'

He grinned.

Her lips lifted in a half smile. 'Of course. You're Mitch Bailey. Why did I bother to ask?'

She turned rapidly on her high heels, dashed out of the room, and returned seconds later with a stylish leather satchel flung over her shoulder.

'Let's go,' she said.

Walking more briskly than he'd imagine anyone else could in those heels, she took off across the wooden dock at the harbourside front of the building, past the small marina and around to the car park.

He pressed his key fob and lights flashed as the doors unlocked on the innocuous mid-range sedan he'd rented for the few days he was in Sydney. It wasn't the type of car people would expect Mitch Bailey to drive, which was exactly why he'd chosen it. Choose a top-of-the-range European sports car like the one he had back in Madrid and he'd be inviting attention he didn't want.

So far he had evaded anyone outside his family and close circle of friends knowing he was back in Sydney. And Zoe too, of course. Where did she fit in? Friend? Lover? He found it impossible to categorise her.

She broke into a half run to get to the car and flung herself into the front passenger's seat after he'd opened the door for her. The car was suddenly filled with her energy, with her warm, heady scent—immediately familiar.

As he steered the car out of the car park she apologised for the rush. 'One of the bigger accounting firms has approached me to buy my business. My meeting this morning is with them.'

'That sounds impressive.' It didn't surprise him at all to hear she was doing well in the corporate world.

'It's flattering—that's for sure. They think I've tapped into a niche market they want a part of.'

'You don't sound one hundred per cent enthusiastic.' Since when had he been able to read her voice?

'I am and I'm not. They propose that my company would be absorbed by them as a specialised division, with me as the manager. But I worry that the vital personal touch might get lost if I lose control. My clients are an eccentric bunch and they could get scared off—even see my move as a betrayal. But I could help more people, expand the business to other states where there's a need for it.'

'It's a big decision.' He liked the way she was considering her clients—not just the potential gain for herself.

'There's pros and there's cons. I'll go in there this morning with an open mind.'

'You can tell me all about it tonight. I'll be interested to see what happens.'

As they spoke Mitch drove as fast as he could around the steep, narrow streets of Balmain, one of the oldest inner western suburbs of Sydney. The streets were lined with quaint restored nineteenth-century terrace houses and historic shop fronts. The area suited Zoe.

He turned into Darling Street and headed down towards the water. Ahead was the ferry terminal, framed by a view of the Sydney Harbour Bridge on the other side of the harbour.

'Thank heaven,' Zoe breathed when they saw the ferry was still docking. 'I wouldn't have made it without you.'

'You wouldn't have been late if I hadn't distracted you.'

'I'm glad you distracted me,' she said, tucking her satchel over her shoulder.

Mitch didn't know whether to read that as flirtatious or as a mere statement of fact. She was giving nothing away. Was she happy to see him or not? Had Bali meant anything to her?

She started to open the door before the car was completely stopped, then scrambled out. 'Gotta dash.'

She paused, half out and half in the car, revealing a stretch of slender leg that Mitch could not help but appreciate.

'I live on the floor above the office. Pick me up at seven-thirty tonight.'

'Right,' he said.

He reached out and put a hand on her arm. She stilled, and for a moment he thought she might shake his hand away from her.

'Good luck with the meeting,' he said. Had she thought he was going to say something else?

'I might need it,' she said, moving away. 'Thanks for the ride. See you tonight.'

She headed down to the ferry, which was now loading people across the gangplank. Commuting by ferry was an attractive part of Sydney living, he'd always thought.

The sight of her shapely back view in the bright pink suit as she broke into a half run down to the ferry was very appealing. She might be a different Zoe from the one he remembered from their time together in Bali, but she was just as hot in that subtly sexy way he'd found impossible to forget.

Which Zoe would he see tonight?

CHAPTER NINE

MITCH SAT ACROSS from Zoe at the harbourside restaurant he had booked for their dinner. He was not usually a man who found himself tongue-tied in conversation with a female companion. But tonight he was scraping around for something to say.

He and Zoe had already exclaimed over the spectacular view—the restaurant was situated on the north side of the harbour, right near the north pylon of the Sydney Harbour Bridge—and together they had marvelled at the sight of the lit-up ferries and pleasure boats criss-crossing the darkened waters of the harbour. They'd commented on the swimmers braving the winter to do laps below them, in the black-marked lanes of the Art Deco-style North Sydney Olympic Pool. And they'd each said how fond they were of the big grinning face that marked the entrance to Luna Park, the harbour-front amusement park next door.

Trouble was, that elephant was back. It was sitting below them, in the pale blue waters of that big swimming pool, looking up at them, taunting them. He and Zoe had spent the night together two months before, had shared the fear of possibly losing their lives, and yet neither of them had mentioned it. They were just acting as though they were old acquaintances catching up, skimming the surface with dinner table talk.

This morning he'd seen Corporate Zoe. Tonight he was with Sophisticated Zoe, stylish in a simple purple lace dress that covered her arms and chest but revealed glimpses of her creamy skin, the enticing curves of her breasts through the gaps in the lace. Her hair was slicked back smoothly to her head and she wore long drop earrings that moved when she turned. She was striking, elegant, self-assured.

Heads had turned when they'd walked in to the restaurant together—and they hadn't been looking at him. But he wanted the Zoe who'd turned *his* head wearing nothing but a skimpy white towel.

He remembered the flower he had tucked behind her ear that night in Bali—a prelude to the intimacy that had followed. Next morning he had found it, crumpled on her pillow. Never would he admit to anyone how he had scooped it up, wrapped it in a tissue from the bathroom and taken it back to Madrid with him.

He picked up the menu. 'Perhaps we should order?'

'Good idea,' she said.

'The menu looks good. Are you hungry?'

How inane was this conversation? He was flying back to Madrid the next day. The way this was going it didn't seem likely he would get a chance to talk to Zoe about anything important—let alone anything intimate.

He resisted the temptation to glance at his watch.

'Not excessively,' she said. 'I don't know that I've ever got over the Bali belly.'

At last—a reference to their recent shared past. He hoped the elephant was appeased.

'You're still feeling unwell?'

'Off and on.'

He frowned. 'That's a worry. You should get it checked out. You might have caught a tropical bug. They can have long-lasting consequences.'

He thought about telling her the story of his teammate who'd picked up a parasite through his bare feet in some country or other, but decided that was hardly dinner date conversation.

Zoe sighed. 'I know. I should go to the doctor. It's just I've been run off my feet at work—it's our busiest time of the year. All I do is work, work and more work.'

And date? Had she been going out with other guys? Had she found dating as unsatisfactory as he had?

The thought of her with another guy had tortured him back in Madrid. Had the ex-boyfriend come sniffing around? If he, Mitch, had had Zoe in his life he wouldn't have let her go easily.

Mitch gripped the side of the menu. *He had let her go.* He had made love to her all night and then just let her go.

Had he seriously expected he could just fly into Sydney, show up on her doorstep and everything would be as it had been in Bali? He gritted his teeth. She wouldn't be independent, feisty Zoe if she just fell back into his arms. This was up to him. Unfinished business or not.

'Promise me you'll get to the doctor as soon as possible?' he said.

She smiled. 'I promise. Thank you for your concern.'

Their eyes met across the table. To his relief, he saw genuine appreciation in hers. That was at least a step up from guarded politeness.

'Good health is important,' he said. 'As I know only too well.'

'Your knee,' she said. 'I keep meaning to ask about it. Is it holding up?'

'So far, so good. I'm back to match fitness. Let's hope it stays that way. I've still got a lot to prove.'

'And your father?' She laughed, and her laughter had

a nervous edge to it. 'No different from this morning, I guess. Sorry. Dumb question.'

'It wasn't a dumb question. He gets grumpier by the hour. Hates being inactive.'

'Did you get your interest in soccer from your dad?'

This wasn't how he'd pictured his reunion with sexy, passionate Zoe. Talking about his father. But if that was the way it was going he might as well throw his grandfather in too.

'Dad liked to kick a ball around. But it was my grandfather who really got me into soccer.' He smiled. 'Grandpa is English, and he would hate to hear me refer to football as "soccer".'

Zoe tilted her head attentively and her earrings swung. He wanted to reach over and still them. But would his touch be welcome? Her 'hands off' shield was very much in place.

Mitch realised that this evening might not go as he'd anticipated. After their meal was served he might get a polite brush-off and a cool kiss on the cheek like the one she'd given him this morning. He wasn't used to that. It stymied him.

'I didn't know your family was English?' she said.

'My father was born in England and grew up there. In his twenties he came out to Australia on a gap year—only they didn't call it that in those days—met my mother here and stayed. We lived in north London, near my grandparents, for a year when I was eight. My grandfather got me hooked on soccer then. He used to take me to games...got me on a local team. He played for a London team himself when he was young. He lives and breathes the game.'

'He must be so proud of you now.'

'Not proud of me playing for a Spanish team. In fact he's disgusted.'

'Why don't you play for an English team?'

'I did. But a Spanish team bought me.'

'*Bought* you? Like a commodity?'

'I guess you could put it that way.'

'I know so little about the game.' She smiled. 'If an old schoolfriend hadn't become a soccer superstar I'd know even less.'

'Just ask if there's anything you'd like to know,' he said.

An old schoolfriend? He wanted to be so much more than that to her. Passionate, playful and sensual—that was the Zoe he remembered from Bali. He couldn't settle for just friendship after she'd been all that to him. But then he couldn't offer her a relationship either.

In that regard nothing had changed since they'd last met in Bali. He could *not* let himself be distracted from his game by Zoe or any other woman. *He just couldn't.*

Last year he'd been briefly involved with a woman who had been too temperamental for his taste. When he'd broken it off with her there had been scenes, threats, confrontations—until he'd been forced to take out a restraining order against her.

It had been during that time when he had suffered his knee injury. Had the stress caused him to miss that split-second warning that two opposing players were headed towards him, clearly with the intent to take him out? He believed there was a good chance it had. It wouldn't happen again.

'Why do they call it "The Beautiful Game"? It sounds so...so *romantic*,' Zoe said.

His grandfather had often used the term, and had explained it to him many times as a kid. 'It's because the game is beautiful in its simplicity. It's not loaded with complex rules. If you have a ball you can play anywhere. Kids in their back yards or on dusty streets all over the world...

highly paid players on a perfectly groomed pitch. It's an intelligent game—an individual's game as well as a team game. They say the first person to officially call it "The Beautiful Game" was the great Brazilian footballer Pelé.'

Mitch paused, conscious that he sounded as if he was preaching.

'I don't want to bore you…'

'You're not boring me at all. I can see how much you love your game. I admire your passion. No wonder it comes first with you.'

There was a hint of the Bali Zoe's teasing in her smile.

'Even if you *are* bought and sold like a racehorse.'

Zoe obviously had no idea of the money that changed hands at the top level of soccer. It wasn't the huge deal in Australia that it was in Europe, where players' incomes were splashed all over the press. Even he'd been astounded at the amounts that had poured into his bank account since he'd made it to the top. And that didn't include the sponsorship and endorsements his agent was always negotiating.

He was glad Zoe didn't seem to have any interest in his income. Lara had been only too aware of every possible euro, pound and dollar that might come his way. It had been a bitter realisation that Lara had been more in love with the money and the spotlight than she had been with him.

Ultimately she'd pressed for marriage—to secure that income, he'd believed. That had resulted in their final split—and a pay-out from him to stop her selling the story of their relationship to the media. To be fair to Lara, she'd stuck to the deal. It hadn't come as a shock when she'd taken up with another player not long afterwards.

Since then he'd steered clear of women he suspected of being interested not in the real Mitch Bailey but in his image and wealth. There were plenty of them around. Star footballers could be a target for the unscrupulous.

The waiter came alongside their table and asked if he could take their order. Mitch quickly chose white fish and steamed vegetables in a lemon yogurt sauce. Zoe ordered a cheese and spinach vegetarian dish, explaining that she had lost her taste for meat since she hadn't been feeling well.

The conversation dwindled to virtually nothing. The elephant in the pool below was wallowing in the shallow end and spraying water through its trunk all over the swimmers. But neither he nor Zoe seemed able to call it to heel.

Zoe pleated the edge of her linen napkin, drew her finger around the edge of her water glass, played with her dangly earrings. She must be feeling as uncomfortable as he was. This was untenable.

Mitch reached across the table and stilled her hand with his. He looked into her eyes for a long, still moment.

'Zoe, I wish I could see what was in your thought bubbles,' he said. 'Because we're not making any headway talking and I don't have much time.'

Zoe gripped his hand in deep, heartfelt relief that Mitch had found the courage to say what she had been too knotted with nerves to say. He'd been so formal, his conversation so stilted—unless he was talking about soccer—that she'd feared the connection they'd shared in Bali had been completely severed. That she'd never see again the Mitch she'd shared both danger and ultimately pleasure with in the seclusion of her villa back in Seminyak.

'My thought bubbles?' she said, knowing her voice sounded shaky but unable to do anything about it except follow her words with a nervous laugh. 'Please don't ask me to sing them, because there's a guy over there with a cell phone who seems a tad too interested in us.'

In fact it looked as if the onlooker was about to snap a photo of them. Zoe withdrew her hand from Mitch's, kept her hands firmly on her lap.

'No need to sing,' Mitch said, with the disarming smile that struck straight to her heart.

He looked so impossibly handsome in that dark suit. She could still hardly believe he was here with her in Sydney. Her pulse quickened at the thought of what the evening might bring.

She took a deep, steadying breath. 'Okay. My thought bubbles say: "Apprehensive". "Awkward". "Curious".'

'"Curious"?' he said, his head tilted to one side, his eyes narrowed.

'Curious as to why you looked me up when you'd made it so clear you didn't want anything ongoing between us.'

'Fair enough,' he said. 'What about "awkward"?'

Under cover of the tablecloth overhang Zoe wrung her hands together. 'I'm anxious that I'll say the wrong thing—I'm second-guessing every word. I'm over the moon that you're here, but I don't want to appear too glad to see you in case...in case you think I'm wanting more from you. You made your agenda for the future very clear.'

'Which explains "Apprehensive"...' said Mitch.

She nodded, unable to speak through a sudden lump of emotion. She blinked against unwelcome, mortifying tears. 'Yes,' she forced herself to say.

'My thought bubbles are pretty much the same,' he said slowly. 'I'm worried that we seem like strangers to each other.'

'Exactly,' she said. 'And I don't know what to do about it.'

Mitch leaned across the table. 'I thought about you a lot when I was back in Madrid, Zoe.'

'I...I thought about you too.' She didn't want to give too

much away. Such as the fact she still awoke from dreams of him to find herself in tears.

'We didn't get to say goodbye in Bali.'

There was accusation in his voice and affronted pride in his eyes.

Zoe realised that Mitch, the celebrity sportsman, was not used to being left by a woman. Not in those circumstances. She hadn't meant to take the upper hand by creeping out of the villa without awakening him to say goodbye. It had saved her an awkward moment. Mitch might be used to such no-strings encounters. She was not.

'It seemed better that way,' she said, finding it difficult to meet his eyes. 'We'd agreed it…it would only be for that night.'

'When I woke up and you weren't there I was gutted.'

'It…it was difficult to leave you, but it would have been worse to face you. I…I had never been in that situation before. I didn't know how to deal with it.'

She'd sobbed in the taxi all the way to the airport. Then huddled into her seat on the plane for the entire six-hour flight home to Sydney, desperately trying not to sob some more.

His mouth twisted wryly. 'Severing all contact between us seemed the right thing at the time. When I got back to Madrid and had time to think, it seemed all kinds of wrong. I wanted to get in touch. But I thought that wouldn't be fair on you. My situation hadn't changed.'

'I wanted to contact you too. But I…I didn't want to seem like a…like a groupie. I…know you're probably plagued by them.'

Mitch's so-expressive eyebrows rose. 'Don't ever think that. You are nothing like that. Not that I've had anything to do with groupies, and nor am I criticising them, but I see what goes on.'

'Each to his own,' she murmured, glad that Mitch had distanced himself from that aspect of his fame. But still... She couldn't believe their one night in Seminyak had been the first no-strings incident for *him*. He was idolised by women.

'You're smart, gorgeous, funny. I couldn't stop thinking about you.'

On the surface, those words should have sounded romantic. But Zoe detected an undertone of annoyance—even anger. It was as if she were some unwelcome prickly thorn, pressing into his consciousness. She wasn't at all sure she liked it.

She swallowed hard. 'I...I couldn't stop thinking about you either,' she said. 'I tried, though. I really tried. Otherwise I would have gone crazy. I purposely avoided the sports pages, the international sports news. That's why I got such a shock to see you this morning. I had no idea you were in Australia.'

'I was going crazy in my own way, trying to find out what *you* were doing. You've got such rigid privacy settings on your social media.'

'You tried to stalk me on social media?' Zoe tried to suppress her laughter so it didn't attract attention. 'Imagine...Mitch Bailey stalking me—I'm flattered.'

'I wouldn't say "stalking" you,' he said, with what she took to be more affronted pride. 'More...attempting research into your comings and goings. And failing dismally—courtesy of your firewalls.'

'I told you...I'm a private person.' She looked sideways at the guy on the other table with the camera phone. His attention was now on his meal, not on Mitch, thank heaven.

'Did you date other guys?'

The directness of Mitch's question stunned her. But she didn't have to search for an answer. 'No. I didn't want to.'

How could any other man have compared to Mitch? Trouble was, no other guy she'd met in the meantime had attracted her. That night in Bali had shown her what it could be like between a man and a woman. Not just the lovemaking. It had also been about the shared laughter, the joy, the connection that to her had been so much more than physical.

She wanted Mitch but he could not offer her what she needed—commitment, love. One day she'd meet some-one who could offer her more than one night in his busy schedule. She had no intention of putting her life on hold for Mitch Bailey.

No matter that just sitting opposite him at a restaurant table was thrilling her in a way being with any other man never had. No. She hadn't even looked at another man in the last two months.

His relief was palpable. 'Good,' he said.

Zoe gasped. His reaction was a bit rich. What did he mean, *'good'*?

He had no rights over her personal life. They'd made no commitment—hadn't even exchanged contact details. She was free to date whom she darn well pleased. The fact that she hadn't met anyone who came anywhere near him was beside the point.

She wanted to say something but bit her tongue. It was an unexpected bonus to see Mitch again. She didn't want to ruin it by being combative. What was the point?

'What about you?' she said.

He shrugged. 'I went out with a few women.'

Jealousy—fierce and unexpected—stabbed her so hard she flinched. She couldn't bear to think of him with some-one else. And that was crazy, considering the nature of their relationship. Not that you could even call it a rela-tionship. Heck, you couldn't even call it a *friendship*. She couldn't find a label to paste on whatever it was with her and Mitch Bailey.

She didn't say anything, just raised an eyebrow. While she churned inside with jealousy.

'It was a disaster,' he said. 'I kept comparing them to you and they fell short. I gave up on dating.'

What was she meant to infer from that? 'Oh...' was all she managed to choke out, with her jealousy somewhat appeased.

For a long moment their eyes met. But if she was searching for more she didn't find it. His gaze was guarded.

'It's good to see you, Zoe.'

'It's good to you, too,' she said.

'There's something there...more than friendship,' he said.

A secret thrill that he had acknowledged it pulsed through her. 'So what are we going to do about it?' she asked eventually. 'Fact is, I still live in Sydney and you still live in Madrid.'

'And that isn't going to change,' he said. 'For all the reasons I explained to you before. But we could keep in touch on the internet.'

'You mean I'd have to let down my firewalls for you?' she said, in a feeble attempt at humour.

'Yes. You'd have to let me scale those walls.'

Did she detect a note of triumph in his voice? Mitch liked to win. *For what purpose?*

She found herself pleating her napkin again. 'Will you be back in Australia any time soon?'

It would be torture to wait months and months to see him.

'It's not likely,' he said. 'Not until next year, when the season ends. Playing league football is more than a full-time commitment.'

'That…that's a long time.' How could they possibly maintain anything resembling more than a casual friendship on that time scale?

'Are you planning a trip to Europe any time soon?' he asked.

She shook her head. 'I'm not sure…'

She'd blown her vacation budget with the Bali trip. There was no spare cash for an expensive trip to Europe, and she didn't believe in paying for vacations on credit.

'That's a shame. You could have visited me in Madrid,' he said. 'I have a very nice apartment in old Madrid. You'd like it.'

'I…I'm sure I would,' she said. 'I'd like to see Spain some day. That would give me an incentive to study Spanish again.'

Would it be worth a credit card binge to see Mitch in Madrid? Excitement started to bubble up at the prospect.

'Let's think about how we can make it work,' he said. 'I have a full schedule of training, then pre-season matches in England, France and Italy before the season starts the last week in August. We could fit in a visit when I'm playing at home? That is if it coincided with your trip?'

Zoe was about to engage seriously with Mitch about what might be a good time for her to visit Madrid if she happened to be travelling to Europe—and then it hit her.

Mitch wasn't actually *inviting* her to visit him. He wasn't putting himself out in any way. Such a trip would be all about her running around the world to meet him at his convenience. For *what*? A bootie call? If she just happened to be in the neighbourhood? He was hedging his bets in a major way.

She swallowed down hard against a sudden bitter taste in her mouth. There would be no trip to Madrid for her to chase after Mitch in the hope of spending time with him. In her book, old-fashioned as it might be, the man did the chasing.

Before she could explain this to Mitch the waiter arrived at their table with their food and proceeded to describe in detail the meals they'd ordered. She put down her napkin— by now pleated to a narrow strip—and thanked the waiter.

She looked at the food on her plate—beautifully cooked and presented. But she didn't feel like eating. As the aroma of the food filled her nostrils a wave of nausea overtook her. Mitch was right. She needed to check out this recurring illness. Or was it disappointment that was making her feel like this?

Mitch picked up his fork. 'You haven't told me how your meeting went today with your potential purchaser?'

Zoe was grateful for the change of subject. She pushed her food around her plate with her fork. 'They made me a generous offer,' she said. 'Set out some attractive if constricting terms and conditions. We talked about expanding my specialised service into other states.'

'And...?'

Zoe shrugged. 'I'm still not convinced. I'm a very independent person—used to running my own show. I'm not sure how I'd take to being at the beck and call of a boss.'

'I believe that,' said Mitch. 'So, how did you leave it with them?' He seemed genuinely interested.

'I told him I'd consider it. In the meantime I talked with my friend Louise, who works with me. I've been thinking of bringing her into the company as a full partner. She'd have to *buy* in, of course. Then we could think of expanding. We already spend quite a bit of time commuting to Melbourne, to service the clients we have there.'

'You're very ambitious,' he said, and she appreciated the admiration in his voice.

'Yes,' she said. 'That's one reason I'm seriously considering the offer. Perhaps I can move higher in a bigger firm than I could on my own. It's all worth considering.'

'You've got a big decision to make. It will be interesting to see what you decide to do,' he said. 'Be sure you let me know.'

Was he just saying that? Did he really want to stay in touch?

'Yes…' she said non-committally.

'We've both come a long way since we were seventeen,' he said, his brows drawn thoughtfully together. 'Me where I am—you with your own business.'

Startled, she looked up. 'I guess we have.'

'We've both still got a long way to go,' he said.

She knew his career was all-important to him, and he'd made it very clear that he'd put his personal life on hold. But she aspired to more than business success. Success for her also meant a fulfilling personal life one day. That lifetime love she aspired to—and a happy family life.

With a wrench to her heart that was almost physical she realised it would never happen with Mitch—no matter the strength of her feelings for him. By the time he reached a stage when he wanted to settle down she would be long in his past.

CHAPTER TEN

MITCH PREDICTED ALMOST to the minute the time when the guy with the camera phone Zoe had been keeping her eye on would make his way to their table: after he and Zoe had finished their main courses and the waiter had removed their plates.

Mitch knew from the guy's respectful attitude and the phone held so visibly in his hand that it wouldn't be a problem. But Zoe's eyes widened in alarm.

He remembered what she'd said about being a private person. Even a casual friendship with him opened her up to possible confrontations with the paparazzi.

'Mitch, I'm a huge fan—so is my son,' the guy with the camera said. 'Could I have a photo with you, please?'

'Of course,' said Mitch, looking around for the waiter.

'I'll take the photo,' said Zoe, jumping up from her seat.

Full marks to Zoe. That was one way of avoiding being in a photo. Maybe he didn't need to worry too much about her coping with any possible publicity.

She took the guy's phone and made a fuss of posing Mitch and his fan.

'Thank you,' the guy said to Zoe. 'Can I get one of me and you two together now?'

'I... I...' Zoe stuttered.

'Of course,' said Mitch.

'It's for my wife,' his fan explained. 'She didn't like Lara one little bit and will be happy to see you with such a lovely young lady.'

Again Mitch was struck by how public his life had become. It was highly improbable that this man's wife had ever actually met Lara. The woman just hadn't liked the Lara she'd seen in the media.

'Zoe is an old friend of mine,' said Mitch, 'and she is indeed lovely.'

Zoe was obviously too stupefied to object. Mitch called the waiter over to take the photo. That would save both him and Zoe from any unflattering 'selfie'.

After the fan had gone happily on his way Zoe turned to him. She shuddered. 'Do you have to put up with that all the time?'

'I'm never rude to a fan. He was a good guy. We made his evening—his wife and son will be chuffed.'

'I found it disconcerting, to say the least,' Zoe said, in a tone so low it was nearly a whisper. 'Especially what he said about Lara.'

She looked nervously around her, as if there might be a photographer at every table. Fact was: there could be. Everyone with a smartphone was a potential paparazzo these days. But that came with the turf. Mitch had learned to deal with it.

'C'mon—let's leave if it's making you uncomfortable,' he said. 'We can grab a coffee somewhere else, if you'd like.'

'There are a few nice cafés around here,' she said. 'We could walk along the boardwalk by the harbour.'

'Good idea. We can work that dinner off.'

Not that she'd eaten much.

She hesitated. 'I...I won't end up on some gossip website, will I? You know—"Mystery brunette on harbourside stroll with visiting soccer star"?'

Mitch thought about her helicopter fears back at the villa in Bali. She was right—they did exist on different planets. Zoe was so unlike Lara, who would have been preening at the thought of being in the spotlight.

'That guy? Highly unlikely,' he said. 'He'll show the photo around to the other parents at his boy's soccer club though, I'll bet.'

Although freedom from other, less scrupulous people, who cashed in on opportunistic amateur shots, he couldn't guarantee. But he'd seen no one suspicious tonight. No one would imagine he'd be in Sydney when he should be in Europe, playing 'friendly' matches to warm up for the season to come.

But he'd had to see if his father was okay. And then there was Zoe. He'd be kidding himself if he denied that he'd leaped at the opportunity to see Zoe.

Now he realised that if at the back of his mind he'd hoped meeting with her again would leave him cold—would rid him of his attraction to her—then he'd been totally mistaken. She was even hotter than he'd remembered. There was nothing he wanted more than to take up where they'd left off in Bali.

Of course Zoe tried to pay her share for the dinner. He'd anticipated that, and had already settled the bill when Zoe came back to the table after going to the ladies' room.

'I insist on paying for the coffee, then,' she said, with that already familiar stubborn tilt to her chin.

Yes, Zoe was *very* different from the other women in his orbit.

They walked out of the restaurant into the narrow back street of Milson's Point. It was a typically mild Sydney winter night, but Zoe wrapped her arms around herself and shivered. She reached into her purse and pulled out a filmy scarf she wrapped around her shoulders.

'I can't imagine *that* will keep you warm,' he said.

'I'm fine,' she said, with an edge to her voice, not meeting his eyes.

'No, you're not, you're shivering,' he said. 'Come here.'

He pulled Zoe into his arms and held her very close, until her shivering stopped, and finally she relaxed against him with a small sigh, her head resting against his shoulder Mitch didn't know whether to interpret that sigh as relief or defeat.

He closed his eyes, the better to savour the sensation of having her close. He inhaled the sharp sweet scent of her—a Balinese blend of lemongrass and jasmine, she'd told him when he'd asked—that brought back heady memories of that brief, intense time they'd spent together in her villa.

This. This was what he'd longed for back in the echoing emptiness of his apartment in Madrid. He should not be letting himself feel this. But he heaved a huge sigh of relief that she made no effort to break away from him.

'Warm now?' he asked, his voice a husky rasp.

'Yes,' she murmured against his shoulder.

She pulled away, but remained within the circle of his arms, her own arms around his waist.

She looked up to him. 'Thank you.'

Her face was in semi-shadow, her earrings glinting in the reflected light from the illumination of the giant grinning face of the entrance to Luna Park that loomed behind him. The sounds of carnival music and kids screaming on rides travelled on the still air.

'What next, Zoe?' he asked.

Her eyes told him that she knew he wasn't talking about the direction of their walk.

'Whatever we both want,' she said slowly.

She lifted her mouth to him. He didn't hesitate to accept the invitation. He bent his head and kissed her. But his kiss was brief and tender—he was as aware as Zoe of the possibility of interested eyes on them.

'I've been wanting to do this all day,' he said.

'Me too,' she said, a catch to her voice.

A taxi drew up and a noisy group of people got out, obviously heading for the restaurant. Zoe turned away from his embrace. As if by silent consent he took her arm and they headed away, to leave the restaurant behind them.

He walked beside her down the steep steps near the giant smile at the entrance to Luna Park to reach the harbour walk that ran by the harbour's edge, from Lavender Bay to Milson's Point. Despite the mildness of the night there was a hint of a breeze blowing off the water.

As they reached the boardwalk Zoe shivered again, and pulled the flimsy excuse for a wrap tighter to her. 'I don't know why I didn't wear a coat,' she said.

Mitch didn't hesitate to put his arm around her and pull her to his side. To hell with the possibility of cameras. He and Zoe weren't the only couple strolling along the boardwalk with their arms around each other. They would just blend in. He wanted her near him.

It had been such a long time since he'd lived in Sydney, and he found himself caught up in the magic of Sydney Harbour on a calm, clear night. He blocked the thought that being with Zoe was part of the magic. He could not allow himself to think that. Not when he was leaving tomorrow. Not when he didn't know when he would see her again.

In silence, they walked past the Art Deco façade of the pool and under the arch of the bridge. He didn't know whether the silence was companionable or choked with words better left unsaid.

Once they reached the eastern side of the bridge he

and Zoe paused and leaned on the cast-iron railing to look across the water to the Opera House, its giant white sails lit up with a beauty that was almost ethereal.

'Do you think you'll ever come back to live in Australia?' Zoe asked.

He shrugged. 'Maybe. I don't know. Sydney will always be home. But for the foreseeable future Europe is where I want to be.'

At the age of twenty-seven he saw that future stretch way ahead of him, exciting with possibilities. He was cautiously optimistic about his knee. Who knew how far he could go?

'Tell me again when you have to go back to Madrid? It really is tomorrow?'

'Yes,' he said.

The single word seemed to toll like a warning of impending doom.

Zoe was looking ahead at the view so he couldn't see her face. But he felt her flinch.

'So…so we only have tonight,' she said, again with that little catch to her voice that wrenched at him.

'Yes,' he said. 'I fly out in the afternoon.'

A big harbour cruiser went by and a blast of brash music shattered the tranquillity of the scene. Did Zoe like that kind of music? Probably not. He realised how much he didn't know about her. How much he wanted to know. One day, perhaps…

'I wish it wasn't such a long way between Australia and Spain,' she said wistfully.

It remained unspoken between them that it wasn't only the twenty-two-hour flight that separated them. His need to prove himself over and over without distraction stood in their way. Mitch liked Zoe. *Really* liked her. But he couldn't let that liking and his attraction grow into anything deeper. This wasn't the time for him. No matter how he might find himself wishing it could be different.

'Me too,' he said. 'But even if we lived closer I still couldn't promise anything more than—'

'Friendship with benefits?' she said.

He followed her gaze as she looked down into the dark green water of the harbour. Small waves from the cruiser's wash were smashing against the sandstone supports of the railing.

'Very occasional benefits,' she added, in a tone so low he scarcely caught it.

Put like that, it sounded so callous.

With his fingers, Mitch tilted her chin upwards so she had to meet his gaze. 'Zoe, I wish it could be more. Who knows what could happen in the—?'

'Future?' she said. She reached up to silence him with her finger on his mouth, as she had done before. 'Let's not talk about the future.'

The thinly veiled sadness in her eyes made his resolve waver. 'Who knows? One day...' he said.

Slowly she shook her head. 'It seems to me we can only take this one day at a time. So we'd better make the most of the hours we've got left.'

'Agreed,' he said.

He hoped her idea of a wonderful way to fill the hours coincided with his. Alone. Private. Clothes optional.

'How long since you've been to Luna Park?' she asked.

He paused, surprised at the question. 'Years and years,' he said.

'Me too,' she said. 'Not since I was at uni. The noise and music coming from there sounds fun. Let's walk through before we go and find a coffee shop.'

Mitch was too startled to reply. It was hardly *his* idea of making the most of the hours they had left together.

'Sounds like a plan,' he said, with an effort to sound enthusiastic.

'We can just walk around and look,' she said.

His parents had taken him and his brothers to Luna Park when he was very young. Then it had been closed for years, and he hadn't revisited it until he was a teenager. He'd taken his training so seriously that amusement parks hadn't been much on the agenda. Besides, Lara had looked down her nose at what she'd thought was a plebeian form of entertainment.

'That could be fun,' he said.

He took Zoe's hand in his as they walked along the harbour back towards the bright lights and clashing noises of Luna Park. She looked up at him and smiled, and he smiled back.

Holding hands with Zoe. Who would have thought something so simple, so everyday, would make him feel so…? He thought hard about what this feeling was. *Happy*. Being with Zoe made him feel happy.

As they walked under the big grinning face into the entertainment park he gave it a mental salute.

CHAPTER ELEVEN

ZOE HAD NO IDEA why she'd suggested going to Luna Park with Mitch. Panic, perhaps? Prolonging the inevitable? What she really wanted was to be alone with him, somewhere quiet and romantic.

But she was struggling with the 'friends with occasional benefits' scenario. She wanted Mitch with a deep, yearning hunger—a craving. It was impossible to stop sneaking glances at him to admire his profile, the shape of his mouth, the set of his shoulders. She found everything about him exciting. The thought of the sensual pleasures they had shared made her shiver with remembered ecstasy. But she balked at the idea of being his occasional lover.

Bali had been different. The circumstances had been extraordinary. She'd believed there would be only the one time. That she would be able to put their encounter behind her almost as if it had been a dream. It hadn't been easy to forget him. And now he was back in her life, but on very uncertain ground. It might be commonplace for a celebrity sports star to do the 'occasional lover' thing. Not so for an ordinary girl with dreams of a once-in-a-lifetime love. A girl teetering on the edge of falling in love with him.

Walking hand in hand with Mitch like any other couple strolling along the harbour walk on a mild Thursday evening felt so *right*. She loved the feel of his much larger hand enfolding hers, the way their shoulders nudged, the subtle intimacy. As if they were meant to be together.

But tomorrow he would be on his way to Madrid again. And she would be left with perhaps the comfort of an occasional phone call. She had no illusions. Once he was again immersed in his game she would not be at the front of his mind.

Luna Park was chaotic and fun. It was the perfect distraction from the hollow feeling of loss Zoe felt at the thought of Mitch flying back to Madrid the next day. Her spirits had lifted as soon as she was surrounded by the bright lights, music and carnival atmosphere.

Set right on the harbour, surrounded by some of the most expensive real estate in Australia, the old-fashioned fun fair operated in the evenings during school vacations despite the protests of its well-heeled neighbours. Zoe supported its right to be there—the Sydney icon had existed since 1935, built on land that had been the construction site for the building of the Sydney Harbour Bridge.

For many older Sydney-siders the place was loaded with nostalgia. Zoe's maternal grandmother had brought her here a few times by ferry when she was a little girl—it was one of her only memories of her as she had died when Zoe was seven.

She sometimes wondered how different her life would have been if *that* grandmother had been alive when her parents had died and she had been put into *her* care.

Once through the entrance, she and Mitch were surrounded by rides and sideshows on both sides.

She looked around and laughed. 'Just watching the rides is making me feel dizzy.'

'They're fast and furious, all right,' said Mitch. 'What do you want to ride first? The Wild Mouse rollercoaster?'

What had she got herself into? Zoe pretend to cower, but her fear was real. 'Uh…I'm actually terrified of it.'

Mitch couldn't mask his disappointment. He looked longingly upwards to where the brightly painted carriages rattled at great speed along the tracks. Excited squeals and shrieks rang out every time a carriage swung around.

'I didn't take you for such a wimp, Zoe,' he said, but the way his eyes crinkled and he squeezed her hand let her know he was teasing.

She looked up at him. 'I have a confession to make. When it comes to rides I *am* a wimp. When I'm on something like the Wild Mouse, screaming, it's not from excitement but from genuine fear.'

'You *have* to be kidding me?' he said, raising his expressive eyebrows. 'A fun fair is all about exhilaration and terror and regretting that last hot dog you ate. Why did you bring me here if you weren't prepared for the screaming? Does that mean we don't even get to go on the Hair Raiser?'

He waved his arm towards a ride where strapped-in riders were raised up high in the sky, only to be plummeted back to earth at a frightening pace, screaming all the way.

To Zoe's eyes it was terrifying. She pulled a repentant face. 'Sorry. You wouldn't get me up on that thing in a million years. It would be an amazing view of the city, up so high, but I'd have my eyes tightly shut and wouldn't see a thing. I'd forgotten how scary these rides are.'

'So we're only going on *girly* rides, are we? Don't expect me to ride with you on that wussy carousel.' Mitch glowered, but ruined the effect with a smile that insisted on breaking through his frown.

'Actually, I rather like those pretty ponies. Sure you wouldn't join me on one? Safe and sedate—just how I like it.'

Safe and sedate? There was nothing safe or sedate about the way she felt about Mitch…

Mitch crossed his arms across his chest. 'No to the painted ponies. You will never, *ever* get me on one of those things.'

'I love the giant slides. Or I could challenge you on the dodgem cars?'

'Now you're talking,' he said.

They only had to wait a few minutes for the next dodgem session. Zoe liked the way Mitch wasn't the least bit self-conscious about lining up with a crowd of mainly teenagers. Looking around her, she saw she wasn't the only woman in a dressy dress and heels.

'Shall we share a car?' she asked as they got ready to run and claim one.

'I want one of my own,' he said.

Once Zoe was strapped into her bumper car and the music started she stepped on the accelerator too hard—and crashed her rubber bumpers straight into Mitch's car.

'Gotcha!' she called, smiling.

'A challenge?' he said, assuming a racing driver's position behind the wheel, his expression deadly serious. 'We're talking professional, here. I drive to win.'

'You're on,' she said. 'I drive to destroy.'

As they took to the circuit and thumped and bumped their electric cars into each other, and the surrounding cars, Zoe started to laugh. By the time the session came to an end she was paralysed by giggles.

Mitch helped her out of her car. 'That was so much fun,' she said as her giggles subsided.

'You were determined to thrash me,' he said.

'And I did,' she said.

'I would dispute that. I counted the bumps and I came out ahead.'

'Oh, really?' she challenged. 'How many bumps?'

'I was five more than you. Do you concede defeat?' he said, grinning.

'I wasn't counting, so I have to believe you,' she said, narrowing her eyes in mock anger.

'That said, I'll allow that you were a worthy opponent.'

'I just wish I'd thought to count the bumps—I'm sure I came out on top.'

'I enjoyed it,' he said. 'Kids' stuff, but fun.'

'The thing is,' she said, 'I don't think I ever acted that childish when I was a child.' She tucked her arm through his. 'C'mon—let's try another ride.'

They wandered through the fun fair until Zoe stopped at the Laughing Clowns sideshow.

'I was so scared of these things when I was little,' she said.

A row of motorised vintage clown heads with open mouths moved from side to side, ready for people to throw small balls in the hope of winning a prize.

'You seem so fearless, Zoe, and yet you have all these hidden fears,' Mitch said.

He rested his hand on the back of her neck and the casual contact sent shivers of awareness coursing through her.

'Not so hidden,' she said. 'Lots of people are frightened of clowns. There's even a name for it—coulrophobia. I still don't like them.'

He leaned in closer. 'What else are you frightened of, Zoe?' he asked in an undertone.

Of falling in love with you and getting my heart pulverised, she thought, but she would never put voice to that.

She forced her voice to sound unconcerned. 'Earthquakes, of course. But we've been there—done that.

Nothing much else—what about you?' she said. 'Snakes? Spiders? Sharks?'

He shook his head. 'I wouldn't go out of my way to encounter any of those, but I'm not scared of them.' He paused. 'I…I fear failure.'

She stared at him, too surprised at his admission to speak. 'But you're so successful,' she said eventually.

'You're only as good as your last game,' he said. 'Failure on the world stage isn't a pretty thing.'

'So if you don't come back fighting this season, with your knee fixed, you'll consider it failure?'

He stilled and went silent, and Zoe sensed his thoughts had turned inwards.

'Yes,' he said, after a long pause.

The single word was a full-stop to the thought and she knew there was nothing further to be said.

Mitch looked at the clowns, challenge in his stance. 'I'm not scared of *these* things. I'm going to beat 'em,' he said with confident arrogance. His eyes narrowed as he assessed the clowns' state of play before taking out his wallet.

The young guy behind the counter explained that Mitch needed to get five balls into the clowns' mouths—each clown varying in points scored. Mitch paid for and took the balls. Then he focussed his gaze, took aim and, one at a time, shot all five balls into the gaping mouths of the clowns.

Zoe clapped her hands together, doing a little dance of excitement. 'Well done!'

'Not bad,' said Mitch, with studied nonchalance.

It was nothing—absolutely nothing—compared to his achievements in soccer, but she was there with him and that made it special to her.

Would she ever be able to come to Luna Park again without him? There would be memories everywhere.

The sideshow attendant handed over a bright blue teddy bear as Mitch's prize. But Mitch pointed to a little white stuffed dog, wearing a miniature Aussie-style hat.

'That one, please,' he said. He turned to Zoe and handed it to her. 'For you,' he said. 'To remember what fun we've had this night.'

Zoe took the toy and clutched it to her, ridiculously pleased. Unwelcome tears stung her eyes. She swallowed against a sudden lump in her throat. 'Th...thank you. It's very cute.'

Did he have to remind her how fleeting their time together was?

Before Mitch had a chance to say anything more, a thirty-something man who had been standing behind them, waiting his turn for the clowns, turned to Mitch. 'That was awesome, mate.'

Mitch nodded in acknowledgement of the praise. 'Focus is what it takes,' he said.

Zoe could see recognition dawn in the man's eyes before a big grin split his face.

'As Mitch Bailey knows only too well!' he said. 'Mitch, you're meant to be in *Spain*.'

He reeled off an impressive list of European fixtures in which Mitch's team was scheduled to play. Then he pulled out a crumpled flyer for a restaurant.

'Can I get your autograph?'

Mitch obligingly autographed the piece of paper, then shook the man's hand. As the man walked away he looked back over his shoulder to Mitch several times, grinning. Zoe didn't have to be able to read his thought bubbles to understand the man's delight in having met his idol.

The full weight of Mitch's responsibilities to his fans seemed to settle on her shoulders. She began to comprehend his determination that nothing could come between his return to top form. Not her. Not any woman. But she refused to let it suppress her spirits.

Tonight was hers.

Mitch looked down at Zoe. Her face was flushed, and strands of her dark hair had come loose from its severe style to waft around her face. Laughter still curved the corners of her mouth and her eyes shone.

He reached out and smoothed the errant hair back into place. He had never wanted her more.

'Thank you,' she murmured. 'I must look a mess.'

'You could never look a mess,' he said. 'You look like a woman who's faced a mighty dodgem battle and won through.'

She was breathtaking. Attractive, yes, but also vibrant, smart and straightforward. Zoe Summers was unlike any other woman he'd met.

Something deep inside him seemed to turn over as he looked into her eyes. When they'd been battling with so much fun, intent on the dodgem car circuit, he'd been struck by how effortlessly they got on together. There were no games, no pretence. It had taken him back to their water fight in the pool in Bali—how much he'd enjoyed that too. And that was on top of how superlatively they'd got on in bed.

It struck him what it was that drew him so strongly to her—she grounded him. He knew she didn't give a toss about his money or fame. She'd been on his side when they were teenagers. He firmly believed she was on his side now. He could be himself with her, in a way he couldn't with anyone else outside his family.

Her idea to come to Luna Park had been inspired. She'd relaxed, and so had he. He could think of no other place he'd rather be right now than here with her.

Not even Madrid.

That was a dangerous thought.

He had to block it.

If he wasn't careful this woman could change his life. And he did *not* want to deviate from the path he had set himself.

All he had with Zoe was tonight. He'd better remember that.

'Time to go?' she asked.

'Yes,' he said. 'We can drive to a coffee shop.'

'Or have coffee at my house?' she said.

Coffee or something more? He just wanted to spend time with her, no matter how it might end up.

'Great idea,' he said.

'Let's go, then,' she said. 'Before more of your fans realise Mitch Bailey is in town.'

He took her hand and led her out of Luna Park, striding so fast she had to ask him to slow down, breathlessly reminding him that she was wearing high heels.

He slowed his pace on the steep stairs up to the narrow street where he'd parked the car. Then, in the shadows the streetlights did not illuminate, at last he kissed her—fiercely, possessively—and she kissed him back with equal fervour.

CHAPTER TWELVE

ZOE DIDN'T EVEN MENTION coffee when they got back to her place. Mitch didn't give her the chance to. He made sure she scarcely had time to draw breath between urgent, drugging kisses. He was too conscious of the hours, the minutes, the seconds ticking by until he had to say goodbye to her.

She didn't protest. Laughing, breathless, she took him—stumbling as they tried to walk and kiss at the same time—through the reception area, where he'd waited for her that morning, past an office and into a large living room. She fumbled with light switches, missing half of them with unsteady fingers, so they could see where they were going.

Between kisses he registered that the room was all industrial chic, with soaring ceilings, open beams, rough old brickwork and wide hardwood floors. Further through was another living area with sleek modern furniture. Open metal stairs led to a mezzanine that Mitch assumed was her bedroom. The east-facing wall comprised floor-to-ceiling industrial windows that framed a night-time view across Mort Bay to Goat Island.

But he was too busy feasting his eyes on Zoe to bother with the view, no matter how spectacular.

Still kissing, they landed on the white sofa, laughing as their limbs tangled and tripped them. A large slumbering tabby cat yowled its protest at their occupation of its sofa and shot off towards the kitchen.

Mitch found the zipper of Zoe's purple dress and tugged it down over the smooth skin of her shoulders. Her scent filled his nostrils: warm, womanly, arousing. Her curves, soft and lovely, moulded to his chest, her thighs pressed to his. *At last.* This was what he had been wanting for two long months. *Zoe.* There had been no other woman in between.

He shrugged off his jacket as she divested him of his tie and fumbled with fingers that weren't steady at the small buttons on his shirt.

A pulse throbbed at the base of her neck and he bent his head to press a kiss there. She clutched at his shoulders with a murmur of pleasure deep in her throat that sent his senses into overdrive. He broke the kiss. Pulled back. Her eyes were unfocused with passion, her mouth swollen from his kisses.

'Zoe, are you sure?'

All Zoe could think of was how much she wanted Mitch. Her heart was frantically doing cartwheels; her body was pulsing with desire. He was irresistible. And she didn't want to resist him for a moment longer.

Just one more time. Please. Just one more time with this once-in-a-lifetime man.

She was going into this with eyes wide open, not prompted by fear or anything other than the overwhelming need to have Mitch with her while she had the chance. *One last time.*

'I'm very sure,' she murmured, not even wanting to waste a minute on words when she could be touching instead of talking.

She wound her arms around his neck to kiss him again,

parted her lips for his mouth, his tongue, and felt the slide
of her dress over her hips as it fell to the floor.

Zoe awoke several hours later. Somehow she was up in
her mezzanine bedroom. How...?

She blinked to bring herself to full consciousness. Memories of Mitch carrying her up the stairs to the bed after
they'd made love on the sofa filtered through. They'd made
love again and she'd fallen asleep in his arms, her head
pillowed on his chest, feeling the thud, thud, thud of his
heartbeat reverberate through her being as she'd swallowed
the words she'd longed to utter: *I love you, Mitch. Don't
leave me, Mitch.*

Now she was alone in the bed and she could hear him
softly padding around the room. His clothes must be downstairs. She should get up. Go down with him. Watch him as
he dressed to leave her and go back to his life that had no
room for her. But she couldn't expose herself to that particular form of torture. Instead she drew her knees to her
chest and curled her naked self into the tiniest ball possible.

'Zoe? Are you awake?'

She heard his hoarse whisper but she was too weary for
words. For platitudes. For promises made in the aftermath
of passion and not likely to be kept.

'Mmm...' she murmured, pretending to be asleep.

She felt him stand over the bed. 'I have to go back to
my parents' house, Zoe, to pick up my stuff, say goodbye
to them. But I'll call around to see you on the way to the
airport—around ten. We can say goodbye properly, swap
contact details.'

He waited for her answer.

'Okay,' she murmured, hoping she sounded convinc-
ingly sleepy.

But when he leaned over to kiss her on the cheek she

lost it. Lost all dignity, lost all pride and clung wordlessly to him until he gently unwound her arms and lowered her back onto the bed.

'See you in a few hours,' he whispered, kissing her again before he left.

She held herself rigid in the bed as she listened to him move around downstairs, heard his footsteps walk through the office, the quiet slam of the door closing behind him, the sound of his car disrupting the stillness of the night.

After he'd gone Zoe lay there for a long time, unable to sleep, her thoughts churning round and round. *She couldn't deal with this.* Couldn't allow herself to be picked up and put down at a man's whim.

She wasn't a cool girl—could never be a cool girl able to handle a casual relationship with aplomb. Underneath her stylish clothes and smart haircut she was still Zoe the nerd who longed to be loved.

She didn't want to engage in some battle of the sexes scenario. But it did appear that men were able to make love to a woman—make it seem special and memorable—and then walk away without a backward glance.

As Mitch had done to her in Bali. And had just done again. And she, to save her pride, her heart, had pretended that it didn't hurt.

But to a woman—*this* woman, anyway—it was more difficult to separate sex from emotion. From love. She couldn't just write off an intimate connection like the one she'd just shared with Mitch as a mere physical fling.

She'd been dumb enough to fall in love with him. All he wanted was no-strings fun while she wanted to be bound by ribbons of love and commitment to the man she gave her heart to.

Mitch wasn't that man. He'd made that very clear, much as she might long for it to be otherwise. The lovemaking they'd shared last night had meant nothing to him, though he'd made sure she enjoyed it to the fullest. She'd gone into it willingly. Did not regret it. But she deserved more than Mitch was prepared to give.

Friends with benefits didn't do it for her—no matter how spectacular the benefits.

If Mitch came to see her as promised, later this morning, she would make all the right noises. The *Let's keep in touch*, the *I'll look you up when I'm next in Europe*, the *I hope to see you next time in Sydney*, conversation. But after he left she would wipe Mitch from her mind, from her heart.

At last she dozed off into a fitful sleep. When she awoke again, to early-morning sunlight filtering through the blinds, it was like a repeat of the dreams of him she had suffered since Bali: waking to find she was alone after all. Only this time she could still see where the sheets had twisted around his body, inhale the scent of him, feel the imprint of him on her. He had been only too real.

She got out of bed, staggered with sudden dizziness and a wave of nausea. Coffee. That was what she needed.

She clung to the railing as she made her way down the winding metal stairs that led from the mezzanine to the living area. There was no trace of Mitch left—not even a lingering scent.

Then she saw the toy dog Mitch had won for her, propped on the coffee table. Mitch had joked that he didn't want it watching them and turned its back to them.

Zoe took the few steps over to the coffee table, hugged the fluffy toy to her and let the tears come.

CHAPTER THIRTEEN

AN HOUR LATER Zoe yawned and stretched as she let herself out of her front door. The coffee had done nothing to quell the nausea—in fact just a sip had made it worse. She'd been lucky enough to get a cancellation for an early-morning appointment with her doctor in Balmain village. It was a crisp, sunny morning and she'd decided to walk.

Even after eating only a few bites of her meal last night she'd awoken feeling unwell again. It was annoying to feel like this when she was so used to perfect health. If, as Mitch seemed to think, she had picked up some long-lasting exotic bug she needed to get it fixed. Or maybe it was stress. Or a food allergy. Half the people she knew these days seemed to have some kind of food intolerance.

Then again, maybe it was caused by heartbreak.

She didn't have to wait long to see the doctor. Straight away, Zoe told her how she'd got food poisoning the first day she'd been in Bali and hadn't seemed to get over it. She was astounded when, after listening to her recital of tummy-twisting woes, her doctor suggested she take a pregnancy test.

Zoe shook her head. 'It couldn't be that,' she said. 'I'm on the pill. We were careful. It was only one night.'

Her doctor gave her a reassuring smile as she handed

over a pregnancy-testing wand and directed Zoe to the medical practice's bathroom. 'It's a good idea to rule it out for sure.'

Zoe had thought she'd felt fear when the earthquake had hit. But that fear was nothing to what she felt in the privacy of the medical centre's bathroom. She had to wait three endless minutes before she dared to look at the result panel of the testing stick. One thin pink line meant she *wasn't* pregnant. Two pink lines meant she *was* pregnant.

She thought her eyes were blurring when she saw two distinct pink lines. Pink lines as deep in colour as the suit she'd been wearing the day before. She closed her eyes and opened them again, but the two lines were still there. She shook the device, in the hope that it might shake back down to one line, like the mercury in a thermometer. But the two pink lines were still there, glaring at her.

This couldn't be.

Those thin pink lines were turning her life upside down more than any earthquake.

Too numb to move, she stayed a long time in the bathroom. Eventually the practice nurse knocked on the door and asked if she was all right. She staggered back down to the doctor's consulting room, holding on to the corridor wall for support.

'You okay?' her doctor asked.

'Not really,' she said. 'It says I'm pregnant. That's not possible. I…I don't *feel* pregnant.'

But when she really thought about it maybe she did. The off-and-on nausea. Her aversion to certain foods. The inexplicable craving for oranges she'd put down to a need for vitamin C. A tendency to be over emotional, which was not like her at all. And when she'd dressed last night, in that gorgeous purple dress she'd bought just before she went to Bali, she'd been surprised when it had seemed tighter across the bust than she'd remembered.

But her brain refused to accept the possibility.

'Don't I need a blood test to be sure?' she asked.

'The test you've just taken is extremely accurate,' the doctor said. 'But just to be certain I'll ask you to hop up onto the bed so I can examine you.'

Zoe moaned under her breath. Could the day get any worse?

'You're definitely pregnant,' the doctor said, after a series of palpations. 'About eight weeks along, I'd say.'

She was eight weeks pregnant.

It seemed impossible. But the timing was spot-on.

'The sickness you're feeling should start to ease soon, as your hormones settle down,' the doctor said.

'How could this have happened? We took precautions.'

'No precautions are one hundred per cent effective,' the doctor said. 'My guess is that your digestive upset in Bali negated the effectiveness of your pill. Put simply: it wasn't absorbed—it didn't work.'

Zoe squeezed her eyes tight shut. This couldn't be true.

When she opened them it was to see the concerned face of her doctor.

'You have…options…' the doctor said.

'No.' Zoe was stunned by the fierce immediacy of her reply. 'No options. I'm keeping it.'

She couldn't bring herself to say *the baby*. Not yet. Not now.

Mitch's baby.

'The father…?' the doctor probed discreetly.

'We're not…not in a relationship,' Zoe replied. 'I…I'm in this on my own.'

She hardly heard another word as the doctor handed her a bunch of pamphlets. Talked of blood tests. Nutrition advice. Referral to an obstetrician. Choice of hospital. Antenatal classes. Nothing really sank in. This couldn't be happening.

She was going to have a baby in February.

It took her twice as long to walk home as it had to get to the medical centre. Her feet felt leaden and it seemed as if she was walking through dense fog. The more she thought about being pregnant, the more complicated the situation got.

She dreaded telling Mitch. He'd made it so clear he wasn't ready for commitment—certainly not for a family. *'Not until I'm thirty. Maybe thirty-five.'* His words echoed in her head over and over.

Then worse words seeped into her thoughts like poison. Her grandmother. *'I won't have you getting pregnant and ruining the future of some fine young man the way your mother ruined my son's.'*

In Bali she'd told Mitch what her grandmother had said. Was that how Mitch would see it? Would her getting pregnant ruin *his* future? It would certainly change it.

Her breath caught on a half-sob. *Not as much as it would change hers.*

Would he think she'd tried to trap him? That she'd demand money? Even marriage? *The oldest trick in the book.* She couldn't bear to think he would believe that of her.

Imagine if the press got hold of it. How sordid they would make it look. A one-night stand. A holiday fling. A scheming woman. It would not reflect well on him.

Mitch's career was all-important to him. He'd been so clear that he couldn't have distractions at this vital stage of his career. What could be more of a distraction than an unplanned baby—with its mother a woman he was only just getting to know?

A mother. She was going to be a *mother*.

From nowhere came a fierce urge to protect her baby. *Her baby.* This baby would be wanted. Would be loved. This was far from the way she'd dreamed of starting a family, but it had happened. She was strong. She was independent. She could do this on her own.

By the time Zoe got back home she'd made her decision. She would not tell Mitch she was pregnant.

Mitch had an early breakfast with his parents, feeling sad to say goodbye to them while his father was still in a cast and a sling and so obviously in discomfort. But that was another price he paid for his international career—being so far away from his family.

His mother had been determined to drive him to the airport. Much as Mitch loved his mother, he had been equally determined that she would be staying home in Wahroonga. He wanted to drive himself, so he could detour to Balmain and see Zoe one last time before he flew out to Madrid.

As he drove his rental car into Balmain, Mitch realised he was excited—heart-pounding, mind-racing excited—at the thought of seeing Zoe, even for only an hour. He had never felt like this about a woman. Always the game had been first and foremost—his emotions and energy channelled into his relentless drive to the top level.

Realistically, now was not the best time to get involved, to be thinking there might be some kind of future with her. But his attraction to Zoe was as out of his control as the earthquake had been. He had to ride with it.

Their night together had shifted something in his thinking. On the drive back to his parents' house he had found himself wondering if Zoe could play a part in his life.

Could she be a support rather than a distraction? Would having her with him in Madrid be less of a distraction than *not* having her there?

Because deep in his gut he knew Zoe was important. *Very* important.

One thing was for sure: he had to see her again, and see her again as soon as possible. Being back in Madrid would be easier if he knew he would be seeing her as soon as they could make it happen. He wanted to make a definite arrangement for her to come and visit as quickly as she possibly could. Her first-class airfare paid by him, of course.

On his third knock, Zoe answered her door.

As a footballer, Mitch was good at reading other players' intentions. Some commentators saw his skill as uncanny. He believed it was because he had been blessed with a well-developed subconscious antennae that picked up on the slightest variations in body language.

But he didn't need more than a basic knowledge of body language to know that something was wrong. Zoe looked washed out and drawn; her hand braced against the doorframe didn't look steady. His first thought was that she was ill.

'Mitch,' she said, offering her cheek for his kiss, but her greeting wasn't over-burdened with enthusiasm—and certainly not with passion.

He swallowed his dismay. Last night she had been so responsive in his arms.

Today she was wearing skinny black jeans and a loose black top that swamped her slender frame. It drained the colour from her face, making the contrast of her red lipstick appear garish. Her eyes seemed shadowed and dull.

He drew back. Searched her face. 'Are you okay?'

Her gaze slid away from his. 'Just tired. It was such a late night last night.'

Worry for her coursed through him. Fatigue. Illness. *Please don't let there be something seriously wrong with her.*

'You look unwell,' he said, more bluntly than he'd intended.

'I actually went to the doctor this morning,' she said.

'And? Did he test you for tropical bugs?'

'It's not a tropical bug. It's...it's... She's testing me for food allergies.'

'That's great. Not great that it could be an allergy. But great you didn't bring something home from Bali with you.'

Zoe choked, and then started to cough. He patted her on the back until her coughs subsided.

'I'm okay now,' she said.

He frowned. 'I don't like the sound of that cough.'

Her smile was forced. 'There's nothing to worry about. I...I'm not sick.'

Mitch wasn't convinced.

She turned on her spike-heeled black boots. 'It's cold out here. You'd better come in.'

The shiver that went through him had nothing to do with the weather.

Mitch followed her through into her living room. The view was, indeed, as spectacular as he'd thought it would be last night.

'This is a wonderful space,' he said, looking around him.

For the first time she smiled, but it was a wan imitation of her usual smile. 'It is wonderful, isn't it? I get it for a very good rent.'

For the first time Mitch felt an intimation of fear. Was

she having second thoughts about them keeping in touch? He regretted not telling her last night that she was so much more to him than a 'friend with benefits'. They'd vaguely discussed her visiting him in Madrid. But nothing concrete. He wanted to remedy that this morning—before he left for the airport.

He looked over to the sofa, where they'd made such passionate love. The cat was firmly ensconced once more, curled up in a ball. It opened one yellow eye, inspected him, and went back to sleep.

'No one working today?' he said. 'Except the mouse-catcher, there, of course.'

His joke about the cat fell flat.

'Louise and our office manager are on a course. I cancelled all my appointments because...'

He wanted her to say it was because he was going to call by and she wanted privacy. But he had a sinking sensation that wasn't what she was going to say.

'Because...because I wasn't feeling well,' she said.

She didn't wait for a reply from him, but turned away so all he saw of her was her black-clad back. Then she spun round to face him. She crossed her arms in front of her chest, seemed to brace her shoulders.

'I can't do this—with you, I mean,' she blurted out. 'I've thought about it. Not knowing when I'll see you again. Being a...a part-time lover. Sleeping with you with no kind of commitment. It's not me. It...it can only lead to heartbreak—for me, anyway. Why pretend otherwise?'

Mitch was too astounded to answer for a moment. 'I don't get it. Last night we talked about you coming to Madrid.'

'Did we? I don't recall a definite invitation. Just *Drop in for a bootie call if you happen to find yourself in Europe.*'

'Zoe, I didn't meant that.'

But that was exactly what it would have sounded like to her. He cursed under his breath.

'Last night we were kidding ourselves that we could keep something going. But all the barriers are still there and...and they're insurmountable.' Her voice broke.

'I don't agree,' he said. 'We can—'

She put up her hand in a halt sign. 'Don't say it. I've made up my mind. In any case, even if you *were* offering more than friends with benefits, I couldn't deal with the public attention. For a private person like me it would be hell.'

'But last night—'

She spoke over him. 'We...we need to get on with our own lives. I'm sorry, Mitch.'

Her words sounded rehearsed. Was this why she was tired? Had she been up since he'd left here, practising how to dump him?

He fisted his hands by his sides. 'I'm surprised. And disappointed.'

And angry as hell.

'I've thought about it a lot since...since last night.'

'So that's it? It's over between us before it even started?'

Dumbly, she nodded, her eyes bleak.

'Then there's nothing further to be said.'

He turned and walked out. She made no effort to stop him. If she'd been able to read his thought bubbles all that would be visible would be dark, thunderous clouds.

Mitch was so churned up he was scarcely aware of how he got out of Balmain and on the road to the airport.

What in hell had gone wrong? He couldn't believe Zoe had had such a complete turnaround of feelings.

But he couldn't *make* her feel what he felt—make her

see what a good chance they had of something special if they both worked at it.

He had to put her behind him.

It wasn't as if he'd be short of feminine attention once he got back to Madrid.

Oh, yes, there were plenty of eager women around for a player of his standing in La Liga. He was only alone by choice.

But none of them was Zoe.

His hands clenched tightly to the steering wheel. As he drove towards the airport his thoughts spun around and around, unable to make sense of his confrontation with her.

It hadn't seemed right. There had been something about her. She'd seemed…*cowed*. The thought of her face brought back a flash of memory. The way her shoulders had been hunched over, the way she'd kept her eyes to the ground. She'd been like that Zoe he'd wounded long ago in high school.

But he'd done nothing to hurt her this time.

Something else had happened. Something she was hiding from him—for a reason he couldn't fathom.

As he neared the industrial area of Mascot, home to Sydney's Kinsgsford-Smith Airport, he was still puzzling over what he might have missed.

He thought about her doctor's diagnosis. How could the doctor know straight away that Zoe hadn't contracted a tropical disease? There would have to be tests—tests that would take days to come back from a pathologist.

The more he thought about it, the more he was convinced something was seriously wrong. Something Zoe was determined to hide from him.

Twice before she'd left him with unfinished business. The first time when they'd been teenagers. The second in Bali, after a night of passionate lovemaking. There wouldn't be a third time.

He still had a few hours until he had to check in for his flight.

He swung the car around and headed back to Balmain.

CHAPTER FOURTEEN

AFTER MITCH WALKED OUT Zoe was in such a state of shock she couldn't think straight. She immediately began to worry if she had done the right thing in concealing her pregnancy from him.

She hadn't just concealed it—she had *lied* about it. She had out-and-out lied to Mitch by telling him she was being tested for food allergies to explain her symptoms.

Zoe smothered a semi-hysterical laugh. She wasn't very good at deception. She'd always prided herself on her honesty. Mitch must think she was at best unbalanced; she didn't dare think what he might call her at worst. The confusion, hurt and barely suppressed anger on his face at her ill-thought-out words had distressed *her*. Heaven knew how awful it had been for *him*.

She had decided not to continue their friendship before she'd gone to the doctor. But she'd had no intention of blurting it out to him this morning. She just wouldn't have answered his texts, replied to his emails, until he'd got the message. She'd wanted to avoid a messy confrontation.

But that had been before she knew she was pregnant.

She paced the length of the apartment—back and forth, back and forth—totally at a loss to know what to do, until she began to feel dizzy. It seemed surreal that in the space of a few hours her world had been turned so totally upside down, leaving her staggering and disorientated—way worse than after the earthquake.

She'd discovered she was pregnant, and she'd lost Mitch when she'd only just found him.

Finally, when she truly thought she might topple over from a crippling combination of fatigue and angst, she sank into the sofa. Einstein, her dark tabby cat, looked at her with baleful eyes but allowed himself to be hugged tight.

'What am I going to do?' she asked the cat as she stroked him.

The rhythmic motion on his soft fur was soothing to both of them. She often talked to her cat; he was a great listener. It didn't matter that he only answered with the occasional meow that she fancifully imagined to be a reply.

'I'm going to have a human kitten, Einstein, and I don't know how I'm going to cope.'

Her words echoed through the empty space, emphasising her aloneness. Einstein just purred.

In some ways she identified with the cat. He'd been a disreputable-looking stray, hanging around the warehouse complex car park. With patience and cans of tuna she'd tamed him. Once she'd established that he didn't belong to anyone she'd adopted him.

She and Louise had called him Einstein because, as Louise had put it, 'He's a genius cat to have found *you* to dance attendance on him.'

Einstein was as fiercely independent and self-sufficient as Zoe liked to think she was. After all, she was the girl who had emancipated herself from her grandmother aged just seventeen. She'd put herself through university on her own. Got admitted as a chartered accountant. Established her business by herself.

She'd become very good at solving problems without

seeking help. But she was totally unprepared for a surprise pregnancy and for bringing up a baby on her own.

Suddenly she was overwhelmed by a fierce longing for her mother. A woman desperately needed her mother with her at a time like this. And her father too. He would have given her good advice on what to do about Mitch.

Should she have told Mitch she was pregnant? Presented it as an issue they needed to look at together? After all, they'd made this baby together. Did he have a right to know he was going to be a father? Was it the wrong thing to do to keep him out of the picture? Should she tell him and make it clear she would make no demands on him—financial or otherwise?

Zoe clutched her head with both hands against the throbbing of an impending headache. Conflicting thoughts and questions she could find no answer to were banking up in her brain and banging to be let out.

She glanced at her watch. It seemed like for ever, but Mitch hadn't been gone long. If she was quick she could catch him on his mobile phone and ask him to come back. Or meet him at the airport.

She didn't have Mitch's number.

They hadn't actually exchanged phone numbers or addresses. There'd been no need to as yet. They'd planned to swap all their contact details this morning, if things had gone differently.

Could she get hold of his number from somewhere? Maybe look up his parents and call them? What kind of reception would she get from his mother? A strange young woman, calling to get her famous soccer star son's personal phone number so she could tell him she was pregnant? As if *that* would happen.

She didn't even have a clue about which airline he was flying with. And no airline would divulge passenger details to tell her if he was booked on their 2:00 p.m. flight to Madrid. If she wanted to talk to him she would have to scurry around the terminal, trying to find him. No way could she bear to do that. If he were flying first class he'd go straight to a private lounge anyway.

It seemed she'd missed her chance to tell him face to face that she was pregnant.

If she decided to tell him at some time in the future she would have to try and contact him in Madrid. Maybe she could find out who was his agent or his manager and get a message to him through them. *Yeah, right.* They'd think she was a groupie or a stalker—or worse.

What a mess she'd made of this.

But she'd had her reasons for not telling Mitch and they'd seemed valid at the time. For the moment she'd stick with them.

Louise would have to be told, though, when she got back at lunchtime. They were good friends as well as work colleagues. Her pregnancy would have implications for the business. It would affect the possible buyout and her plans for expansion. Nothing they wouldn't be able to work through, though. Women got pregnant and managed their careers all the time.

It was Mitch who was her concern.

She sighed and yawned—exhausted, overwhelmed, and weary beyond measure.

'Move over, Einstein,' she said to her cat, so she could stretch out on the sofa beside him.

As she settled herself next to the purring cat at last she allowed herself to think about her baby—the new little person she would be bringing into the world in February. Would she/he look like her and Mitch? Her black hair with his green eyes?

Or a little boy or girl who looked just like Mitch.

She smiled at the thought and put her hand protectively on her still flat tummy. But as she drowsed into sleep she thought about how delighted her mother and father would have been to be grandparents and her smile melted into tears.

Zoe was awoken by an insistent buzzing. She struggled through layers of sleep to recognise it as the front door buzzer. *Please don't let it be a client.* She couldn't even face a delivery person, let alone some number-befuddled artiste who'd got themselves into a huge mess with their tax reporting or their quarterly Business Activity Statement.

Right now she couldn't cope with someone spilling a shoebox full of scrappy invoices and receipts all over her desk and begging for help. Usually she'd see it as a challenge, and be delighted to assist. But today it would be the befuddled leading the befuddled.

She moved a protesting Einstein and swung herself off the sofa. Once on her feet she staggered, and had to steady herself against a sudden light-headedness. With clumsy fingers she pushed her fingers through her hair and rubbed under her eyes for smeared mascara.

'Coming!' she called.

It seemed to take for ever to reach the door, and Zoe took a deep breath before she opened it. She thought she was hallucinating when she saw Mitch standing there. She wiped her eyes with the back of her hand and looked again. But he was still there, as billboard-handsome as ever but with his face set in unfamiliar grim lines.

Mitch.

Joy filtered through her shock to warm her heart. *He'd come back.*

'You're...you're meant to be at the airport,' she managed to choke out.

He didn't explain but rather launched straight into tight-lipped speech. 'Zoe, you obviously have your reasons for saying what you did this morning. But I'm not leaving until I know the truth.'

'I...I wanted to... I didn't have your number and...'

The words seemed to stall in her throat. She stared at him until the lines of his face seemed to go fuzzy. Her hand flew to her mouth. She felt flushed, light-headed, nauseated. She clutched at the doorframe. For the first time in her life she was going to faint.

Zoe felt Mitch catch her, lift her into his arms, cradle her to his chest. She could hear his voice as if it were coming from a long way away.

'Zoe... I've got you, Zoe.'

He carried her to a chair in the waiting area and forced her head between her knees. She was aware of his hand, warm and reassuring on her back.

'Breathe,' he said, his voice coming back into normal range. 'Breathe in and out, slowly and deeply. You told me you've done yoga. Use your yoga breathing.'

She did as he instructed until the fog cleared. But it was an effort to lift her head.

'Slowly,' Mitch said. 'Lift your head slowly.'

He handed her a paper cup of water from the cooler.

'Just sip it,' he said.

Obediently, she took a few sips of the cold water.

He hunkered down in front of her, his green eyes narrowed. 'Are you going to tell me what's going on?'

Not here. Not now. Not with her at such a disadvantage. She needed her thoughts to be clear.

Weakly, she bowed her head and didn't answer.

'So there *is* something?' he said gruffly.

She nodded.

'I knew it,' he said.

'I…I'm sorry about…this morning…the way I….' She couldn't force the words out. She swallowed hard but it didn't make it any better.

'How long since you've eaten?' he said.

'Last night…I think.'

'When you just nibbled at your dinner? You didn't have any breakfast?'

She shook her head. 'Nothing. I thought the doctor might want to take blood for tests. I didn't want to have to go back another time, so I decided to fast so I could have the tests done straight away.'

It had seemed a good idea at the time. Then, after her visit to the doctor, food had been the last thing on her mind.

'What have you got in your refrigerator? I'll make you something to eat.'

'There's some bread in the freezer. Some toast, maybe?'

'You stay here and keep sipping on that water. Whatever else might be wrong with you, it's my bet you're dehydrated.'

She heard him rattling around in the kitchen. Soon the smell of toast wafted towards her. Suddenly she was starving. But she took Mitch's advice, leaned back in the chair and kept sipping water.

Within minutes he returned, with a plate holding two pieces of wholewheat toast, cut into squares. 'I think you should eat it dry until you see if you can keep it down. Just nibble on it to start with.'

He was so kind. She flushed. What if she didn't keep it down? How humiliating would *that* be in front of Mitch?

But she did keep it down. And she started to feel better. Stronger. Who knew? All she'd needed was some food.

'Thank you so much, Mitch, for looking after me. I feel fine now.' She wasn't used to being pampered—found it difficult to accept it.

'And, from that coolness in your voice, you think you're dismissing me and that I'm going to go away. Not happening. I told you—I'm sticking with you until I get to the bottom of what's going on.'

He'd come back to her.

It changed everything. She would have to pick her moment to tell him the truth. He was every bit as wonderful as she'd thought he was. And more. She would not find it easy to tell him she'd lied to him about something so important. That he was going to be a father.

Mitch was relieved to see the colour return to Zoe's cheeks, the light come back to her eyes. She'd given him a fright by fainting. But it was nothing he couldn't handle. It wasn't uncommon for a player to pass out from the sudden pain and shock of an injury.

Why she'd fainted was what he was determined to know. And why she'd behaved the way she had earlier this morning. It didn't make sense.

At the back of his mind was still the suspicion that there was something very wrong and she was trying to protect him from a painful truth. That was the kind explanation. What he knew for sure was that she was concealing *something* from him.

He didn't give up easily—he would never have got to where he was if he had. He wasn't going to give up on Zoe. Or leave her here to suffer by herself. She had no family. Was so fiercely independent that she wouldn't ask for help from anyone.

He needed to catch that plane and get back to Madrid.

But he'd left her on her own once before, in a corridor at a high school. In all conscience he couldn't to it again.

Who was he kidding? He felt more for Zoe than he ever had for a woman. It would nag at him if he left her—if he didn't look out for her. She awoke in him a deep, almost primeval urge to protect her. He would stay with her, no matter the cost to him.

'You said you'd cancelled your appointments for the day. Is that still the case?' he asked.

She nodded.

'Today's Friday. I assume you don't have any business plans for the weekend?'

'No.'

'Social engagements?'

'None to speak off.'

'Good.'

'What do you mean, "good"?'

'Because I'm taking you away. Somewhere you can get the rest you so obviously need. Somewhere we can talk. Talk until there's no more pretence or prevarication between us. I just need to make a few calls.'

She gripped the arms of the chair. 'You're taking me away? What the heck do you mean by *that*?'

He waved his hand around to encompass her office, the living area, the view to the harbour. 'This isn't working for us. The city. Being in Sydney. It's some kind of barrier. I thought we'd breached it last night. Got back to how we were in Bali. But obviously not.'

'No,' she said softly, looking somewhere near her feet.

'I'm not letting you go without a fight, Zoe. If it were at all possible I'd fly us back to Bali. But that can't happen. So I'm going to take you somewhere else.'

She looked directly up at him. 'You're kidnapping me, Mitch?'

'You could call it that.' She sure as hell wasn't going to get away from him.

Zoe smiled. It was a watery smile, but a smile just the same. 'I think I like the idea of being kidnapped.'

She pushed herself up from her chair. He took her elbow to support her.

'Please don't faint on me again,' he said. 'When your eyes rolled back in your head I thought—'

Those same brown eyes flashed indignation. 'My eyes did *not* roll back in my head.'

'They did.'

'They did not. I would have felt them if they had.'

'Okay, they didn't,' he said, unable to suppress a grin. 'They just...tilted a bit.'

'I don't know whether to take you seriously or not.' She shuddered theatrically. 'That would be such an unattractive look. I wouldn't want you to think of me as an eyes-rolled-back kind of girl.'

'Now I don't know whether to take you seriously or not,' he said.

'You'll never know, will you?' she said, with a challenging tilt to her chin.

She was cute. Very cute. And he was relieved to see a spark of *his* Zoe back again. But he wanted so much more than just a spark. He wanted the Zoe he'd been with in Bali. The Zoe he'd developed feelings for and didn't want to let go.

She frowned. 'But what about Madrid? Shouldn't you be back there? I'm worried that—'

'Let *me* worry about that. I can stretch my absence until Monday. I have to fly out tomorrow evening, come what may, but I'm going to keep you locked up in my kidnapper's lair until tomorrow afternoon. We either sort things out—'

'Or...?'

'Or we say goodbye for good.'

She stood very still. He could hear the ticking of the large clock on the wall behind him, the ding of incoming emails on the computer in the next room, even the faint slap of the water against the wooden piers below the building.

'Okay,' she said at last. 'But I hope you don't intend to gag and bind me and throw me in the back of your car?'

He laughed. She looked so washed out, her eyes shadowed, but that Zoe spirit was still there. 'I wouldn't dare,' he said.

'So...where are you taking me?'

'I can't take you to Bali, so I'm taking you to Palm Beach.'

Her face brightened. 'Palm Beach? I *love* Palm Beach. Even though I've only ever been there a few times. Even though it's winter.'

'There's a heated pool at the house.'

'I've never been kidnapped before. So what do I pack...?'

'Casual...comfortable. Something warm. It can get chilly by the sea. Oh, and walking shoes.'

Those sexy little boots wouldn't do for long walks on the beach.

He made a few calls on his mobile phone—one of which was to postpone his flight back to Madrid. He had to admire the efficiency with which Zoe packed her small red overnight bag and flung on a black-and-white-checked coat. In less than ten minutes she was ready.

'What about the cat?' he asked.

'I've left a note for Louise. She'll look after him.'

'I'm glad we don't have to take him with us,' he said.

She looked up at him. 'Would you really have brought Einstein with us?' she asked.

'Einstein? You call your cat *Einstein*?'

'Long story. I'll tell you later.'

'Yes. I would have brought Einstein with us if I'd had to. I don't mind cats.'

She went very quiet again. 'We haven't even established whether we like dogs or cats yet, let alone—'

'We can talk about that on the way down to the beach,' he said. 'Though, for the record, I love dogs and I like cats too. We had both when I was growing up. Not having a dog or a cat around the place is one of the things I miss, living in Spain.'

But they didn't get a chance to talk about dog and cats, or favourite movies or their taste in music, let alone the reasons Zoe had stonewalled him earlier this morning.

Because almost as soon as he'd driven the car out of Balmain and over the Anzac Bridge, heading north to the Harbour Bridge, Zoe had fallen asleep.

CHAPTER FIFTEEN

ZOE WAS ANNOYED with herself to find she had slept for most of the one-hour drive to Palm Beach—the most northern of Sydney's northern beaches. Her time with Mitch was so limited, and she didn't want to waste a minute of it.

But by the time her eyes had started to flicker open they had already driven past every one of the long, sandy beaches and the surrounding suburbs that lay between Manly and Palm Beach.

By the time her eyes were fully open they were on Barrenjoey Road, with the blue, boat-studded waters of Pittwater on their left, and cruising into Palm Beach. She barely had time to notice the handful of shops and restaurants that formed the hub of this exclusive, resort-like suburb as they flashed past.

Zoe didn't know how many times she'd heard Palm Beach referred to as 'the playground of the rich and famous'. When Hollywood celebrities jetted into Sydney in the summer it was often to stay in luxurious beach houses owned by themselves or their billionaire Aussie friends up here on the Barrenjoey Peninsula. Real estate was prized on this strip of land that jutted out into the sea, bounded by the surf beach on one side and the calm waters of Pittwater on the other.

Still feeling a tad drowsy, she allowed herself the luxury

of watching Mitch as he drove. He made even an everyday thing like driving a car look graceful and controlled. Both hands were firmly on the wheel as he concentrated on the road ahead. She noticed he wore one of the expensive watches he endorsed in an advertising campaign. He'd told her he only endorsed products he believed were of the best quality and design. His face—already so familiar to her—was set in such a serious expression. Designer sunglasses masked his eyes.

She wished she could see his thought bubbles. Was he looking ahead to a future—if his knee continued to hold up—as an elite athlete at the top of his field?

He was a determined, driven man who had made his thoughts about not settling down until he was in his thirties very clear. And yet it appeared he was serious about wanting her as part of his future in some way—he wouldn't have turned around at the airport otherwise.

But it wasn't just about *her* now—or even about *him*. They'd made a baby together. The way he'd looked after her when she'd fainted gave her cause to think that despite his celebrity status he was not the kind of man who would deny his own child. *He would make a good father.* It would be up to her to make sure he played some role in their child's life.

'That trip went fast,' she said, trying out her voice and finding it to be back to normal. She had never, ever fainted before.

'The lady awakes,' Mitch said, giving her a sideways glance.

Zoe remembered waking up next to him in Bali, after a night of sensual pleasure. How wonderful that time together had been—as it had been last night. She longed to be something more in his life and not to have to say goodbye in the morning. Would it ever happen?

'I missed the whole drive down. I wish you'd woken me up,' she said.

He smiled. 'So you could quiz me about my preference for dog over cat?'

'Something like that.' She'd planned to segue into his thoughts on having kids.

'You obviously needed the sleep,' he said. 'Feeling any better?'

'Much better,' she said, stretching her limbs as best she could in the confines of the car. 'Thank you.'

'We're nearly there,' he said.

'So I see.'

It was a magnificent winter's day, the sky cloudless, the sea a deep blue.

'It's ages since I've been down here. I'm a city girl—I don't stray over the bridge too often.'

'We came down here for a couple of vacations when I was a kid and I loved it. A friend of my parents had a house here.'

'Nice,' she said.

Now the road ran parallel to the surf beach that stretched to the Barrenjoey headland at one end and Whale Beach at the other. Even on a weekday in winter there were people swimming, and others in wetsuits, riding boards or paddling surf kayaks out into the breakers.

She opened her window to enjoy the salty air.

'We lived in Newtown,' she said. 'My parents weren't much for the outdoor life. They were arty, musical, and preferred to hang out in coffee shops rather than on beaches. Though when I was older I went with friends to the eastern suburbs beaches, like Bondi and Coogee. That was… that was before I moved to Wahroonga.'

'I was always a north shore boy. I learned to surf here, how to handle a surf kayak. My brothers were older than me—they taught me.'

'Knowing you, you probably overtook them at it your first day in the water.'

'Yeah. That's how it happened. They weren't too happy, having their kid brother beating them so quickly. But that was the way it was in my family. I was the brawn—they were the brains. And that's how it's played out. Just like my parents planned—they got a doctor, a lawyer and a banker.'

'And one of the best sportsmen in the world,' she reminded him.

'They appreciate that—don't worry. They're very proud of my success. They always supported me in anything I wanted to do,' he said.

'But why did they pigeonhole you?' she said, indignant on his behalf.

'They recognised our aptitudes early on, I suppose.'

'You've got plenty of brains. I know that for sure. You even ended up writing a halfway decent piece of poetry for that last essay.'

'You mean the essay that got the big red "fail"?' he reminded her.

'I don't know how that awful teacher could have thought you had plagiarised that poem,' she said.

'You mean because it was so very, very bad?" he said with a grin.

'It wasn't bad. She just didn't appreciate the analogy between scoring goals in a soccer game and goals in life. It was wonderfully rich in similes and metaphors and—'

'And more similes and metaphors, and a whole heap of words I didn't understand. It was *bad*, Zoe,' he said. 'Admit it.'

'It didn't have to be a masterpiece to get you a pass,' she said. 'I liked it, and that's that.'

He glanced sideways at her. 'Thank you for your loyalty. I didn't deserve it.'

She put up her hand in a halt sign. 'No need to go there again.'

She wondered how loyal he would feel towards *her* when she told him she was pregnant.

'I got a place to study engineering at the University of New South Wales. Did I tell you that?'

'You didn't—that's fantastic. You must have done well in the final exams.'

'I had no intention of taking up the place, of course,' he said. 'To play football was all I'd ever wanted to do since my grandfather took me to my first game at White Hart Lane in London. I applied to university just to prove I could get in.'

At the south end of the beach Mitch turned off and swung into a street a few hundred metres back from the water. He pulled up in the driveway of an elegantly simple house, rising to two storeys, all whitewashed timber and huge windows. It was surrounded by perfectly groomed tropical gardens. In an area of multi-million-dollar houses, it fitted right in.

'Is this your parents' friends' house?' Zoe asked. 'It's fabulous.'

'No, it's mine,' he said simply.

'Oh,' she said, not attempting to hide her surprise. Mitch hadn't mentioned owning property of any kind. But then she hadn't asked.

He opened her car door and went around to swing out both her small bag and one of his own.

'This house looks like a very posh kidnapper's lair,' she said.

'I don't think you'll object too much to the conditions of captivity,' Mitch replied with a smile.

They took a small glass-fronted elevator from the garage to the second floor. Zoe stepped into an airy, spacious living room that opened out through folding glass doors to a deck and an infinity edge swimming pool. Beyond that was a magnificent view of the sea, right up to the Barrenjoey headland, filtered by a stand of the tall cabbage palm trees that gave the area its name.

She turned to Mitch. 'Can you forgive me if I can't come up with anything more than *wow*?' she said. 'Except maybe *wow* again? I could look at that view all day.'

'I bought the house for the view.'

'The house itself isn't too shabby either,' she said.

The interior looked as if it had been designed by a professional, in tones of white with highlights of soft blue and bleached driftwood. Large artworks with abstract beach and marine life themes were perfectly placed through the room. It was contemporary and stylish, straight from the pages of a high-end decorating magazine. And yet there were homey touches everywhere—like a shabby-chic old pair of oars, a glass buoy covered in ancient knotted rope, tiny wooden replicas of fishing boats—that took away any intimidating edge.

What an idyllic place for children.

She slipped off her coat. The sun streaming through the windows made it superfluous.

'The house is awesome, isn't it?' said Mitch. 'I bought it with all the furniture included when the market was down, for a very good price.'

Zoe's money-savvy brain recognised that he'd got a good deal by buying at the right time. But around here a 'very good price' would still measure in the multi-millions.

Great. Just great. Mitch must be very wealthy. Wealthier than she'd thought he must be. And, from her experience with her clients, the wealthier they were, the more protective they were of their money—and defensive against people they suspected of wanting to take a bite out of it.

Like a girl who got pregnant on a holiday fling and came looking for a pay-out.

She forced the negative thought to the back of her mind. If she wasn't to tie herself up in knots of anxiety again she had to trust in Mitch that he wouldn't believe she'd had any other motive that night in Bali than to be with him. No matter what else he might come to believe when she told him about her visit to the doctor.

'Let me show you around,' Mitch said.

He took her for a quick tour. The kitchen seemed to be stocked with every appliance and piece of equipment possible. The bathrooms were total luxury. Each of the four bedrooms had ocean views.

Mitch took her overnight bag to the master bedroom, with its enormous bed and palatial en-suite bathroom. 'I'm putting your bag in here,' he said.

She stilled. 'And where are you putting yours?' she asked.

'That's up to you,' he said.

Whatever happened here in this beautiful house, whatever transpired with Mitch, she didn't want to sleep in a different bedroom from him.

'Put your bag with mine. Here. Please.'

The bedroom opened up onto a balcony. While Mitch went to get his bag she stepped out onto the balcony, breathed in the salt air. A flock of multi-coloured lorikeets took flight from the orange flowering grevillea that grew next to the pool. This truly was a magnificent place.

Mitch placed his bag next to hers and came up behind her on the balcony. He put his arms around her and pulled her back to rest against his chest. After a split second of hesitation she let herself relax against his solid strength. She felt safe, secure—and terrified.

This. Mitch. His arms wrapped around her, his breath

stirring her hair, his powerful body close. It was what she wanted. Now. And in the future. She was terrified that would never happen. Not when he discovered how dishonest she'd been with him.

That she was pregnant.

Mitch held Zoe close, relieved she hadn't pushed him away. He didn't want to let her go. Out of his arms—out of his life. They had twenty-four hours to sort out whatever was troubling her. He just hoped it was something he could work with—or solve for her.

He wanted her with him.

The more he was with her, the more he realised that a 'now and then' relationship wouldn't satisfy him for long. What he felt for her couldn't be blocked or passed or sent off the pitch.

'A good substitute for Bali?' he asked as they both looked ahead at the view.

'Oh, yes,' she said. 'It must be glorious in summer.'

'One day, maybe, I'll get to see it in summer. Usually I don't even get back to Australia for Christmas.'

'So you bought the house as an investment?'

'An investment for now. A home for later. When my football career is over.'

He hated to say those words. Right now he couldn't bear even to think about a life without playing.

'Is that inevitable?'

'It's a young man's game. I've still got good years ahead of me.' If the knee stood up to it. And if he didn't suffer any other serious injuries. 'But, yes. It will end.'

'What do you plan to do? Afterwards, I mean?'

Mitch liked it that Zoe didn't seem to realise he would never have to work again. He'd been careful with invest-

ments and he would continue to be. That was where banker
and lawyer brothers came in handy.

'I was bored witless while I was recuperating,' he said.
'I had a good look into some of the injury prevention de-
vices for sportsmen. Shin guards, ankle wraps, mouth
guards. That kind of thing. I reckon they could be better.
I'm looking into that.'

'Sounds good. You'd still be involved in sport.'

'But that all seems a long way away, Zoe. I don't want
to think about it too much. I'm concerned about the now,
not the future.'

'Of course,' she murmured, her voice subdued.

The change in her tone signalled a warning. They had
limited time. He had to try and recreate the atmosphere
that had brought them together in such a spectacular way
back in Bali at her villa.

'I can't promise roosters.'

'Just parrots?' she said.

'Or Indonesian food,' he said.

'Or earthquakes?' she added.

Mitch could think of various ways he might make the
earth move for her, as he had last night. He could carry her
right now to that big bed behind them in the bedroom. But
first he had to find out why she had behaved the way she
had this morning. After the fun they'd had at Luna Park,
after the lovemaking they'd shared, he still wondered why
she had dismissed him so coldly.

'However, there *is* a swimming pool—that's bigger and
better than the one at the villa.'

'With colder water?' she said pretending to shiver.

He looked over to the sparkling blue pool. There was
no elephant in residence. Both he and Zoe knew what had
to be tackled.

'The water should be heated up enough to swim,' he said. 'Not quite the same as Bali, but warm enough.'

'It's the most beautiful pool—I've never swum in a wet edge pool before. Are you sure I won't drift over the edge?'

He laughed. 'There's a ledge below. It's quite safe. Anyway, I'm here to catch you if you get into trouble,' he said.

'Are you, Mitch?' she said, in that tremulous voice that worried him.

She went to ease away from him but he hugged her tighter. 'Of course I am.'

They stood without speaking for a long moment.

Zoe broke the silence. 'So. The pool. Do you leave the heating on all the time?'

'The pool is solar-heated. But there's a gas-fired booster. I called the manager this morning and got her to switch it on.'

'You have a manager?'

'She looks after several of the properties here for absentee owners. My family use the house too. And sometimes I let it out to carefully vetted guests.'

'That makes sense. If the house is earning income you can get tax benefits too.'

'Of course you *would* know that,' he said. 'I also got the manager to stock the fridge with basics.'

'I was wondering about that. I wasn't sure what kidnappers did about feeding their victims. And it's been a while since that toast. It must be lunchtime.'

'Some of the restaurants here do delivery service. I asked the manager to pick up their latest menus.'

'So we can get room service? Like in Bali?'

'Yes,' he said. 'We can order lunch now.'

Zoe twisted in his arms so she faced him. He refused to let her go.

'Mitch, before we order lunch, and definitely before I get into a bikini, there's something I have to tell you.'

Mitch held his breath. *What was coming?*

She looked up at him, her eyes huge in her wan face. 'I'm pregnant.'

CHAPTER SIXTEEN

MITCH COULD NOT BELIEVE what he was hearing. *Zoe was pregnant?* He gently pushed her away from him. Stared at her as if he she were a stranger as he tried to process what she had just told him. Then the reality of it hit him. He cursed loud and hard.

How had he let this happen? He had trusted her. What an idiot he had been to lose control in Bali. Not to take absolute charge over contraception. What the hell had he got himself into?

Damn. Damn. *Damn.*

She didn't say another word, just stood on the veranda facing him, the glorious view stretching behind her. He knew she was nervously waiting for his response, but he was too shocked to say anything. Nothing in his twenty-seven years had prepared him for this moment. He cursed again.

He didn't know a lot about pregnant women—in fact he knew virtually nothing. He hadn't been in Australia when his nephews—the children of his oldest brother and his wife—had been born.

But some of the cards began to fall into place. Sickness, fainting, fatigue—all symptoms of a worrying serious illness. *Or a pregnancy.* What a blind fool he'd been.

'You're pregnant? And you didn't tell me?'

She flinched at the harshness of his voice but he didn't care. He'd been so careful to protect his future. Now a moment's lust, a moment's carelessness, had thrown everything off course.

She didn't look any different—still slim. But when he thought about last night he remembered that her breasts had seemed larger. He'd appreciated that. It must be a symptom too.

'I only found out myself this morning,' she said.

Her bottom lip was quivering, and she looked near to tears, but she met his gaze fearlessly. She gripped the veranda railing so hard her knuckles showed white.

'This morning? When you went to the doctor?' Strangely, he believed her.

'Yes. I got the shock of my life,' she said. 'I wasn't expecting it at all.'

He looked again at her slender figure in the tight black jeans. 'You're absolutely sure you're pregnant?'

She nodded. 'There's no doubt. The doctor gave me a test and examined me.'

Zoe pregnant.

He was struggling to get his head around it.

'But how did it happen?' He realised what a stupid remark that was the second the words were out of his mouth. He and Zoe had made love with passionate intensity all through that sizzling tropical night two months ago.

Through her misery, a spark of *his* Zoe emerged. 'The usual way,' she said. 'You know—basic biology.'

'But we were careful. You're on the pill.' He ran a hand through his hair in frustration. He should have taken care of the contraception.

'I know. But the doctor told me the pill doesn't work if it's not absorbed. And the Bali belly meant it didn't get digested. So no protection.'

It was the first time Mitch had seen Zoe so downcast; her lovely mouth set tight, her face strained, her eyes shadowed.

'So your illness wasn't an illness at all?'

'The initial food poisoning, yes. But once I got back to Australia it was what's called morning sickness.' Her mouth twisted wryly. 'Or, in my case, sometimes all-day sickness.'

Percolating through Mitch's shock was real anger. He'd been worried half-crazy about her. Driving back from the airport earlier, he had been imagining her with a serious, possibly fatal illness. What angered him was how dishonest she'd been.

He'd been stupid. She'd lied.

He made no effort to mask his anger. 'So when did you intend to tell me you were pregnant?'

He doubted she was even aware she was wringing her hands together. 'I...I didn't know how you would react. What...what you'd think of me.'

'You were going to let me fly back to Madrid without a word? What was I going to get—a lawyer's letter, demanding maintenance?'

She cringed from him. 'No! I was in shock. I was... frightened.'

Mitch took a step towards her. 'You were *frightened*? Frightened of *me*? What did you think I would do to you?'

Her face crumpled. 'I didn't know. I was so shocked. Trust me when I say it never entered my head that I could be having a baby. I didn't want you to think I...I'd tricked you into...into some kind of commitment. Or that I expected anything from you. I know how important it is to you to be...unencumbered. A baby certainly doesn't figure anywhere in your plans.' Her chin rose. 'It didn't figure in mine either.'

A baby. The actual word 'baby' hit him. Pregnancy was one thing. Baby was another. The reality was that Zoe was bearing a child—*his* child. Realising that sent Mitch into a deeper state of shock.

He and Zoe were going to be parents.

'Did you *ever* intend to tell me that I was going to be a father?'

He a father. Zoe the mother of his child.

The thoughts were so shocking, so unexpected, whirling around his head.

'Yes. No. I didn't know what to do.'

'You lied to me, Zoe. You said your sickness was caused by food allergies.'

'It was the first thing I could think of that might sound plausible. I didn't want you going back to Madrid worrying about it. Not when I know how extremely important the next few months are for you.'

'You're damn right about that,' he said.

Her chin tilted. 'I don't expect anything from you, Mitch. Not money. Not support.' Her mouth twisted bitterly. 'I know I'm nothing to you except a casual bedmate. If I ever thought anything else this sure as heck proves it.'

She headed for the bedroom, pushing past him. She picked up her red bag.

'I assume I can get a taxi from here? I'll walk down to the surf club to wait for one.'

He took a step towards her. 'Zoe—stop.'

She put a hand up to ward him off. 'Don't come near me,' she said, her voice as cold as her eyes.

She was leaving him again.

He grabbed her arm. She went still.

'Touch me again, Mitch, and I'll have an assault charge on you so fast your head will be spinning.'

He stared at her, shocked. How had it come to this?

After all they'd shared last night? What had happened to his plans for her to become part of his life? He'd been wrong to react the way he had.

She turned and walked away from him, her back ramrod-straight. But he could see her shoulders shaking.

As she left the room the enormity of what he'd done hit him. Zoe hadn't planned this. She'd tried to save him worry. He cared for her. *She was having his child.* And she was walking out of his life. A life he'd begun to hope she could share with him.

He took the strides necessary to reach her. 'Zoe. Stop. I'm sorry. I was out of order, speaking to you in that way. It was a shock. But I was wrong to react like that.'

She turned back to face him, her lips set in a tight line. 'I want nothing from you, Mitch.'

'But what about the baby?'

'There's just one thing. For his or her sake I'd like you to acknowledge the child as yours. To play a role in its life.'

The truth slammed into Mitch and left him reeling. *He wanted Zoe. He wanted the baby.*

'Zoe, I really am sorry. Please don't walk away. It was an accident, but we're in it together. *My* child. *My* responsibility. You don't have to go through this by yourself.'

To his intense relief she put down her red bag.

No way was he going to 'play a role' in his son or daughter's life. He was going to be a father. A *good* father. Like his father had been to him. And his grandfather before him.

'When is the baby due?'

'February, the doctor said.'

The reality of it hit him with full force. Something akin to anticipation, even a stirring of excitement, began to infiltrate his thoughts.

'My parents will be beside themselves,' he said. 'Especially my mother—she's desperate for more grand-children.'

'You…you'd tell your *parents*?' Zoe's eyes were huge with trepidation.

'Of course I'll tell my parents. This isn't just about you and me, Zoe. Not any more. This will be the next genera-tion of my family. A Bailey grandchild. A Bailey great-grandchild. A niece or nephew. A cousin. In my family our child will be a reason for celebration—not commiseration.'

Zoe shook her head in seeming disbelief. She put her hand on her belly in an age-old gesture of protection that shot straight to Mitch's heart.

'I…I'm still coming to terms with this. That we've made a little person.'

'You're thinking about what your grandmother said, aren't you?'

That mean old witch had a lot to answer for, the way she'd treated her hurting, vulnerable granddaughter. She wouldn't be getting her claws into *his* child, that was for sure.

Mutely, Zoe nodded.

'This baby won't ruin my life,' Mitch said. '*You* are not ruining my life. We're twenty-seven—not seventeen. Our careers are established. We've got more than enough money.'

Zoe had no idea just how much money.

'All true,' she said.

But Mitch could sense a big Zoe *but* coming up.

The more he thought about this baby, the more he thought it wasn't such a disaster. He wanted Zoe. He had to look after her and the baby. They had to be with him.

'Zoe,' he said. 'Come here.'

He held out his arms to her. Her eyes widened but she took the few steps needed so he could draw her into his arms. He held her tight, close to his heart. He allowed relief to flood through him. She was okay. Not ill. Not terminal. *Pregnant with his child.* He would look after her. He would protect her.

'I'm not angry. Not any more,' he said. 'I'll admit it was a shock. But this child is our responsibility. We need to get married as soon as possible.'

Zoe froze in Mitch's arms. She pulled away. Looked up at him. 'Get *married*?'

Mitch drew his brows together. 'Of course, get married. You're pregnant.'

He sounded so certain, so matter-of-fact.

Problem solved. Let's get on with it.

Not a word about love.

Could you actually feel a heart breaking? That must surely be the explanation for the sudden pain that stabbed her somewhere in that region.

During those long, sleepless hours this morning, when she'd decided to end things with Mitch, she'd allowed herself a single moment to dream of the impossible. She'd let herself fantasise that Mitch would fall in love with her the way she'd fallen in love with him. That their planets might end up permanently aligned.

Her pregnancy had put paid to those dreams.

Those ever-present tears started to sting her eyes again but she fiercely blinked them back. *Darn hormones.*

'Just because I'm pregnant it's no reason to get married,' she said.

Mitch's frown deepened. 'Of course it is. I'm old-fashioned, Zoe. I want us to be married before you have the baby.'

She broke away from him, turned, looked blindly out at the view. Then spun back to face him.

'Mitch, I appreciate your gesture. It's honourable of you. Gentlemanly. But I can't marry you.'

'I don't get it. You're having my child. I want it to have my name. I want us to be together when he or she is born. To bring our child up together. Give him or her a good life.'

'That's impossible.'

He shrugged. 'There'd be some logistical problems—I acknowledge that. You'd have to come to Madrid to live with me. I can't live here. Not now. Not yet. But I know you want to travel, learn European languages, so I hope you won't mind that. We'd have to sort something out with your business… You could even bring your cat if you wanted.'

The pain in her heart intensified. She wanted to be with Mitch in Madrid more than anything—but not like this.

'No, Mitch. I can give my child a good life here in Sydney. But I want my child to know his or her father. I want you to be involved. Maybe…maybe when our baby is older he or she could spend time with you in Madrid, or wherever you end up living. It should be possible to have some kind of shared custody, if that's what you want. I don't know… I haven't had time to think it through.'

If only it could be different—him, her and their baby together.

Mitch's mouth set in a hard line. For the first time she saw the toughness, the aggressive strength she knew must be there for him to have got where he was in his ultra-competitive world.

'I don't agree,' he said. 'A child needs both mother *and* father, and I want to be a father to my child.'

'You *can* be a father, Mitch. I would encourage you to have a relationship with our child. I…I just don't want to get married.'

How it hurt to say that. *To lie.*

'Why, Zoe? Surely it's the only answer.'

Slowly, she shook her head. 'Mitch, I don't think I'm getting through to you.' It was difficult to keep her voice steady and reasoned. 'Don't you remember what I told you in Bali? I only want to get married if...if I'm head over heels in love.'

'I remember,' he said slowly.

The love was there on her side. There was no doubt about that. She'd been in love with him when she was seventeen—a hopeless, unrequited love. And it had been ignited again in Bali, she now realised.

'The man I marry has to love me in the same way. I...I can't settle for less. Not...not even to give my baby its father's name.'

'But, Zoe, I *do* love you,' Mitch said.

Her poor wounded heart soared. But she yanked it firmly back to the ground again.

'Mitch, you don't have to say that. It doesn't change things.'

Mitch took her by the shoulders, his voice low and urgent. 'Zoe, I'm not just saying this. I *love* you. Why do you think I came back this morning? Brought you down here? You know I'll get a hell of a fine and a reprimand from my club for not being on that plane to Madrid, for missing a game.'

'You're missing a *game*? But, Mitch, that's so important to you. Your knee—your—'

'Not as important as you, Zoe. When I drove home from your place last night I was determined you'd come and visit me in Madrid as soon as you could. Once you were there, I might not have been able to let you go. I'm asking you to marry me now. Most likely I would have asked you to marry me when you came to Madrid.'

'But it... But... I want to believe you, but it seems so sudden.'

'Does it?' He tilted her face so she was forced to meet his gaze. 'I wasn't completely honest with you in Bali.'

She shrank back from him. 'What do you mean?'

'I left out part of my story about when we were at school together. When I came back from soccer camp I kept looking out for you at school because I wanted to say how sorry I was for the way I'd behaved. But that wasn't all. I missed you. *Really* missed you. School wasn't the same without you. I missed our talks. I missed the way we laughed together. The way you believed I was so much more than anyone else thought I was.'

'I still think that,' she murmured, not expecting an answer.

'When I went round to your grandmother's place and she told me you wouldn't be coming back I was gutted. I got moody—bad-tempered. Lara didn't like it. "What's the matter with you?" she taunted me. "Were you in love with that geek girl?"'

Zoe felt herself blush for her seventeen-year-old self. 'Surely she didn't say that?'

'She'd hit on a truth I hadn't recognised until she put voice to it. It all made sense. I *did* have feelings for you—feelings I hadn't acknowledged. That's why I missed you so much. I snapped back at Lara. Denied it. I realised then why she'd been so mean to you. She was jealous. She'd seen how it was with you and me from the get-go.'

'I can't believe this,' Zoe said, slowly shaking her head. She wanted to believe it. But it seemed surreal.

'Believe it,' said Mitch. 'My first break-up with Lara was over you.'

'But you got back with her. Stayed with her for years, on and off.'

'You weren't around. I was seventeen. Lara was persuasive. What can I say?' Mitch said with a rueful grin.

'So how do you explain what happened in Bali?' she said, still reeling from what Mitch had confessed.

'You caught my eye straight away. I thought you were hot even before I recognised you.'

'Really?' she said, pleased. It didn't hurt a plain girl's ego to hear that she'd caught Mitch Bailey's eye.

'You were wearing a towel that scarcely covered your amazing body. Of *course* I noticed you.'

'I don't know what to say to that,' she said. 'I was terrified the towel was going to fall off.'

'I was hoping the towel *would* fall off.'

'Mitch!' she said with mock indignation, and laughed.

'I thought I was long over you. That my feelings for you had been a teen thing. I was glad to see you and to be able to put things straight. That was all. I didn't expect to fall in love with you all over again.'

'And...did you?' She couldn't control the tremor in her voice.

He nodded with a smile that set her heart racing. 'But I didn't realise how hard I'd fallen until I was back in Madrid. I tried to deny it. *Man*, did I try to deny it. The timing wasn't right. Like the timing of this baby isn't right. But we can't control that, can we? Life can have a way of making up our minds for us.'

'My getting pregnant, you mean? Or...or you falling in love?'

'Both,' he said. He cupped her face in his strong, gentle hands. 'What about you, Zoe? Could you fall in love with me?'

The look of mingled hope and expectation in his eyes made her knees feel weak and shaky.

'Oh, Mitch, I'm already in love with you.'

'Head over heels?'

'So head over heels I feel dizzy. I had a crush on you

at school, but I never dreamed it would be reciprocated in any way.'

'It was such a long time ago. We were kids.'

'But the emotions were real,' she said slowly. She thought back to those hours she'd spent with Mitch in the privacy of her villa. 'I…I think I fell in love with you during our water fight.'

'I can't pinpoint when. It was just…*there*,' he said. 'And everything changed. I tried to tell myself it was just a vacation thing. Reaction to fear of the earthquake. All that. Then when I saw you in Sydney, looking so hot in that pink suit, I knew the attraction was genuine. But you were so glamorous, so contained—so unlike the Zoe I'd known in Bali. I wasn't sure it was the same person.'

'I was terrified of saying the wrong thing. It took a while for us to relax with each other.'

'Yes,' he said. 'Until I wiped you out on the dodgems.'

'I'm glad we worked it out,' she said, hoping he could tell the depth of her feelings for him.

At last he kissed her, his mouth warm and possessive and tender.

Kissing a man you loved, who loved you, who wanted to spend his life with you, felt so different from the other kisses she'd shared with Mitch. Just as exciting, just as sensual, but taken to a new level by love. She wanted Mitch's kisses for the rest of her life. Never anyone else's.

There never had been anyone else, she realised. This was true love—first love.

And they were going to have a baby. A little boy or girl to bring more joy and love into their lives.

She pictured a little boy who looked just like Mitch, kicking a soccer ball around with his father's skill and talent. Or a little girl doing the same thing. A little girl with her dark hair and—

She broke the kiss 'Mitch, one little thing...'

'Yes?' he said.

'You know how you didn't recognise me at first?'

'It didn't take long. You were still the same Zoe. You just looked a bit different. Your hair, your—'

'My nose. I had a nose job when I was twenty-one. I thought I should let you know that. Just in case the baby... Well, the baby won't inherit this expensive new nose. The old one is still there, lurking in my genes. With a horrid bump in the middle.'

Mitch laughed. He gently stroked down her nose with his finger. 'This is a very nice nose. But I never even noticed you had a bump in it before.'

He kissed her again, deep and slow. She looked over his shoulder at that big, imposing bed. It would only take a few steps to take them there.

Mitch broke away from the kiss. His breathing was heavier, his eyes a shade darker with desire.

'So, will you marry me, Zoe?'

She didn't hesitate. 'Oh, yes, Mitch. *Yes*.'

They kissed for a long, long time. Then Mitch started to walk her back into the bedroom.

She broke the kiss to murmur against his mouth. 'Do you want to know what's in my thought bubbles?'

'Yes,' he said.

'No words. They're just filled with beautiful rainbows of joy,' she said.

CHAPTER SEVENTEEN

The following June

ZOE LEANED FORWARD in her VIP seat in the president's box of the Madrid stadium, where the final game of the Spanish La Liga season was being played at the home of Mitch's club. They only needed to draw to win the league and become the champions—the most sought-after of honours.

Mitch was below on the pitch, playing the toughest and most important game of his career to a packed stadium of nearly one hundred thousand spectators.

She could only imagine how it had felt for him as he had run through the players' tunnel onto the pitch to be greeted by the mighty collective roar of the fans. The game was being beamed worldwide by satellite to millions more fans—maybe billions.

Mitch, the only Australian, had become a star in a starstudded team. Over the course of the season that had been a test of his injured knee, he had scored ten goals in a total of twenty-seven league games—the best of his career.

But now the vast stadium was silent as, in the dying seconds of the game, her husband lined up to take the free kick that would decide the outcome of the game against his team's closest rival.

Five of the opposition's players had lined up to form

a wall, each of them with their hands cupped over their nether regions for protection against a possible hit by the ball.

At any other time Zoe would have found that action amusing. But not now. Her fingernails were digging into her hands so hard they were drawing blood, but she didn't notice.

All she was aware of was Mitch as he took the free kick and curled the ball up over the heads of the players in the wall and into the top corner of the net. It was a breathtaking demonstration of his skill that left the goalkeeper helpless.

Goal!

Zoe jumped up from her seat, fists pumping in the air, as she cheered for her husband. He had scored an equal-ising goal to clinch the title for his team. *They'd won the league!* Mitch's team were now the champions—the most important title for any major club.

The crowd erupted into a deafening roar of approval.

On the large-screen monitor she saw a close-up of Mitch's face, his expression one of triumphant ecstasy, his grin huge. He acknowledged the crowd's cheers and pulled off his team shirt, leaving his perfectly sculpted chest bare as, arms outstretched, he ran a victory lap in only his shorts and long white socks. He looked breathtak-ingly handsome and the fans went delirious.

Then he was overtaken by his jubilant teammates in a great show of hugging and back-slapping that culminated in the players throwing their grinning coach above their heads in the air.

Part of the gig of being married to a soccer star was that Zoe had to share his bare chest with the world. There were internet video channels dedicated to just that—shots of Mitch with his shirt off. But she had to deal with it, knowing that while Mitch might be public property to his fans he came home to share *her* bed and enjoy the private family life they cherished. He had never given her cause not to trust him implicitly.

She looked down to where baby Isabella still slept in the carrycot by her feet, oblivious to her famous daddy's triumph.

Zoe's heart seemed to flip over with love for her daughter. Mitch called her the most beautiful baby in the world. With her mummy's dark hair, her daddy's green eyes and straight nose, she was very pretty. Her sweet nature and bright ways made her a joy to have in their lives. If she would just learn to sleep through the night Bella—as she was already called—would indeed be perfect.

It remained to be seen if she would grow up to be the soccer star her father predicted she would be.

In the next seat to her Amanda Bailey, Mitch's mother, wiped away tears of pride in her youngest son. She looked dotingly on her only female grandchild.

'The little pet didn't stir—even with all that commotion,' she said.

Zoe met Amanda's eyes in a perfect communication of shared joy. From being initially wary of Zoe, Amanda had become the best mother-in-law Zoe could ever have imagined having.

Even though they had at first questioned the haste of their son's wedding plans, Mitch's parents had come up trumps in helping them organise the ceremony and reception at short notice.

The ceremony had been perfect—held in the small chapel of an ancient monastery just outside of Madrid. Her dress, from a leading Spanish fashion house, had been exquisite in its simplicity and style—and cleverly cut to disguise the growing presence of baby Isabella.

Zoe had hoped for an intimate reception, but with

Mitch's fame that had not been possible. But it, too, had been perfect, with all his family and friends there. Mitch had flown over a number of her friends too, as their guests.

Louise, who was doing a brilliant job of steering The Right Note to further success as a full business partner, had been among them. She had moved into the Balmain apartment and taken over Einstein's care, as both she and Louise had agreed that he wouldn't have been happy with a move to another country. Louise had brought with her to the wedding a card signed with Einstein's pawprint that had made Zoe both laugh and cry.

When the time had come Amanda had insisted on flying to Madrid to be with Zoe and Mitch in the days after Isabella's birth, to help out. In an unobtrusive, loving way she had given her the help and support Zoe knew her own mother would have given her as she, in turn, had learned to be a mother.

Amanda had flown back to Australia once Zoe was managing motherhood on her own. Now she was back to watch Mitch's big game.

In marrying Mitch, Zoe had gained not only an adoring husband but also a warm, welcoming extended family that had filled the painful gap left by the loss of her own parents. It was an outcome she hadn't ever dreamed of.

Now she and Amanda looked again to the monitor, to see Mitch being interviewed on the pitch by a gaggle of sports media representatives. He switched effortlessly from English to Spanish in his replies, and Zoe was pleased with herself for being able to understand the Spanish. She had fitted right into life in Madrid and could happily converse with most people.

The main commentator for one of the big sports networks was interviewing Mitch now. Her husband's beloved face filled the screen.

'You've come back from your knee injury in spectac- ular form, Mitch,' the interviewer said. 'And I hear talk that you've been nominated as Footballer of the Year. Is this your greatest moment?'

Mitch looked directly into the camera. 'Yes, it's the greatest moment of my career,' he said, in that deep, fa- miliar voice. 'But the greatest moment of my life was when my beautiful wife, Zoe, agreed to marry me, followed by the birth of our precious daughter, Isabella.'

Zoe stared at the screen long after Mitch had finished the interview. She knew he would be with her as soon as he could, and it wasn't long before she heard murmurs among the other guests in the VIP area that let her know he was on his way.

Dressed now in his team tracksuit, and wearing a medal on a ribbon around his neck, Mitch headed towards her, politely accepting the congratulations being showered on him but making it clear that he had eyes for only one per- son—his wife.

He swept her into his arms and hugged her close. Cam- eras flashed, but Zoe didn't care.

'We did it,' he said.

'*You* did it. I just cheered,' Zoe said. 'It was your vic- tory.'

'It was *our* victory,' Mitch corrected her. 'I could never have done what I did this season without your love and support. Having you by my side has made all the differ- ence. Thank you, wife.'

Mitch and his team had won the grand prize today. But Zoe knew the greatest prize of all was the love of her hus- band—and *she* had won it.

* * * * *

LET'S TALK

Romance

For exclusive extracts, competitions
and special offers, find us online:

- facebook.com/millsandboon
- @millsandboonuk
- @millsandboon

Or get in touch on 0844 844 1351*

For all the latest titles coming soon, visit
millsandboon.co.uk/nextmonth

*Calls cost 7p per minute plus your phone company's price per minute access charge